I0761202

THE GREAT FORGOTTEN

THE GREAT FORGOTTEN

K.L. MURPHY

CamCat Books
2810 Coliseum Centre Drive, Suite 300
Charlotte, NC 28217-4574

This is a work of fiction. Names, characters, places, and incidents are either products of the author's imagination or are used fictitiously.

Hardcover ISBN 9780744311907
Paperback ISBN 9780744311921
eBook ISBN 9780744311938

Library of Congress Control Number: 2025939318

Book and cover design by Maryann Appel

5 3 1 2 4

For Those We've Loved,
For Those We'll Never Forget.

“The train is a small world moving through a larger world.”

—*E. B. White*

“What’s done cannot be undone.”

—*William Shakespeare*

AUTHOR'S NOTE

THIS BOOK CONTAINS newspaper articles and speeches which include language and words that are not acceptable today; however, in an effort to preserve the accuracy of these sources, I did not change the articles or the text of the speeches. In every other area of the book, an attempt has been made to be accurate without the use of offensive language.

PART 1

UNLOCKED

CHAPTER ONE

Nashville, Tennessee
Summer 1988

GINNY CAMPBELL SURVEYED the boxes stacked in all four corners of the living room, surprised by how much she'd managed to bring to the new house. Footsteps sounded on the stairs, and she looked over her shoulder. The movers, their faces shining pink with exhaustion, marched down the stairs, arms swinging.

"That was the last of it, Mrs. Campbell," the larger of the two men said. A fresh bead of sweat dripped from his temple, and he mopped it with the sleeve of his coveralls. "What do you want me to do with the trunk?"

Her brows creased. "What trunk?"

"The one in the attic." He glanced at his partner and shrugged. "Probably left by the old owners."

The other man, as skinny as a pogo stick, chimed in. "Looks like it's been there a long time."

The young woman frowned. The house was supposed to have been empty before she moved in, cleared of all her grandmother's belongings that hadn't already been given away. Tired as she was, Ginny figured she might as well deal with it sooner rather than later. "Can you bring it down?"

Minutes later, the movers set the trunk in a corner of the living room. "Well," the first man said, "I think we're done here, unless you need something else."

"No," she told him and thanked him again. After the movers had gone, she busied herself with the business of unpacking, focusing on essentials where she could. Towels for the bathroom. Sheets for the bed. Cups for coffee and tea. The hours slipped into late afternoon and golden sunlight warmed the old house. Ginny yawned and fell back onto the couch. This exhaustion, the overwhelming need to sit down and rest still surprised her—even months into her pregnancy. Her hand found its way to her belly, and she settled back, letting her eyes drift closed.

The sharp trill of the phone cut through the quiet, jerking her awake. Looking around, she blinked, momentarily confused. Remembering, she shook her head, got to her feet, and made her way to the kitchen and the phone hanging on the wall.

"Hello?"

"Did they break anything? Movers always break something, you know."

Ginny's grip on the phone loosened. "Hi, Mom."

"You have to watch them like hawks." Ginny couldn't help but smile. Her mother might be short on pleasantries, but she was long on opinion. "When we moved to Tallahassee, they broke an entire place setting of Grandma Betty's china. Do you remember it? The plates had those tiny pink flowers in the middle with gold trim along the edges. Maybe you don't though. I can't say I ever used it except when Grandma Betty came for Christmas which wasn't often—thank the Lord. It wasn't my style. Not modern at all. Please don't tell your father I said that. His mother was a dear when she was with us, of course, but we never did have much in common."

Ginny choked back a snort and dragged a chair closer to the phone. Her mother liked to imagine that she and Grandma Betty were quite different, but they definitely had one thing in common. Both women could talk and neither cared to whom—as long as the body was warm, and even that wasn't absolutely necessary. It was no wonder Ginny's father was a quiet man.

"Anyway, I hope none of your china has broken like Grandma Betty's. Though I guess yours is plain enough that you could probably replace it with any old white plate, and no one would notice the difference. Now, if it were one of the Florentine patterns or the Scandinavian designs we considered, that would be quite upsetting. I really wish you'd gone with that Wedgwood. Can you imagine how gorgeous your table would be during the holidays? And with the crystal that—"

"Mom, stop." Ginny's fingers tightened around the receiver again.

Maggie Piler made a clucking sound. "Surely, I'm entitled to my opinion, Virginia."

"I know your opinion." Ginny heard the sharp inhale over the line and groaned. "Please, Mom. Can we talk about something else?"

"Maybe you'd like to talk about that husband of yours. I swear, Virginia, I don't understand that man. Letting you move all on your own. He should have told his boss no, that it wasn't a good time for him to go to London. I can't understand why he had to go halfway around the world. Couldn't they have done one of those conference calls? Your father did them all the time before he retired."

"No, Mom." Ginny raised a hand to her temple, massaging the soft flesh. "We've been over this."

"Well, in my day, a man would never let his pregnant wife move alone."

"I'm not due for almost six months, Mom. I'm fine. Perfectly capable of handling a move by myself."

"It's not right." The words were spoken in a way that made Ginny know her mother's chin was lifted to the sky, her red-stained mouth puckered in disapproval. "You can't tell me I'm wrong about this."

Ginny had no intention of discussing Shawn with her mother. "I'm hanging up now."

"Wait. I haven't even had a chance to ask how you're feeling or how the baby is."

"The baby's fine."

"You would tell me if anything was wrong, wouldn't you?"

Ginny looked up at the ceiling. "Yes, Mom."

"Good, because I would get on a plane if you needed me. I'd do it right now. All you would have to do is ask. Your father too. We could be there in a few short hours."

Ginny's lips parted. "You hate flying. You're terrified."

"I'd still be terrified, but for you and the baby, I would do it. Promise me that if you need me, you'll let me know."

"I promise."

"Good." Maggie changed the subject again. "Well, how's the house? Is it as dreary as I remember?"

Ginny's gaze swept past the half-emptied boxes to the large window overlooking the small backyard. The grass could stand to be cut, and the fence needed to be repaired, but there was room enough for a swing set and a patio.

A huge oak shaded the front porch, and there was a fireplace. Now that her grandmother's heavy furniture and brocade drapes had been removed, the house felt brighter. Still, the wallpaper would have to go. "It's not dreary, Mom. It needs a little updating, that's all. But you can help me with that when you and dad drive up next month."

"Will you let me help with the nursery?"

Ginny hesitated. It wasn't like her mother to ask permission for anything. Maybe it was being a grandmother that was softening Maggie. Either way, Ginny wasn't one to argue. "I would love your help."

"I've got so many ideas. What do you think about pink and yellow with—"

"Why don't we wait until you're here?"

"Sure, we can do that. I've been going through boxes of your old things. Make sure you save room in the attic for the baby's clothes as she grows older."

"Mom, we don't know the baby's a girl."

"It's only a feeling, Virginia. Don't make too much of it. But I do have some dresses of yours I've kept stored all these years."

"That reminds me," Ginny said. "The movers found a trunk in the attic."

"One of your grandmother's?"

"I don't know. Hold on a sec." Dragging the long phone cord behind her, she crouched down beside the trunk and ran her hand across the dusty surface. There, under the grime, she spied a set of faded gold initials. AMK. Ginny's teeth caught her lower lip. Grandma Betty's initials were EVP, not AMK. She sat back, studying the top and sides of the case. It was large enough for travel, but there were no stickers or anything to indicate where it had come from. Suddenly remembering her mother waiting on the line, she said, "It looks like it belonged to someone with the initials AMK." She touched the gold letters again as she spoke. "It's definitely old."

"AMK . . . AMK." Ginny heard the clink of a spoon against a teacup. "I can't think who that could be."

"Me neither," she said with a sigh. "I guess I'll have to decide what to do with it."

Her mother snorted. "What's to decide? It's probably filled with spiders and mouse droppings by now." Ginny laughed, imagining her mother shuddering at the idea. "Toss it in the trash before you regret it, Virginia. I'd do it today."

"But what if it's filled with family heirlooms or," she paused, her lips twitching, "very valuable china?"

"Well," Maggie said, dragging out the word. "I suppose you could open it and see, but I'm telling you, Virginia, if you don't find jewels or money, you need to get rid of that thing."

"How sentimental of you, Mom."

"Ha! Being sentimental is dead these days, or haven't you heard?"

"Whatever you say, Mom. I'm hanging up now. For real this time."

Finding the teapot, Ginny made herself a cup and carried it back to the living room. She surveyed the pile of boxes stacked against the far wall, the smallest catching her eye. Written across the surface in giant letters were the words WEDDING ALBUMS. Surrounding the words were pink hearts drawn with a magic marker. Shawn had laughed when she'd drawn them, and she'd countered, "Make fun, but it's my favorite box of all." He'd grinned and wrapped his arms around her. That had been three moves and three apartments ago. Once more, her hand dropped to her growing belly, and her chin fell to her chest. This was supposed to be a happy time. The gift of Grandma Betty's house. Shawn's new job. A baby. So, why was she fighting back tears?

"Stop it," she said to the empty house. "You can do this."

Taking her tea, she turned her back on the heart-covered box, her gaze coming to rest on the old trunk from the attic. The late-afternoon sun poured through the large front window, spotlighting the leather-wrapped case. Sun-speckled particles of dust danced above it, reminding her of fireflies on a hot summer night. She set her tea aside and crossed the room, falling to her knees in front of it.

"Who do you belong to?" she asked the trunk, her voice a whisper.

Breathing in the musty scent of dried leather and dead flowers, she was instantly transported back to childhood and playing in Grandma Betty's cedar closet. How many times had she hidden among the heavy woolen coats and perfumed gowns? Her heart swelled with the memory as she stared down at the old case. There was no telling what could be inside. Her mother was wrong. Sentimentality wasn't dead. It couldn't be. Besides, there were other reasons to value photos, books, or artifacts. Those things were someone's story, and more important, history.

She sneezed and knew her mother was right about one thing though. The trunk was dirty and looked as if it hadn't been moved in years or possibly decades. She bent closer, inspecting the case for spiders or rotted wood or splits in the seams, but saw nothing. She exhaled a slow breath. With clumsy fingers, she loosened and unbuckled the bindings. The leather straps crackled and fell away, sending clouds of dust into the air. Coughing again, she leaned back, her mind racing. How had this trunk ended up in her attic? Did it contain family heirlooms? Books? Photographs? And who was AMK? Had he or she searched for the trunk only to give up? Squaring her shoulders, she told herself there was only one way to find out. She reached out and turned the key.

~~~~

Ginny pulled into the small lot, slowing at the sign.

Welcome. Nashville Home for the Infirm.

Hands resting on the wheel, she studied the three-story building. Dark streaks stained the concrete from the roofline to the lowest window. Cracks and broken pavement marked the lot and sidewalk, and dandelions pushed up through the weed-choked front lawn, their yellow faces the only bright spot to be seen. *There's nothing welcoming about it,* she thought. Not for the first time, she wondered if this was a good idea.

"Are you sure it's the right lady?" Shawn had asked when he'd phoned.

"Yes. Well, no. I suppose there could be another woman with the same name, but it doesn't seem likely."

"Gin, I'm not sure you should go. I don't have a good feeling."

She wanted to laugh but thought better of it. "What do you think's going to happen, Shawn? I'm going to see an old woman in a nursing home."

It had been an easy argument to win, yet she wasn't sure if that was because she was right or because they were both too tired to make the effort. Despite her brave words, she had doubts of her own. What if it was the wrong woman? What if the trunk did belong to her, but she didn't want it back, or worse, didn't want to be reminded of it? Images of the things inside flashed through her mind. Everything in the old case had been so carefully wrapped and preserved. It didn't make sense that it had been abandoned. A new idea struck her. Maybe the trunk wasn't left but lost.

Ginny got out of the car and raised her sunglasses on her head. At the front door, she peered through the glass. Inside, a woman in a white nursing uniform sat behind the front desk of an empty waiting room.
~~~~

"Good morning," the nurse said when Ginny walked in. The name tag she wore read JEAN. "Visiting?" she asked.

"Yes."

Nurse Jean flipped a page in her book and pointed at a wooden clipboard. "You can sign in there. Who are you seeing today?"

Ginny picked up the pen and wrote her name. "Anna Mae Kennedy."

The woman's head came up. "Anna Mae Kennedy?" She closed her book and tented her hands, appraising Ginny in a way that made the young woman's palms sweat. "Are you family?"

"Daughter." Ginny hadn't planned to say that, but the lie popped out of her mouth before she could take it back. The nurse lifted one brow. Realizing her mistake, she forced a laugh. "I mean, granddaughter."

"Granddaughter, huh?" Jean pursed her lips and looked past Ginny to the mostly empty lot. "Are you alone?"

"Yes." Ginny's face flushed under the woman's scrutiny. It occurred to her that maybe she shouldn't have shown up without having called first. What if the woman's real family showed up? How would she explain herself?

"Anna Mae doesn't get many visitors," the nurse said. "Actually, she doesn't get any visitors."

"Oh." While Ginny was thankful that she wouldn't be running into actual family, she found the nurse's declaration sad. "Then I'm glad I came."

Jean tapped her fingers for a minute, as though considering. "She gets tired," the nurse said. "She's one of our oldest patients."

Ginny exhaled. "I won't stay long."

"Fifteen minutes," the nurse said, handing Ginny a visitor pass. "Second floor. Room Five."

On the second floor, another nurse sat behind a larger desk. Ginny waved her pass in the air and kept walking. The door to Room One was open, the interior dark.

A man in a wheelchair was parked outside of Room Two. Ginny slowed. The crown of his head shone pink and white under the unforgiving fluorescent lights. The hair he did have fell in a gray sheet to his shoulders, partially obscuring the cracked lines of his face. With his chin tucked close to his chest, he twisted his hands in his lap, half talking, half ranting, his words rising and falling in a drone.

"They're coming, I tell you. Coming. Watch for the night. That's when they come." His hands moved faster, his body rocking. "They're coming, I tell you. Coming." Spit dribbled down his chin. He repeated the words and his head snapped up, his pupils searching, unfocused in the light. "Watch for the night. That's when they come." Ginny backed away and his head dropped down. "They're coming, I tell you."

When she arrived at Room Five, she tapped lightly on the wood. Silence. She knocked louder, glanced around once, and pushed the door open.

An elderly woman sat in a wheelchair, her face angled toward the window. Wispy white hair like soft-spun cotton candy floated around her head. She wore a high-necked nightgown with pink lace trim and pearl-colored buttons. A colorful quilt lay across her lap, and pink slippers poked out from under the coverlet.

"Mrs. Kennedy?"

The old woman shifted toward Ginny. "You don't look like a nurse. Where's your white uniform?"

"I'm visiting." She lifted the pass again.

The woman in the chair blinked. "Oh, my. Did they tell you the wrong room?" She tipped her head to one shoulder. "I might be able to help. Who are you here to see?" she said, a hint of curiosity in her tone.

"No. I'm in the right room." Ginny's arm dropped. "At least I think I am."

The woman's forehead wrinkled. "Do I know you?"

"No. We've never met, but I found something of yours, at least I think it's yours."

"How mysterious." The lines that fanned out across her cheeks softened and she settled back. "Why don't you sit down?" She lifted a graceful hand toward a wooden chair. "You can pull it closer."

Following directions, Ginny dragged the chair closer. Perching on the end, she clutched her purse in her lap.

"And what is it that you think you've found?" the woman asked, colorless lips turned up in a small smile.

"A trunk. It was in the attic of my house."

The woman made a choking sound, and Ginny sprang to her feet, purse spilling to the floor. "Oh, my God, are you all right? Should I call someone?"

Waving her hand, the woman's breathing slowed enough for her to speak. "No, no. I'm fine. You surprised me is all." Color returning to her cheeks, she pointed at the chair again. "Sit down. I'll be fine in a minute."

"I'm sorry. I didn't mean to upset you."

"Nothing to apologize for," she said, light eyebrows drawn together, "but I must ask: What makes you think this trunk belongs to me?"

Ginny swallowed. "Well, there are initials on the outside of it, AMK, or I think that's what it says. And there were some letters inside, addressed to Anna Mae Kennedy."

"I see." The woman's gaze drifted to the window, and a stillness fell over the room. Ginny didn't know what to think. Was the woman angry? Sad? Both? Maybe Shawn and her mother had been right. It occurred to her that this was one of the few things those two had ever agreed upon.

"What else did you find?"

Ginny looked up to find the woman watching her now. "Some photos, hats, a diary. Oh, and sheet music." There was more, but when the woman nodded, she knew she'd said enough.

"And where did you say you found this trunk?"

"In the attic of my house. I moved here a couple of days ago."

"What house?" the woman asked, her voice arched.

"On Sunset Place, not too far from Vanderbilt. It was my grandmother's house."

The old woman blinked and sat back slowly. "Sunset Place. I don't think I've ever been there." She tilted her head to her shoulder, openly studying Ginny now. "What did you say your name was?"

"Oh, I didn't," she said. "Ginny Campbell."

The old woman stared at her so long, Ginny's cheeks flushed. "Is something wrong?"

"Not at all. For a second, you reminded me of someone, but it seems I'm mistaken."

Ginny's cheeks warmed. "I have that kind of face."

"Did you grow up in Nashville, Ginny Campbell?"

"Chicago."

"Ah. Then I really do have you confused with someone else. What brings you to Nashville?"

"Lots of things," the young woman said, keeping her answer vague.

"Well, welcome to Nashville. How do you like the city so far?"

"It's nice. I used to come here and visit Grandma Betty when I was younger. It's part of the reason I wanted to come back here."

"It's her house that was on Sunset?"

"Yes."

"Well, that really is a mystery. I don't believe I ever knew anyone named Betty on Sunset, but if I had a nickel for every mystery in life . . ." She gave a short laugh and eyed Ginny again. "But none of that is the reason you came here, is it? I believe you expected to ask me what I wanted you to do with the trunk."

"Yes," Ginny said, relieved to get back to the reason for her visit. "I could bring it here for you."

The woman gestured at the four walls. "I'm afraid I don't know where I would put it."

Ginny didn't think the trunk would take up much room, but she didn't say so, offering an alternative solution instead. "I can donate the items to charity if you want."

"Oh, I'm not sure I'm ready for that." The old woman's voice grew husky. "You know, I haven't thought of that trunk in a long, long time. So many memories inside. Some good, some not, which I suppose is how life works. Joy and grief are two sides of the same coin, aren't they? It's hard to recognize one without the other." She paused, her face clearing. "Your eyes are lovely, dear. You should wear green whenever you can."

"Oh. Thank you." Shawn had said the same more than once, but it had been a long time since she'd heard it. "Mrs. Kennedy, about the trunk—"

"It's Miss."

"Oh," Ginny said again, groaning inwardly. She wasn't doing this very well. "Well, maybe there's someone else in your family who'd like to have the trunk. I could send it for you."

"Oh, you're very kind, but I'm afraid there's no one left who'd want it."

Ginny's forehead creased. The woman didn't want the trunk brought to the home, donated, or sent to a relative. What did that leave?

"I hope you won't think me presumptuous," Anna Mae said, the words coming slowly, "but would you mind holding on to my trunk a bit longer, until I decide what to do with it?"

Ginny could already hear her mother's answer: "*Absolutely not.*" And Shawn's: "*I don't think that would be wise. Why are you encouraging her?*" But she wasn't her mother or her husband.

"Why not?" she said with a shrug.

"Wonderful. And I hope you won't mind, but I was wondering—"

A swift knock sounded, and Nurse Jean pushed the door open, shooting a dark look in Ginny's direction. "It's been longer than fifteen minutes." Crossing the room, she addressed Anna Mae. "Are you tired? I could help you back to bed."

Anna Mae patted the nurse's arm. "I am a bit tired. Thank you, Jean."

"Why don't we say goodbye to your visitor, then?"

"Yes, thank you for coming, dear."

Jean kept her eye on Ginny as she returned the hard chair to the corner and exited the room. Ginny was almost to her car when the nurse called her name.

"May I have a word with you, Mrs. Campbell?"

Ginny spun around slowly, heart pounding.

"Is something the matter?"

Jean's hands went to her hips. "I know you're not Anna Mae's granddaughter or any other kind of daughter. Anna Mae didn't have any children. Makes it kind of hard to have grandchildren, don't you think?" Before Ginny could answer, the nurse said, "Anna Mae is my favorite patient. She's a really nice lady, and I don't like seeing her upset."

"I didn't mean to."

Nurse Jean nodded. "Well, make sure it doesn't happen next time."

"Next time?"

"She wants you to come back. Tomorrow morning at ten o'clock."

Surprising herself, Ginny agreed. "Okay. I can be here then."

"Fine. For the record, I'm not sure it's such a good idea." The nurse squinted in the bright light. "There's one other thing. She said to tell you to bring the letters. Do you know what that means?"

Ginny nodded. "I do."

Nurse Jean met her at the door. "I wasn't sure you'd show."

"I said I'd be here."

"Do you know how many times I hear that?" the woman asked, lifting a dark eyebrow, the kind that looked painted on with dark ink. Ginny thought maybe it was meant to accentuate her small eyes, but the exaggerated black arches only succeeded in highlighting the unhealthy pallor of her skin. Still, she had a kind face. "They promise to come, but most times, they never show." She pointed a finger at the bleak waiting room. "It's not a popular place to visit, you know."

Ginny remained silent. Grandma Betty had died surrounded by family, her heart giving out while she slept. Anna Mae had no one. A lump formed in her throat, and she looked away.

The nurse handed her a pass and gestured toward the elevator. "She's expecting you."

Stepping onto the second floor, Ginny searched the hallway.

The man from Room Two was nowhere to be seen. She hurried past the rooms to Anna Mae's door.

"Come in."

Anna Mae sat in the same chair with the same quilt, but on this day, she wore a silk housecoat over her nightgown and her fine hair had been combed into soft waves. The hard chair sat across from the old woman. "Sit down, dear."

Ginny did as she was told. "Thank you, Miss Kennedy."

"Call me Anna Mae."

"Okay. Anna Mae."

"Is it warm outside?"

"Yes, ma'am."

"Summers are like that in Tennessee." She squinted at Ginny. "Tell me about yourself, Ginny Campbell."

It occurred to her that the old woman was lonely, and while that certainly wasn't Ginny's doing, what harm could kindness do? Besides, she felt drawn to the woman in a way she didn't understand. Was it because she, too, sometimes felt alone?

"I teach history, but we just moved to Nashville, so I don't actually have a job for the fall yet."

"We?"

"Me and my husband, Shawn." She didn't mention the pregnancy, that Shawn was in Europe, or that she wasn't sure if she still had a husband. Ginny held up the bundle tied with string. "I brought the letters you asked for."

"Have you read them?"

The truth was, she'd started to. Although the words had been difficult to make out—the writing looped and the once-dark ink now pale as stone—one letter had touched her, its message clear enough.

My Dearest Anna Mae,

As I write this letter, my heart is full of gladness. Never did I imagine that I would meet a woman like you, a woman of great courage and kindness and beauty. Having found you, I am most afraid of losing you. Forgive me for my advances last night. I am aware that things that seem wonderful in the night can look different in the light of day. I pray that is not the case with you. If so, I can only hope you will allow me to make amends upon my return. I want nothing more than to take you in my arms again, my darling.

Looking at Anna Mae now, a wave of guilt washed over her. "I read one, well, part of one. I'm sorry. I know you shouldn't open another person's mail, but—"

"I understand, dear," the elderly woman cut her off. "You were trying to find me." Taking the stack, Anna Mae untied the string and sifted through the letters. She lingered over each but none more than the one Ginny had opened.

Caressing the worn edges of the envelope, she lifted it to her heart before scooping the letters into a pile and retying the string. Finished, she deposited them in the drawer of her nightstand.

Ginny knew the letters didn't belong to her, but she felt something close to disappointment now that they were gone—or at least no longer in her possession.

"Do you like stories, dear?" Anna Mae asked, yanking Ginny from her thoughts. "Stories of the past?"

"Sure," Ginny said with a shrug. "I'm a history teacher. Stories of the past is kind of what I do."

The old woman seemed to perk up at that. "Good. I've waited a very long time to have someone to tell."

"I," she started and stopped, closing her mouth again. She didn't want to hurt the lady's feelings, but she didn't know about a story. How long would it take? And what about the trunk?

"I don't mind saying I'd given up hope," Anna Mae went on. "I'd thought with time, but . . . well, it doesn't matter what I thought now." She lifted her chin and locked eyes with Ginny, her gaze unwavering. "Do you know what that feels like? To give up hope?"

Ginny shifted on the hard chair. There was a directness in the old woman's manner that caught her off guard, that demanded an answer. Did she know what that felt like? To give up hope? She couldn't be sure. "I don't know," she said finally.

Anna Mae nodded. "Well, I hope you never do, but life doesn't ask your permission, does it?" She smoothed the soft fabric of her nightgown. "It's not an easy thing, you know. Which is why I'd like to tell you my story—everything that happened that day in July of 1918."

Ginny went still. July of 1918? Her mind jumped to what she knew of that year. The First World War, of course, and the flu epidemic, but that wasn't until after the summer. And there were the early days of prohibition.

Anna Mae gave her a small smile. "I was twenty-three that summer."

Ginny did a quick calculation. That made Anna Mae ninety-three. "1918," she repeated.

"Yes. Quite a lot going on in the world back then." She chuckled. "Well, of course you know that. You're a history teacher. But there are some things that aren't taught in schools. Things that should be."

She sat forward. "Like what?"

"We'll get there, but you have to trust me, and you have to let me tell you the story my way, if you're willing to listen."

Was she? Ginny had known this woman for less than a day. No doubt Anna Mae would be grateful to have someone to talk to besides Nurse Jean, but was that a good enough reason to stay? She knew what her mother and her husband would say, but the softer voice of her father came to her then.

"Helping people is what I do. It's why I went into medicine," he'd told her. "When I was a boy, we had a neighbor who was a doctor. I didn't think much about it at the time, but after one of my friends fell ill, this doctor took care of him, sometimes staying for long periods of time. He saved him just by being there. I've never forgotten that." His face had grown somber as he'd picked up his medical bag and shrugged into his coat. "Taking is easy, Gin. Giving can be harder, but it doesn't always have to be."

Her mind slid back to the trunk, to the photos and tissue-wrapped mementos inside. 1918. *There are some things that aren't taught in schools.* Goose bumps dotted her bare arms.

This wasn't history from a textbook. This was living history. Anna Mae was only asking for a little of Ginny's time, an easy thing to give. It hardly counted as a difficult sacrifice at all.

Besides, what else did she have to do?

"I'm willing."

~~~

"Are you comfortable, dear?"

"Yes, ma'am." In truth, the room was too warm, the chair was too hard, and she didn't know if she'd ever get used to the medicinal odor of the place.

"Good. Do you like riding trains?"

Ginny hesitated. "I've never really thought about it. I've done it a few times, but I probably prefer flying."

"Yes, that's the way now, isn't it? In my day, trains were the most efficient way to travel—the most glamorous too. There were sleeper cars and dining cars. Union Station was really quite something back then. If you could have seen it . . ." The old woman's voice drifted, caught in a memory. "My mother would take us sometimes. There was a candy shop and large waiting rooms with fireplaces." Her fingers fluttered through the air as if she could reach back in time.

"I think my grandfather might have worked for the railroad once, before my father was born," Ginny said.

"Oh? But he stopped?"

"He had his own insurance company when he died."

"And your father? Did he take over the family business?"

"No," Ginny said with a laugh. "He's a surgeon. Or he was. He retired a few years ago."

"You seem very young. He's retired already?"
~~~

"Oh, he's older than my mother. He likes to say it took him a long time to find the right woman."

"Ah. I'm glad for him, then. And for you, of course," Anna Mae said, fingering a shiny gold locket that dangled from her neck. "Well, before we get started, I need to explain a few things. You may think I'm going to tell you the story of my life, but you would be mistaken—though I will make an appearance from time to time." Ginny's brows rose, a question on the tip of her tongue, but Anna Mae either didn't notice or was unwilling to explain. "Although this story is not about me, it is no less true. I daresay you won't be disappointed." She paused and took a sip of water. "This is the story of five men. One train engineer, one porter, one salesman, one farmer, and one thief. It is the story of a series of moments at a particular time in history leading up to one, very big, very terrible moment that changed things forever." Anna Mae lifted her chin, the motion smoothing the crinkled skin of her neck. "You probably wonder how I have come to know the stories of these five men." She didn't wait for Ginny to answer. "I promise to tell you, but not before I finish. Until I've told you everything, I ask that you simply listen."

Ginny considered the woman's request. How often did a historian get the chance to speak to a woman—to anyone—who'd lived through both world wars, the flu epidemic, polio, and who knew what else? Could she stop herself from asking questions? "I don't know if I can."

"Thank you for being honest. I understand it will be difficult, but I'm afraid this condition is nonnegotiable."

While there was nothing unkind about Anna Mae's tone, Ginny heard steel behind the lilting accent and thought maybe the old woman was tougher than she appeared.

"It was quite a time," Anna Mae said, her voice turning wistful. "Very different from today and yet, not in some ways. So much happened though."

In spite of herself, Ginny slid forward on the chair, her curiosity getting the better of her. "I don't know if it's enough, but I'll try."

The old woman's eyes danced, and she gave a nod of approval. "It's enough. I'll begin, then." She laced her hands together in her lap. "This story begins on July fourth of the year nineteen hundred and eighteen. Independence Day. The country was at war over in Europe, but back here, patriotic feelings were running high. There were parades and picnics and parties in the city and at the parks. Everywhere you looked, you could see red, white, and blue." Anna Mae drew in a long breath. "That day, five men got up as usual. The first was a train engineer who worked for the L&N Railroad. No one loved trains more than he did. He'd worked for the railroad most of his life. He was pleasant and kind, but his son was in Europe, in the war, and it weighed heavy on his mind."

Ginny sat forward; her fingers wrapped over her knees.

"That engineer was my father. His name was David Kennedy."

CHAPTER TWO

Thursday, July 4, 1918
Dawn

OUR HONOR ROLL

Washington, July 3.—The army casualty list today contained 85 names, divided as follows:

Killed in action, 18; died of wounds, 9; died of accident and other causes, 6; died of disease, 4; wounded severely, 12; missing in action, 36.

—*The Tennessean,* July 4, 1918

〜〜〜〜

David Kennedy slowed as he approached Union Station, his railroader's box swinging from his right hand. Looking up, he craned his neck. A statue of Mercury sat atop the train station's tower, more than two hundred feet in the air. Mercury was said to be the Roman god of travelers. David didn't know much about the gods of Rome, but he figured it fit the tower just fine. Under the statue, the tower housed a digital clock, one of the earliest of its kind. Reading the time, the railroad engineer shook his head. The darn thing was wrong again.

A viaduct ran along one side of the station. For a time, the viaduct had fed two pools where Major James Geddes had housed his beloved alligators. When the exotic animals had first arrived in Nashville, they'd attracted large crowds. David had brought his own children when they were young. Anna Mae and Katie Belle had drawn back at their first visit, their hands over their mouths.

"Will it eat me?" Katie Belle had asked, clinging to his leg.

David had laughed and patted her head. John George, though, had inched closer. It wasn't long before the girls lost interest, but David brought John George many times. Major Geddes himself would stand nearby, sharing what he knew about the fearsome animals. When the alligators had gone for good and the pools stood empty, John George cried and cried, as though the wild animals were his own.

David frowned, stopping short. He hadn't thought of the alligators in years, and he wondered why this day was any different. Perhaps it was the excitement in the air, the anticipation of the holiday. With that in mind, he opted not to go directly to the train's shed. Instead, he walked through the portico, under the gray stone archway to the interior of the station. Red, white, and blue decorations hung on the walls, the colors vivid in the early-morning light. The chandelier twinkled as if it, too, had been shot through with patriotic color. He felt a measure of pride as he moved past the ticket office and the half dozen long, pew-like wooden seats in the center of the lobby. Glancing at the clock over the ticket counter, he lingered only another minute, then hurried on. Passengers for his train would be arriving soon.

Descending to the shed, David inhaled the grimy scents of oil and smoke, the odors comforting. Union Station was grand, but it was the shed where David felt most at home. It was constructed entirely of steel and housed all thirteen sets of tracks, the passenger platforms, and an assortment of offices and repair shops. The size and expanse had seemed excessive when it was built in 1900, but David knew that was no longer true. Since President Wilson had entered the war, joining the fight against Germany, the station and the railroads operated day and night. The voices and sounds of mechanics, porters, and dispatchers floated across the platforms. As the morning crews arrived and the night workers finished their shifts, the shed teemed with energy. Some of the railroaders departed for the bathhouse. Others headed home. David walked on toward the stationmaster's office. His conductor, Shorty Eubank, was waiting for him outside.

"Good morning, Uncle Dave. Happy Fourth of July." David couldn't remember when he'd earned the familiar nickname, but it was no secret he was the oldest engineer with the railroad. He'd been there so long, everyone seemed like family. "How are you today?" Shorty asked.

He answered as he did every morning. "Never better."

"As it should be."

David glanced down at Shorty. The conductor had earned his own nickname the old-fashioned way, being a stub of a man with a belly almost as round as he was tall. David waved a hand toward the door. "Shall we?" Together, the pair retrieved the day's orders, each reading them aloud in front of the dispatcher.

Number One being hauled by Engine #281—hold at double tracks until Number One passes.

"Have you ever seen the trains so crowded?" Shorty asked as they walked down the platform.

"No, can't say that I have."

Shorty licked his thick lips. "I collect the tickets as fast as I can," he said, tipping his head back to look into David's face. "But when we have to look for the Number One too, well, you understand, don't you?"

David took off his glasses and wiped them on a clean handkerchief. He did understand, but orders were orders. Both men would be expected to watch for the other train before leaving Shops and continuing on the single track they shared

"It's the war," Shorty was saying now. "Can't end too soon, I say. Wouldn't you agree?"

A half dozen soldiers came down the steps, stealing David's attention. A quick scan of the young faces only reminded him of the face he wished to see but couldn't. He moved closer to the waiting soldiers. Two stood apart from the others. Both leaned against the stone wall, their supply bags at their feet.

"My cousin is in the Thirtieth," one said. The younger soldier tapped his chest. "That's where I want to be. Infantry." David's ears perked up. John George was in the Infantry. "My daddy was in the Thirtieth and my granddaddy before him." The boy lifted his hairless chin as he spoke.

"Is that so?" The second soldier tapped his foot, ran his hand over his hair.

"Yes, sir. My cousin's in France now, getting ready to show those Germans who's boss. They'll be sorry they started this now."

"You know everything, do you, kid?" asked the second soldier.

The boy flinched. "You don't have to be that way."

David studied the second man. His uniform fit close to his chest; it didn't hang off his bones the way the boy's did. His beard was flecked with gray, and his skin was lined where the younger man's face was smooth.

The older soldier's tone took on a hard edge. "You don't know what you're talking about."

"My cousin is at the front," the boy insisted. "And that's where I'm going."

The second man's jaw tightened. "Look, it's not the way you think it is. You talk like you think this is going to be fun. It's not like that. It's the opposite of fun. People are going to be killed, or worse." His nostrils flared. "Kid, you might think dying is the worst, but it's not. I've seen it. Way worse."

David heard the anger and weariness in the man's voice, recognizing the words as those of a man who had seen too much, knew too much. His own blood ran cold.

The boy, however, heard only the sound of his own voice, interrupting to repeat himself. "I'm going to the front with my cousin."

The man pressed in, the bulk of his body closing the gap between the two soldiers. The boy shrank back against the wall. "It won't be only Germans that die or get their legs shot off. Americans are going to be killed too. Lots of them. It might be you or your cousin. Does that sound like fun?"

The boy's voice quivered. "That's not what I meant."

"Isn't it? You're all the same. You think it's some kind of game. It's not."

The boy screwed up his mouth. "But we're winning, right? I saw it in the papers. President Wilson says we're winning."

The older man snorted and lifted a hand. "Sure, kid. We're winning." He walked away and planted himself farther down the wall, his arms folded across his chest. The young soldier started to follow, his mouth open to argue, but seemed to think better of it. Kicking the floor, he settled back against the wall, crossing his arms in imitation of the other man.

David's stomach churned, his mouth dry. John George had been gone for months and there hadn't been a new letter in weeks. David had only the newspapers. The young soldier wasn't wrong. The papers and the president said America was winning. Some even said the war would be ending soon. For David, it couldn't be soon enough. As he walked down the platform to the engine, the words of the older soldier echoed in his mind.

Americans are going to be killed too. Lots of them.

~~~~

George Hall peered at the balled-up figure that was his wife. Her body, no more than a shadow in the semidarkness, looked small under the covers. He reached out and traced the gentle curve of her body with his fingers. She stirred and he backed away, careful not to make a noise. Later, she would rise, lift her arms, and stretch like a cat, purring in that way that made him want to wrap her up and pull her close. He considered waking her, but it was her day off, and he wouldn't take that from her.

He tiptoed from the room, his heavy porter's coat over his arm. At the washbasin, he plunged his hands into the tepid water, splashing it over his face. Sleep washed away, he dressed and ate the hard bread his wife had left for him. He picked up the lunch she'd made and tucked it under his arm. He paused at the door, listening. There was only silence.
~~~~

He left the house, went right at Sixteenth Avenue, and walked south toward the train station. He walked to work most days, except when it rained or the wind blew cold. Those times, he took the trolley to the station, riding in the section for people of color, but he preferred walking. It didn't cost anything, and more important, he could do it alone.

George soaked in the quiet of the empty streets. It was his favorite time of day, the time when he liked Nashville best. There were fewer electric lamps on this side of town, but the sky had brightened in anticipation of the sunrise and he didn't need them. He could taste the morning dew with every breath, the air warm and sweet. George kept walking, the blocks passing quickly. His mind strayed back to his sleeping wife. She'd be up soon to wake the children. For his family, it would be a day of celebration. No work. They would join their neighbors and friends at Greenwood Park to celebrate the Fourth of July. There would be food, laughter, and fun. He didn't mind missing the crowds—he got enough of that every day—but he would miss the music.

The sun rose higher, and the trees emerged from the shadows. He passed Pearl Street and took a right on Charlotte. He left the familiar neighborhoods behind, skirting the white sections. He walked faster toward Twelfth Avenue and then rounded the corner at Broadway. As it did every morning, his gaze drifted upward. The station's clock tower caught and held the sun. The size of the station alone was impressive—and he'd been in enough of them to know. In his mind, none could hold a candle to Union Station. He appreciated the giant arches and the marble floor, but it was the stained-glass ceiling he liked best. He walked faster toward the station, thinking of the day ahead. The new gunpowder plant would run trains every hour for the Fourth of July celebrations, and the regular passenger trains promised to be full too. Since the government had taken over the railroads, he was busier than ever. Longer hours, increased demands. Even though working hard was all he'd ever known, they couldn't keep this up. No one could.

Making his way around the station, he bypassed the main entrance and the passengers out front. Most of the ladies wore fine dresses and hats.

The men, too, were dressed well, in suits and derby hats. The children stood close to their mothers, their little faces reflecting awe and wonder. The air buzzed with anticipation. He caught sight of a young couple coming up the platform. First timers. George could always tell the new travelers from the seasoned ones. The first timers had that lost look, the kind where they didn't blink enough, their mouths hanging open. Most tried to hide it, of course, but George always knew. He liked the first timers. He liked their excitement, the way they gaped at the scenery speeding by and the gratitude in their voices when he brought them a warm blanket on a cool day. The regulars were different. Not all bad, but different.

George buttoned his porter's coat over his starched white shirt and smoothed the creases. He inspected his shoes, deciding they'd need a polish by the next day or the day after. Finally, he picked up his hat. A brass-colored sign was stitched above the brim, fourteen letters etched into the plate. *Railroad Porter*. He fit it on his head. He was ready.

~~~~

POST OFFICE TO BE CLOSED ON FOURTH

The Nashville post office will be closed all day today in order to allow the employees to enjoy the Fourth. No deliveries to the city or on the rural routes will be made, but collections will be made in the city at certain times in the day. No stamps will be sold or money orders taken on that day.

—*The Tennessean*, July 4, 1918

~~~~

Clyde Lewis opened the newspaper, the pages rattling as he flattened the inked paper. He skimmed over the war stories, turning instead to the social columns. None of the names were familiar, but he hadn't expected them to be. Even so, he filed them away for future reference.

"I hate this town," Carl said, upper lip curled.

Clyde lowered the paper, saying nothing. His brother Carl didn't need much prompting to talk, keeping at it whether Clyde wanted him to or not. The truth was, Clyde was inclined to agree. Nashville wasn't really his kind of place. There were too many people, too many buildings; everything and everyone too close together. Hell, the papers even bragged about it. *Nashville. The quarter million people city.* It was right there at the top of the front page of the *Tennessean.* Why would he want to live with a quarter million people? He liked open spaces and riding alone. He was counting the days until he could get back to the mountains of West Virginia.

"It's too hot here," Carl complained. "And the ladies. Too high and mighty if you ask me." His brother ran a large hand through greasy locks. "Why'd you pick this hotel anyway?"

Clyde grunted, noncommittal. There was nothing wrong with the hotel and Carl knew it. The Hermitage was nicer than most, and best of all, it wasn't far from the train station. If Carl had a problem with it, the reason had nothing to do with the accommodations. More likely, it had to do with the beauty shop at the Sixth Avenue entrance. Clyde didn't know why his brother bothered. The ladies that frequented that salon were either married or took one look at Carl and knew him for the good-for-nothing scoundrel he was.

It wasn't that Carl wasn't handsome enough. A certain type of woman might give Carl a chance, but that woman wasn't having her hair curled at the Marinello beauty shop. Clyde had cleaned him up as best he could, but there was no taking the slither out of a snake. Their father had been famous for saying that one.

Clyde set the newspaper aside and got to his feet. "It's time," he said.

Outside the hotel, a streetcar passed by, mostly empty at that hour of the morning. The brothers walked up Sixth and crossed Church, the train station looming in the distance. The marble and gray stone turrets and tower reminded Clyde of castles, the kind he'd seen in pictures. He slowed, glancing at his brother. "This is where it starts," he said. "First real step."

Carl spit on the ground. "'Bout time something happened."

The brothers walked under the marble archways into the station. Sunlight poured through the glass overhead, bathing the lobby in sparkling light. Clyde took in the red, white, and blue decorations and the long line of passengers in front of the ticket window. More passengers filled the wooden seats lined up in rows across the tiled floor.

Carl whistled under his breath. "Fancy."

Clyde cut through the clusters of folks milling about, passed the waiting rooms, and headed directly for the wide staircase. He skipped down the steps to the platform. At one end, he spied ladies and children standing together waiting to board. In the opposite direction, a porter carried valises and luggage to the baggage car.

"This way," Clyde said. He pulled his hat lower and led his brother up the platform. They skirted the bags and stopped in front of an open car. Stepping back, they watched the activity from a distance, close enough to see but far enough away to speak without being heard. Clyde gestured at the first car behind the engine and steam. "That one is the mail car, has some baggage. The other one is bags only."

Carl gave him a sideways glance. "I don't see any mail."

"It's the Fourth. Declared a holiday for the post office today."

"Then why are we here?"

Clyde gestured toward the combination mail and baggage car. "I want you to see which one it is." He described the way the system worked in the combination car. One man would stack the baggage. Two others would pull mail from large bags, sort each piece, and place them into compartments. Clyde hadn't needed to see the specifics to understand there was a well-established system.

Carl shifted next to him. "Okay. What else?"

"There's a postal worker I want you to meet. He works that car, sorts the mail."

"Yeah? Who is it?"

Clyde gave him the name. "You'll meet him tonight."

"How'd you arrange that?"

"While you were out spending our money on booze, I was doing what was necessary."

Carl stiffened. "That's not fair. I can't be cooped up in—"

Clyde raised a hand. "I've been here every morning, every evening. I know the train schedule inside and out. I know how many railroaders are on the train. I know how many cars there are most days. I know our man. I know his name and where he lives. I know what he likes to do in his spare time."

Carl made a huffing sound and spit again.

From under his hat, Clyde watched the porter finish loading the bags, disappear, and reappear with more. A tall man in overalls walked by. Clyde tracked him as he made his way to the front of the train. "Are you done pouting?" he asked his brother.

Carl shoved his hands deep in his pockets, took his time answering. "Okay, I'll bite. What does the postal worker like to do in his spare time?"

Clyde nodded. He'd made his point. "Gamble."

"Is that so?" Carl drew out the words.

"Yep. I've arranged for you to join his game tonight."

He rubbed his hands together. "Well, don't mind if I do."

"Easy, brother," Clyde said. His attention was drawn to the activity on the platform. Dozens crowded the platform. He knew the white passengers were afforded the coaches farthest from the engine and the smoke. The white women and children would board the two coaches at the rear of the train while the white men would occupy the middle coaches. The others would be crowded into the Jim Crow car, closest to the engine. As he watched, a portly man made his way through the crowds to the center of the platform. Clyde elbowed his brother. "Conductor there."

"Okay. Who else?"

Clyde gestured toward the front of the train, finding the tall, silver-haired man in the overalls. "Engineer."

"Huh. That all they got?"

"There's another guy doing the steam. You got the guys in the baggage cars. The porter. A flagman at the back. So, no more than seven or eight that I can tell."

"What about—"

"Haven't seen one, but that don't mean anything." Carl had been right to ask about the Pinkertons. The railroads had been using them for years. Although he hadn't spotted any on the Nashville trains, that didn't guarantee there wouldn't be one or more when the money was loaded onto the mail car. Clyde had a plan for that too.

They watched as the combination baggage and mail door closed. "Getting ready to board," Clyde told his brother. "Let's go."

Behind him, his brother bumped into the porter. "Watch it." Carl's tone was sharp, and Clyde tensed.

"I'm sorry, sir. It won't happen again."

Clyde moved behind his brother, his hand finding Carl's arm. The porter blinked, his gaze suddenly wary. "Not now," he said, leaving no room for discussion. He could feel the twitch of his brother's muscles, the quick anger that vibrated under his skin.

"Better not," Carl said, finally, and let the porter go by.

Clyde exhaled. Carl followed him up the steps, grumbling all the way. Clyde ignored his brother's complaints, his mind on the plan. Everything had been the same as the day before and the day before that. Same time. Same train. Same railroad staff. He felt a small amount of satisfaction. Clyde didn't like the unexpected. The only thing that could come from that was a whole lot of trouble—or worse. Outside, lifting his face up to the sun, he felt the weight of the plan in the hollows of his belly. Everything had been the same. He wouldn't fail. He couldn't.

~~~~

Out of the corner of his eye, George Hall spotted Mr. Mason, a regular, making his way down the steps from the lobby to the platform. He limped
~~~~

across the floor, a cane in his right hand and a small case in his left. He rode twice a month, every month, always alone, boarding the early train to Hickman on the first and third Thursday. Mr. Mason rode all the way to the end of the line and always returned the Sunday after. He rarely spoke, other than the occasional question. "Is the smoking car full today, George?" he might ask, or "Would you mind raising my window, George?" At the end of every trip, he pressed a nickel into George's hand. He didn't say thank you, but after more than two years loading the man's bag, George knew better than to expect it.

After helping Mr. Mason, George found himself following a large woman with three small children in tow. Her long skirt swished as she walked, and the children hurried to keep up. George carried her trunk to the baggage car. Since the first baggage car was full, George took the lady's luggage to the second car. After loading it, he followed her to the rear of the train, one hat box under each arm.

The lady and the children stopped at the last car. "The children and I are traveling to visit family over in Hollow Rock," she said. "Mr. Dinkins won't be able to join us until Monday. I'll need you when we arrive, so don't forget."

"Yes, ma'am," he said, swallowing a sigh behind a practiced smile.

"The children are very excited, aren't you, children?" She bent toward them, her voice cheery. Three heads moved in unison.

First timers, he thought.

"See? Traveling is such fun!" She clapped her hands together, and the children snapped to attention. "Will we be able to board soon?"

"Any minute now, ma'am," he said. The porter took a step back from Mrs. Dinkins and gave a slight bow. "I'd best be helping other passengers."

"Of course," she said, already looking over his shoulder. "Why, children, there's Mrs. Thompson."

Greeting the other passengers, he carried bags and boxes, taking them one by one to the baggage cars. He moved back and forth between the white folks and the baggage cars. He spoke softly, smiling and nodding when he knew it was expected. His muscles burned under the heavy bags. Head bowed as he zigzagged through the crowd, he didn't see the tall man before they collided.

"Watch it," the man barked.

"I'm sorry, sir. It won't happen again."

The tall man's dark eyes bored into the porter's and George's skin prickled under his heavy coat. A second man appeared behind the first, placing a hand on the first man's arm. After a moment, the bigger man spit on the ground. "Better not," he said.

Letting out a shaky breath, George retreated, keeping his eye on the men as they walked away. His brows furrowed when the pair didn't stop in front of the white coaches but climbed the stairs to the sunlit station instead. Had they forgotten something? Or gotten the wrong train?

"George. Oh, George." A woman waiting at the top of the steps, her small foot tapping the marble floor, called for the porter. "Goodness, what took you so long?" she asked when he hurried forward. "I've been calling you for going on five minutes now. I won't be missing this train because of you." She lifted her finger in the direction of her bags. "Take these, won't you?"

"Yes, ma'am."

"And don't be slow about it, George."

"Yes, ma'am," he repeated, but she didn't respond, already hurrying down the steps to the waiting train. Sighing, he picked up the lady's bags, carrying one under each arm, the two strange men a memory.

~~~~

David waited near the end of the platform, his hands tucked into his engineer's overalls. The black metal of the engine glowed, the number 282 painted in large gold letters. An imposing mass of steel, the engine had four small leading wheels in the front and six heavy, cast-iron wheels in the rear. It was a popular engine on the railroad, massive in size and with enough power to
~~~~

pull either passenger or freight trains. On this day, as most days, David and the 282 would drive the passenger train. Instead of freight cars, he would pull two baggage cars and six coaches.

The steam engine hissed as Luther Meadows, his fireman, worked. The porter loaded the baggage, and Shorty inspected the train. The flagman took his position at the rear. These things were a matter of course, part of an ordinary day. Although David knew that, he still felt a measure of anticipation each time he stepped onto his train. Decades on the tracks hadn't diminished his love of the railroad or trains. Each time was like the first.

At the center of the platform, Shorty pushed his way forward until he was only a few feet from the train. Raising his arm, the conductor cupped his hand near his mouth. "ALL ABOARD," he called, the words echoing over the waiting passengers.

The women and children headed for the back of the train to the pair of ladies' cars. Through the crowd, David caught sight of George's dark uniform and shiny buttons trailing behind a lady in a red, white, and blue-ribboned hat. The men in suits and uniforms came next. There were three wooden coaches for them, each outfitted with rows of seats. The newer trains had steel cars, but rumor had it the railroad bosses weren't eager to part with the money needed to replace the older, wooden cars. David had heard the grumbling among some of the other engineers, but he didn't pay it any mind. Like him, the old cars did the job. The last set of passengers allowed to board trudged forward, climbing into the Jim Crow car.

After Shorty signaled that everyone was on board, David stepped up to the engine. He glanced briefly at Luther Meadows, who hunched over the firebox shoveling coal in one continuous motion, his arms bulging as he worked. The job of the fireman was a thankless one, and David was glad of Luther's presence on this day. Nodding at the other man, he reached up and pulled the heavy cord of the train's horn. A few seconds later, he pulled the cord a second time. He never tired of the sound or the squeaking and grinding of the steel wheels as they rolled over the tracks. He leaned his body into the motion of the train as it chugged forward. *Click clack. Click clack.* The train gathered speed. He checked the time on his clock. Seven a.m.

Behind David, Luther stood upright and lowered the bandana from his mouth. "On time?" David told him yes, speaking loudly to be heard over the rumble.

"Orders?"

David touched a hand to the pocket of his striped overalls. His copy was there, but he didn't need to read it again. He knew the orders by heart.

Aloud, he said, "Wait for the Number One."

A shadow passed over the younger man's face, but he said nothing. Instead, he replaced the bandana and bent over the box again.

David didn't like the orders any more than Luther did, but the war had forced the government to increase the number of freight trains. To keep as many passenger trains running as possible, the government had altered the routes, creating tight timetables and longer hours. As it was, if the Number One was on time, it would arrive in Nashville only minutes after David's train left Union Station. If it wasn't, which had been the case more often than the engineer would have liked—for safety reasons—his train would be forced to wait at Shops, where the parallel tracks converged to a single track. Only after the Number One passed and continued on to Nashville could he continue his route. Sometimes he waited only a few minutes. Other times longer. Every time made David's train late.

"Come on, Number One," the engineer mumbled over and over, the words lost in the noise of the train. "Come on, Number One."

~~~

Shorty gestured to George. "I've got the orders."

The porter noted the tightness around the conductor's mouth and steeled himself for the news. "I'm ready, sir."

"You understand?" Shorty asked after he'd recited the orders. "I'm going to need you to watch for the Number One. I've got tickets to collect."
~~~

George knew better than to mention that the conductor always had an excuse for why he couldn't keep an eye on the track ahead. Instead, the porter held himself erect, though he was eager to move away. "Yes, sir. Watch for the Number One." He wrinkled his nose as Shorty brushed past. The conductor smelled vaguely of sweat and something else foul that George couldn't name, but the porter didn't mind that so much. It was the whiny quality of the man's voice, the way he spoke in a way that shifted the blame when it suited him.

Engineer Kennedy was different. He had a calm demeanor and a kind manner. George didn't know if he drove the train better than other engineers, but he did know that Uncle Dave—as he was known among the railroaders—was better liked among the porters. Only thing was, when Uncle Dave was the engineer, most times Shorty was the conductor.

George sighed and squared his shoulders. The passengers wouldn't care that George needed to watch for the Number One. He would need to do his own job too.

Moving to the front of the car, he checked on passengers, all the while looking out the windows, searching for the other train. Shorty found him in the second coach.

"George, you're needed in the ladies' car. It's Mrs. Dinkins." George waited to see if there was more. "One of the children."

The porter stood another moment, waiting.

"Well, get going, George." Shorty waved his hand at him. "You'll see when you get there. And don't forget to watch for the Number One."

"Yes, sir." The porter made his way through the men's coaches, his footsteps slowing as he approached the ladies' car. He'd been asked to mind children, feed children, any number of things he would not be allowed to do off the train, but he understood his job. Pulling open the door to the car, the odor knocked him back. There on the floor were the nasty remains of a child's breakfast or dinner or whatever had been in their stomach before they'd boarded the train. He held tight to the door and breathed through his mouth. Mrs. Dinkins sat in the front of the car, the smallest of her children next to her. The rest of the ladies had moved to the back. They held handkerchiefs over their noses.

"Thank goodness you're here, George. Can you clean it up?"

"Yes, ma'am," he told her, his expression unsmiling now. "I'll be right back with the supplies." He slid the door closed. Hurrying away to gather the mop and cloths, George gulped clean air, the Number One momentarily forgotten.

~~~~

David stuck his head out the window, the hot air blurring his vision. Peering ahead, he watched for his sister train but saw only empty track. A knot hardened between his shoulders.

Checking the time, David pressed his lips together. He was already halfway to Shops, the train yard where he would be required to wait for the Number One. He couldn't be expected to be on time with these types of constraints. A quarter mile in front of them, he spotted the Number One barreling toward him on the parallel track. He looked over at Luther. "Number One ahead."

His fireman raised his head briefly, the lines of his forehead clearing, and resumed shoveling.

With one hand on the throttle, David exhaled, the tension in his upper body easing. Waving a hand at the Number One, he continued on, passing through Shops to the single track that would take him west of the city. David's train picked up speed, hurtling toward its first stop.

~~~~

"How'd you arrange it?" Carl asked. He pulled a cigar from his pocket and chewed the tip. "Me joining their game?"

Clyde shrugged. "I followed him. After he leaves here, he walks home. It's not far, only a few blocks."

"And?"

"And I waited. Sure enough, he came out again. I followed him to Black Bottom."

Carl chuckled. "Where a good time is had by all."

Clyde said nothing. It was no surprise to him that his brother had already acquainted himself with this particular section of town. Like so many growing cities, Nashville was eager to wipe away all that was considered evil and ugly. As of late, that included liquor and gambling, but in spite of the efforts of the good citizens of Nashville, both could be found in the Bottom.

"Where'd he go?" Carl asked.

"A saloon called Rowena's. Know it?"

"Haven't been in that one."

"Good. Better if they don't know you. Some hard drinkin' going on down there, but our boy didn't stick around for that. Headed straight for a room in the back."

Carl lifted one brow. "And you?"

"No. Stayed where I was. Asked a question or two, but no one was talking. I dropped it."

"A room in the back, huh? A game or a woman?"

"I wasn't sure. Followed him again the next night."

"You have been busy," Carl said with a smirk.

The pair rounded the corner. "Went to the same place at the same time. Rowena's. I stayed longer. Watched who went to the back, who came out. And then I saw them."

"Who?"

"The brothers from the hotel."

"The bellhops?"

"One and the same."

"Small world. Did they see you?"

"I made sure they didn't. The next morning, I saw them in the lobby, casually mentioned how you liked to play, were looking for a game." It hadn't taken much more than a dropped reference and a friendly manner. Spotting the bellboys was the kind of good luck Clyde needed. Carl would call it fate, but Clyde didn't believe in such things. Luck was different. Luck came and went with the wind. Still, he knew better than to count on good luck. It was bad luck that blew in most times.

"That did it?"

"I might have mentioned that you're not very good."

Carl laughed. "I guess they're in for a surprise."

"Not tonight."

His brother shot him a questioning look. "You want me to lose?"

"Has to be that way. Tonight is about making friends."

"I don't need any new friends."

Clyde did his best to keep his voice even, hide his growing irritation. "I want you to get to know him, make him trust you. I was told the delivery wouldn't happen before next week. We have some time to get the information we need."

"So, lose and make nice?"

"That's right."

Carl hooked his thumb through his waistband. "Whatever you say, big brother. What time?"

"Ten o'clock. After most of the festivities are over."

"I'll be ready." They arrived back at the hotel, the sun brighter and higher in the sky.

"I'm counting on you, Carl."

"Don't be so serious, Clyde. I know what I'm doing," Carl said with a laugh, clapping him on the back. "It's our destiny, big brother. We're going to be famous."

Clyde frowned. He didn't believe in destiny any more than fate. He was not a superstitious or spiritual man. He liked facts and plans. According to the papers, DuPont had built the largest gunpowder plant the country had ever seen. The plant had gone up fast, and word had it that it had already started producing. Clyde didn't care about the war or the gunpowder. He cared only that a plant that size had large amounts of gunpowder to sell and that meant money. A lot of money. And like banks, DuPont would be forced to move those funds by train in order to pay the workers and grow their own coffers. A large shipment of funds was scheduled to take place soon. Those were facts that meant something. He had no grand ideas about destiny, the way his brother did.

Clyde knew about the money and how it would be transported, but he didn't know which day the money would be loaded onto the train. Although Clyde had a man on the inside—a man working at the plant—so far, he'd come up with nothing. Without that knowledge, he was stymied. Knowing they'd only get one shot, he'd studied the mail sorting system, watched the workers. He'd learned the money would be loaded into the combination car and stored in the large safe behind the sorting tables. The safe came with its own set of challenges, but that didn't worry Clyde. That was Cooper's specialty. All he needed now was the day. The postal worker was the key.

Clyde watched his brother stride through the hotel lobby and plant himself outside the entrance to the hair salon. Carl bent one leg at the knee and propped his booted heel against the wall, hands shoved deep in his pockets. Carl never gave up. Clyde had to give him that.

Leaving his brother to scare the ladies, Clyde headed through the lobby. He planned to take Carl out to the site later, though he knew he'd need to keep Carl away from the liquor in the afternoon. His brother had a date to keep that night, and he would be on time and sober if Clyde had anything to say about it. It would all come together. It had to. He needed this job. They all did.

CHAPTER THREE

Summer 1988

THE AFTERNOON SUN sank low in the sky, casting shadows across the room. Anna Mae blinked as though coming out of a trance. She brushed absently at a wisp of hair, a tremor in her hands. "What do you think so far, dear?"

"Well, it's interesting." Ginny spoke slowly. She didn't want to hurt the old woman's feelings, but as far as she could tell, the story didn't seem directly tied to the war or any other major event she knew of. "David seems nice."

"Oh, he was a very nice man," Anna Mae said.

"And the others . . ." Her words trailed off.

"You wonder how I know them?"

Ginny nodded. David Kennedy was Anna Mae's father. As his daughter, she would have heard him speak of his worry for John George and his life with the railroad. And Ginny could also believe that Anna Mae might have met the porter or knew of him, but how could she have known Clyde or his brother? It didn't make sense. "Your story is quite detailed. I'm not sure how you remember all that."

"It's hard to forget, my dear."

Ginny stared down at her hands.

"I can see that you're too polite to say what you're thinking." Ginny looked up, but there was no accusation or disappointment on the old woman's face. "But I must ask you to trust me. Listening—just listening—isn't as easy as it sounds, is it?" Anna Mae tapped a finger to her ear. "There's an art to it, you know. Listening. My mother was deaf, and she was the best listener I ever knew. She heard with her eyes and her hands. She watched what you said and how you said it. More than once, my father commented that nothing got by her, and it was true." She drew herself up, shaking off the memories. "I'll answer all of your questions when I'm finished."

~~~

Walking through the bleak lobby, Ginny slowed at the sound of Nurse Jean's voice. "Are you coming back?"

Ginny flinched at the woman's gruff tone. "I don't have to come at all."

The nurse's face softened. "You're right. I'm sorry." She pulled at the fabric of her starched uniform. "I really care about Anna Mae, and she seems to want you to visit. That's a lot to put on a stranger." She paused again, and Ginny waited, rummaging through her purse for her keys. "It's almost like she's been waiting for you."

Ginny's eyes snapped back to the nurse, the keys forgotten. "What do you mean?"

"I don't know what I mean. Forget it," Nurse Jean said with a shrug and backed away. "Forget I said anything at all."

~~~

Ginny wiped the lid of the trunk with a soft cloth, clearing away the last of the dust. While the old case had seen better days, it hadn't entirely lost its luster. Lifting the lid, she studied the contents inside. Pulling out the hat box, she opened it to find a straw hat decorated with red ribbon and a single red silk flower. She smiled, imagining it perched on the head of a young Anna Mae. Setting the hat aside, she reached in to find an ivory hairbrush and matching mirror, a stack of embroidered handkerchiefs, and a pipe wrapped in crinkly tissue. Some items were more delicate than others, and she laid them out in a row on the floor behind her. All were items of interest, but none were the one she was looking for. Near the bottom, she found the small wooden box.

Inside were a dozen photographs. In one, a tall man with silver hair, a strong chin, and spectacles stood next to a younger woman with eyes as dark as her dress. She wondered briefly if the man was David Kennedy. She turned it over, but there was no name. Underneath the photographs was a book, remarkably preserved. Although the edges had lost their dark color, the title, *A Line a Day,* was clear enough and the spine remained intact. Ginny had seen one of these before, in her father's house.

"Your grandmother gave it to me," he'd said with an embarrassed grin. "She wrote something about me every day starting not long after I was born. A baby book of sorts. Although I have to admit, reading 'Michael ate all of his peas and most of his carrots' is not interesting or entertaining. I'm afraid I was pretty boring." His smile widened. "Now, maybe if I'd thrown those nasty peas against the wall, that would have been something."

They both laughed.

The memory receding, she traced the lettering of the book with her fingers. She understood the concept. The owner of the journal would write a couple of lines about their day. Clearly, that didn't leave room for spilling innermost secrets or detailing stories of love, but it was something. And since Anna Mae had restricted her from asking questions, the trunk and its contents would have to do. Her heart pitter-pattered as she opened the book to the first page, the first day of 1917.

We went to mass today to celebrate the new year. Father even stayed awake—probably because Mother promised a roast for supper.

Amused by the young Anna Mae's comment, she flipped the pages until she came to the first day of the old woman's story, July 4, 1918.

It seemed like all of Nashville was at Celebration Park today. I danced and danced until it was time to go, although I think I would have liked to stay.

Ginny read the words a second time. The park and dancing, but nothing about David, George, or Clyde. She kept reading.

July 5, 1918

Last night, Father gave me permission to teach music. I hope to start next week. At Sol's, I got a new hat today and, I think, a new friend.

Not exactly enlightening stuff, although the friend part showed promise.

July 6, 1918

Katie Belle and I went down to the Women's Center this morning and M. was there to surprise me. I can't remember feeling this way before. It feels like I've known him forever, but I'm not sure Father would approve.

Ginny's fingers tightened over the book. Was M. the new friend? Was this the same man who'd written the love letter? And why wouldn't her father approve? She read on.

July 7, 1918

I'd hoped I was wrong about Father, but I don't think so. I don't like to keep this from him or Mother, but they wouldn't understand. I won't let it stop me though.

Wouldn't understand what? Ginny looked up. Anna Mae's cryptic words didn't make sense. She turned the page.

July 8, 1918

I'm not afraid about tonight, only about tomorrow. The war makes us all afraid.

Ginny scanned the page but there was nothing more. She flipped to the next week and the week after. All blank. Ginny frowned. There had been nervousness and excitement in Anna Mae's words, and more than a touch of defiance, but there had also been happiness. She was sure of it. And then there was nothing.

~~~~

The next morning, Ginny itched to ask Anna Mae about the daily journal, but the old woman was eager to get started, tucking the quilt around her legs. "Now where were we?"

"Your father was driving the train and George was the porter," Ginny said, reluctantly pushing thoughts of Anna Mae's new friend to the back of her mind. "And there were the brothers too."

"Oh, yes, that's right. Well, you've been introduced to three of the men in my story, so it's time you met the others." Anna Mae settled back in her chair. "About two hundred miles away, over in Mississippi, there were other folks celebrating the Fourth. One of those folks was a young man, a boy really, only nineteen years old. His name was John Lang, and he worked on a farm with his uncle. He liked farming, but like a lot of young men, he yearned to sign up for the war, to join his cousin Robert."
~~~~

CHAPTER FOUR

Thursday, July 4, 1918
Afternoon

THIS IS THE crisis of the world. For all the long years to come men will point to the year 1918 as the great Day of Decision, the day when the world decided whether it would submit to military despotism and an endless armed peace—if peace it could be called—or whether they would put down the menace of German militarism and inaugurate the United States of the World.

We of the colored race have no ordinary interest in the outcome. That which the German power represents today spells death to the aspirations of Negroes and all darker races for equality, freedom and democracy. Let us not hesitate. Let us, while this war lasts, forget our special grievances and close our ranks shoulder to shoulder with our own white fellow citizens and the allied nations that are fighting for democracy. We make no ordinary sacrifice, but we make it gladly and willingly with our eyes lifted to the hills.

—Editorial, *The Crisis*, July 1918

~~~~
~~~~

John Lang leaned against a large oak, the thick green leaves of the tree offering the only shade for miles. Sweat coated his skin, making it slick with salt. Behind him, the voices of his momma and his aunts rose and fell as they told one story after another. It didn't matter that every story had been told dozens of times, changed, and retold a dozen more. They could keep at it for hours. Just listening to them made him glad. It had been a good day, a day of celebration, and he didn't want it to end. His mother giggled like a young girl before the sweet sound was drowned out by his Aunt Ruth's cackling.

A lone cloud passed overhead, broke, and splintered into threads. Sighing, John donned his hat and pushed off the tree. His stepfather and uncles passed around a jug.

"I'm worried," his uncle Elijah said, his wiry gray brows drawn into a single line. "If we don't get rain by next week or the week after, the corn ain't gonna be no good. And the cotton neither." It wasn't the first time John had heard the complaints about the weather. Sometimes it was too dry, and other times it was too wet. John knew his uncle didn't like being dependent on the weather, didn't like being dependent on the landowner either, but as far as John could tell, his uncle didn't do a whole lot about it.

Abel House got to his feet. John watched his stepfather, a sinking feeling in his stomach. Years of labor had taken their toll on the man. His hair was more gray than black now, and his hands were studded with callouses, but he could still take most of the men at the picnic. He had wide-set features and skin that cracked like dried-out leather, but it was his eyes that people noticed. Lighter than most folks—on account of his white daddy—House's eyes caught and held the light. John's momma said they were shot through with gold, but John didn't know about that. He thought maybe it was something else.

"There's rain comin'," House said. "Feel it in my bones. Tomorrow or the next day for sure."

"I hope you're right," Uncle Elijah said.

As the men droned on, John relaxed and stopped listening. His momma sat on the rocks with his aunts, their skirts heavy with the dirt and dust kicked up by the children. His sister, Leah, sat nearby, whispering with one of the other girls. Behind his aunts, he caught sight of Sabina. She held her baby on her hip, her gaze unfocused, far away. He watched as the baby pulled at the long braid she wore, bringing her back from wherever she was. She glanced up then, and his pulse quickened. He waited, but she didn't see him. She never did.

"Who's that?" Uncle Elijah asked, arm raised, finger pointing.

John squinted in the bright sunshine. A man in a brown rumpled suit lingered at the far edge of the clearing. Flanked by two other men, he held a wad of folded papers in his hand. Studying the man, John felt sure he'd never seen him or the others before. Voices dropped to murmurs, all the bright laughter from earlier gone. The stranger's dark gaze, unblinking and somber, fell on John and settled. He didn't smile, didn't nod. A shiver crawled up John's spine.

The stranger walked to the center of the grounds, the clomp of his boots the only sound. A second man followed and set a wooden box before him. John watched as the stranger climbed onto the box, his face stony, thick lips set in a hard line. Waving the papers at the crowd, he opened his mouth to speak.

"Good people of Hernando, Mississippi. I've been asked to come here today by the government of this great country of ours." His voice rang out over the whispers, loud and knowing. He didn't talk like he came from Mississippi or from anywhere around there. Yet he had a way of drawing out his words that commanded attention, making them listen, and John inched forward. "Even as we celebrate our country's independence, we are at war with Germany. I know what you're thinking. Has nothing to do with us. It's far, far away." He pointed a finger to the east. "What can we do about it here in Mississippi? And that's what I'm here to tell you today." His skin was dotted with perspiration, but he didn't remove his suit jacket. He bowed his head to read from the papers in his hand. "This is a world struggle for democracy and win it we must. How can we win it? There is but one way. Everyone—man, woman, and child, be he a millionaire or a day laborer—

must do his level best at his work, wherever he may be, whether on the farm, at the docks, in the machine shop, in the mill, at the White House in Washington, in the kitchen, in the home, or in the trenches."

John eyed the man as he read. The war had been going on for more than a year. His own cousin had signed up—hadn't waited to be called—leaving Sabina and their baby. Robert might even be in the trenches, might be dead, but no one knew for sure. John had wanted to go too. At nineteen he was old enough, but his stepfather wouldn't let him. Uncle Elijah needed John now that Robert had gone. If they couldn't get the crops planted and harvested in time, Mr. Hadley would give the land to someone else. They'd seen it happen before.

"And do not forget that any person, black or white, who does not work hard, who lags in any way, who fails to buy a Liberty bond, or a War Savings stamp if he can, is against his country and is, therefore, our bitter enemy." The crowd stirred at the man's words. As though sensing the unease, the stranger's face split wide, his white teeth shining. "I am happy to say that the majority of our men and women are working like all other good Americans to make their labor win the war. Only a few weeks ago the world's record for driving rivets in building steel ships was broken by Charles Knight, a Negro workman at Sparrows Point, Maryland. In one nine-hour day he drove 4,875 three-quarter-inch rivets in the hull of a steel ship. The newspapers of the country have lauded him for his work. The British government sent him a prize of one hundred twenty-five dollars." There were a handful of gasps followed by a smattering of applause. John had never seen that much money at one time and was fairly sure no one else had either. "Now is the time to work every day we can. Now is the time to work every hour we can. Now is the time to make and save every dollar we can."

The man spoke again of hard work and flags and stars. "Negroes are being asked in every city, town, and rural district to join in this work of winning this war. We, like other folk, are having an unusual chance to work and save our country. Let every one of us be wide awake and make the most of this opportunity. Let him bear in mind that every time he makes good on his job, he helps his country and the race. Let him also remember that every time a Negro falls down on his job, he pulls down his country and the entire race, and thus makes winning the war less possible."

John's shoulders tightened and he sensed the same in the men around him. The stranger said, "A few months ago—" but the shorter man with him took him by the shoulder and shook his head, nodding toward the audience, now tight-fisted and grim. A look passed between the men, and he lifted his head, smiled wide, and started again. "My fellow patriots, you and those who came before you are to be admired." He went on to commend those who had fought in previous wars, praising the way they'd bravely protected the country's flag. Uncle Elijah and House and the others relaxed again. Voice booming, he spoke about those who were now at the front in France, risking their very lives in this new war. "Will you, because of your refusal to work six days in every week, or because of your failure to save as much food as you can, or because of any lack of interest whatever on your part, have to answer to our boys on their return, maimed in battle or even to men who never return?" The man pointed a finger at the crowd, eyes bugging as he concluded. "We are our brothers' keepers; we, too, are soldiers on duty, and in our hands rests the destiny of our country and our fellow men. America needs, expects, and asks every man to do his duty."

The stranger paused to take a breath, his arm falling back to his side. "There's a new gunpowder plant outside of Nashville," he said. "DuPont, a very patriotic company, is in charge of it. But they need men to do the work, to make the gunpowder. They need men like you. How can our good men at the front fight without gunpowder?"

John's heartbeat quickened under his sweat-soaked shirt.

"What about our land?" Uncle Elijah asked. "If I don't have a crop, they'll give the land to someone else."

Unfazed, the stranger had a quick answer. "That's true, and that's why the work at DuPont is temporary. You'd be back in lots of time to harvest your crops, and you could also serve your country." He explained that while there were new munitions plants everywhere, the Nashville plant would be the largest. He told the men they needed help to complete the construction as well as work inside the plant. "Three months, men. That's all we'd need. There's a train leaving come Monday to take the next men ready to report for work."

"How much money we talkin' 'bout?"

"Well, I'm glad you asked that. Some of our best workers are earning six dollars a day." The stranger grinned at the chorus of approval. "Now mind you, that's for the best. But even the lowest are earning two to three dollars a day."

John turned the words over in his brain. *Back before the harvest. Six dollars a day.* House didn't earn six dollars in a week. But Monday was only a few days away. John licked his parched lips, his hands leaving his pockets.

"Don't you be thinkin' 'bout anything just yet, boy." The voice belonged to House. His stepfather stood at his shoulder, his lips close to the young man's ear.

Matt Toles, John's oldest friend, stepped forward. "What about the factories up north?"

The stranger swung toward Matt. He saw the challenge in the tilt of Matt's chin, in the hard line of his mouth. "What about them?"

John watched Matt as he spoke, recognized the set of his jaw. They'd known each other since they were big enough to walk, big enough to go to school, and big enough to work. Matt's daddy worked the Wingold farm, one of the biggest this side of Memphis. Matt worked the farm, too, when his daddy made him, but Matt didn't like farming. He didn't like Hernando or Mississippi either.

"There's been lots of folks coming down and trying to get us to come up north," Matt said. "They have plants and factories too. Why should we go to Nashville when it's no better than around here? At least up north, folks like us have more of a chance." A hush fell over the crowd.

The stranger spun around, surveying the small crowd as he spoke. "It's true that the factories up north have needed help since President Wilson decided to enter the war. And many good people like yourselves have answered that call. But this is a new call. The needs are in Nashville now." He paused. "This isn't only the war with Germany. It's a war about democracy and it is our duty to defend our flag and our country."

Matt snickered. One or two others grumbled at the man's words, too, but most stood silent, listening. It was true that while most of the men wanted change—like Matt—there was good reason to fear speaking up.

The man raised his voice again. "In the words of W. E. B. Dubois, I say, 'Let us, while this war lasts, forget our special grievances and close our ranks shoulder to shoulder with our own white fellow citizens and the allied nations that are fighting for democracy. We make no ordinary sacrifice, but we make it gladly and willingly with our eyes lifted to the hills.'" Another pause. "Train's on Monday. And don't forget the pay. Six dollars."

The stranger stepped off the box and was soon surrounded. Throwing up his hands, Matt pushed his way out of the crowd.

"Three months," one man said. "Guaranteed pay," said another, and then, "Before the harvest."

Lingering outside the circle, John's mind buzzed. If the men who went to the plant were back before fall, how could his stepfather argue with that? He cast a sideways glance at House.

"Your momma's tired, boy," the older man said. "We best be getting home."

John looked back at the crowd where more than a few men took flyers from the stranger. House's fingers pressed into his shoulder, and John let out a long, weary breath. "Yes, sir."

NASHVILLE TO OBSERVE THE FOURTH

Nation's Birthday to Be Elaborately Celebrated Today.

In the city there will be a patriotic celebration and pageant at Centennial Park this afternoon and evening for the benefit of the Red Cross. The city and county divisions of the Women's Committee of the Council of National Defense are giving this in compliance with President Wilson's request that all citizens assemble to their respective cities and truly celebrate the Fourth of July. There will be dances and community singing. Mrs. Celia Grady Reddy and Mrs. Ruthbeth Binford will be in charge of the pageant.

—*The Tennessean*, July 4, 1918

Milton Lowenstein weaved to the right, sidestepping the crowd. He could hear the band behind him, finishing their set. He'd left Uncle Leopold and Aunt Rikki at the pageant stage, the performers grouped around them. Uncle Leo had brought an array of hats for the young ladies to wear. It was a brilliant marketing move, of course, but most things Uncle Leo did were not without purpose. The song ended, the band quieted, and a restless hum filled the air. The pageant would start soon.

He walked on. To his right, there were tables piled high with sandwiches and sweets. He knew there were more tables like these spread in a semicircle around the perimeter of the stage. Surely, no one would go hungry on this day of celebration. A pair of former schoolmates hovered near the closest table, each balancing a plate laden with food. He kept moving. He couldn't remember when Centennial Park had seen so many people. The city's streetcars were full, dropping load after load at the gated entrance. It seemed half of Nashville had turned out for the Fourth.

Milton slowed as he approached the Parthenon. The monument sat perched on a small hill, a massive rectangular structure with thick, marble-like columns and an imposing statue of the Greek goddess Athena. He'd been inside once, though he didn't think it was much to see. At one time, it had been the centerpiece of the city's centennial exposition but had since fallen into disrepair. He passed through a sunken garden bright with summer blooms. Through the trees, he caught a glimpse of Lake Watauga, the afternoon sun making the surface shimmer. He walked toward it, hands in his pockets. There were fewer people here. A trio of young boys sat on one side of the lake, fishing poles dangling from their hands. A smattering of couples sat under trees on their blankets, escaping the crowds. At the water's edge, he reached into his pocket and pulled out a crust of bread. Breaking it into crumbs, he tossed it over the surface. Fish darted to and fro, their hungry mouths breaking through the water to snatch the tiny morsels of bread. He stood transfixed, watching until the last crumb was gone.

He kept walking until he found himself on the other side of the park, far from the festivities. Seeking shade and solitude, he rested his back against the fat trunk of a large oak. He stoked his pipe and sucked in the smoke, savoring the pungent flavor. He thought about the friends he'd passed earlier. It seemed there were fewer of them now. The draft was taking them one by one. He touched a hand to his jacket. He carried his papers with him, a reminder of his own commitment.

He'd thought Uncle Leo would be angry that he'd signed up for the war, but Uncle Leo had proved him wrong.

"It is a good thing to be patriotic. Love of country is a gift, Milton." Uncle Leopold's accent thickened as he spoke. "It's a good thing you will go. This war." He shook his head. "America must end it. It's not good for anyone."

Although the young man had heard similar speeches from his peers, he couldn't keep his thoughts from spilling out. "But you're German."

"Bah." His uncle stamped his foot. "I'm American. I've been here longer than I was in Germany."

"Why though?" Again, Milton wanted to clap his hand over his mouth, but it was too late. Uncle Leo and his brother were legendary in Nashville and all of Tennessee for their hats and dresses and equally legendary for their German ways. Aunt Rikki cooked German meals, and sometimes they spoke quietly in German, knowing he couldn't understand. More than once, the young man had wondered why they'd left their families, why they'd never gone back to their home.

His uncle sat down, exhaling. He spread his hands across the table and chewed his lower lip. "Germany is not the country I once loved," he said. "It is a country seeking something else. It is . . ." Milton tensed, then started when Leo slapped a hand against the wood. "Doesn't matter. What matters is that you will serve your country—our country." He threw his hands up in the air. "What? You have no joke about this?" He didn't wait for Milton to answer, his voice gruff. "You will go, and you will come back." It was the second time that day that his uncle had surprised him.

In a rare moment of affection, his Aunt Rikki cupped his face with her hands, the pads of her fingers hardened after years of work in the millinery. "I will miss you, Milton."

Milton leaned against the tree now, the smoke from his pipe drifting upward. As the day he was to report neared, his aunt and uncle had grown more distant. They rarely spoke of the army or the war anymore. Instead, they grumbled about who would travel to Memphis and Kentucky and Mississippi to sell their wares. He knew better than to take it personally. His own enthusiasm had waned. Two weeks. Only fourteen days until he would leave.

It wasn't that he didn't want to serve his country. He did, but he wondered if they'd be all that happy to have him. He'd never hunted. He'd never even shot a rifle. His hands were soft. Most of his life had been spent in school and his uncle's millinery. He could discuss fabrics, lace, and the latest trends in hats. What if he couldn't do it? Worse, he worried, what if he got someone killed?

~~~~

Outside the city, Clyde stood with his brother near a white bridge, his finger extended toward the horizon. Green stalks with browning leaves covered the ground as far as a man could see. A single train track cut through the field, the shiny metal and wooden ties arcing from east to west. "There's a train yard between the station and here."
~~~~

Carl chewed on a leaf, his brows knitted. "I don't like it. The city is too close."

"That's why it works. No one would expect it."

Carl pointed up the hill at a large, brick building with tall windows. "What about that place? Is it empty?"

"Nothing to worry about. Bunch of nuns and orphans. Even if they did see something, what are they going to do?"

"I don't know. Something."

Clyde hid his smile. Carl had an aversion to preachers, nuns, and all things religious. Clyde had little use for the church himself, but it went beyond that for Carl. No doubt, their own father's fire and brimstone speeches had something do with it. "It'll be dark when we get here. By the time anyone from the orphanage could spot us, it will be too late."

"Before sunrise?"

Clyde nodded. "At my signal, the men will ride."

"What if the train's not on time? We'll be exposed."

"It will be." Clyde shoved his hands in his pockets. "I don't know how much time we have, but no need to rush things tonight. Laying the groundwork is enough. We don't need you to do more than that."

Carl reddened. "What are you saying, big brother?"

"I'm saying it's a holiday. The men you meet tonight should be feeling fine. They'll be less suspicious of a stranger." He paused. "Save the strong-arm tactics for another day."

His brother's jaw clenched. "It would be quicker the other way."

Clyde sighed. His brother had always preferred to act first and think later. That type of behavior usually got men in their business killed.

Neither brought up the game Carl had botched in Colorado a few months earlier, but it was there just the same. Carl had been lucky that time, lucky the knife hadn't caught him a few inches higher—even if he didn't say so.

"You lose tonight, Carl. Stick to the plan." He told his brother everything he'd learned about the postal worker, his family, and his friends.

Carl tucked his fingers into his waistband. A single vein in his neck pulsed. "And the sister?"

"Later. If we need it."

The minutes ticked by, and the hardness around Carl's mouth softened.

"Fine. You're the boss."

It was Clyde's turn to grunt. He needed Carl to follow orders this once. Together, they walked back to their horses and swung their legs over the saddles. Carl squinted up at the orphanage on the hill. "Bunch of nuns, huh?"

"And orphans."

Carl shuddered, steering his horse away from the large brick house. "I don't care what you say. Place gives me the creeps."

~~~~

POWDER MAKING BEGUN AT BEND

The first unit of Old Hickory, the Government's new powder plant here has now started the manufacture of smokeless gunpowder. The initial charge of guncotton was started through July as per schedule.

—*The Tennessean*, July 4, 1918

~~~~

"I saw you watching her."

John stopped walking, shooting his sister Leah a dark look. House and his mother were barely ten feet up the road.

"They can't hear us," she said, but she slowed her pace. "Why don't you talk to her?"

He had no answer. It wasn't that he wouldn't like to, but what was the point? Sabina was someone else's wife and a mother now too. If he'd had a chance, it was long gone. There was nothing to say.

"I think she's lonely."

"Please stop."

"What did I say?" she teased.

He ignored her, and for several minutes, neither spoke. House and his mother carried baskets, empty now. The food had been eaten. The games had been played. Stories had been told and countless songs sung until they were all hoarse. It was the best Fourth of July John could remember, and yet, he felt vaguely dissatisfied. Leah would say it was about Sabina, but he knew that wasn't it.

House called back over his shoulder, "Stop your lollygagging. Tomorrow is another day and there's work to be done." He didn't wait for a response, lengthening his own stride.

Leah rolled her eyes and stuck out her tongue. John bit his own tongue to keep from laughing. They passed the grocer and the school.

"What did you think of that man today?" she asked. "The one talking about going to the gunpowder place?"

He stayed quiet a moment, remembering the stranger and the words he said. Matt had walked away, not bothering to hide his scorn. There were others, too, who'd felt the same, but there were more who didn't. The promise of a job was one thing. The promise of good pay was another. "He was okay," he said finally.

It was no answer and they both knew it. "Do you want to go?"

"Shhh." He waved his hand.

"He can't hear us," she said again.

John wasn't so sure. House had big ears to match his broad shoulders and strong hands. "It doesn't matter what I want."

His sister leaned in closer. "It doesn't have to be that way," she said. Her fingers tightened over his. "We don't always have to do what he says."

The sun slipped lower in the sky, and the summer light faded to soft gray, and John squinted to make out their small house in the shadows. He loved her spirit, but for all her brave words, she'd never defied House. She wouldn't dare.

He pulled his hand back. "Don't we?"

THE PAGEANT AT CENTENNIAL PARK

In accord with the celebrations observed throughout the United States, the citizens of Nashville will assemble at Centennial park this afternoon at 5 o'clock to take part in the expression of patriotic observance of the glorious Fourth.

—*The Tennessean*, July 4, 1918

Milton took a long puff from his pipe. From somewhere in the park, the horns blasted again. The pageant must be over. His aunt and uncle would be expecting him back. He let a few minutes pass before he pushed away from the tree. Even as it sank lower in the sky, the sun blazed, and Milton slipped off his jacket, slinging it over his arm. A shout went up from nearby. A pack of boys ran across the park, baseball gloves in their hands. Behind them, three women sauntered up the gentle slope of lawn, arms linked at the elbow. The tallest of the three wore a navy-blue hat with a red ribbon around the brim and a day dress in the same shade of blue. A wide sash in white satin circled her waist. The skirt fell softly to her shins, a few inches above her slender ankles. He recognized the new style, wondered if it was a Jonas dress. As they crossed in front of him, she looked his way, and he drew in a breath, his pipe going slack in his mouth. He'd seen her before. He knew that heart-shaped face, that sprinkling of freckles that matched her golden-red hair, knew that long stride.

The first time he'd caught sight of her had been weeks earlier. She'd been wearing red, a color that made her hair seem even brighter somehow. He'd seen her again a month later, strolling down his own street. Only after she'd passed by him did he close his mouth. Last week, he'd seen her on the corner near his uncle's shop, handing out flyers with a half dozen other women, all dressed in white and yellow. At first, he hadn't understood, and then he'd remembered. Yellow and white were the colors of the women's suffragette movement. His aunt, a tiny woman with a powerful belief in her own voice, had tried to join one of the marches a few years earlier, but his uncle worried it would hurt business. Against her wishes, Aunt Rikki had stayed home, but the cause had stuck with Milton, nonetheless. And here was this mesmerizing woman again, head thrown back in laughter, skipping past him.

All three women, arms still linked, headed in the direction of the music and celebration. His legs trembled and his breath caught in his throat. Heart drumming faster, he hurried past the lake, the sunken garden, and the tables of food. Reaching the throng crowded around the stage, he searched for the tall woman's hat but lost sight of it among a sea of similarly colored hats. Without thinking, he wiped the sweat from his brow and plunged into the mob.

A new band took to the stage, each of its members wearing matching red, white, and blue vests. The bandleader stepped forward.

"Happy Independence Day," he shouted. The crowd roared in response. "Before we get started, we want to remind you that the Women's Committee of the Council of National Defense has organized this celebration to benefit the Red Cross and our soldiers." A second roar sounded. When it died down, the bandleader lifted his horn. "So, without further ado, let's celebrate."

Milton scanned the faces of the couples taking their places on the dance floor, twirling in time to the sounds of "Tiger Rag." There she was. She sailed by, her hand resting lightly on the shoulder of a dark-haired gentleman. He counted the minutes and seconds until the song ended. Spotting his chance, he moved quickly.

"Cutting in," he said, tapping the dark-haired man on the shoulder. When the man bowed out, Milton found himself standing nearly eye to eye with the woman. "If the lady doesn't object."

He took her hand in his.

"For now, I don't. But I reserve the right to change my mind."

Milton's hand fell before he realized she was laughing. He forced himself to relax, and the pair glided over the lawn to the sounds of the music. The band changed tunes again, slowing to a waltz. He placed one hand on her back above her waist and held the other high in the air. Almost floating, their bodies moved across the floor as one, as though they'd spent a lifetime as partners. She smiled at him in a shy, almost surprised way, and for the first time, he was grateful for the dance lessons his aunt had insisted he take. As the song came to an end, however, she was no longer smiling. Her attention had been drawn to something or someone else. His mouth went dry.

"Is it something I said?"

She seemed to startle. "Oh, I'm sorry. That was rude of me, wasn't it?"

"It wasn't, but you do seem a bit distracted." He spun her across the lawn. "And I haven't even told any of my famous jokes yet."

Her laugh, when it came, was full-throated, not the tinkling laugh of the girls his aunt usually introduced him to. "I'm sorry," she said. "Are they famous? Really?"

"No," he admitted. "My uncle doesn't think I'm funny at all, but I did get you to laugh."

"You did, didn't you?"

He gestured behind her. "Were you looking for someone? A minute ago?"

"My mother and my sister. They were over there, but I don't see them now."

"Oh." He dropped her hand. "Do you need to find them? I can help."

"That's nice of you." She started to pull away, but stopped, appraising him again. "Maybe after. Right now, I need to dance."

He took her hand once more. "Dance it is, then."

They moved together once more, their bodies swaying in time to the music. The song ended, but if she noticed, she didn't say. When a stocky man with a shock of white hair tapped him on the shoulder, Anna Mae proclaimed her dance card full. Milton said nothing, unsure whether she meant him or someone else. But as the music played on, she held on to his hand.

"You don't mind, do you?" she asked, her cheeks flushing pink. "If there's someone else you want to ask . . ."

"Oh, no," he said quickly. And so, they danced to the next song and the next and the next, until the band stopped to take a break.

Reluctantly, he stepped back. "May I get you something to drink?"

"That would be nice."

"I don't even know your name," he said as they walked.

"Anna Mae Kennedy."

"Well, Anna Mae Kennedy, it's nice to meet you." He bowed at the waist. "I'm Milton Lowenstein."

"It's nice to meet you, too, Milton."

"I hope this won't sound terribly forward, but I've seen you before."

"Oh?"

He told her about seeing her handing out flyers with the other women on the corner. With each word, her smile slipped until she stared at him, stone-faced.

"Have I said something wrong?" he asked, his pulse jumping under his skin.

"That depends," she said, eyes narrowed. "On which kind of man you are."

"Which kind of man?"

"Well, the last man who came around had quite a bit to say about my suffragette activities."

In an instant, he felt sure he understood. Perhaps his aunt hadn't gone to the march that day, but she'd done plenty since, educating both Milton and his uncle along the way. "And why would he do that?"

"I don't know. Why would any man?"

"Most likely because he's a fool."

She drew back, studying him now. His cheeks reddened, but he said nothing, waiting. When she finally smiled, her eyes glowing, his shoulders loosened again.

"You are not what I expected, Mr. Lowenstein."

She was everything he'd expected, but he knew better than to say so. "I'm glad." He gave a half laugh. "At least I think I am." She laughed with him, and he gestured back toward the dance floor. "I hope you'll want to dance some more. I hear the band playing tonight is even better than this one."

A tiny line appeared between her brows. "I'm afraid I'll have to miss it. We have to get home before my father returns for dinner." She raised her hand and waved. He spun around, spotting her sister and mother moving in their direction. "I need to go," she said. "I'm sorry."

He touched her lightly on the arm. "Maybe I could see you again." Before she could decline, he suggested the first thing that popped into his mind. "At Sol Frankland's shop?" If she was surprised, she hid it well.

"That would be nice," she said. She slipped by him then, intercepting her mother and sister before they could be introduced.

He watched the three of them veer toward the gates until they disappeared behind a row of trees. Only after they were gone did the racing of his heart calm and his breathing slow.

"Anna Mae Kennedy." He shoved his hands in his pockets, mouth wide in a toothy grin. "Until tomorrow."

CHAPTER FIVE

Summer 1988

GINNY SAT FORWARD, her fingers closing over the hard edge of the chair. She remembered the entry in the *Line a Day* journal and felt transported. *I danced and danced until it was time to go, although I think I would have liked to stay.* She could see the couple twirling across the dance floor and hear the band playing, feel the crowd swelling around them. Milton—M. in the journal—had to be that man.

"Do you believe in romance, dear, or is that old-fashioned now?" Anna Mae asked her.

"Romance?" It wasn't something Ginny thought she knew much about—at least not the kind you saw in movies, the kind where lovers saw fireworks at their first touch. Her own first date with Shawn had been less stars and butterflies and more full-on dread with a little curiosity thrown in.

"You fixed me up with a lawyer?" she'd said to her friend. "Aren't all lawyers on power trips and love to hear themselves talk?"

"Not this one. He's corporate law."

"Great. A boring lawyer," Ginny said with a groan but promised to give the date a chance.

They met at a popular restaurant crowded with people. Safe and unintimidating, she thought, and easy to leave when the one-way conversation she expected got to be too much.

He showed up out of breath, his hair damp from a shower. Over his shoulder, he carried a long, oblong bag—too large to be a briefcase and too oddly shaped to be luggage.

"What's that?" she asked.

"If I tell you, I'll have to kill you."

She drew back and folded her arms over her chest.

"Not funny?"

"No."

He shrugged. "Fine. I'll tell you, but after that, I don't want to talk about it."

She agreed.

"It's a foil. A sword," he told her in a matter-of-fact tone, as though that explained everything. But his short answer only fueled her curiosity.

"And why would you bring a sword to a first date?"

"I wanted to impress you?" He flashed her a smile. "Is it working?"

She leaned over to take another look at the bag he'd slid under the table and thought maybe she'd give the date a chance after all. He was definitely not boring. "Will you tell me why you have a sword after dinner?"

His smile widened. "If you still want to know, then yes."

She looked back at Anna Mae now, the memory washing over her. "Maybe. It depends on what you mean by romance, I guess."

"Well, romance is a bit like life, isn't it? It seduces you, wraps around you, pulls you along, and then one day, it ends as suddenly as it began."

Ginny half laughed. "To be honest, you don't make it sound that great."

"Oh, but it is, dear, it is. It's the most wonderful thing in the world. It comes in all shapes and sizes. It makes the sky bluer and the sun brighter. It sweeps you along, grabbing you whether you're looking for it or not." Her fingers rose, brushing at the air. "The slightest touch—to your hand or your cheek—reaches into your soul and holds you in a way that you just know."

Ginny's brows puckered. A touch that reached into your soul? Had the old woman read too many romance novels?

"But, the thing is . . ." Anna Mae started, her dreamy smile fading, "true romance can be fleeting. Far too fleeting. Like life. Not always, but sometimes." She spread her hands wide. "The trick is to be grateful to have had it at all." Spotting Ginny's expression, Anna Mae wagged a finger. "You're wondering if I've lost my marbles. Don't deny it. If I were in your shoes, I'd wonder the same." Her smile broadened. "You're young and have many years ahead of you, years of triumph, failure, love, and romance, and like it or not, loss. These are the things that define our lives."

Her words reminded Ginny of conversations growing up. "You sound a little like my father."

"Do I?" she asked, seeming pleased. "Well, I'll take that as a compliment."

Although she'd promised not to ask questions, the way in which Anna Mae spoke of romance only piqued Ginny's curiosity. "Anna Mae, about you and Milton? Was there—"

"Why don't we leave that for another day, dear?" Anna Mae cut her off, her hand closing over the gold locket around her neck. "We've lots of time for questions after I've finished. Lots of time."

Ginny found herself on the floor once again, the lid of the trunk pushed back. She'd reread the journal, but other than guessing Milton must be the unnamed man, she remained stymied, unable to puzzle out what it meant. Setting the journal aside, she rifled through the photographs once more but found none of Anna Mae with a young man. Reaching into the bottom of the trunk, she pulled out a set of books. The first, *Anne of Green Gables,* had a mint-green cover and the profile of a young girl in the center. Ginny's fingers traced the golden letters, remembering how much she'd loved this story as a girl. Along with the first book was *Anne of Avonlea, Anne of the Island,*

and *Anne's House of Dreams*. Each had the well-worn look of a book that had been read over and over. Clasping *Anne of Green Gables* to her chest, Ginny felt her heart swell for Anna Mae.

With a yawn, she repacked the trunk, save for the books. Those she carried up to her room.

It was the books she'd been looking at when Shawn called that night.

"You're doing it, Gin."

She rolled onto her side, the phone pressed against her ear. "Doing what?"

"Getting attached. You're going there every day now. I'm going to be in Nashville at the end of next week, and I'd really like to spend time with my wife."

The snort escaped before she could stop it. "Why start now?"

"Ginny . . ." He drew out her name as if speaking to a small child, but she didn't apologize. She wouldn't. "I'm trying here," he said.

"Are you? By criticizing me?"

"I don't think it's too much to ask that I not have to share you with a stranger in a nursing home."

She exhaled. "She's not a stranger."

"Do you hear yourself? You didn't even know this woman a few days ago. Now you see her every day. She's not your grandmother, Gin, as much as you miss her."

It occurred to her that he thought she was lonely. The idea made her want to laugh. She'd been lonelier in those last weeks in their apartment, each of them dodging the other, their few conversations stiff and oddly formal. At least Anna Mae's story had given her something to think about other than her own problems.

More than that, the old woman's quiet strength and resolve had somehow chipped away at the edges of her pain. The hurt wasn't gone—not by a long shot—but the humiliation and anger that had driven her for weeks had ebbed, eclipsed by sadness and maybe a bit of reflection. Either way, Ginny didn't have the energy to argue.

"Shawn, do you ever miss fencing?" She didn't know which of them was more surprised by her question.

There was a brief pause, and the sound of crumpling paper. "Yeah, I miss it."

The foil he'd carried had been his hobby, his weapon in the sport his English father had insisted he learn as a boy. Despite its lack of popularity, he'd managed to keep at it through high school, college, and law school, finding clubs where he could practice. But in recent years, there'd been no time. When he wasn't working, he was traveling for work. The things he had made time for were things she didn't want to think about. It was a double-edged sword.

"Maybe I'll start again," he said.

The idea made her glad. Another surprise. "That would be nice for you."

"Yeah, it would." He cleared his throat. "Gin, the story—the one she's telling you. Is it any good?" His voice held none of the judgment of earlier.

She didn't have to think about the question long. Although she didn't know where it was going, she realized she wanted to. Milton, Clyde, George, John, and David. She wanted to know more about all of them. "Yes, it's good."

"Do you believe her? About it being true?"

Overhead, the ceiling fan turned on its axis, the whir the only noise in the room. She blinked, considering. "I don't know, Shawn. I don't know."

~~~~

The man from Room Two glared from his wheelchair. He mumbled under his breath, the same phrases she'd heard before. "They're coming. In the night."

Ginny started to pass by him, stopped, and went back. "How are you today, Mr. Morris?"

The man's head jerked up, his mouth screwing up in an ugly scowl. "THEY'RE COMING," he shouted. "In the night." The second-floor nurse got to her feet.
~~~~

"Quiet down, Mr. Morris," she said, "or I'll have to put you back in your room. You don't want me to do that, do you?"

His chin fell. He averted his face, hands twisting over and over in his lap. The nurse went back to the files on her desk.

"Oh, there you are," Anna Mae said, hands fluttering up when Ginny entered the room. "Would you mind pulling open the blinds a bit more, dear? I want to show you something."

Ginny pulled the cord, raising the blinds.

"Do you see that track? The one that goes under the bridge? That's New White Bridge. Well, I guess it's called Old White Bridge now, but not when I was a girl." Ginny followed the line of Anna Mae's finger to see a short bridge constructed of white concrete. "That was the bridge that led to County Road. And do you see that track? That's the one that brought the overnight train from Memphis. See how it passes right under the bridge? None of those buildings you see now were here—only the orphanage up on the hill. If you walked the track, you would see nothing but cornfields for miles." She pointed farther up the track where it arced and seemed to disappear. "There. That's Dutchman's Curve."

"Dutchman's Curve?"

Anna Mae dropped her hand. "It's part of the story, but I'm getting ahead of myself. Sit down, dear."

Ginny settled onto the chair, doing the best she could to find a comfortable spot on the hard wood.

"In those days, Blacks and whites did things separately. It was before civil rights and the desegregation of schools."

A look Ginny couldn't place crossed the old woman's face. Embarrassment? Regret? Or something else? She didn't know Anna Mae well enough to guess, but she did know this was the South, and for some, the change that came with the civil rights movement wasn't welcomed. Her shoulders tensed.

"And the Fourth of July, Independence Day, was no different. Blacks had their own parades and celebrations at their own parks. I can't say exactly what they were like because I wasn't there—that would have been quite a scandal, although I would have liked to have gone." This time, there was no mistaking Anna Mae's wistful expression, and Ginny relaxed a little. As she'd taken to doing, the older woman tapped a silent tune in her lap as she talked. "Sometimes, you could hear the music from their concerts for miles . . ."

CHAPTER SIX

Thursday, July 4, 1918
Evening

AT PARKS FOR NEGROES.

At Hadley and Greenwood parks, the amusement parks for colored people, will be held Fourth of July celebrations today.

The main feature of the Hadley park celebration will be a thrift parade, a patriotic program and music by Abel's band. Greenwood will have all amusements open and a local colored band will furnish music.

—*The Tennessean,* July 4, 1918

~~~~

George dragged his bread over the plate, sopping up the last of the gravy. "Another great meal, Celeste."

His wife cleared the table. "Was it still warm?"

"It was fine," he told her. "How was Greenwood Park today?"

Before Celeste could answer, his daughter, Anita, jumped in. "There was a parade, Daddy. Everyone was singing, and we played games. There were contests. The boys even won candy."
~~~~

He laughed. "I guess that means it was good."

"It was," Celeste said. "The boys are exhausted."

"Are they in bed?"

"Yes. Fought me all the way, but since I put them to bed, I haven't heard a peep."

George shifted his attention to his young cousin. The boy hadn't spoken much at dinner, but the porter hadn't missed the way he stabbed at his food between sighs. "And what about you, Ben? Did you enjoy yourself at the park?"

The younger man dropped his fork onto his plate. "It was okay. Band was good."

George waited, but the boy said nothing more. "That's fine, then," he said and pushed away from the table, settling into his favorite chair. He stretched his legs, his muscles loosening. A copy of the latest *Crisis* and the previous week's *Globe* were folded on his side table. Like most nights, he meant to read them, but more often than not, he faded before he could finish an article or two. After the day he'd had on the train, he wasn't sure he could manage even that. Behind him, he heard the clink of silver and plates being washed and dried.

His cousin sat down across from him and clasped his hands together. "I've been thinking about this porter thing."

Ah, George thought. Perhaps that explained the boy's mood. He lowered the paper he held. "You took the test, right?" George asked. Ben nodded once. "I'm sure you did fine. And you're the right height. Smart young man like you, you'll hear soon enough."

"It's not that." Ben licked his lips, ducking his head. "I'm thinking I don't want to be a porter after all."

The sounds at the sink quieted. George, too, bristled. Porter jobs didn't come open often, but when they did, the railroad was good about giving preference to family members of porters in good standing. If a man could read and write and follow the rules, he had a chance. "Can I ask why not?"

"I don't think I can do what you do."

George understood his cousin's hesitation. A porter worked six days a week, sometimes more than eighty or ninety hours with little sleep. But a man got used to it, and Ben was strong in that way that young men were, his muscles not bulging but sinewy and solid under his skin. "Well, it is hard work, but it's not too bad. I'm sure you can handle it."

"That's not it. I can work hard."

"What, then?"

Ben leaned forward, his elbows on his knees. "The way they talk to you."

George drew back. He didn't like Ben's tone or his words, but there was something else he liked even less—the smell of liquor. "You've been drinking."

"That doesn't answer the question."

"What question is that?"

"Why do you let them talk to you that way?"

George gave a slow shake of his head and reached for the paper. He was too tired for this argument.

But Ben wasn't finished. "It isn't right."

George set the paper back on the table. Ben hadn't been in Nashville a week, spending his nights on George's sofa. As far as George could tell, Ben was short on funds—had no job—but he was long on knowing. The boy had the hands and skin of a much younger man—soft and without a whisker in sight—but that didn't stop him from spoiling for a fight. "You don't know what you're talking about."

"I do know. You think because I'm not a porter, I don't know what it's like. I've heard how they order you around."

The silence at the sink filled the room.

George shot a glance at his wife and daughter. "Part of being a porter is doing things for people," he said.

Ben sneered. "Things white people order you to do."

"I do my job," he said. George stopped short of reminding Ben what happened to men like them when they failed to follow orders or stay on their side of town. He thought of Mrs. Dinkins and her children, his own stomach twisting at the memory. The conductor and even the flagman were above being asked to clean up after a child who'd stuffed their belly with sweets, but a porter wasn't. If the job came with difficulties, it wasn't something he couldn't manage for the sake of his family. That didn't mean it didn't rankle.

"See, that's what I'm saying. 'I do my job.'" Ben mimicked George, slurring his words. "You say it like it's some kind of badge of honor. Being a porter, you think you're better than everyone else."

George drew back. "I don't think that."

Ben snorted. "All you porters stick together, but that doesn't change things. Ordering you around. Calling you all George. You can't tell me you like that."

"George is my name."

Ben jabbed his finger under George's nose. "But not the other porters down at the station. They can't all be named George, can they? None of those white folks can even be bothered to order you around by your own name. It's no better than being called Boy—as if that was ever anyone's name. Every porter is George, and you know it." His mouth was wet with spit. "I've been on that train. I see the way you're always jumping to get things or carry things and always with that stupid smile—like you love being at some white lady's beck and call."

George heard his daughter gasp. His own anger swelled, and his hands no longer rested on the arms of the chair but curled into fists at his side. Ben couldn't see beyond his years, but he was right about one thing. Porters were a proud lot—whether you were a Pullman porter or a railroad porter. They stuck together, and whatever grievances they had—and the groundwork they were laying now to change things—were not for Ben's ears. He breathed in and out, reminding himself that the boy was drunk, not in his right mind.

"Well, I don't know about that, Cousin." He forced a lightness he didn't feel into his next words. "But I do happen to love being at a certain lady's beck and call." George nodded at his wife and winked.

Celeste, eager to ease the tension in the room, draped her arm over her daughter's shoulder and joked, "Don't you be telling stories over there, George."

"Never." He got to his feet. "How about some coffee, Ben?"

Ben grunted but stood, listing to the left before grabbing George's arm. The porter stiffened. The boy wasn't his son, and he didn't know how much longer he could put up with the kid. "I'm serious. Everyone knows the first porters were former slaves." George said nothing. "Maybe porters are still slaves."

George jerked his arm back, his skin hot. It didn't matter that he'd heard the same from others. The boy had spoken the words in front of George's wife and daughter. His chest heaved, and his jaw worked until he could answer. When he did speak, his voice hummed with barely contained fury. "I'm my own man, Ben. I support my family. I own this house that you're standing in right now. It might not be much, but it's ours. Slaves don't do that."

The fire in Ben's eyes faded, replaced by something that pierced George's heart more than all that had come before—disappointment. "Some do, George. Some do."

~~~

AMERICANS SMASH ENEMY ATTACKS

(By the Associated Press)

WITH THE AMERICAN ARMY IN FRANCE, July 3,—During the serial fighting today, four more enemy machines were brought down. Victories are claimed for Lieutenants J. H. Stephens, New York; K. L. Porter, Dowagine, Mich.; Ralph O'Neill, Denver, and Maxwell Perry, Indianapolis.

All told, on Tuesday and Wednesday the patrols from American pursuit squadrons in the sector engaged in about twenty combats, bringing down seven enemy planes.
~~~

Two American aviators were lost and one was seriously wounded. Among the airmen engaged in the fighting today was Quentin Roosevelt, youngest son of Colonel Theodore Roosevelt.

—The Tennessean, July 4, 1918

~~~~

Most days, David Kennedy could be mistaken for a younger man, but sitting across from his wife, her lovely mouth pursed in worry, he felt every one of his seventy-two years.

"Does that mean there's no letter, Father?" Katie Belle asked. Candles flickered in the evening light, casting soft shadows over his youngest daughter's face. She shot an anxious glance at her mother before turning her attention back to her father.

"I'm afraid not. No mail today with the holiday." He knew Mary would be watching, reading his lips.

"What about in the papers?"

"Nothing new." He told her the little he'd learned in the *Tennessean,* but since they didn't know where John George had been sent after he'd arrived in Europe, David didn't know whether the news was good or bad. He laid his fork on the table, his appetite gone.

David was too old for this war, but once he wasn't. In 1862, he'd been sixteen, the same age as John George, when he'd signed up. Like his son, David had defied his father. The irony was not lost on him now. Raised in Alabama, he'd broken ranks with his family, fleeing to Ohio. There, he'd joined up with the Union Army, the 38th regiment. Back home, there'd been widespread conviction the South would prevail. As the months and years passed, that certainty had turned to disheartenment, desperation, and then defeat. The Union had won, and David had been glad, but in the wake of victory, he'd seen houses burned to the ground and lifeless bodies left in blood-soaked fields. His own family had been lost to him. The memory tasted sour in his mouth.
~~~~

His eldest daughter, Anna Mae, reached out and squeezed his hand. "Father, I'm sure John George is fine."

He held his breath, not wanting to hear again how everyone said they were going to win. Winning didn't come without loss—often of the worst kind. That knowledge kept him up at night, tossing and turning, his head aching more and more.

Anna Mae wasn't one to sugarcoat the truth though. "If John George wasn't okay, if something had happened, you would have heard, don't you think? Isn't that how it works?"

Some of the tension seeped from him. Wrapping her hand in his, he leaned over and kissed her on the cheek. Anna Mae was right. No news was good news.

"There is no letter today, but I have reason to believe all is well." Again, he spoke slowly to allow Mary to read his lips. His daughters, too, offered assurances. He felt a surge of pride. Mary was by no means weak or even in need of help, but her worry for her only son sometimes required more reassurance than he alone could give. A change of subject was in order.

"How many young men were at the dance today?" he asked.

"Oh, more than a few," Katie Belle said. Her impish grin grew wider. "Why, Anna Mae—"

A thump sounded, and Katie Belle looked over at her sister, her mouth open wide.

"Actually, I have something I'd like to discuss with you, Father," Anna Mae said, talking over Katie Belle.

She leaned forward, placing both hands on the table, palms pressed against the wood. Katie Belle's lips were closed tight now, grin gone.

David stifled a sigh. On most days, his worries were few, but the hours on the train and the war seemed to sap his energy more and more. "Well," he said after sitting back, "let's hear it then, Anna Mae."

"I've been offered a position as a music teacher."

"Ah." He ran his long fingers over his white beard. He'd been worried for an instant, but he was grateful now. A job? It wasn't the first time Anna

Mae had made that type of proposition. She'd worked as a clerk at a department store for a while, but it had been temporary. He hadn't minded her taking the job as he recognized his daughter was quite bright and liked to be busy. He understood her better than she thought. Her pronouncement, while polite and dutiful, was but a ruse. Most likely, she had already accepted the position or promised to. Her insistence on being more self-supportive made him uneasy, made him hesitate. The last serious suitor had not been enamored with her independent ways, and that had been two years earlier. There'd been no one of importance since, and soon she would be twenty-four years of age. Katie Belle was twenty-one. With so many young men signing up for the war, he wondered what would become of the women left behind. Aloud, he said, "Tell me about it."

As she talked about the position, he couldn't help noticing the way Anna Mae vibrated with excitement. He stole a glance at his wife and knew in an instant that she had already been told and approved. Although Mary had embraced her life as a railroad engineer's wife, she possessed a deep strength of her own, a strength she had passed on to her eldest daughter.

Anna Mae's words faded, and a silence fell over the table.

He sat back in his chair, and Katie Belle jumped up to retrieve his pipe. He took it, knowing even as he did that he was prolonging the moment he would give Anna Mae an answer. Again, he felt a surge of pride. Both his daughters were lovely, but more than that, they were lovely in spirit. And though Anna Mae was often headstrong and impetuous and Katie Belle stubborn, he didn't really mind. They were good girls. He recognized the way they watched out for and helped their mother. Her lack of hearing had never bothered him. He was a man of few words himself, but sometimes he wondered if it had ever bothered them. And yet, there was nothing lacking in these daughters of his. No father could ask for more.

"Well, I take it you're interested in taking the position, then."

"Yes, Father."

"And it won't interfere with helping your mother?"

"No, Father."

Katie Belle chimed in. "I can help."

He took a puff from the pipe and thought about the young men he'd seen on the train. More would go the next day and the next. A job would fill the time, serve his daughter well. "Then of course you should accept the position."

After dinner, Anna Mae played the piano. Mary sat on the bench next to her as she always did, the best place to feel the vibration of the keys. The music washed over David, and he settled deeper into his chair, his eyelids growing heavy. The days stretched longer since the government had taken over the railroad. Although he was up to the challenge, an unsettled feeling—a feeling he would not share with Mary—had been gnawing at him these last weeks. With no news about John George, that uneasy feeling had grown to be something more like dread.

A blinding pain behind his eyes jolted him forward and he clutched at the arms of the chair.

"Father." Katie Belle flew across the room, kneeling at his feet. "Are you okay?"

He didn't know how many seconds passed—five, maybe ten—before the throbbing subsided, gone as quickly as it had come. Vision cloudy, he found his pipe again, grateful he hadn't been burned.

Anna Mae and Mary watched him from the bench.

"Yes, of course." He waved a hand in the air, spoke slowly for Mary. "I'm afraid I must have dozed off, had a bit of a start."

"You work too much, Father," Katie Belle told him.

"Yes, I'm sure that must be it." He settled back again and relit his pipe. The deliberate action of lighting and puffing calmed him. In a moment, the pain was forgotten.

Anna Mae picked up her songbook. "What would you like to hear next, Father?"

The light from the lamp cast a halo over her and he thought, *Anna Mae is glowing.*

"Yes, what do you want to hear?" Katie Belle asked.

He smiled at his youngest daughter. "Will you sing?"

"I'd be happy to."

"It's settled, then. 'By the Light of the Silvery Moon.'"

Anna Mae laughed and opened her book. "You always pick that."

"And I always will."

Watching the exchange, Mary laughed too. Anna Mae's fingers hovered over the keys and from the first note, his heart lightened. Katie Belle lifted her face and began to sing, her voice sweet and pure.

~~~~

A WONDER

The poker crew
Must praise Tom Cases;
He knows when to
Lay down three aces.

—*The Tennessean,* July 4, 1918

~~~~

With a whiskey in one hand, Milton watched the boys and the game. With his other, he patted his vest pocket, satisfied his mother's golden chain was where it should be. His grandmother had worn it for years, and after she was gone, it had belonged to his mother. He remembered how she would let him play with it when he was a boy, laughing along with him. Now he carried the heirloom with him each day, mostly out of habit, and also perhaps for a bit of luck.

He sipped his drink, only half paying attention to the card game. A loud shout from the front of Rowena's followed by a crash and broken glass made all eyes in the room look around. Heavy footsteps clomped down the hallway. Milton straightened, his fingers tightening around his glass. The men at the table put down their cards and stood, all focused on the door. No one spoke, each remembering the raid the week before at another Bottom establishment. The footsteps came closer then, slowing outside the door. Inside the room, the heavy silence expanded. Every man held his breath. A body hit the door. Next to Milton, Frank Danielson jumped. A man's voice, slurred with drink, cried out. Another bump and more steps. No one moved until the sound of heels hitting the floor faded and the back door of Rowena's slammed closed. Milton exhaled, his fingers loosening.

He told himself it was the holiday that had everyone on edge. The saloon was more crowded than usual after the city-wide celebrations, and by the sound of it, the booze had been flowing since early in the day. Not that the Women's League or any of the other party organizers endorsed drinking or gambling. Definitely not. It was no secret that while half the town had turned into teetotalers since the push for prohibition, the other half could be found drunk on bootleg whiskey. Milton sipped from his glass and savored the warmth of the liquid as it slid down his throat. He was quite sure his own aunt and uncle would be appalled at his behavior—gambling and drinking in the back room of a tavern—but he felt no shame. Rather, the thought pleased him.

Smoke hung over the table like a cloud, shrouding the four men in shadow. The Smythe brothers, Hank and Joseph, sat on one side of the table. Inseparable, they worked at the Hermitage Hotel as bellboys. Sometimes they were in their uniforms, as they were on this night, but other times, they slicked back their hair and wore their Sunday best. On those nights, they were more interested in the ladies than the games.

Larry Minor, a postal worker with the railroad, sat across from them. He held his cards by the corners as though he didn't want to smudge them with railroad grime. The fourth man was a stranger to Milton.

Milton tilted his head toward the table. "Who's the new guy?"

"Don't know," Frank said. "Must know someone though."

Milton checked the time on his pocket watch. After eleven already. Whether he liked it or not, his uncle expected him to arrive early the next day. "Won't be able to stay long tonight. I've got two morning appointments."

"Business must be good."

He lifted a shoulder. "Could be better, according to my uncle."

Frank leaned against the wall and lit a cigarette. "Things okay at home?"

Milton didn't speak for a minute. Life with his aunt and uncle was never bad. They weren't unkind. They housed him, fed him, gave him a job. But it wasn't the same. He touched a hand to his pocket again. "Sure. Fine."

"You're gone soon anyway."

"Right."

"Hey, I thought I saw you at Centennial today."

"I was there. Uncle Leo was helping with the pageant."

"After that. By the refreshment table." Frank's brows arched. "With a redhead."

Milton's hand dropped. Frank was his oldest friend. They'd known each other since before Milton's parents had died. They'd been schoolboys together at Hume-Fogg, taken dance lessons together, and attended meetings at the YMHA. They'd shared their boyhood, talked about girls plenty of times, but on this night, he hesitated. He couldn't have explained why, even to himself, except that she was different—at least he thought she was. Anna Mae didn't feel like the dalliances of his past or even like one of the girls his aunt insisted on inviting to dinner until he'd asked her to stop.

Frank chuckled when Milton didn't answer. "What's the matter? She already turn you down? Don't worry about it. A girl like that probably already has a fella anyway."

Milton took a long swallow, not looking up from the floor. Did she have someone? It hadn't occurred to him to ask. They'd spent most of the afternoon together, dancing and talking, but what did that really mean? It was a celebration. Everyone had been in fine spirits. Could that have been all it was?

"Don't let it get you down. I hear all the girls are writing to soldiers, finding war fellas. You'll be army soon. Maybe you'll get a girl too." Before Milton could answer, Frank hooked his chin toward the table. "Almost done."

At the table, the last cards were dealt. Larry pointed at the pile of chips. "Lot of money there."

Milton and Frank exchanged a glance, and Milton moved closer to watch the action.

"Sure is," the stranger said.

Larry bounced his leg up and down.

"Take your time," the stranger told him.

Hank threw his cards on the table. "I'm out," he said.

Joseph followed suit. "Me too."

Larry's leg bounced higher. He placed his cards face down on the edge of the table, his fingers tapping them lightly. Milton smiled to himself. They'd had a regular game off and on for months, and Larry had the worst poker face he'd ever seen.

"You in or out?" the stranger asked.

Larry picked up his cards again, his mouth screwed up into a tight circle. Milton could almost see Larry's brain churning, working to calculate what the stranger was holding. Hank and Joseph exchanged looks. Milton held his breath. It was a fool's game, and Milton knew Larry to be a fool.

"I'm in," Larry said.

The stranger held his cards. "Give me a minute." No one spoke, the only sound Larry's shoe tapping against the wooden floor. "Okay. I'm in too." He pushed the remainder of his money across the table, nearly doubling the pot. "I'll see your bet and raise you."

Larry's mouth fell open. If he stayed in the game, he would have to put in everything he had. "Th-that's a lot of money."

The stranger's thin lips stretched wide. "It's more fun that way."

"Is this guy crazy?" Frank whispered.

Milton studied the man. Where Larry was a man in motion, the stranger remained still. There were no telltale movements or tics, nothing. A dark beard hid the hard lines of his mouth and shaggy hair fell over thick brows. In spite of the pile of money on the table, he appeared as cool as a cucumber, his face unreadable.

Larry stopped bouncing long enough to push his money forward. "Call," he said and laid his cards on the table, hands shaking. Two pair. King high. It was a good hand. Milton would give Larry that, but the smug look on the face of the stranger told him it wouldn't be good enough.

Seconds passed and the stranger got to his feet. "Well, friend, I'm afraid you got me." He tossed his cards on the pile with the others. "You win."

Milton's mouth fell open. He'd been sure the stranger had Larry beat.

"Larry finally got one," Frank said.

Joseph clapped Larry on the back, and Hank began counting the pile.

The stranger held out his hand. "A pleasure to play with you men tonight."

Larry stood. "Good game."

"Gotta be going, boys, but I'm in town for a few days more. Hope you don't mind if I pop in again."

After the stranger left, Larry grabbed the bottle of whiskey and poured a drink. "Best win I've had in months," he said, raising his glass. "Maybe my luck is turning. About time."

Milton, his back to the group, reached out and flipped the stranger's cards over one by one. Ten, Jack, Ace, Ten, Ten. Three tens. Three of a kind. He frowned. Every gambler knew that three of a kind beat two pair.

"What've you got there?" Frank asked, coming up behind him.

Milton slipped the cards back into the pile and swept them together. "Nothing," he said. "You ready to play?"

Frank sat down. "You know it."

The Smythe brothers joined them and Milton shuffled, the cards fluttering easily through his fingers. Separating the cards, he cut the deck, then dealt, starting on his left. Two games later, he called it a night. Walking home, he couldn't stop thinking about the game. It bothered him. The stranger bothered him. He'd been too comfortable, too smooth. His poker face was everything Larry's wasn't. He'd let Larry win. Milton was sure of it. What he didn't know was why.

PART 2

THE ROAD DIVIDED

CHAPTER SEVEN

Summer 1988

GINNY'S PALMS WERE damp with sweat, and she was surprised to realize she'd been holding her breath. "And then what happened?"

Anna Mae stirred, her hand coming up to her throat. "Oh, so much. You have no idea." Saying no more, she reached for the cup of water on the nightstand. Her hand shook as she lifted it to her lips. "Do you play poker?"

"Not really. My father plays cards with his friends down in Florida, I think. I don't know if it's poker though."

"It's a marvelous game, really. You absolutely must pay attention to the other cards played. It takes a certain amount of skill."

Ginny couldn't hide her astonishment. "You play?"

"Oh, no, but I did once. I wanted to know what it was about, why men liked it. After I played, I understood." She spread her fingers across the quilt. "But I was much more interested in music than cards, I suppose."

Ginny was reminded of the sheet music she'd found in the trunk. "You played piano."

Anna Mae rubbed at the nobs and veins of her hands. "Oh, yes, for a long time. I gave lessons. There were some lean years though. I had other jobs. Music lessons tend to be a luxury when money is tight and food is short."

"You have the hands for it. I wanted to take lessons once, but I have stubby fingers like my mother. It's my dad who has the long fingers. He says that's what made him a good surgeon."

"Does he?" Anna Mae asked, her face thoughtful. "Did he ever play?"

"Definitely not," Ginny said before switching gears again. "Did you always live alone?"

"No, I lived with my mother for a time, but she passed away in 1948. We were very close before she died."

"I'm sorry," Ginny said. "It must have been hard for her—being deaf."

Anna Mae lifted one frail shoulder. "If it was, she never said. She was a wonderful mother, a wonderful wife." She cocked her head. "Though she wasn't my father's first wife."

Ginny sat up straighter. "She wasn't?"

"His first wife died, leaving my father with a young daughter, my half sister. My sister's name was Mary—like my mother's—but everyone called her Birdie. We didn't see her much after she got married though." The afternoon light faded, bathing the old woman's face in shadow. "I suppose she had her reasons."

"That must have been hard for your father."

"Yes, I do believe you're right. I'm sure he missed her. We all did." She tapped her fingers. "I suppose that's as good a place to start again as any. Shall I continue with my story?"

Ginny had already been at the nursing home for several hours, and she'd never stayed this late before. "Only if you're feeling up to it. Are you tired?"

"Ha! Not a bit. For once, I think the question is whether or not you're up to it. I feel like I could talk straight into the night."

"Then I can listen."

"Atta girl," Anna Mae said, beaming. "Here we go, then. On July the fifth, the sun rose high as it had every day for weeks. Not a cloud in the sky or a single breeze to break the endless heat of that summer. Each day brought more news of the fighting in Europe, but in Nashville, life went on. And like every other day, David Kennedy dressed in his overalls and walked to Union Station and down to the train shed for his orders."

CHAPTER EIGHT

Friday, July 5, 1918
Morning

VICTORY OF AMERICANS AT CHATEAU THIERRY DESCRIBED
The Nashville Tennessean, July 5, 1918

Washington, July 4.—In a continuation of Tuesday's communique, Gen. Pershing today reported in graphic details on the successful American operations near Chateau Thierry Monday, and described activities along the various fronts held by Americans during several preceding days.

"At 3:45 o'clock in the morning the Germans counter attacked. Thanks to the thorough consolidations of the position which had been made, the counter attack was repulsed with heavy losses to the enemy in killed and wounded. It also resulted in the taking by us of additional prisoners. The number of prisoners so far counted is over 500 and includes six officers. Our casualties were light, considering the success obtained."

—*The Tennessean*, July 5, 1918

~~~~
~~~~

William Jones crossed the platform under a cloud of steam. He walked toward the dispatcher's office with quick steps, his dark expression matched by his suit.

"William." David caught the other man by the shoulder.

The younger man spun around, stuck out his hand. "David. I thought I recognized that voice. It's good to see you." His skin grew pink. "I know we were going to come by last week, but it couldn't be helped."

David said nothing.

"My job—you know how that is—and Birdie and the children have been busy," William said, spreading his palms. "But not to worry. Everyone is well."

David's face softened. "How is Birdie?"

"She's good," William told his father-in-law. "The children have been a handful of late, and I've been a bit shorthanded myself."

"Your business is well?"

"Oh, yes." Loud voices echoed through the rafters as some of the maintenance crew changed shifts. William stepped closer. "Any news?"

David shook his head. "No news is good news, they say."

"Birdie is so worried. She loves John George like one of her own. And the girls, of course."

Nodding, David stayed quiet. Birdie might love her half siblings, but she rarely visited. She would never speak of why and he would never ask, but he had his suspicions. She'd been old enough to remember her own mother, to miss her, to resent another taking her place.

A train arrived then, the wheels squealing as the locomotive came to a stop. When the noise died down, William spoke again. "Did you see the papers?" he asked, changing the subject. "We're defeating the Germans in the air and on the ground. Taking prisoners. It's possible this could all be over in a matter of months, weeks even."

David wasn't sure if William believed the war was nearing the end or only repeating what he'd read and heard. He only knew he wanted it to be true. "I hope you're right."

The young man placed a hand on his father-in-law's shoulder. "I'm sure I am. And about Birdie. It's not you, David. You're a good father. You are." Before the engineer could respond, William stepped back. "I've got to be going," he said, "but we'll be around soon. I promise." He raised a hand and was gone.

David's vision clouded. *You're a good father.* Was he? His oldest daughter harbored some unknown resentment toward her stepmother and avoided time with them. Had he done all he could to help them forge a relationship? His younger daughters were home with no prospects in sight. John George had run away to the war. Had he been too hard on him? Driven him away?

Shorty came up beside him. "Everything okay, Uncle Dave? You look a million miles away."

"Sorry," he said. He said it again, louder, determined to sweep away the pain in his head and his heart. "I was thinking about something." He checked the time on the clock that hung from the rafters. After six thirty already. "I'm about to pick up our orders. Care to join me?"

"Love to. Looks like a perfect day for a train ride."

~~~~

THIRTY THOUSAND BRAVE NEGRO SOLDIERS SOMEWHERE "OVER THERE" IN FRANCE.

Thirty thousand brave, unflinching, uncompromising American citizens representing a people of over Thirteen million Negroes who are true, loyal, American citizens, are now fighting under the Stars and Stripes, in the trenches, somewhere in France. While the figures given out have not been officially confirmed, it has been learned from authentic sources in this city that with the arrival of Lieut. H. A. Cameron and Captain M. V. Boutte and H. H. Walker, with quite a few others who are stationed in various camps in the country, that the number in France was augmented to this increase and that the Negro soldier
~~~~

without fear or hesitation has made a gallant dash at the Huns and they are now pushing their way to the very gates of Berlin . . . While accurate information that would give details of the heroism of the Negro troops has been slow in coming across the Atlantic either by cable or wireless, returned officials and men have been extravagant in their language and in their compliments of what the black man has been doing and is still doing to help win the world's war for Democracy.

—*The Nashville Globe,* July 5, 1918

A prickly heat rose from the dry and dusty ground, choking the air and tickling John's throat. Using the sleeve of his shirt, he wiped his forehead and walked across the field. His fingers brushed over a half-grown stalk of corn, the brittle leaves crackling. He squinted up at the cloudless sky and mumbled a short prayer. It wasn't that he thought God cared so much about the corn exactly, but it had been weeks since they'd had more than a spit of rain, and John knew what a bad season meant. There were other farms, but Uncle Elijah was too old to move again.

John set off for town. He walked down the center of the road, deep wagon ruts on either side of him. Dirt swirled under his boots and clung to his damp skin. He rounded a corner, avoiding the big houses on Elm. The road narrowed at the next block. After a few more turns, he came to another row of houses, smaller and plainer. None had white porches or staircases. He passed the small, square building where his mother taught school. There would be a few kids there now, although the rooms would be close to empty come harvest season.

"The town is growing," she'd said. He knew that to be true. Hernando had an electric power plant now and even an automobile agency over on Commerce Street. John stopped sometimes to see the shiny machines—Fords, they were called—black with gleaming metal. He'd stand, mouth open, pulse racing. Some had tops, some didn't. He liked the way they rolled past, the wheels turning, motors purring. They wouldn't be much use on a farm, he figured, but he longed to touch one, ride in one someday.

"John." A voice called to him from across the road. "Hey, John."

Matt Toles. Breaking stride, John wavered. His sister was waiting.

Matt trotted over, waving a paper in the air. "Got the latest from Chicago. The *Defender*. Want to hear what it says?" He began reading, his voice growing stronger with each word. "See?" Matt asked, looking up from the paper. "Don't you want to get out of this town? It's no good here. In Chicago, we could have our own farms, our own places. Not like here."

"You don't like farming."

"That's true enough," Matt said with a laugh. "But still."

John's gaze wandered down the street. A large horse and buggy came toward them. "Besides, I thought you said Chicago was a big city. Doesn't sound like there's much farming to be had to me."

"What Chicago has is jobs." Matt pointed at a spot on the page. *Men Wanted. Come to the Aid of Your Country.* "They need men like us." He tapped the advertisement. "Good pay too. It's different than here. You can be your own man."

"I'm my own man."

Matt laughed again. "Sure you are. With House around?" Heat rose under John's skin. He thought of his stepfather's hand on his shoulder at the picnic, the words he'd whispered in his ear. "Don't get mad," Matt said. "I don't mean anything by it." He tapped the paper again. "But they do need men."

Matt kept reading, but it was the stranger's words John heard instead. The government needed men too. They needed them at the gunpowder plant in Nashville. That pay was better than good. Better than around Hernando anyway.

"C'mon, John. We could go to Chicago together."

John scratched at the dirt with the toe of his boot. He didn't want to go to Chicago.

"At least think about it."

John heard the clop of a horse's hooves and stepped back from the road, saved from answering. Reverend Hawkins sat atop the bench, reins in his hands.

"Hello, boys," he said.

"Hello, Reverend Hawkins." John touched a hand to his hat and bowed. Matt stood behind him, lips pressed together.

"Shouldn't you boys be out at the farms?"

Before Matt could answer, John said, "Already been."

"I see." Reverend Hawkins craned his neck to see Matt. "What's that you're holding, Matt?"

John stepped to the side, and Matt held up the paper. "The *Defender*. It's out of Chicago."

"I know what it is, young man." His voice was cool. "It's a paper written by men who live to stir up trouble."

"I disagree."

"Oh?" The preacher's hands tightened on the reins. The horse kicked his hoof and tossed his mane. "I suppose you think you know better."

"Yes, sir." Matt held the *Defender* up like a prize. "It's a paper that's not afraid to speak the truth. It's where a man can read about getting a better life."

"A better life? Papers like that can get a man—or a woman—lynched, and you know it."

John dropped his gaze. Mention of the lynchings three months earlier in Georgia—some of the worst anyone had heard about—made both young men close their mouths and bow their heads. What neither said was a man didn't have to be reading the *Defender* to get lynched. They didn't have to be doing anything at all if someone had a mind to do it.

"Hard work is what gives a man a better life," Reverend Hawkins was saying. He leaned forward and pointed a long, bony finger. "I hear you haven't been helping your daddy as much as you should. It takes hard work, young man. That's what makes a better life and makes us rich in God's eyes." Matt muttered something under his breath and shook his head. The preacher glared, his voice rising. "Don't you be forgetting that, son. We are all working for God." He snapped the reins with a sharp crack. "I expect to see you both at Sunday services."

"Yes, sir," John said, exhaling.

The horse kicked up dust, and John raised a hand to his mouth and nose. He watched the preacher move down the road, his mind swirling. Uncle Elijah worked hard, but that wouldn't stop him from losing his land on the farm if it didn't rain. His momma worked hard at the school. Leah worked hard doing white folks' laundry. As far as he could tell, none of them had gotten rich in anyone's eyes. And hard work hadn't saved Mary Turner, her unborn baby, or the others back in Georgia from being strung up in the night.

Matt slapped the paper against his thighs. "Reverend Hawkins doesn't know what he's talking about. He's just a stupid old man." He spit on the ground and wiped his mouth. "Someday, he's gonna learn that what the *Defender* says is true. They're all gonna learn." He stomped off, leaving John standing on the street.

John had heard the talk about how Matt was lazy and too big for his britches, but he admired his friend. At least Matt knew what he believed, knew what he wanted. And Matt wasn't the only one. He'd heard two farmers gave up and left for Boston only the week before. The Hollis family left before that. He didn't have to think about it though. He didn't want to go to Boston or Chicago. What he wanted was to earn good pay and have his own land.

He crossed the street to the sign tacked up next to the general store. Written in bold black letters, it was like the one the stranger had been handing out, advertising for men to work at the plant in Nashville. He stared at the words for a long time. *Train leaves Monday*. It wasn't a farm of his own, but it was a start. Matt wanted him to think about Chicago, but he didn't need to. It was Nashville he'd been thinking about. If only House would let him. But it wasn't just House. There was his mother. And his sister. They needed him. Shoulders sinking low, he tore his gaze from the flyer and walked away.

~~~~

L. Jonas & Company's millinery sat at the corner where Commerce Street intersected Eighth and Ninth Avenues, dominating the block and the stores around it. Milton's Uncle Leopold had emigrated from Germany to the United States when he was a boy of sixteen. Landing in Maryland along with his brother Adolph, the pair had made their way to Nashville by 1885. Together, they'd founded their apparel company. By 1918, the firm had grown to employ dozens and was situated in a building several stories high. Milton's uncle routinely ran ads in the paper calling the company the South's Greatest Wholesale House.

Even with all his success, Uncle Leo was not a man to rest on his laurels. He had his fingers in many pies, including the Chamber of Commerce, the Board of Trade, and the Retail Merchants Association. Milton knew most of the businessmen that Uncle Leo and Uncle Adolph worked with and regularly visited their shops on Fourth Avenue. They sold men's and women's finery, yet hats remained his uncle's first love. More than once, he'd witnessed his uncle's hands moving across a piece of brown felt or lace until he'd created the right look, the right hat.

Nothing had changed.

As a boy, Milton had visited the millinery with his mother. He stared open-mouthed at the ladies' hats—many the size of turkeys—each wider and more colorful than the one before. The hats themselves held little interest for the boy. He loved the ornaments affixed to them, whether wide-brimmed, straw, or felt. The type of hat didn't matter so long as it had flowers or ribbons or the most exotic thing of all: feathers.

On one occasion he stepped closer to the hats, his pulse quickening. He ignored the brightest feathers, awed instead by the long, white, gray, and black ones. He knew in an instant: ostrich feathers. He reached out to touch one.

"The child, Nannie," his uncle said, scowling.

The boy's outstretched hand froze midair.
~~~~

"Milton, dear," his mother said. "I'm sure we've taken enough of your uncle's time. Why don't you say goodbye, then?" His uncle grunted, barely looking up from the array of ornaments spread out in front of him. Milton followed his mother dutifully but couldn't resist looking over his shoulder one more time at all those feathers.

His mother was long gone now, as were the enormous hats decorated in brightly colored plumes. Simpler times called for simpler hats—smaller and plainer. There were still flowers and silk, but the feathers were disappearing. A public outcry to protect migratory birds had altered the industry, and the Migratory Bird Treaty Act of 1918 made it official. Hatmakers across the country were banned from using the feathers of songbirds and other endangered species. Some milliners had been left saddled with hundreds of feathers no one would dare wear in public. "It's a crime," his uncle had been heard to say—though he'd never said which was the crime, and Milton had never asked.

On this day, Milton walked through the warehouse with Leo, his eye on the clock. "The hat order for Crump's store will be ready by tomorrow," his uncle said. The order wasn't large, but the need for men's derby-style hats seemed to have increased in the months since the war. "I expect you will get to Memphis in plenty of time if you leave Monday. Mr. Crump wants this shipment Tuesday, Wednesday at the latest."

"Tuesday or Wednesday. No problem." He didn't mind the trips to Memphis or the other cities where his uncle sold hats. Besides, soon his travel would be of a different kind. Perhaps he could make the most of this final trip as a salesman. "Hey, Uncle Leo, have I told you the one about the—"

"Don't have time for your jokes today, boy," Leo said, cutting him off. "There's work to be done." He sat down at his sewing machine, fingers pushing fabric, his nephew already forgotten.

Sighing, Milton left him to check on the inventory that he would take to Memphis. As he inspected the rows of brown and black hats, his mind wandered. There would be a card game later at Rowena's. He frowned, wondering if the stranger would be there. The man and his play hadn't sat well with Milton, keeping him up part of the night.

Across the floor, his aunt Rickie placed a glass and plate of cheese and hard rolls in front of Uncle Leopold before spotting her nephew.

"Is something wrong, Milton? You look so far away." As she spoke, she kept one eye on her husband. "Leopold, eat." She marched straight back, waving her hand. "Eat. Eat."

After checking the time, Milton left them both to find an an empty hatbox. He surveyed an assortment of women's hats and was pleased to see the newest styles in a rainbow of colors. Many were destined for shops throughout Tennessee and the bordering states. He moved down the row and stopped. The hat in front of him was smaller than most and made of straw. A summer hat. A red ribbon had been attached to the crown, anchored by a red silk flower. It was perfect. He opened the box and laid the hat inside.

"What are you doing?" His uncle stood at his elbow. He smelled of cheese and wool.

Milton placed the lid on the box, a white lie rolling off his tongue. "A customer came into Sol Frankland's shop last week to buy a hat like this one. I thought I'd take it over now."

Leopold lifted one wiry brow. "Why didn't I hear about this customer before?"

"You're hearing now," Milton said, keeping his voice even. He pushed the box toward his uncle. "I'm sure Mr. Frankland would be happy if you wanted to bring the hat personally."

"Bah," his uncle said with a low growl. "I've got work to do. You're the salesman."

Milton left the warehouse with the hat under his arm. Arriving at the shop, his pulse raced, and he wiped his palms on his pants. Was he early? Was he late? He pushed open the door, the hatbox in his hand. Inside, his sight was slow to adjust to the darker interior.

A half dozen ready-to-wear dresses were draped on wooden mannequins in one corner. Two shelves on the back wall housed a small assortment of hats. Many of them were Jonas hats. Sol stood behind the counter, a bolt of lemon-colored fabric rolled out before him. A woman fingered the delicate fabric, her back to Milton. Ginger curls peeked out from under her hat.

"Mr. Lowenstein," Sol said, looking up. "What have you brought me today?"

The woman swung around to face him, and his heart thumped. She wore a cornflower-blue dress that matched her eyes and brightened her porcelain skin. The freckles sprinkled across her nose glowed when she offered a shy smile. Milton felt quite sure there had never been anyone lovelier.

"A hat." He held up the box, his fingers trembling. "For the lady."

~~~~

Advertisement

TAKE THIS BOOK

It is a Complete History and Manual Of the Colored Knights of Pythias

This Is The First and Only Complete History Ever Compiled

This book is over one thousand pages. Contains over five hundred photos of the noted Pythians and Calanthians of the United States, covering a period of more than fifty years.

Bound in Fine Cloth and Leather, Price $2.50 and 25 Cents for Postage.

—*The Nashville Globe*, July 5, 1918

~~~~

George dragged the brush across the tip of the shoe, moving it in small circles. Holding his shoe up to the light, he inspected it for the proper shine. His sword lay across the table. He paused to admire its weight and intricate design.

"You love that sword, don't you?" Anita stood over him. She held a large book tight against her chest.

"Well, I guess I do." He touched the heavy hilt. It was the sword of a major, his rank in the Knights of Pythias. Indicating the book, he asked, "What's that you've got?"

She sat down, sliding it across the table. "Mrs. Charles gave it to me."

George flipped it over. The book, bound in cloth, had golden letters on the cover and spine. *The Life and Times of Frederick Douglass.*

"Do you know who he is?" she asked, opening the book to an engraving of a man with deep-set eyes, a strong nose, and a thick beard.

George doubted there were any men from his part of town who didn't know the name Frederick Douglass. He'd achieved fame when he wrote the story of his life of slavery and subsequent escape. He was often given credit for pushing the movement to abolish slavery. "I learned about him when I was a boy. I believe he's been gone awhile now."

Anita beamed, and he marveled at how like her mother she was. She had the same butter-soft skin, pointed chin, and curled lashes. But she was brighter, more educated than all of them. He and Celeste had worked hard to make sure of that.

"Mrs. Charles says Mr. Douglass was the most famous slave ever."

"Don't know if that's true, but I guess it's right enough."

"But did you know that Mr. Douglass was on the side of the suffragettes?"

"Was he now?"

"Definitely." Anita reached across the table and tapped the book. "It's amazing, Father. You should read it."

Her enthusiasm tugged at his heart. "Why don't you read me some now?"

She rewarded him with a smile and eagerly turned the pages. He listened as she read, her voice strong and sure.

When she finished, he praised his daughter. "You're right. Quite amazing. We should thank Mrs. Charles for sharing it with you." He shifted on his chair. "Well, I'd better get to polishing these shoes."

He'd dipped the brush in the thick black paste and started on his other shoe when his daughter's voice interrupted his thoughts. "Father?"

"Yes?"

"I've been thinking about what Ben said last night."

He regarded his daughter, not missing the way she chewed her lower lip and averted her gaze. "He didn't mean anything by it."

It was clear his answer didn't satisfy her. She rubbed her fingers over the cover of the book as though drawing courage from the story inside. "He said being a porter was no different than being a slave."

George set the shoe to the side. Ben's words had stayed with him through the night too. His cousin was wrong, but that didn't mean he didn't have points to make.

Labor unions had been popping up since the war; there'd even been talk of one for the porters. George and a handful of others who worked the trains at Union Station had formed their own kind of internal union, and they'd begun making plans to push forward.

But that kind of action came with risks, so up to now, the idea of an official union was only talk.

"How long have I been a porter, baby girl?"

She shrugged. "A long time, I guess."

"Do I call myself a slave?"

"No."

"You know most of the other porters. Do they call themselves slaves? Do the bosses at the railroad? Do our neighbors?"

He watched as she pondered his questions. George and his fellow porters took leadership positions within the community, in their churches, and in their business. They were hard workers with good families. Their children were her schoolmates, her friends. After a minute, she said, "No, but they wouldn't, would they?"

Her words stung.

"I don't have to be a porter." He didn't, of course. The working conditions could be better—hell, they should be—and the pay wasn't always good, but he got by. In 1916, the Pullman Company had raised the monthly salary for their porters. The railroads had followed suit, and their porters had also received a higher salary. George made close to fifty dollars a month in wages, but like most porters, he couldn't survive on that alone. He relied on tips. Without those and his wife's pay, his family would likely starve. "I could quit tomorrow. Do something else."

"Mama would kill you."

"You're right," he said with a laugh. "She would. But it would be my choice just the same." He glanced at the book again, considering how best to explain. "Look, you'll graduate from Pearl High School next year, won't you?"

She nodded.

"Does everyone graduate?"

"Well, no."

"So, you choose to graduate?"

"That's not the same."

"You're right. It's not. But if I didn't have my job as a porter, you might not be graduating." He saw the confusion, the flicker of doubt. "You'd be working already, not just going twice a week to help your mama. You know I want you to get educated. More than I did."

"But I don't see—"

"Better jobs come from being educated." He wasn't ashamed of being a porter, but he wanted more for his daughter, for all his children. He wanted more opportunities than had been available to him.

"You're educated."

"Not like you. But it's because I can read and write that I got the job all those years ago. Now I get educated on the trains. I listen. I hear what people say. I know places and things. Because of that, I can bring home what I learn and make sure you get educated. Go to college. I choose to be a porter, but I can also choose not to be a porter." He gestured toward the book she held. "The slaves, like Mr. Douglass when he was a young man, didn't get to choose. Everything was chosen for them."

She sat quiet a moment before saying, her voice soft, "Okay, but some things are still chosen for you—for us—aren't they? That's what Ben meant, wasn't it?"

He wished he could tell her that wasn't true, but he wouldn't lie to her. She made him proud, was smarter than all of them. "See, that's why you and your brothers are going to stay in school."

"Thank you, Father," Anita said and wrapped her arms around her father's neck. Her voice dropped to a whisper. "I think you're the best porter there ever was."

~~~~

Milton and Anna Mae strolled through the park, their questions starting and stopping. The hatbox—the one containing the new straw hat—swung from her right hand.

He racked his brain for something clever to say, but his tongue felt stuck, as if it had doubled in size.

Anna Mae broke the silence. "Do you like selling hats?"

"I don't mind it," he said.

"That's not the same as liking it." She slowed when he didn't answer. "I've offended you."

"Not at all." He'd never spoken to anyone but Frank about his uncle and selling hats. "I haven't worked anywhere else, and I'm good at selling hats, but . . ."

"But you don't enjoy it much," she said. "If you could do something else, something you enjoyed, what would that be?"

"Ah, that's the thing," he said, palms facing up. "I'm not really sure. I'm not like my uncle. He's never wanted to do anything but make hats. Even when he was in Germany."

"My father is like that," she told him with a nod of understanding. "He says he was born to drive trains."

"What about you?" he asked. "What do you want to do?"
~~~~

"What do I want to do?" she repeated slowly, pulling back to study him. New lines appeared between her brows.

"Am I the one who's said something wrong?" he asked.

"No," she said, tilting her head to one shoulder as though considering. "I guess I don't know what to say. No one's really asked me before. What I want to do."

"Why not?"

"I suppose because the answer is assumed. What is any woman supposed to want? To make a home with a husband and children." She waved a hand in the air as though that was nothing. "Quite a few of my friends are already married and have families."

His brows inched higher as he studied her. "You say that like it's a bad thing."

Anna Mae laughed. "Not at all. It's not that I don't want that. It's just that I don't want only that."

"Ah," he said as they rounded the corner. "But you don't know what else you want?"

"No. Like you, I guess." She offered him a small smile. "That's why you signed up for the army, isn't it? To find out what you want?"

His eyes opened a bit wider. No one but Frank had understood. There were brains behind that beauty. "Partly. I figured it was one way to try something different from hat sales."

"Well, I think it will be *that*." A shadow passed over her face. "My brother is in France."

"I didn't know that."

Lines appeared at the corners of her mouth. "We've only heard from him once since he went to Europe. My mother is awfully worried. We all are."

"I'm sorry," he said even as he wondered if his aunt and uncle would worry after he was gone.

They walked on until Milton spotted a fat white oak, its branches twisted high above, its large green leaves hanging like drapes. He spread his suit coat on the ground, and she leaned back against the trunk, taking off her hat. Wisps of red hair spun with gold curled at her temples, framing her face. He longed to reach out and touch them, to hold the soft strands in his fingertips. She raised a hand to her hair. "Is something wrong? Do I look a fright?"

"No," he said, fighting the urge to take her hands in his. "The truth is, I think you might be the loveliest woman I've ever known."

"Oh." Pink splotches dotted her cheeks, and her hand jumped to her throat. "Thank you."

Behind them the voices of children and their mothers filled the silence. A bird chirped in a nearby tree and a stray breeze blew the leaves overhead, the rippling sound like flapping wings.

"Milton," she started, her voice soft, "I—" Anna Mae's words fell away, and she ducked her head to hide her face. "Oh, my."

Looking around, Milton spied two women passing, their heads close together, their skirts swaying in unison. He didn't know them or why Anna Mae was hiding. Even so, he shifted his weight to shield Anna Mae from their view. Neither spoke until they'd passed.

"Do you know those ladies?"

"One. Letitia Nolan. She's the wife of John Nolan." She didn't meet his eye as she spoke, keeping her head down. "From the railroad. They live in our building. Lots of railroaders do."

"I see. You didn't want to be seen," he said slowly, plucking a blade of grass, the taste in his mouth bitter. "Is it because I'm Jewish?" The question slipped out before he could stop it. He'd never known being Jewish to be a problem—most of his uncle's clients and friends were also Jewish—but he'd never liked a woman like this one before.

Her head came up. "I don't mind that you're Jewish."

He heard what she didn't say. "But your father would."

"I don't know." She glanced over at him. "Do you mind that I'm Catholic?"

"No."

"What about your aunt and uncle?"

Milton's mouth closed and he thought back to the previous week.

"When are you going to bring home a nice Jewish girl?" his aunt had asked. "It's time for babies, Milton."

He laughed, having heard the same question countless times before. His aunt and uncle were strict, and traditions ran long and deep. Until now, until Anna Mae, he hadn't thought much about it.

Milton took her hand in his and lied. "I don't know either."

~~~~

EVENING

Bits of By-Play
By Luke McLuke
"A gambler's ways, I understand.
Are crooked," said Tom Tottom;
"He tries to get the upper hand,
By dealing from the bottom."
—*The Tennessean,* July 5, 1918

~~~~

"What do you think they'll call us?" Carl asked, propping his feet up on the table. He stroked his beard, lids half-closed. A glass of whiskey rested in his lap.

"Shut up," Clyde answered with a hiss.

"C'mon, big brother. You gotta give us a name. We're gonna be in the papers."

Clyde reached out and swept Carl's feet from the table. The glass tilted and the amber liquid spilled onto his trousers.

His younger brother jumped to his feet, wiping his pants. "Hey, what'd you do that for?"

Clyde jerked his thumb toward the door. "Keep your voice down. There are ears in this town." He spun a chair around backward and sat down, resting his arms across the top rail. "Besides, they aren't going to call us anything 'cause they aren't going to know who we are."

"Oh, yeah? How're you planning to pull that off?" Carl refilled his glass and sat down again.

"We'll cover our faces."

"That never works, and you know it."

Clyde didn't bother to respond.

Carl tossed back his drink. "I like the 'Lewis Boys.'" He leaned back and crossed his feet again. "Not some stupid name like Hole-in-the-Wall Gang. That don't sound right for us."

Clyde sipped his own whiskey. He had no interest in being anything like the Hole-in-the-Wall Gang or Jesse James or anyone else. They'd done all right for a while, but they got caught. He didn't care about being famous like his brother did, and he didn't plan on getting caught.

"No nicknames," his brother was saying. "Remember Billy the Kid? Who wants to be called a kid forever?" His voice took on a hard edge. "And I'm not afraid to draw my gun if I need to. Billy the Kid did know how to shoot though. Remember that? They say he liked his rifle, but myself, I like a six shooter. You can—"

"Are you going tonight?" Clyde asked, cutting into his brother's ramblings.

A train horn sounded in the distance and Carl waited until the call faded. "I already told you I was."

"I want you to do better tonight. Lose a little, but not enough to draw attention."

"I can't win?"

"Once or twice. Small though."

Carl snorted. "That's not an easy thing to do. These guys are terrible. They couldn't even get in some of the games I've been in."

"It's not about the cards, Carl. We need to stick to the plan. Let's go over it again."

"How many times are we gonna do this?" Carl's jaw jutted forward and his lips clamped shut.

"As many times as it takes," Clyde shot back. "It needs to be so embedded in our brains that neither of us could make a mistake even if we tried. There's too much riding on this. We can't take any chances." Leaning in, Clyde could hear Carl grinding his teeth. "We're going to go over it again." A tic pulsed at his brother's temple. "Think of the payoff, Carl."

His brother rose, poured another drink, and swallowed it down in one gulp. After a moment, he shrugged his shoulders. "Fine. We'll go over it again."

The brothers discussed the plan for another hour, picking apart the details they could. Outside, the sky darkened, and Clyde switched on the electric lamps. "It's time."

Wordless, Carl pulled on his waistcoat and hat.

From the window, Clyde watched his brother leave the hotel, his long shadow following behind. Over the shops and buildings on Church Street, he spotted the marble-like tower of the train station, glowing under the night sky. He raised his glass, relishing the burn of the whiskey. His brother was right.

They would be famous whether they wanted it or not. He didn't, but it couldn't be helped. Carl was right about another thing too. The "Lewis Boys" had a nice ring to it, a very nice ring.

THE NEGRO DOING HIS PART

Without any great urging and at most times at a sacrifice the Negro measures up full and free to all of his country's needs during these perilous times. He has given the flower of the manhood of his race to the army, he has cheerfully subscribed for Liberty Bonds at each and every call, he has bought Thrift Stamps, contributed to the Red Cross and is now standing eagerly awaiting the next demands. We feel we

> *have done right in helping our country. We are willing and anxious to do all that can be done to make the world really safe for democracy. And a fit habitat for all races of people.*
>
> —*The Nashville Globe*, July 5, 1918

~~~~

"I heard you were talking with Matt Toles today."

John's mouth went dry and he stared down at his plate, the seconds passing.

His stepfather's voice dropped an octave, his words slow and deliberate. "I'm talking to you, boy."

"Yes, sir," John said, palms damp. He liked it better when House yelled. His anger came on in a flash then, burning hot but flaming out just as fast. Not that he couldn't hurt a man in under a minute, but at least it was over quick. That was easier somehow than the forced calm he heard now. John stole a glance at Leah. At the stove, his momma paused as she filled his sister's plate, her ear cocked in their direction. "He was on the street when I went to get Leah today."

House's chin jutted forward. "I thought I told you I didn't want you hanging around that boy."

"I wasn't. I was talking with Reverend Hawkins. We both were."

Essie smiled at her son. "I don't know what we would do without Reverend Hawkins. Ever since he's come to Hernando to preach, it's brought so much comfort to so many folks. And especially now with the war on."

House leaned forward in his chair, his lips pursed. "And that's all you did?" he asked as though Essie hadn't spoken.

John had no intention of sharing what he and Matt had talked about. House liked the *Defender* fine when it suited him and less so when it didn't.

"We don't need men taking jobs from each other and getting good men killed," his stepfather had said after a copy of the paper had been passed around a community meeting. "All this talk about leaving the South and
~~~~

promises that things are better for our kind up North. How do we know that's true? Is it a wise man who gives up a known job for talk?"

John knew many men felt the same, and yet, the rumblings were growing. The promise of more money and more jobs sounded good to a lot of folks. It was no secret that Matt Toles was one of the more vocal young men in that group.

Answering House, John chose his words carefully. "I think we talked a bit about the news and jobs. Reverend Hawkins said men who work hard are rich in God's eyes." He saw Leah's lips curve upward before she lowered her head.

"Well now, that's the kind of thinking we need more of around here." House picked up his fork, waving it in John's direction. "I don't want you hanging around that Matt Toles. He's been nothing but trouble these last months, and if I were his daddy, I would've taken a switch to the boy." He poked at a potato. "That boy thinks he's better than the rest of us. Your momma and I don't need him giving you ideas. You got that?"

"Yes, sir," he said, a pang of guilt making him mumble. Matt didn't think he was better than House or anyone else, although he did have a lot of ideas that made folks nervous.

"Smithson and the boys came by today," House said. "They were passing around that flyer again, the one about the gunpowder plant. There's signs hanging up in town too." John's head shot up to find House watching him, his gaze hard as marbles.

"That doesn't concern us," his momma said.

"Maybe not. But there's talk a few men can be spared from the farms. 'Course I'm not one of them, mind you." He turned his attention back to John. "It's no secret that money is tight for a lot of folks. Gives people ideas."

John swallowed hard, not liking the way House was looking at him.

"Since when hasn't money been tight?" Essie asked. House grunted at that. "Whatever talk you've been hearing will not be tolerated in this house," Essie continued, palms flat against the table.

"Or at the farm," House said with a pointed look at John. "I don't like this war, and I don't want anything to do with it, no matter what any paid government man tells me to do." He slapped the table, rattling the dishes, and John wondered who his stepfather was most angry at—God for the drought or the government for the war. According to House, both were costing the farms and towns too much. A raised chin from Momma calmed him quick enough though.

"Those signs'll be gone soon. After Monday," House said with a nod for his wife.

After Monday. John heard the words in his head like the *tick, tick, tick* of a pocket watch. Monday. Monday. Monday.

His stepfather pushed away from the table, getting up to stand behind John. One large hand dropped onto his shoulder. "And then all the talk about leaving and gunpowder plants will be gone too." His fingers tightened before loosening again. "And good riddance, I say. Good riddance."

~~~~

JACK DEMSEY KNOCKS DEVERE OUT IN FIRST

JOPLIN, Mo., July 4.—Jack Dempsey knocked out Bob Devere here this afternoon in the first round of a scheduled twelve-round fight. Devere apparently was not in good condition, while Dempsey was hard and fit. A short left hook landed as the men separated from a clinch, put Devere down for the count. The fight lasted less than two minutes. The men are heavyweights. Dempsey and his manager left tonight for Atlanta, Ga., where Dempsey meets "Porky" Flynn Saturday night.

—*The Tennessean,* July 5, 1918

~~~~

Milton studied his cards. He would need a bit of luck if he didn't want to fold. Across the room, the door opened. The stranger was back.

Joseph raised a hand. "Hullo, Carl. We got a game going already. Maybe you'd like to play the next hand?"

Carl shrugged. "Why not? I can wait."

"You hear about the fight last night? About Dempsey?" Joseph asked.

"Don't believe I did," Carl said, pouring a drink. While Joseph detailed what he'd read, Carl found a chair and dragged it over to the table. "So, he fights again tonight?"

"That's what they say," the bellhop said as he dealt the cards.

Carl positioned his chair behind Larry and took a long swallow from his glass. He reached out, clapping Larry on the shoulder. "How's things, friend?"

Larry almost dropped his cards at the man's touch. "Good." He leaned forward and Carl's hand fell away. "Got a game going here though." Larry squinted at his cards, concentrating.

Carl gestured at the small pile of bills on the table in front of Larry. "Seems you do." He sat close. "Maybe I could learn a little something from you."

Joseph laughed out loud, poking his brother in the ribs. "Hear that? Carl's gonna learn from Larry."

Carl winked at Larry before he could protest. "He took my money. That's good enough for me."

"That's right. I did," Larry said.

"Seems to be taking yours too," Carl said.

Larry sat up straighter in his chair.

Milton studied the stranger. With his longish hair and heavy beard, he looked more like a rancher than most of the businessmen he knew. Carl was tall, with the kind of sloping posture that suggested he'd been forced to duck through doorways for much of his life. The stranger drained his glass, got up, and grabbed the bottle from the side table. He set it on the floor next to him.

As always, Joseph did most of the talking. "Hank and me might miss a few nights next week. Hotel's expecting some of those DuPont bosses to come into town."

Carl's hand froze midair. He set his glass on the table.

"The way I'm playing tonight," Joseph continued, "I could use the extra wages."

"What DuPont bosses?" Carl asked.

"It's that gunpowder plant," Frank said. "Word has it that even though there's still some work left to be done on the building site, they've begun operations. They've been hiring too."

Milton had heard the same. "Some good things about the war, I guess."

"Right. Anyway," Joseph said, "didn't want you to be surprised when you didn't see us a couple nights next week." He shifted back toward the stranger. "How long you and your brother staying, Carl?"

The man scratched at his beard. "A few more days. Got some business to take care of."

Milton watched the stranger pick up the bottle and pour again. "What kind of business are you in, Carl?" he asked.

"Kind of a nosy question, ain't it?"

"Is it?" Milton squirmed in his seat but returned the stranger's stare. "I'm in sales. Thought we might have something in common, that's all."

"It's a fair question," Larry said, his voice soft.

Carl took a long swig of whiskey. "Sales, huh? What d'ya sell?"

"Hats mostly."

Carl exploded in laughter, his spit spraying the table. "Hats," he said in a half shout and slapped his thigh. Whiskey slopped to the floor, and he laughed harder.

Milton's face flamed. What was so funny about selling hats? It was an honest job, and he was good at it. Uncertainty gave way to a growing anger. He wanted to drag the guy off his chair and throw him out, but based on the man's size alone, Milton would probably be the one on the floor. "I don't see what's so funny about it."

Carl's laughter slowed to a hacking guffaw. "Nothing's funny about it," he said when he could speak again. "Nothing at all." He raised his empty glass in the air. "Let's drink a toast to hats." No one moved. "Come on, now. I didn't mean anything by it. Hell, maybe I'll even buy one from you."

"Hear that, Milton?" Joseph said. "Might buy a hat from you."

Hank chimed in. "His uncle makes the best hats, Carl. No joke there."

"Well, it's settled, then. Before I leave town, I'll get a hat from our sales boy."

"My name is Milton."

Carl's lips twitched. "Sorry. I'll get a hat from Milton." He raised his glass again. "Let's have that toast."

Joseph and Hank lifted their glasses. A minute later, Larry joined them.

"Didn't mean nothin' by it," Carl said again. He placed a hand over his chest. "Honest."

Milton's anger slipped away. Maybe selling hats was a little funny after all, although Uncle Leopold wouldn't think so. He definitely wouldn't think it funny that Milton was not at home, observing the day of rest, but to Milton, rest was subjective, in the eye of the beholder. Like selling hats. He raised his glass. "To hats."

"To hats." A chorus of cheers went up, everyone drank, and Carl waved a hand at the table. "Finish your game, boys. That's what you're here for, ain't it?"

They played out the hand. Unable to concentrate on his cards, Milton folded. Carl took his place and Milton watched from the corner, sipping his whiskey. Carl won a single hand, folded a few times, and lost the rest. When he had no money left to wager, he pushed back his chair, standing over them.

"Well, boys, it's been fun."

"You leaving, Carl?" Joseph asked.

"I'm afraid I'm out of money. Guess I shoulda been watching Larry more."

Milton followed the line of Carl's outstretched hand. The pile of money in front of Larry was twice the size of any other at the table.

Larry beamed. "Can't remember when I've had a winning streak like this one."

Joseph snorted. "You can say that again."

"Call me your good-luck charm, then," Carl said. "Same time tomorrow night?"

Hank lifted a hand. "We'll be here."

After he'd gone, Milton took his seat at the table again. After a few more hands, the game fizzled out. Milton walked home alone, his thoughts skipping from Larry to hats to Carl. This night had been the same as the night before. The stranger hadn't fiddled with his cards or picked them up to check them. He hadn't jiggled his leg or squinted or worn the smug expression he sometimes saw when a man felt sure he held the winning hand. He'd given no signs at all. Milton had seen players like that a few times before. If Milton were asked, he'd swear Carl knew the game better than most, but his play said otherwise. He was reminded of the three of a kind Carl had thrown away the night before, and the hairs rose on the back of his neck. It was only then that he remembered. Carl had never said what business he was in. Milton walked faster, his hands deep in his pockets. What did they really know about Carl anyway?

~~~~

OUR HONOR ROLL

Washington, July 4—The Army casualty list today contained 52 names, divided as follows: Killed in action, 9; died of wounds, 6; died of accident and other causes, 3; died of disease, 5; wounded severely, 26; missing in action, 2; prisoner, 1.

—*The Tennessean,* July 5, 1918

~~~~

David moved through the rain as fast as he was able, his walk turning to a run.

"Help me."

A crash sounded. He slipped, catching himself. Was it thunder or shots? David struggled to find his footing in the mud, the land uneven with trenches and craters. He ran faster, the rifle he carried banging against his back. Lightning flashed and lit up the field. Bodies were strewn across the rain-soaked land. He raised his face to the sky, the storm drowning out his curses.

"Help me."

The voice pulled him from despair. John George. There was no time. His son needed him. David searched in the darkness, straining to see. He cupped his hands around his mouth. "John George!" He spun around, calling his son's name four times, five, ten.

"Help me."

The voice came from somewhere to the north of him. David picked his way across the field, checking each body, stumbling in relief when none were John George. The bodies around him seemed to multiply and the mutilation got worse. Arms and legs missing. Faces unrecognizable. Blood mixed with the rain, and he stopped more than once, retching.

"Help me." The words were faint, weaker. David wiped his mouth and kept moving. His feet stuck in the muck, and he felt himself growing weaker. The acrid odor of burning flesh stung his nose. He fell to his knees, crawling when he could no longer walk.

"John George," he croaked. The darkness pressed in on him, and he shivered in the cold. "Where are you?"

He listened as hard as he could but heard nothing. He crawled onward, rocks and broken branches cutting his hands and shredding the skin on his knees. His strength nearly gone, he threw off the rifle. He had to be close now.

"John George? Please say something." There was only silence. He dragged himself onward, hot tears flowing with the cold rain. He crawled until his hands found cold flesh. He froze, blinking, but he could see nothing but a lump half buried in the mud. Digging with icy fingers, he uncovered the man.

"John George?" He didn't recognize his own voice. "Is that you?" There was only the sound of pounding rain. Thunder crashed again. Lightning cracked, casting its sharp white light over the blood-soaked ground. David recoiled, opened his mouth, and screamed.

PART 3

AFTER THE DARK

CHAPTER NINE

Summer 1988

ANNA MAE CLASPED her hands to her chest and sank low in her chair, the burden of her father's nightmare too much for her to endure. Her eyes shimmered in the dim light.

"David didn't know—"

The door slammed open. "Exactly as I thought. You," hissed the night nurse, her finger pointed at Ginny. "Visiting hours ended two hours ago."

The younger woman jumped to her feet. "I must have lost track of the time." She shot Anna Mae an apologetic glance. "I'm so sorry."

"It's not you who should apologize, dear," Anna Mae said, looking at the nurse with pursed lips. She tapped a finger to her chest. "It was I who kept Mrs. Campbell here after hours. If you must be angry at someone, then it should be me."

"It's against regulations," the nurse said, crossing her arms over chest. "I'm afraid I'll have to report this."

"If you must, although I didn't realize those rules applied to a woman in my weakened state. Of course, I'm quite sure you already took that into consideration when you decided that the only visitor I've had in years should be ordered to leave. Rules are rules." She lifted her hands as though the woman had handcuffs at the ready. "Do whatever you think best."

Ginny couldn't look at Anna Mae, afraid she might laugh if she did.

"Well, maybe I don't have to report it this time," the woman said with a heavy sigh. "But lights go out at nine, which is in"—she paused—"twenty-five minutes. No exceptions."

"I'll be gone before then," Ginny said quickly.

After the nurse had gone, Ginny whirled back around, no longer able to contain her amusement. "You're something else, Anna Mae, you know that?"

The old woman smiled, but without the sparkle Ginny had come to know. It was then that Ginny noticed the sallow tint of her skin and the fine red lines that crisscrossed her eyes. *Weakened state.* She'd thought it part of the old woman's ploy to make that nurse feel guilty but she wondered now. "Are you okay, Anna Mae?"

The old woman nodded. "It's nothing."

"It doesn't seem like nothing. You said—"

"Not to worry. When you get to be my age, everything is something, which is the same as nothing. There is nothing wrong with me but old age," Anna Mae said, patting Ginny's hand, her fingers cold against the young woman's skin. "I hate to ask, but would you mind sending in that infernal floor nurse before you leave?"

Before Ginny could get out the door, Anna Mae's head lolled against the back of her chair, her eyelids already drooping. Ginny took one more look at the old woman. "Sleep well, Anna Mae," she whispered. "Sleep well."

~~~~

Ginny jerked awake, a sheen of sweat coating her skin. Her hands flew to the soft mound of her belly, and she let out a breath. Calmer, she struggled to remember the dream, but it slipped away before she could snatch any memory. Was it George or Milton or Clyde who'd crept into her
~~~~

subconscious? Shaking off a feeling of foreboding, she pushed herself up on her elbows, flicked on the lamp, and reached for *Anne of Green Gables*. Reading was something she'd always done to soothe her mind. By page twenty, she'd forgotten about the dream, lost in Anne's world. Turning page after page, she didn't notice the letter until it fell from the book.

Sitting up, she turned it over, studying the envelope. No name or address. Sliding a finger under the flap, she found a single page. She unfolded the letter, the fine paper crackling. The writing was familiar, not the angular, slanted loops she'd seen in Milton's letter to Anna Mae but something more elegant and fluid, like the script in the *Line a Day* journal, Anna Mae's journal. Lips moving silently, she read:

My Darling,
I saw you in Centennial Park today.

Ginny's heart rose up in her throat. Was this to Milton? And if so, why wasn't it sent? She read on.

You didn't see me—at least I don't think you did—but every part of me wished you had, although I daresay you wouldn't have known me. I'm not the woman who held you in my arms. These last months and years have changed me. So much loss here and in the world. I fear it got to be too much for me. Sometimes, it still is, but I am better now. I've been going to the park every day since I've been able, hoping to catch sight of you, even though I know you're better off without me. The days in court and the trial itself surely took their toll. The testimony, so very cruel, was especially difficult. That's behind us now, but I am glad you weren't brought into it, that you couldn't be. If ever I needed another reason for the decision I made, that is surely a good one.

"Oh," Ginny breathed. Milton had lost her. Or was it the other way around? She turned the paper over. Nothing. She searched the book for a second page but there was nothing more. Confused, Ginny read the letter a second time. It didn't make sense. What trial? What decision? The phone rang then, jarring her from her thoughts.

"I hope I didn't wake you," Shawn said.

She looked at the clock. While it was early in Nashville, for him it was nearly lunch. Unable to keep her discovery to herself, she told him about the letter.

"Maybe whatever she's talking about in this letter is why she never married," she said, turning the idea over in her mind.

"Maybe. Does it matter?"

"Come on, Shawn. Aren't you the least bit curious why she ended up alone? Milton loved her."

"And you know this from one love letter?"

She knew how foolish her words sounded. Milton might have written that same letter to half a dozen girls and forgotten about Anna Mae before the week was out.

Silly as it sounded, she didn't want to believe that.

"It's romantic," she said.

"Gin, what's gotten into you?"

She said nothing, unable to explain what she didn't understand herself.

"Look, I know you like this lady and her story, but don't make this into something it's not."

"Like what?"

"I don't know. Some big tragedy or something. It's a lady who didn't get married. What did they used to call them? Old maids? Spinsters?"

She groaned out loud. "Really? That's where we're going?"

"Sorry, I didn't mean anything, but I don't think you should go there today. Go shopping or do something else. Clear your head."

She knew what he really meant. Clear your head of all the nonsense.

"Maybe," she said, knowing she had no intention of going shopping or anything else. The letter had only fueled her curiosity. Nothing would keep her from Anna Mae's bedside now.

~~~~

Ginny walked in to find Nurse Jean, her hands resting on the handles of Anna Mae's wheelchair. "We've been waiting for you."

Anna Mae, her skin translucent in the bright light of the morning, beamed at Ginny. "We're going outside today. Isn't that wonderful?"

Jean led the small group to the elevator and out the back door. She parked the wheelchair next to a pair of splintered picnic tables. "How's this?"

"Perfect, thank you." Anna Mae wrapped her shaking hands around Jean's. "You take such good care of me. I don't deserve it." She let go of Jean and sighed. "Though it won't be for much longer, I'm sure."

"Don't say things like that, Anna Mae. I can't lose my favorite gal." The smile Jean forced couldn't hide the lines that had deepened between her brows. She straightened. "Who else is going to listen to Hank Williams with me?" Jean tucked her hair behind her ears and winked at Ginny. "Did you know we're in the only home in all of Nashville where none of the staff likes country music?"

Ginny shook her head. She didn't know much about country music.

"Except you," the old woman said.

"And you, Anna Mae." Jean shook her head. "I can't understand it." She waved at the women as she went back inside. "Not too long out in this heat."

The older woman tipped her face up to the light. "Isn't the sun glorious?"

Ginny squinted and put on her sunglasses. Glorious or not, the sun was a fireball on her skin. A trickle of sweat slid between her shoulder blades. Despite the heat, Anna Mae looked cool enough. On this day, her colorful quilt had been replaced by a lightweight wrap.

"I've always loved summers in Nashville," Anna Mae said. "I know there are those who complain about the heat, but I never minded. Of course, we wore hats in my day. Milton's uncle made the most fashionable hats in the city. It's a shame they went out of style." Her faraway look faded. "And nowadays, people are practically naked."
~~~~

Staring down at her own bare legs, Ginny was reminded of the things Anna Mae would have seen in her lifetime. She'd have seen the flapper era, the Depression, and the birth of rock and roll. She'd lived through both world wars, the Korean War, and Vietnam. Ginny had more questions than ever, but she wouldn't spoil the moment. Not yet. This was Anna Mae's time now.

"Would you like to know more about trains?" Anna Mae asked.

"Sure."

"My father used to tell us stories when we were young, sometimes the same one over and over, of course. My favorite, I think, was about the first railroad. It was something of a legend among us railroad families." She paused, gathering the wrap around her shoulders. "As the story goes, on July fourth of 1828, Charles Carroll dug a shovel into the ground. It was a ceremonial gesture to celebrate the creation of the Baltimore and Ohio railroad, the first in the United States. Carroll was an old man, though not as old as me," she said with a chuckle. "Anyway, as he stood among the other leaders of this newly formed railroad, he said something like this." Her voice dropped an octave. "'I consider what I have now done to be among the most important acts of my life, second only to my signing the Declaration of Independence, if indeed, it be even second to that.'" She finished with a flourish of her hand. "My father said it was with those words that the railroads were born." Her smile softened. "Now I can't say for sure if that story is true or a myth, but I've always like the sound of it."

"I like it too."

Anna Mae waved a hand in the air. "Enough about that. Where did I leave off last night?"

"Your father." The unease the young woman had felt during the night came rushing back. "He was looking for John George. It was raining, and he was screaming."

Anna Mae's brows creased. "Oh, yes. That horrible nightmare." She angled her head as she spoke, and the present fell away. "Well, as you can imagine, when he woke up, he was quite distressed."

CHAPTER TEN

Saturday, July 6, 1918
Dawn

OUR HONOR ROLL

Washington, July 5.—The army casualty list today contained twenty-three names, divided as follows:

Killed in action, 5; died of wounds, 7; died of accident and other causes, 1; died of disease, 2; wounded severely, 3; missing in action, 5.

—*The Tennessean,* July 6, 1918

~~~~

David's heart thudded in his chest, and he sat up, his hands curling over the sheets. The room was dark, but if he concentrated, he could make out the dresser against the wall. Listening, he heard the gentle snores of his wife. He was home. But the images—the rain, the blood-soaked mud, and the bodies—those were seared on his brain. They would fade over time, like tears, but they couldn't be forgotten.

Mary stirred next to him, rolling onto her side. He breathed a sigh of relief, grateful she had slept through the nightmare. More than once, he'd
~~~~

startled her with these dreams. She'd hold him in her arms, rub his back and neck. She would make soothing noises—the kind she once did for the children—but she wouldn't be able to hide her concern. His dreams scared them both.

He pulled back the covers and padded to the window. The sun had not yet cleared the horizon, the sky still dark. Even so, it would be impossible to sleep now, the frightening visions too close, too real for comfort. He dressed, peeked at his wife again, and left the room.

The quiet in the apartment calmed him and eased some of the tension that had settled along the base of his neck and shoulders. He tiptoed down the hall to the parlor, lit a candle, and crossed the room to his desk. Opening the bottom drawer, he gathered the small pile of letters. Even before the war, John George hadn't been much of a writer. Since he'd been gone, David couldn't say if the lack of letters was John George or the difficulties in posting mail during wartime. The last letter they'd received had been dated weeks earlier and had taken another month to make its way to Nashville. Any letter—no matter the date—was a gift, a prize to be treasured. He sat down, stretching his legs. Hands shaking, he clutched the bundle to his chest.

David didn't consider himself a sentimental man. He knew loss. He wasn't afraid of death for himself, but this was different. This was his only son. Memories of their last conversation flooded back.

"I'm leaving today," John George had said. "Leaving Nashville." He stood in the doorway of his parents' bedroom, a small bag thrown over his shoulder. Mary hadn't been able to read his lips, but seeing his bag, she raised a hand to her mouth.

David patted his wife's hand and slid from the bed. "John George, if this is about you going to college, we can talk further. No need to do anything rash." He threw Mary a quick smile and pulled on his shirt. "Running away won't solve anything."

"I'm not running away."

"Good," he said, steering his son out into the hall. "I understand you think you don't want to go to college, but this is for the best. I've made some inquiries and I think you'll find my selections acceptable." Behind them, Mary was climbing out of bed to fetch her housecoat. "We don't need to worry your mother."

John George pulled away. "I'm finished with school. I'm going into the army."

David's steps slowed. "You can't go into the army. You're only sixteen."

"I signed up eight weeks ago."

"B-but you couldn't." His wife appeared at David's side, her hands clutching his nightshirt.

"I did. It's official." John George took a piece of paper from his pocket, unfolded it, and waved it in front of his father. "I ship out today."

Heat rose from David's chest to his cheeks. "I forbid it."

"Too late for that." John George brushed by his father and folded his mother into his arms. He kissed her cheeks and promised to write when he could.

And then he was gone.

Mary sank to the floor, her sobs echoing through the apartment. Stone-faced, David stood alone, staring at the empty space left behind.

He looked now at the bundle in his hands. The anger he'd felt that morning had long since gone, replaced by fear and a yearning to have that day back, to say goodbye in a different way. He ran his thumb across the letters, picking out one of the most recent. The paper inside had worn thin, the once-sharp fold soft. He opened the page, fingers trembling. The writing was as familiar as his own, the words large and bold, not unlike John George himself.

Dear Mother and Father,

The days have gotten longer and the nights warmer. It's even hotter here than at home. Training has been better of late though. It seems they may make a good soldier of me yet. I've made a few friends these past months. Most of the men are from the Carolinas but I've met two others from Tennessee. It's funny. I didn't know I would miss Nashville, miss home, until I wasn't there.

David laid the letter down, rubbing at his temples. His head ached again, but he couldn't be sure if it was due to John George's letter or his own memories. He'd missed home, too, missed the family he'd broken with. Like his son, he'd entered the war of his own volition, never suspecting he wouldn't go home again. The words on the page blurred in front of him, and he forced his mind to focus, to think of happy times and good memories. He took the letter up again.

The news is that we're shipping out next week. They haven't told us who is going or where, but the talk is England or France. Everyone is pretty tight-lipped around here. Even if I did know where I was going, I'm not sure I could tell you. They're pretty strict about what we can say.

Mother, I'm glad to hear you are working with the Red Cross—and Anna Mae and Katie Belle too. We've seen them here delivering packages and supplies to be sent over to the front.

Well, that's all for now.

From your son,
John George

David held the letter in his hand for several minutes. His son could be at the front now, fighting the Germans, maybe fighting for his life. Shuddering, David remembered the bloody battles of America's war. He wouldn't ever forget the sharp sounds of gunfire and the piercing screams rising over the fields. He pressed the letter to his chest. The candle flickered, and he whispered a prayer, his mouth moving from memory. His eyes filled and the tears he'd fought, hot and thick, ran down his cheeks.

~~~~

Boots clomped over the hard dirt, the sound drifting across the field. John's jaw tightened. A dust cloud swirled over the rows of corn. He lifted his hat
~~~~

and squinted. There. A hat bobbing up and down between the curling leaves. He stiffened. Uncle Elijah was supposed to have left early for town, but he'd been checking on John and the crops more often than usual. Maybe it was the lack of rain. Maybe it was Robert being gone. The reason didn't matter. The sound of footsteps came closer, and John braced for a lecture.

"There you are, I've been up and down these rows, and Lord knows, it's hot as the devil out here."

John's shoulders loosened. Matt. He searched the edge of the field but saw only an empty tree line. They were alone.

"What are you doing here?" John asked. "I thought you'd grown scared of farms these days."

"You know I'm not scared of farms. I just don't like 'em. Never have." He ran a hand over the crackling stalks. "I do like cornbread though."

Laughing, John knew this to be true. President Wilson had asked Americans to ration food so more could be sent to the soldiers. Now they had Meatless Tuesdays and Wheatless Wednesdays. Cornmeal had replaced wheat in many households. It didn't bother John, and some, like Matt, seemed to prefer it. He could eat more cornbread than most. "There'll be plenty if we ever get any rain."

Matt pointed at the cloudless sky. "Doesn't look like it today."

Sweating under the hot sun, John guessed Matt was right. "Why'd you come find me?"

"I have news," Matt said, bouncing on his tiptoes. "I'm leaving Hernando." John's mouth fell open. "And guess where I'm going? Chicago."

"Chicago." The word sounded hollow in the open field. "When?"

"Tomorrow. Monday at the latest."

"Monday," he said in a low breath. Matt would be gone by Monday, the same day the train was going to DuPont. How many others would be gone too?

A circle of crows cawed, and John tensed, searching the sky. The black birds hovered near the far side of the field, where a figure darted past the corn. The birds raised their beaks, their sharp call carrying for miles. He caught a glimpse of the figure, saw the delicate line of her neck and the long braid hanging down her back. Sabina. The birds flew off, disappearing over the trees. John watched Sabina move past the field and into the woods where the crows had flown. She crossed the road, ducked through a small opening in the trees, and disappeared behind the thicket.

"I know why you don't want to leave Hernando," Matt said, jabbing John in the ribs.

John picked up his hoe and hacked at the ground. "I like Mississippi. And Hernando," he said, not looking at Matt, his cheeks hot. "And Elijah needs me here."

"If you say so," Matt said, smacking at a cornstalk. "This corn doesn't need you. The only thing it needs right now is rain."

John reached out and fingered the dry leaves of a withering stalk. If the weather didn't get better, there wouldn't be a harvest, and he would have missed his chance.

"Come on, John, there's gotta be somewhere you want to go."

He shrugged. "Maybe." Dragging his hoe through the dirt, John reached the end of the row.

"Wait. Is this about that gunpowder plant?

Sweat dripped from John's temple, and he mopped it with the back of his hand before starting down another row.

"You should do it."

John's hoe stalled. He looked up at his friend. "That's not what you said at the picnic."

"That was about me, not you. Besides, I've been thinking about it, and maybe Nashville's not so bad. Nashville has a college for people like us," Matt was saying. "Fisk is the name. DuBois went there. I saw it in the *Defender*. There's a big train station, lots of jobs."

"Then why don't we both go?"

Matt batted down the idea with a flick of his hand. "I'm a Chicago man, John. You know that."

A lump formed in John's throat. "I don't know what to say. I'm going to miss having you around."

"Say you'll go to Nashville. Promise me."

John looked down at the dry, dusty soil and the rows of sun-beaten, colorless stalks of corn. It wasn't his farm. The house he slept in wasn't his house. He didn't have anything of his own, and in case he ever forgot, House made sure to remind him. Three months with good pay sounded better than the nothing he had now. John said the only thing he could. "I promise I'll try." He shook Matt's hand. "Good luck."

Beaming, Matt said, "I don't need luck. There are plenty of jobs to be had. Maybe I'll even get an automobile." He hopped around as he talked. "Might even meet a nice Chicago girl. Get married. Wouldn't that be something?"

John laughed. "It really would."

Matt lifted his chin toward the edge of the field, toward the thick line of trees. "Sabina misses you."

John's hand tightened around the wooden handle of the hoe. "You don't know that."

"She said you never talk to her anymore. Asked if it was her, if she did something wrong."

John paused. He'd thought Sabina didn't want to talk to him. "She didn't do anything."

"I told her that." A smile crept over his face. "I also told her you couldn't speak to her because you were madly in love with her."

John stumbled backward. "What?"

Matt erupted into laughter. "You should see yourself. If I didn't know any better, I'd swear you'd keel right over." He smacked his leg and laughed harder.

Unsmiling, John failed to see the humor in what Matt had done, but he wasn't sure if that was because he was angry at his friend for embarrassing him or for other reasons he didn't want to think about. "That's not funny," he said finally.

Laughter dying, Matt wiped his eyes. "It is so, but don't worry. That's not what I told her."

"Oh." He sagged, letting out a long breath, but his relief was soon replaced by a vague feeling of disappointment. "What did you say?"

Matt grinned. "Something stupid like you were too busy at the farm."

John looked past Matt to the hole in the trees that had swallowed Sabina. He didn't have to see her to know where she'd gone. "I never said I was in love with her."

Matt laid a hand on his friend's shoulder, his expression somber now. "You didn't have to."

~~~~

WOMAN'S ACTIVITIES IN W.S.S.

Work at the W.S.S. headquarters began in earnest Friday morning and a number of women responded to Mrs. L. B. Fite's call for clerical workers. She announces that there is room for more workers and any competent woman who will volunteer her services for a day, week, or few hours each day will be a great assistance to the committee in charge.

Mrs. Roger Caldwell, chairman of the Girls' Patriotic League, urges all girls of the Patriotic League to come to headquarters of the W.S.S., 221 Fourth Avenue, North, and assist in the clerical work.

A number of ladies from the National League for Women's Service were at headquarters today to assist in the work. Mrs. Jesse Overton, state chairman, urges that every member who can do so to assist in this work. Work begins at 9 and ends at 5 o'clock.

—*The Tennessean*, July 6, 1918

~~~~

Milton leaned against the brick stoop and checked his pocket watch. Nearly nine. Even though his uncle would be expecting him soon, he folded his arms over his chest, determined to wait a bit longer. Ladies, young and old, had been streaming past him all morning, each entering the building behind him. Dazed by the numbers, he'd tipped his hat at each woman who came and went—even recognized some. The building, a two-story square, was unremarkable, however, it had become one of the busiest in recent months. A plain sign over the door marked the address of the Nashville headquarters of the War Savings Stamps. At a few minutes past nine, a trolley sounded. Anna Mae and her sister stepped off the car. Pulse quickening, he straightened and pushed off from the wall.

"Mr. Lowenstein, what a nice surprise," Anna Mae said.

"I hope you don't mind." His glance swung from one sister to the other and back to Anna Mae. "I was passing by and remembered you said you'd be here this morning."

She smiled and pulled Katie Belle forward. "You remember Milton from the park, don't you?"

"I do, but I don't believe we've been formally introduced."

"Allow me to correct that," he said, taking her hand and bending at the waist. "Very pleased to make your acquaintance, Miss Kennedy. I'm Milton Lowenstein, a, uh, friend of Anna Mae's."

"Well, as long as you're a friend of Anna Mae's," she teased. "I feel like I already know you, but it's nice to actually meet you." Katie Belle turned back to her sister and gave her a hug. "I'm going inside. I'll save you a spot."

"Thank you," Anna Mae said and squeezed her hand.

"I'm sorry to show up this way," Milton said after Katie Belle had gone. "But I wanted to see you—even if it's only for a few minutes. I—I missed you. Is that strange?"

"Not too strange. I think I missed you too."

He grinned and waved a hand toward the street. "A walk around the block before you go inside?"

She bit her lip and looked down the road. A couple crossed the street, and a pair of automobiles rolled past. "Yes, I think I will," she said.

They walked in silence a moment. "You told your sister about me."

"Well, she already knew of our meeting at the dance, but yes. I told her about seeing you at the shop yesterday and going to the park, about you being a hat salesman, and how you travel for your job. She thought that sounded nice. Especially riding the trains."

"The war has made that harder now. The trains are so crowded, it's difficult to even take a smoke."

"That's what Father says, too, but there's something thrilling about it, don't you think?"

He laughed. "Spoken like a true railroader's daughter."

"Oh, I don't know," she said. "I envy you. I'd love to ride the train all over the country, see the wonderful cities, watch the world speeding by." Her tone grew wistful. "They have those lovely sleeping cars. The idea of riding for a few hours and waking up in a new place; it's quite exciting."

"It can be, but it would be more fun with you than a bunch of hatboxes."

She wagged her finger at him. "Don't make promises you can't keep, Mr. Lowenstein." They came around the corner, arriving back at the Women's Center. "I should probably get inside," Anna Mae said.

"Yes, I should get back too." He cleared his throat, but before he could speak again, she took a step back to allow a tiny woman carrying a basket full of yarn and needles to pass. The woman gave him a long look before nodding once at Anna Mae and disappearing inside.

"Let me guess," Milton said, face grim. "Part of the railroad family in your apartment building?"

"No, worse," she said with an apologetic smile. "Our parish. By the time I get inside and take up my knitting, ten women will know we were standing together outside this building."

"I'm sorry."

"Don't be. You've done nothing wrong."

He hadn't and neither had she, but that might not matter. "How about this? I stopped you to ask how to get to the millinery and you were kind enough to tell me."

She smiled at the excuse. "The millinery—as in the place where you work?"

"One and the same."

Her eyes danced in the sunlight. "You really are something, Milton Lowenstein."

"I'm glad you think so." He shifted on his feet. "Because there's a film playing at the Strand tonight, and I was wondering if you'd like to go with me. I know it's short notice." His hand rose to the pocket that held his army orders, not that he needed a reminder he was running out of days before he left, running out of days to see Anna Mae. "But if you don't already have plans, I could come by your apartment and—"

"No." She held one hand to her throat. "That's not a good idea."

Her words hit him like a slap. Had he misunderstood this new friendship?

"It would be better if I met you on the corner." His eyes snapped back to hers. She spoke slowly, her voice soft. "My father plays cards on Saturday nights, and he won't be home until late this evening."

"Only your mother and sister will be home."

"Yes." She hesitated. "But only Katie Belle . . ." Her words drifted away.

"Knows about me," he finished.

"Can you forgive me for being such a coward?" she asked.

He supposed he should have been disappointed, or possibly even hurt, but he was neither. He, too, had been reluctant to mention their meeting to his aunt and uncle. "You're not. You told your sister and if you're a coward, then so am I. My aunt and uncle can be stubborn. I'm not sure what they would say."

Her face cleared. "So, you don't mind?"

"No, I don't mind."

She reached up and touched his cheek with her hand. "Until this evening, then."

Milton watched her walk away and up the steps. He raised a hand to his face, skin tingling where her fingers had been. High in the sky, the sun beat down on the city, and he willed it to sink faster. For Milton, the night could not come soon enough.

~~~~

THE WAR

Negro troops, supported by allied tanks, which did great execution, delivered a brilliant counter attack on the western front and recaptured the crest running southwest of Marqueglise, between Perte Farm and Loges Farm.

—*The Crisis*, July 1918

~~~~

John dragged his hoe down the row, digging and scraping at the dry dirt. Each day, he mounded the soil where he could, protecting the roots. His muscles strained against the hard ground. Wiping the sweat from the back of his neck, his gaze drifted to the empty road and the narrow opening in the trees. He stared until the hoe dropped from his hand. He didn't think then. He cut through the fields, the path stamped on his brain. When he reached the road, he wavered less than a second before plunging into the forest.

Under a blanket of thick green leaves, cooler air caressed his warm skin. He'd missed the sweet scents of moss and bark, so different from the earthy odors of the fields. The trees opened up again and the ground sloped downward. The water in the creek was low this year, trickling over stones and sandy beds. The creek widened a few miles farther down before streaming toward the Mississippi.

On the other side of the bank, jagged rocks bordered another cluster of trees. He stood a moment, unsure. He didn't need to see her to know she was there. It had been more than a year since he'd stepped foot across these banks—not since she'd told him about the wedding.

"I'm getting married," she'd said, moving away from him.

He wasn't sure he'd heard right. "Wh-what?"

"Next week." The words when she said them were flat, no trace of emotion. "I'm getting married."

John's legs weakened under him, and he stumbled to the closest tree. He still thought maybe he'd misheard, until he saw the sorrow and uncertainty reflected on her face.

Sabina stepped forward. "Robert asked me to marry him, and I said yes."

His cousin had asked Sabina to marry him? John couldn't understand. Robert knew how John felt about Sabina, didn't he? Had Robert ever said anything about Sabina before? He'd remembered then.

"Sabina is nearly eighteen, isn't she?" Robert had asked one Sunday after services. John had searched for her in the crowd, found her trailing after her parents. There was a chill in the air, and she'd draped a light gray shawl over her narrow shoulders.

"I guess," John said.

"Probably looking to get married soon. A girl like that won't be unattached for long, Cousin."

"There's no rush," John said. He blushed at the innocent words now. Robert hadn't been talking about him. He'd been referring to himself.

A month later, Sabina had made her announcement. His momentary surprise had given way to anger.

"Don't be stupid, Sabina," he said. "You can't marry Robert."

Her hands flew to her hips. "You don't get to tell me what I can and can't do, John Lang. You are not my daddy."

His mouth opened and closed. "But I thought . . ." The words fell away.

The set of her features softened, and her hands fell to her sides. She stood next to him, close enough that he could smell the lavender flowers she'd wiped across the hollow of her neck. "You thought what?"

Fighting back tears, he was unable to face her at first. How could he say he'd thought she'd marry him? That he'd thought they were more than friends? He didn't want her pity, not then, not ever. "Nothing. I didn't think anything."

Neither spoke. He listened to the gurgle and splash of water washing over the rocks as the afternoon shadows gave way to the fading light and the crickets sang their evening song. He didn't know how many minutes they stayed like that, neither speaking nor moving. He thought only that if he made no sound, if he remained motionless, he could stop time, and she wouldn't marry Robert after all. But that never worked.

"Is that all you have to say?" she asked.

If he'd heard pity in her voice before, now he heard nothing, worse than nothing. He lifted his chin and forced himself to face her. "I hope you'll both be very happy."

She recoiled, lips closed tight. Snapping up her fishing pole, she fled, disappearing among the trees.

He stayed there, alone, for hours. The air grew cool and the sky dark. He rose to his feet and walked the miles home in a stupor, sure he'd be in trouble for being late. But it wasn't anger he went home to that night, only the very thing he dreaded. They already knew his shame.

Sabina and Robert had married. She'd borne a child, a son, and Robert had left for the war. John had never visited their spot again. Until now. He stepped on a stone, then another, crossing to the other side. Ahead, the trees seemed bigger than he remembered, their thick limbs stretching over the mossy ground, their green leaves blanketing the knoll in shade.

John heard the sound of her crying before he spotted her. She sat on the ground, curled inward, her back to him. He wanted to go to her, to take her in his arms, but he knew he couldn't. She wasn't his wife. Sabina belonged to someone else now.

LUKE McLUKE SAYS

The one objection to a man who knows what he is talking about is that he doesn't know when to stop talking about it.

—*The Tennessean,* July 6, 1918

"It won't be long until Carl has the information we need." Clyde paced the room, gauging the open-mouthed faces of the men. There were five in all, not counting Carl and himself. He'd picked each personally. Three he'd worked with before. They followed directions, took precautions, and best of all, had proven more than once that they could keep their heads when things didn't go as planned. The new guys were from Memphis. They were young and relatively inexperienced, but Clyde recognized smart when he saw it. They could follow directions and if they couldn't, they'd be outnumbered. "We know the shipment will be on the morning train out of Nashville," he said. "Soon, we'll know which day."

"When are we talking?" Cooper asked, chomping on the tobacco he'd tucked between his lower lip and gums. "Me and the guys are getting kinda tired of being stuck here."

"You've got everything you need, don't you?"

"Sure, but a man needs more than a bottle of whiskey and a loaf of bread. He needs a warm bed and a good woman now and then. How long do you expect us to sit on our hands?" Sandy haired with leather-chapped skin, Cooper had been with Clyde for nearly a decade. It was Cooper who'd found the abandoned house they were using. Situated on the outskirts of town, the house was close enough to the tracks but far away from nosy neighbors. Empty bottles and bedrolls lined the far wall.

"Only a few more days. According to my sources. Tuesday, Wednesday at the latest."

Frowning, Cooper said, "Only going to get one chance at it."

"That's why we wait until we know for sure. Either way, the plan doesn't change." He gestured toward Carl. "We've been down to the site. There's an orphanage up on the hill, so we'll need to get there before light. Can't have any of those nuns or orphans spotting you riding in."

Cooper spit on the floor. "We can handle a bunch of nuns if we have to."

"Wrong," Clyde said, careful to raise his voice enough to make the men sit up. "No one is handling any nuns. No one is handling anyone 'cause no one is going to see any of you before the job. Is that clear?"

"Sure, Clyde," Cooper said, aware the other men were watching him. "We stick to the plan. Go nowhere. Leave the nuns alone." He took the measure of the room and waited a beat. "Got it?" There was a chorus of grunts and ayes.

"Good," Clyde said, pleased.

Carl sat on an old wooden chair, his feet kicked up on a scarred table, his gun peeking out from his waistband. He wasn't alone. All the men in the room had guns tucked in at their hips. Clyde figured they'd been cleaned that morning, caressed like old friends. He understood. But this job needed to be different.

"So, when can we hear the whole plan?" Cooper asked.

Clyde's thoughts shifted, and the details aligned themselves in his mind. "Now's as good a time as any." He told them what they needed to know, clarified the timeline as best he could. More than once, he reminded them of the prize. The new guys practically jumped, elbowing one another. "Patience, boys. That's what will get the job done."

"That and a six-shooter," Carl said with a grin.

"No." Clyde's voice was harsh. "No shooting."

Carl sneered. "I think you're going soft, Brother. First, with the postal worker and now, when we're doing the job?"

There was a new restlessness among the men. They were outlaws, and as such, they were not above killing when killing needed to be done. Clyde didn't disagree, but this was his last job, and he didn't need any extra reasons for the law to search him out, or Carl. His brother was all he had left.

"Shooting is what gets guys caught," he said. "The law can let the money go, but not when there's killing involved. We can wait them out back home, live our own lives, and no one will bother us. But if there's killing, they won't stop until they find us." Clyde recognized there would be disappointment at his orders, but as long as Cooper and Harper agreed, he doubted the others would act on their own. "With this job, we got enough money to last a long time, but that won't be worth nothing if we're swinging from the trees."

"We won't get caught." Carl held his hand in the shape of a pistol. "Dead men don't talk."

"No, Carl. We do it my way," Clyde said. "We won't get caught if we do things right."

The men around him scowled, and the air in the room cooled. Clyde kept his body relaxed, face unreadable. The silence crackled. He was counting on Carl to be the one who couldn't keep it under control. It didn't take long.

The bottle flew across the room and hit the wall, glass exploding. Warm, brown liquid splashed across the floor. "What kind of gang are we that don't have guns? Can't shoot a man when you have to?" Carl leaped up, spit flying from his mouth.

"I didn't say we wouldn't have them. I said we wouldn't use them."

"What's the difference?"

"The difference is one could get us caught or worse, killed. Just having them will be enough to keep people in line, do what we want them to do." He struggled to stay patient. This was taking too long. "They won't be expecting us. Not in the cornfield. Not at that time of the morning. We've got surprise on our side. It's enough."

"Clyde's right." Cooper got to his feet. All eyes landed on the sandy-haired man. He shot a wad of spit in a puddle on the floor. "This could be the biggest job this side of Texas. I don't mean to get caught by no Pinkerton or anybody else." Listening, Clyde exhaled. "We don't need to shoot anyone to do the job. Having 'em is good enough."

Carl snorted, but Clyde knew with Cooper backing him, the others would follow orders. The older men had families now too. They didn't need the Pinkertons on their tails either.

Cooper spoke up again. "You said six in the cornfield. That leaves one of us out."

Clyde steeled himself for what he knew was coming. "You'll be in the cornfield, Coop. All of you but Carl." He took a look at his brother, saw the storm brewing there, and spoke quickly. "I've got another job for you."

"You're cutting me out." Carl's jaw clenched and cracked. "That wasn't the plan. It's my score. I should be there."

Clyde forced a casual tone. "I'm not cutting you out. You already know you're part of the front end with the postal worker, but there's something else I need from you. Something even more important." From the corner of his eye, he saw the others lean in. "I need you on the train. If the engineer decides not to stop, you'll be with the conductor to pull the cord." Clyde didn't want the conductor or anyone killed, so putting his brother on the train came with risks. But he had his reasons. There wasn't a man alive that Carl couldn't scare into turning on his own mother. The conductor would do as he was told; Clyde was counting on it. "You're the inside man. If the train doesn't slow, you're going to make it. And if there is a Pinkerton . . ." Letting the words sit there, he sensed rather than saw the heads of the other men nodding now. He watched his younger brother now. "What do you say, Carl? Would you rather ride? I can get Hoffman to do it if you think I'm cutting you out."

A hush fell over the room.

"Inside man," Carl repeated, his fingers caressing the butt of his gun. A wide grin spread across his face, splitting the jagged scar that disappeared under the heavy beard. "You can count on me, Big Brother."

It was the answer Clyde had hoped for—the answer he'd predicted—but that didn't stop the hair on the back of his neck from standing on end. Was using Carl a mistake? What if the plan didn't work? No. It did no good to think that way now. Sweeping aside the unease that had settled in his bones, he clapped his brother on the back and swung around to face the other men. "Boys, this will be our finest hour yet."

~~~~

Sabina's sobs faded to a whimper. Curled up, she lay on the ground, unmoving. John stood uncertainly, a heaviness settling over him. He shouldn't have come. This hadn't been their place in a long time, and now
~~~~

he understood. This was her place now. He took a step back, snapping a branch under his boot. He froze.

"John?" Wiping away the tears, she got to her feet. She tilted her head to one shoulder. "What are you doing here?"

"Sorry. I was just leaving." He moved to go.

"Wait."

Not trusting himself to speak, he waited, silent.

"Can you stay for a minute? Please."

He wanted to stay—more than anything—but he was afraid. Shifting his weight from one foot to the other, he looked away.

"It's okay. You don't have to stay if you don't want to. I'm used to being alone."

His head jerked back. Her voice was different, far from the pleading warmth of a moment earlier. She showed him her back. He faltered, stuck. Maybe Sabina wasn't the girl he knew anymore. He thought about the times he'd seen her at church or near the fields. Aloof. Distant.

Before he could take another step, her shoulders rolled and she sank to the ground, fresh sobs racking her body. Without thinking, he went to her, dropping to the ground, but stopped short of reaching out. The sobs slowed to long heaves until spent; she seemed to shrink into herself, her chin touching her chest, her knees drawn in close.

"Are you okay?" he asked, finally.

Her voice trembled when she spoke. "I don't know. I don't know anything anymore."

He bit his lip, rocking back on his heels. Where was the confident, laughing girl he'd grown up with, spent so many hours with? It occurred to him then that he'd been so wrapped up in his own sadness, his own small world, he'd been unable to see her melancholy, her pain.

"I can stay," he said, his words halting and unsure. "If you want me to." The movement of her head, almost imperceptible, was enough. Resting his arms on his bent knees, John sat with his back against the rough bark of an old tree. He didn't look at her, watching the shadows instead. Overhead, a crow squawked. Time passed—he didn't know how long—before he heard the rustle of movement.

"I'm sorry you had to see that," she said.

"Don't be."

She plucked at the folds of her skirt, her fingers fluttering over the worn fabric. "I come here when I can. It's not as much as I'd like now with the baby, but coming here helps me think, helps me remember before." She paused, her voice catching. "I don't blame anyone, and I do have my son. He's everything to me. I didn't know it would be like that." She lifted her wet face toward the tall trees. "At least I did one thing right. No one can say any different."

That was true. No one would, least of all him.

"Robert never knew about this place. I never told him." She faced him then. "Remember how you used to come here every day? It was your hideaway, you said. You brought Matt and then me, and it was the three of us for a while."

"Then Matt stopped coming."

She sighed. "It was just us. You and me. I thought it would always be that way, but things changed. We got older."

"You got married."

The sharpness of her breath made him want to take back the words, but he knew it wouldn't matter. He couldn't erase the hurt—hers or his—and either way, he'd spoken the truth.

"Yes," she said, shoulders drooping again. "I got married." She waved a hand in the air. "Anyway, I started coming here again when I found out I was with child. Robert hadn't left for the army yet. At first I only came once a week, then more, whenever I could steal away. I would sit against this same tree and I would feel better, safer somehow. I wondered if I'd see you here, but I never did. Until today."

"I haven't been here since you told me you were getting married."

"Oh." A minute later. "Do you hate me now?"

John's head rolled sideways toward her. She was thinner now. There were shadows in the hollows of her cheeks, and the soft lines of her jaw had sharpened. "I could never hate you."

She nodded slowly, and they sat together for a long time, neither speaking. The sun rose higher in the sky, the light cutting through the leaves and warming his skin. Elijah would be back by now, looking for him, but he didn't move.

He hadn't dreamed he'd be with her again, even like this.

"Robert's not coming back," she said after a while. Her words were a chilly reminder of all that had changed.

"What do you mean?"

Without answering, she stood and wiped the dirt from her dress. "I have to go. I've been gone too long already. My baby needs me."

He scrambled to his feet, his thoughts tumbling through his brain faster than he could put them into words. He only knew he didn't want her to go. "Wait. Is that why you were crying? Because Robert's not coming back?"

"You don't understand," she said and moved to leave, walking toward the water.

"Sabina?" She stopped mid-stride, her back to him. He licked his lips, his mouth dry as sandpaper. "Will you be here tomorrow?"

Her chest heaved once. The seconds dragged on, and she turned slowly. "You shouldn't come here, John." Her words were a kick to his gut. "Don't look at me like that."

"Like what?" he asked.

"Like I've hurt your feelings. I don't know if I can be responsible for that again. Not right now."

He thought about the things she'd said, the things she hadn't said. He had no right to ask anything of her, and he told himself he wouldn't make that mistake again. It was enough to be near her, even if only for a brief time.

"I want to be your friend again," he said.

Her lips parted, but there was no sound.

"If you don't want me to come, I won't, but I'd like to."

She didn't answer right away. "Okay. Friends. If I can be here tomorrow, I will be. And if I can't, I'll come the next day or the day after that."

He didn't hesitate. "I'll be here."

~~~~

EVENING

~~~~

David counted the cards in his hand and studied his partner for the evening. On that night, he'd chosen to pair with Harold Geary. Their opponents were Thomas Spence and William Hadley. William was David's closest friend and a good man, but a poor player.

"You're a hard man to beat," William had said on more than one occasion. David knew it was due more to William's lack of skill than his own good play, but he kept his thoughts to himself. Geary was better than William, but only marginally.

More often than not, the men played euchre, refraining from any type of gambling. David had money. He made a solid living as an engineer, but he preferred to hold on to it, especially now that the girls were older and still unmarried. What if something happened to him?

"David." William's voice cut into his thoughts. "It's your turn."

"Right," he said, the cards coming into focus again. He played the last hand, already knowing he and Geary had won.

After the game, the four men sat in companionable silence, each smoking, half-empty glasses on the table. David couldn't remember how many years they'd been playing together, but he always looked forward to it like it was the first time. It was true he liked to win, but it was more than that. These men were his friends. They didn't work for the railroad, and they weren't family.

Geary raised his glass to his lips. "Marjorie's young man will be leaving this week for North Carolina." He inclined his head toward David, his expression grim. "Might even be on your train."

The engineer stroked his beard. "Possibly. Seems like there's more every day."

"Marjorie's worried. They'd hoped to be married before he left, but he got called up." Geary clucked his tongue. "Been a lot of crying at my house this week. Thank goodness her mother is handling that."

William sat back and laced his fingers over his belly. "He'll come back. They all will."

David said nothing. He'd lost count of how many men had boarded his train in uniform, so sure of themselves, so sure they would persevere. More than once, he'd wished he could keep them on the train. They were safer here than at the front. He didn't need to cross the ocean to know that. He'd feel better when the war was over, and the boys came back.

Thomas Spence recounted the most recent news in the papers before shifting to their upcoming Knights of Columbus meeting. As David listened, the pain in his head returned, a dull, pulsing throb in his skull. He set his glass on the table and concentrated on his breathing. His fingers tightened over his pipe. In front of him, William's face blurred. David's stomach rolled and he felt the urge to vomit. This was the third time in as many weeks. He sat still until the ache lessened. Pain easing, he was startled to find William speaking to him.

"David?" William waved a hand. "Are you okay?"

He wanted to answer but somehow couldn't find the words, as though a blanket had been thrown over his mind.

William sat forward. "You're white as a sheet." He addressed Geary. "Should we call for the doctor?"

David raised his hand and clawed his way through the fog to find his voice. "I'm fine."

The words sounded gruffer than he'd intended, and William's brow wrinkled.

"I'm fine. Really."

"You don't look fine. Are you sure we shouldn't send for the doctor? "

"I assure you I am not unwell." David picked up his glass and drank deeply, the cool liquid sliding down his throat. "It was all this talk of the war. Every day we don't get a letter is hard on Mary and the girls."

"Ah," Geary said. "I understand."

"The men on the train in their soldiers' uniforms. They are so young. It's like a daily reminder . . ." His voice drifted away.

As talk about the upcoming meeting resumed, David sank lower in his chair. The headaches were new enough, an annoyance really, and up to now, he'd chalked them up to concern for his only son. He'd tried to keep them from Mary, not wanting to add to her worry, but this one had been worse, the pain momentarily hot.

For a few minutes, he'd lost track of time. Under the table, he folded his shaking his hands together. For the first time in as long as he could remember, David was scared.

~~~~

INDUSTRY

In the recent increase of wages granted by W. G. McAdoo, Director-General of the railroads, it has been ordered that after June 1 no discrimination in wages shall be made between white and colored men doing the same work. At present Negro firemen, brakemen and switchmen receive only from two-thirds to three-quarters of the wages paid white workmen.

—*The Crisis,* July 1918

~~~~

Ben sat across from George, the *Crisis* in his hands. "See? Even the government knows it ain't right. Men like us making too little money for our trouble."

What money have you made? George wanted to ask but held his tongue. It wouldn't do to argue again, and his heart wasn't in it. Besides, his poor, dead momma wouldn't like it. It didn't take much to imagine her looking down at him, her bony finger tapping him on his chest, her mouth shrunk to the size of an acorn. She'd have some words for sure. Family takes care of each other, she'd say. They found common ground and raised each other up. She would be right.

She usually was.

George reminded himself that his cousin was young and had a young man's view of the world. "That's good news, then."

"What about the porters?"

"What about them?"

"Shouldn't the porters be treated better too?"

George took his time answering. "The Pullmans got a wage adjustment back in 'sixteen. We got something too. But even if the Pullmans get another increase, Mr. Pullman doesn't pay all of us. That's up to the government and the railroads, I suppose."

"So, you're saying nothing can be done?"

"I'm not saying nothing can be done."

Ben missed the warning tone in George's voice and threw up his hands. "Don't you care about making things better?"

Grateful his wife and children had already gone to bed, George did his best to keep his voice level. "We all want things to be better, Ben, but a man can't go off demanding things the way you think."

"There's ways."

Although he admired his young cousin's passion, George no longer had the luxury of acting first and thinking later. Most of the other porters were men like him. They felt the same frustrations and suffered the same indignities, but they had responsibilities. "Let me tell you what would happen if I were to ask the railroad for more money with a war going on. I'd find myself back here in a house I couldn't pay for because I wouldn't have a job. And don't think for a minute that the government would care about that. No, sir. Men would be fighting to take my place even before I could take off my cap and uniform." He paused and licked his lips. "You think this is such a terrible job? Tell that to the men who've done it before me, who do it now. Being a railroad porter means something."

"I don't see how all that's enough. Things should be better than being all glad to have a job where you're"—Ben fumbled over his words—"you're invisible."

George's hands cupped the arms of his chair, his knuckles whitening. Ben was wrong. George wasn't invisible to the people who mattered.

"You want things better?" he said, his voice rising an octave. "I want them better too. That's why I go to work at the train station and do my job the best I can. That's why my children will get educated, go to college." He pointed his finger at Ben. "You're sitting in my house. You're eating my food. That's because I'm a railroad porter, which I do because I want to take care of my family." His hand dropped back into his lap. "That includes you, Ben. You're family. I told your daddy we'd take care of you until you got a job, and that's what we'll do."

Ben dropped his chin at the mention of his daddy. Two weeks in Nashville and no job. Thumbing his nose at a decent job wouldn't please his folks back home.

George's anger sputtered as quickly as it had flared. He reached across and picked up the abandoned newspaper.

"The *Tennessean*'s got jobs listed if you're sure you don't want to work for the railroad. There's lots of work right now." He turned to the want ads. "Here's one. 'Wanted: Colored man experienced in changing tires in our tire shop. Call in the morning.'" He looked up. "'Two in One Tire Co.' How about that one?"

"I don't know how to change tires."

"Okay. There's another." He skimmed the page. "What about this? 'Wanted: Colored wagon driver and porter. Apply at once at L. Jonas and Company.'"

"What's L. Jonas and Company?"

"A fancy place where they make hats and dresses. It's over on the corner of Eighth Avenue and Commerce. One of their salesmen takes the Number Four now and then."

"A porter again—for white folks?"

"And a wagon driver."

The corners of Ben's mouth drooped, and George knew better than to push. Ben was smart, but he didn't go to college. He wasn't a dentist or a doctor.

Young and inexperienced, he didn't have many skills. But like the young and inexperienced, he had big dreams and big talk.

"Is that all there is?"

"There's a few more. Most the same."

"Oh." Ben rocked back on the couch, his feet tapping the floor.

"Want me to read some more?"

"No." His young cousin got up, pacing the floor in front of George. "When's my daddy coming?"

"Next week." George set the paper aside. He didn't want to tell Ben's daddy the boy didn't have a job. He didn't want to tell him the boy had been drinking. "I think there are some fine folks over at L. Jonas. Mr. Lowenstein that rides the train is pleasant, always has a kind word to say."

Ben fell back onto the sofa. "I don't think so."

George struggled to hold onto his patience. "I've heard they're hiring over at the gunpowder plant. It's good pay. Factory work for three months, I've been told."

"Labor work?"

"I guess you could call it that." George stood up. It was late, and the boy wasn't his son. If he were, George would have more to say. As it was, he'd had enough. "Well, I'm off to bed. I'll be gone before sunup." He folded the paper, setting it back on the table.

"I heard about my test."

George stopped.

"My test for the railroad. To be a porter."

The older man sat down again. "How'd you do?"

"They said I got the job if I wanted it. I could start next week."

George drummed his fingers on the chair, unsure he wanted to hear what Ben had said to the bosses down at the station. "What did you say?"

"I didn't say anything. They gave me a list of all the stuff I'm supposed to buy, the uniforms and such. Gave me a book to study with all the rules about being a porter."

"I guess I should be offering you congratulations, but I thought you didn't want to work for the railroad."

Ben shrugged "I might try it for a while."

It was all George could do to hide his surprise. Hadn't his young cousin called it slave's work a few nights earlier? "I have to ask: what changed your mind?"

"What was in the paper, what I read you about the government increasing wages, forcing better working conditions."

George stared, not understanding.

"Don't you get it? That means somebody complained, and somebody listened. Maybe we can do that for porters too."

"And you're going to be the one who complains?"

"Maybe. Not by myself." He leaned forward, his elbows resting on his thighs. "But the white folks have these unions. They fight for fair treatment of all the workers. Up in New York City, the elevator operators did that very thing. Porters can do the same if they join together."

George's breath caught in his throat. He knew what unions were. A formal union was the very idea he'd proposed last month at a backroom meeting. Maybe he and Ben were more aligned than he'd realized. Change didn't happen when a man stood still. As it was, with the hours the railroads demanded, a man could break his back and at the end of the day, have nothing but pennies to his name.

In the discussion that followed his proposal, the men had found only one thing they could all agree on. Any extra money the government had was likely to go to the war effort and not to the porters in Nashville, Tennessee. And so, the union idea—an official one—had died before it was really born. George considered his young cousin now.

"There may be a time for that—a union—or something like it. Maybe after the war," he said, his voice soft. Ben's chin came up and he opened his mouth, but George raised his hand before the boy could speak. "But you can't go in causing trouble. You'll be fired before you even start."

The boy's jaw worked as he considered George. "I'm not going to go in causing trouble, and I'm not going to be fired," he said at last.

"That's good. Your daddy wouldn't like that."

A shadow passed over the boy's face before it cleared again. "I'm going to do my job same as everybody else, ride the trains, see the country. That's what it is, right?" He rose and stood over George. "Someday though, when the time is right, somebody is going to start a union, a porters union. You wait and see."

~~~

"You're late tonight," Frank said, pouring Milton a drink.

"I got tied up."

"Where? The girl from the park?"

"My uncle," Milton lied. He trusted Frank, but he wasn't ready to share anything about Anna Mae yet—not even her name. The hours with her were too precious. Already, he'd forgotten the film, but the smell of her, the sound of her voice—those were things he couldn't forget, didn't want to forget. Frank didn't need to know any of that. He raised his glass in the direction of the table. "How's the game tonight?"

Frank snorted. "Same as always. Larry's losing again."

Milton inventoried the table. The Smythe brothers sat on one side, Larry and the stranger on the other. Carl, a large pile of money in front of him, appeared to be winning for a change.

"The Smythes are sitting out the next hand," Frank said. "We can join in then."

"Sounds good." Milton watched the game. Larry was back to his old ways, staring too long at his hand, his features rearranging themselves with each new card. Larry folded, tossing in his cards. Moving his lips, he counted his remaining money.
~~~

"They're done," Frank said. "We're up."

The Smythes cleared up their piles. Frank and Milton took their places at the table.

"You boys ready to play?" Carl asked.

"You bet," Milton said with a broad wink.

"Good one," Frank said with a chuckle. He nudged Larry. "Never get tired of that one, right?"

"Uh, right." Larry pushed away from the table.

If Carl found the small joke funny, he didn't show it; his attention was focused on Larry. "What about you, friend? You ready to play some more?"

Larry's hand hovered over the tiny pile of coins in front of him. "I don't know. Don't seem to be having much luck tonight."

Carl laughed. "Can't quit yet. Lady luck is a fickle one, my friend, but it only takes one hand to turn everything around. Besides, you're the best player at the table. It's no fun if you don't play."

Milton and Frank exchanged a glance, but Larry perked up. "Yeah. Okay."

Carl pushed the deck of cards over to Milton to cut. "Five-card draw this round. Ante up, boys."

Carl's hands moved over the cards in one quick motion, and he dealt five cards to each player. Across the table, Larry picked up his cards, holding them close to his nose. Frank swept his up in one hand. Carl took his time, taking a long drink of whiskey.

Milton picked up his cards one at a time. Jack of spades. Three of diamonds. Eight of clubs. Not much to work with there. He picked up the fourth card. Four of diamonds. The final card was a two of spades. He tapped the cards with his index finger, eyeing the table. A two, three, and four. It was a long shot, but stranger things had happened. Next to him, Frank squinted at the cards in his hand. The lines around Larry's mouth had smoothed. Milton knew the postal worker's foot bounced up and down under the table.

Carl divided his cards into two piles. "What's it going to be, boys?"

Larry went first. He tossed two cards back into the pile, got two new ones. Milton gave back the Jack of spades and the eight of clubs. He fingered the two new cards Carl had slid to him. He peeked at the first card. The six of clubs. Two, three, four, six. One more card. He forced himself to wait a long second. He picked up the final card. The ace of spades. His hand dropped along with his hope of drawing a five. Well, he told himself, he'd known it to be a difficult hand to get. Straights weren't easy under any circumstance, but five-card draw was a fast game, the chances slim. Milton had nothing. He tapped his cards into a single pile. "I'm out."

Frank tossed his cards on the table. "I fold too."

"Guess it's just you and me, friend."

Larry held tight to his cards. His knees bounced harder, hitting the table more than once. A handful of coins popped up and down.

Carl held his cards loosely in one hand. With the other, he picked up his glass and drained the last of his whiskey.

Larry took two coins from his pile and slid them across the table. "I raise you," he said.

"Well, well," Carl said, drawing out the words. "Looks like we've got a bit of fun tonight after all." He pushed his pile of money to the center with a flourish. "I see your bet and raise you."

"Y-you know I don't got that."

Where Larry was jumpy, Carl stayed calm, and Milton leaned forward.

"I'm sure you've got something we can trade," Carl drawled.

Milton's fingers tingled. He'd seen games come to this before. Sometimes it was a watch or fancy jewelry or even land. But as far as he knew, Larry didn't have any of those things. He earned a decent wage, but like many of the worst gamblers, he lost more than he won. Besides, this had never been that kind of game.

"I don't know that I do," Larry said.

"Well, maybe you do and maybe you don't, but it won't matter anyway if you win, will it, friend?" He gestured at the pile. "Hell, I've been losing more than I been winning, but business has been good lately, so I aim to have a little fun. This is a friendly game, and I'm glad to be here. Besides, I ain't never forced another man to play." He reached out to pull back his money, hesitating. "Still, you raised the bet, didn't you? A man only does that for one of two reasons. Either he has a good hand, a hand he thinks is a winner, or he does it to run a bluff and fool the other players at the table. Now, only you know whether you got good cards or whether you're bluffing." He lifted one meaty shoulder, reaching for the money again. "Guess that's it."

"Wait."

Carl's hand froze over the money. Milton and Frank exchanged a glance.

"I don't know that I've got anything you'd want," said Larry.

"Tell you what," Carl said, drawing back. "Let's see what happens, and if you win, the money is yours. I win, we'll go for a walk, talk about it. I'm a reasonable man. Sound fair?"

Larry blinked. His focus shifted from his cards to the sizeable pile of money. Milton figured it would look good to a postal worker. Hell, it would look good to anyone. "I guess so."

Milton's hands closed over the edge of the table. Frank muttered something he couldn't make out.

Carl sat forward again. "Call."

Larry licked his lips. He laid his cards on the table. Three fours. A good hand. Milton's shoulders relaxed.

It was Carl's turn. He peered over his cards, then laid them down, one by one. Ace. Ace. Five. Five. The hair rose on Milton's neck. Five. Next to him, Frank said something, but Milton didn't hear over the blood rushing in his ears. Full house? How could that be? In one swift movement, Carl raked the pile into a sack and stood, his chair falling backward to the floor.

Larry's head sank lower, and his arms hung limp at his sides. "That can't be right," he said, voice squeaking.

Carl stood over the table. "It's right."

"But—"

"How about that walk?"

Larry held on to the table as he got to his feet. "I need a drink." He poured a whiskey, drank it down in one swallow, poured another. His hand shook, spilling whiskey on the floor. "I don't got nothin'."

"You're a smart man, aren't you? You keep your eyes and ears open?"

Larry gave a slow nod, mouth hanging open.

"Good. Why don't we take that walk?"

They left the back room, threading their way through the tables out front. Without thinking, Milton rose, trailing after them. Carl kept an arm draped over Larry's shoulder and his mouth near the losing man's ear. Milton struggled to hear but caught only meaningless snatches of words. "Train schedule. Postal car."

Suddenly, Larry drew back, hands up in the air. "No, Carl," he said, the words ringing out over the noise of the saloon.

Milton shrank back against the wall.

Carl put his mouth to Larry's ear again, his lips moving. His large hand landed on Larry's back, shoving him outside. Milton followed for another block until the two men disappeared, shadows in the dark. He tucked his hands in his pockets, mind racing. Frank would say Larry had never been a good player and was only getting what he deserved. He wouldn't be wrong. But there was something about Carl, something about the way he hadn't let Larry quit when he wanted to. Then there was that full house, an almost impossible hand to pull in five-card draw. Milton's footsteps slowed, and a hard knot formed in the pit of Milton's stomach. He didn't know how, but in his gut, he was sure. Carl had cheated.

PART 4

FORGIVE AND FORGET

CHAPTER ELEVEN

Summer 1988

"YOU'VE BEEN OUT here long enough." One hand resting on her ample hip, Jean eyed Ginny. "You should have known better." Softening her voice, she inclined her head toward Anna Mae. "You too."

"But it's so lovely out," the old woman said. There was no hint of apology in her voice. "A bit longer?"

"Absolutely not." Jean positioned herself behind the wheelchair. "You need to rest, Anna Mae."

"Please," the old woman said, "I've been resting for years. Being out here with the sun and trees and clouds. It's so much better than being locked up in my room."

Jean drew back, her voice tinged with fresh concern. "You're not locked up, Anna Mae. You know that."

Anna Mae reached around and patted the nurse's hand. "I didn't mean it like that. You take wonderful care of me, the best anybody could ask for." Jean's forehead cleared, though Ginny guessed she was no less concerned. "These last few days . . ." Anna Mae gave a small shake of her head, and her voice quavered. "I feel alive again."

A horn sounded in the parking lot, a series of sharp, angry beeps. The car wasn't visible through the trees, but two voices carried across the cracked pavement.

"I'm coming already! Keep your pants on," a woman yelled.

"Hurry it up, won't ya? It's hotter than a two-dollar whore out here, and I've been sittin' here waitin' on your fat ass for twenty minutes. You think I got nothin' better to do?"

"Oh, yeah? What've you got to do that's so damn important?"

Car doors slammed one after the other—muffling the voices inside—and the women exchanged a glance.

"What do you think was so important?" Ginny asked. The engine coughed and sputtered to life, drowning out any answer one of them might have had. A moment later, they heard the sound of screeching tires.

Anna Mae wore a sly grin. "If a whore's only two dollars, is that good or bad?"

Jean slapped her thigh and howled, the worry from earlier gone, and Anna Mae chuckled along with her. Ginny laughed, too, relieved there was no more talk about feeling alive or otherwise.

After their laughter died down, Jean wheeled Anna Mae back toward the home. "Let's get you inside."

Ginny considered following, but a look from Jean stopped her. Around her, bees buzzed over the weed-choked ground, darting between golden dandelions. The late-afternoon sun sank lower, painting pink and orange stripes over the horizon. The heat from the day ebbed, and the air felt lighter. Ginny pictured Anna Mae back in her room, her quilt over her legs. Ginny wanted to be there too.

She wanted to know what was wrong with David. She wanted to know if John would see Sabina again, if Ben would start a union, and if Milton would figure out what Carl was up to. She stood and sighed, knowing that wanting wasn't enough. Ginny would have to wait.

That evening, Ginny held the phone to her ear with one hand and pressed a cool cloth to her sunburned cheeks with the other.

"Have you heard from the high school?" Shawn asked.

"No, but I can always substitute if I need to." She couldn't hide the irritation in her voice. "Why are you so worried about it?"

"I'm not worried. I feel guilty, that's all. You loved your job and—"

"That's what you feel guilty about?" She cut him off, her fingers curling until her nails bit into her skin.

She heard Shawn suck in his breath. "I didn't sleep with her, Gin."

"But you wanted to," she snapped. Silence crackled over the line. She forced herself to breathe in and out. "I'm hanging up."

"Okay, I wanted to," he said, the words rushing out. "For about one minute. But I couldn't. I wouldn't."

She fell back against the pillow, tears threatening. She remembered how she'd seen them together at the spring dance, part of the group of chaperones. She'd been surprised Shawn had agreed to help at all, but she'd been grateful, until she saw Shawn's dark head bent close to Lila's. Instead of backing away, Lila had closed the gap between them, laying a hand on Shawn's chest. Feeling sick, Ginny had stumbled out into the hall, pushing her way through the curtain of streamers. She told herself she was imagining things. She had to be. Lila and Shawn had to stand close together to be heard over the band, didn't they? She'd almost convinced herself by the time she'd returned to the gym, just in time to see Shawn and Lila exit through the side door, his hand on the small of her back. The tears had welled too fast to stop them.

"Nothing happened," Shawn was saying now. "I swear. We've been over this. I'm sorry that I hurt you. I didn't mean to. I broke it off before it went too far."

Ginny brushed away the tears that never seemed to stop now. *Before it went too far.* He'd said it then and many times since, but she didn't believe him any more now than she had before.

"Ginny? Are you there?"

"I'm here."

"I wish I was there with you."

She considered asking why, but she wasn't sure she wanted to hear the answer. She already knew. The baby. Aloud, she said, "I'm fine."

"You still sound mad." When she didn't answer, he seemed to surrender, changing the subject. "Okay, you're fine. How was the nursing home today?"

"Fine."

"Gin, I know you don't want to hear this, but this stuff she's telling you, it sounds like she's making it up as she goes along. You said yourself she's got no family. No one visits. Now she's got some story that's got you going there every day. I'm worried she'll say anything just to keep you around."

"Why do you even care?" she shot back. "It's none of your business where I go or who I go see."

"Gin, that's not fair."

Whatever satisfaction she got in hurting him was short lived, and she closed her eyes. What if he was right? She thought of Anna Mae's long fingers rubbing the locket and the dream-like look she sometimes wore when she spoke. She could be making it up. Ginny bit her lip. But the trunk, the journal, and the letter, those were real. *I saw you in Centennial Park today.* The letter hadn't been signed but nothing could have convinced Ginny that Anna Mae didn't write it. What she didn't know was why.

"Look, it doesn't matter whether it's true or not. I'm going. I want to hear how it ends."

His sigh echoed across the line. "I can't exactly stop you, can I?"

Her eyes were dry now. "No, Shawn, you can't."

~~~~

"So, Carl wasn't trying to lose anymore?" Ginny asked, her shoulders pitched forward.

"Questions, questions," Anna Mae said with a gentle cluck of her tongue. "But you have an excellent memory. Carl was trying to lose, until he wasn't."
~~~~

Ginny opened her mouth, a dozen more questions on the tip of her tongue, but thought better of it. Anna Mae had indulged her more than once already. She wouldn't push now.

The old woman took a sip of tea from the cup Jean had left. "Are you the religious sort, dear?"

Ginny considered the question. She'd gone to Sunday school as a child. She'd even been married in her childhood church, though in recent years her attendance had been limited to major holidays. "Not really. I was raised Methodist, but I don't go much anymore."

"Well, in 1918, most people were what you might call the church-going kind. I was raised Catholic, as you know. My father was quite devout, and we spent a great deal of time with our parish family. Anyway, back then there were a whole lot of church-going folks who thought alcohol was the work of the devil. Prohibition was taking off then." She gave a short laugh. "But that didn't mean there wasn't plenty of drinking going on. Bootleggers were everywhere. Even the mail was being used to send liquor."

"We teach Prohibition as part of our lessons. It was repealed under Roosevelt."

"Yes, that's true, but before that, there were some who devoted their lives to preaching temperance. And Tennessee was no exception." She settled back in her chair. "Here in Nashville, there was no shortage of believers. There were newspaper articles, signs, and speeches." Anna Mae spoke quietly, her voice like the soft rustle of paper, and Ginny sat back to listen, her body still. "I remember there was a letter in the *Tennessean* on that Sunday after the Fourth."

CHAPTER TWELVE

Sunday, July 7, 1918
Morning

LETTERS

The Whiskey Evil.

According to the laws of Moses, upon which all civilized laws are based, no man was allowed to keep an ox, which was dangerous to the community in which he lived. If a man in Nashville conducts his business in such a way as to make it injurious to the community, should this man be allowed to continue in said business?

Tennessee is a dry state, yet I am told by those who are in position to know, that there is a place in Nashville where whisky and beer are sold over the counter, even on Sundays. I can not vouch for the truth of this statement, but I do know that patients are brought to us at all hours of the night from this place tanked up with whisky and cut to pieces with knives and razors, showing that they have been engaged in drunken brawls.

Having been a nurse on night duty at Vanderbilt Hospital for several weeks, where most of these patients are treated, I can truthfully say that Sol Cohn's old place of business is detrimental to the whole city.

As a patriotic citizen of Nashville, I wish to ask the Governor of the State, Mayor of the City, police force, Woman's Councell of National Defense, Four-Minute Men, pastors of churches and all who are interested in law and order, if there is not a remedy for this great evil. Shall we allow this to continue to make gain through traffic in human blood?

Isabella Alethea Williams

—*The Tennessean,* July 7, 1918

~~~~

Mary poked him in the ribs, her elbow sharp, and David jerked upright, his eyes springing open. It wasn't the first time he'd dozed off during services. Perhaps it was because another sermon had devolved into a speech on temperance, or because the nightmares kept him awake long into the night. Perhaps it was both. He stood now, mouthing an apology to his wife. Looking straight ahead, he felt her gaze upon him still. He'd done his best to hide his aches and pains, but Mary wasn't like other wives. A woman who heard with her mind and her heart understood more than most.

Outside the church, Anna Mae lifted her face to the sun.

"Shall we walk through the park today, Father? It's so lovely out."

He squinted up at the clear blue sky. A single bead of sweat trickled down his back. In the heat, his head pounded, and he wanted nothing more than to go back to their apartment and rest a bit, but he wouldn't. The expectant look on his daughter's face got him moving. "That's a wonderful idea."

The girls walked down the street, side by side, each wearing the newest style of hat. They chatted with each other, giggling occasionally. Mary walked next to him, her chin high, her back ramrod straight.

He remembered when he'd met her. He'd thought her young—too young at first—but he'd found she possessed a wisdom beyond her years. Maybe it was her lack of hearing. Either way, he'd been drawn to her. After
~~~~

he was widowed, there'd been no shortage of women, but David wasn't the fanciful sort. She wasn't paraded in front of him and didn't come with a pedigree, but she possessed a calm demeanor and even temper. She was quieter than other women, aware that her speech was sometimes difficult to understand, but even that only added to her appeal. Mary didn't sweep into a room with a fuss, nor did she fade into the furnishings. No. She caught his attention with her tremulous smile, kept it with her love.

It was hard at first. His young daughter hadn't understood that Mary couldn't hear the words she spoke, that her stepmother needed to see her lips move, and even then, she didn't always get it right. It had taken time, but it had gotten better, or at least that's what he'd told himself. Lately, it seemed he may have been mistaken.

The family came upon the park and the girls walked faster, skipping across the grass. Reaching their favorite tree, Anna Mae and Katie Belle pulled handkerchiefs from their bags and laid them on the ground. They plopped down and arranged their skirts around their legs. Only their shoes peeped out. He wished he could stop time and capture the moment, but he knew better. Time was a fragile thing, handed out to some, taken from others, moving forward in spite of men.

He spread his jacket over the lawn, took his spot next to his wife, and stretched out his long legs.

"Isn't this nice?" Anna Mae asked.

"Oh, it is," Katie Belle said with a happy smile.

A young boy ran past them, laughing over his shoulder. "You can't catch me," he called out. A smaller boy followed, his short legs carrying him as fast as they could. David tried to distract his wife, but it was too late. She stared after the boys long after they'd run out of sight, chin quivering. The girls, unaware, chatted on.

David wondered if it had been such a good idea to come to the park after all. So many memories with the children, with John George.

"Father, do you ever see animals in the sky?" John George had asked one Sunday. He lay sprawled over the ground, legs and arms sticking out.

He raised a hand, pointing at the clouds trailing across the sky. "It's like Noah's Ark right now." David craned his neck to see what John George saw, but to him, they were only clouds. "Two of each kind," John George had said. "Lions and giraffes. Oh, and alligators."

How old had his son been then? Ten? Eleven? David expected he would have outgrown that foolishness by his age. Animals in clouds? Alligators? But John George had never forgotten the alligators in the viaducts at the train station or the hours he'd spent watching them. He'd drawn them on paper, filled his stories with them.

There were no clouds at all on this day—not even a wisp—no animals to see. Tucking his hands under his neck, he wondered if there were animals in the clouds at the front, and if there were, if John George still saw them. He imagined an ark floating overhead, animals climbing on board in pairs. Lions. Giraffes. Alligators. He pictured John George as a boy and answered him now. "I see them, Son, all of them."

~~~~

THE CHURCH

The latest figures for church membership have been given out by the census bureau for the ten-year period ending December 31, 1916: The colored Baptists report 3,018,314 members, with 19,423 ministers; the African Methodists have 552,265 members, with 8,175 ministers; the Zion Methodists have 258,433 members with 3,962 ministers; the colored Methodists have 245,749 members, with 3,402 ministers.

—*The Crisis*, July 1918

~~~~

John walked behind his mother and stepfather, Leah at his side. Although House wore his Sunday best, it was his wife who drew looks of admiration.

In a dress the color of lilacs and a matching hat with a silk ribbon and flowers, Essie House floated over the road like a sweet confection. Normally reserved, his mother didn't care much for calling attention to herself, but Sundays were different. Sundays were about worshipping, and there was no better way to worship than to wear your best finery and show God you were grateful. John had heard it so many times, he could practically recite the words.

"Why, look at me," she'd say. "Widowed with young children—the ones I have left—and God thinks enough of me to give me Abel House, a hardworking man who doesn't mind raising another man's son. Truth be told, it's nothing short of a miracle. Yes, God takes care of those in need."

As they walked, his mother tucked her hand into the crook of House's outstretched elbow. John was six years old when his father had died and younger than that when his brother and sister were lost to typhus. He couldn't recall his daddy's face anymore or the way he'd sounded before he died, but he did remember the way he'd brought him everywhere he went, as though if he didn't, it would be a sad day indeed. House didn't take him anywhere unless it had to do with farming or chores.

The sun rose higher, and John's skin itched under the jacket his mother had insisted he wear. It was another battle he'd lost.

"You will not be showing up at services in your shirtsleeves. No, sir. No son of mine would dare disrespect God that way. Not today. Not ever." John had started to argue that he was going to put the jacket on when they arrived at the church, but he never got the chance.

"Put the jacket on," House had said. "Or it won't be God I'm thinkin' you're disrespecting."

Under his coat, John's shirt was damp with sweat. Next to him, Leah wiped away the perspiration dotting her upper lip. Only his mother could stay cool and comfortable in this heat.

John glanced over at his sister. Small and slight like their mother, Leah had a heart-shaped face, the same high cheekbones, and lips as pink as a newborn piglet. Her trim figure was wrapped in a lemon-yellow dress, and she wore a navy hat with a yellow ribbon to match. At seventeen, she'd been courted, but House was a tough man to get by. More than once, she'd complained about her stepfather's attitude toward her suitors.

"It won't be long before no one's coming 'round," she'd said one night, her tone bitter. "He doesn't have to be so mean."

"He thinks you can do better," their mother said, defending her husband.

Leah snorted. "Like you did."

In a flash, Essie's hand found Leah's cheek, the crack like a shot. Leah gasped, her fingers flying to her reddening skin. Their mother stumbled backward, her hands on her own mouth. House was no stranger to the switch, but Essie had never hit them.

No one spoke for several minutes.

"This is a family," their mother said after she'd caught her breath. "Abel wants what's best for us, for all of us." If the words sounded forced to John, they sounded like something else to Leah.

"He'll never let me get married," she said after her mother had left the room. "So long as I'm working and living here, he collects all the wages." She ran from the house, tears already flowing.

Since that day, there'd been other young men, some John knew from his school days or from the farms, but none came more than once or twice. Money had been tight this year, and he'd begun to think Leah might be right.

Twenty minutes after they'd left the house, Zion Hill Baptist Church appeared in the distance. His mother lifted her chin and walked faster. John and Leah hurried to keep up.

Zion Hill was the largest of the Baptist churches in town. Although Oak Hill was closer, Zion Hill was bigger and had Reverend Hawkins, a man Essie swore had the ear of God. John often thought that if he had the ear of God, Reverend Hawkins should seem a lot happier, but he didn't dare say so. "Never question the hand of God," his mother had said. "Perhaps Reverend Hawkins is only sharing what God wants him to share."

They took their usual place in the church, on the left side, four rows from the front. Over the years, they'd moved forward pew by pew—usually after another family left town or died out. John guessed his mother would surely pack for anyone in the first three rows if it meant she could be in the front and closer to Reverend Hawkins.

John didn't really mind going to church. The hymns and music filled him with something like happiness, a safe and content feeling. He only wished there was more singing and less Reverend Hawkins. Going to Sunday services also meant seeing Sabina. Craning his neck, he saw her next to Aunt Ruth and Uncle Elijah, the baby in her lap. Leah kicked him in the ankle, and he dragged his attention back to the altar.

After the songs, Reverend Hawkins glided to the center of the altar. John's mind drifted back to Sabina. Did she miss Robert? What did she mean, he wouldn't be coming back? A shift in the air shook him out of his reverie.

"Are we patriots?" Reverend Hawkins's voice rang out, startling the oldest members of the congregation. "That is the question posed by men who presume to know what is in our hearts. I am here to tell you. We are servants of God first. The work we do is God's work and the money we earn is God's money. After our allegiance to God—and only after—do we pledge our allegiance to our families and our country." He paused, lowering his voice. "Do not be deceived by those who would lead you astray. Yes, we are Americans. But before that, we are Christians."

John drew up his shoulders, struggling not to leap out of his seat. Robert was a soldier, had gone willingly. What was Reverend Hawkins saying?

"Does that mean a man should not serve his country? That by doing so, he has betrayed his God?" The words hung in the air and the church seemed to hold its collective breath. "A man who loves his God, who worships his God above all else, may choose to join the war effort. If we serve God through serving our country, then so be it. But the spillage of blood, our blood, should be in the name of God first and then America. Patriotism cannot be separated in God's eyes."

There were a few *amens* behind him, but John had also seen a few raised brows, and even mouths twisted in anger.

"President Wilson is our country's leader, but he is not our leader in everything. We—as men of God—cannot enter into war without God's blessing." Reverend Hawkins lifted his face to the wooden beams that held up the roof of the church. His lips moved, but there was only silence in the sanctuary. Around John, no one moved. No one spoke. The minutes passed and the preacher lowered his chin to his chest, blinking slowly. "I've had a vision."

A chorus of gasps sounded. John's mother raised a hand to her mouth. Leah sat forward. Even House's mouth hung open, waiting.

"Our heavenly Father is with President Wilson. It is with God's blessing that we must support President Wilson, support the war effort." Reverend Hawkins opened his palms. "As a man of peace, a man who deplores war and bloodshed, these are not easy times for me. I will not pretend that I understand the ways of God, and it saddens me to see families separated, children lost." He stretched out his arm and pointed at Sabina. Every head turned. As he spoke, his voice grew louder. "Why, right here in our midst, a young mother must wait for her husband, must pray each and every night that he will come home to her and their young baby. The young man's father and mother must take care of their son's wife and her baby. They wait and wait some more, hopeful that he will return, and if he does, that he will not be maimed or injured."

A woman in the front of the church wept. Leah took John's hand and squeezed.

At the altar, Reverend Hawkins stepped back from the congregation. "War is like an empty promise and yet . . ." He raised his arms up high. "We, as Christians, must support this war, must support President Wilson. I am but a servant of God and will not question the word of the Lord."

The energy drained from him then, and he fell into a chair. His lips moved again in prayer.

A minute passed. Five minutes.

The preacher stood at last, and the congregation followed, breaking into song. Essie sang, too, but her voice was soft, without the fire and passion he'd come to expect. A single tear trailed over her cheek.

~~~~

CASUALTIES IN U.S. FORCES NUMBER 11,086

To Date They Comprise 4,414 Deaths, 6,169 Wounded and 503 Missing.

Washington, July 7.—Casualties in the army and marine corps in the American expeditionary forces increased by 703 during the week compared with 407 the previous week, and aggregate 11,086 with the inclusion of today's army list giving 117 names and the marine corps list giving fifty-three names.

—*The Tennessean*, July 8, 1918

~~~~

Leah closed the space between them, searching his face. "Something's different with you today."

John rearranged his features into what he hoped was a blank expression. "Nothing's different."

It felt wrong to lie to her. They'd shared everything after their father had died, and again, after their mother married House. But since finding Sabina on the knoll, there had been a new spring in his step. He'd found himself smiling for no reason at all. Even House had told him to stop acting like a schoolboy.

"What's wrong with you?" he'd asked after John had dropped his cup a second time. "You got mush for brains, boy?"

After church, it was more of the same.

His mother shooed House away. "He's young," she said. "It's normal to be a little distracted." House snorted but let it go. His mother leaned over and hugged him. "Don't listen to him, my son. A little daydreaming is good for the soul, or God wouldn't put those thoughts in our heads."

John wasn't so sure God—or his mother—would approve of the thoughts in his head.

Leah wasn't so easily fooled. She pressed her hand into his arm. "What is it?" she asked.

"Nothing."

"You're a terrible liar, John Lang." She blew out a puff of air. "Don't think you can hide from me, Big Brother. You know I'll find out." She spun around on her heel and stomped away.

House came up beside him. "I heard Matt Toles is running off to Chicago."

John stiffened. He knew better than to mention seeing Matt in the cornfields. "I suppose he isn't happy here."

"Happy? Is that what we're calling it now?" House scoffed. "I call it damn laziness. Running off is just another way to shirk his duties here, his responsibility to his family. How do you think it looks for his daddy when his own son can't help out on the farm? Can't stay long enough to harvest a crop?"

John's shoulders settled lower and he dipped his head.

"I'll tell you how it looks. Like he's a good-for-nothin' son, that's what."

Matt's defection—or at least that's the way House described it—appeared to be the talk among the men after services. "Reverend Hawkins said he'd pray for the boy, but he's a lost cause in my book."

John didn't like the look in House's eye and kept his mouth closed, but his stepfather moved closer until there were only inches between them, and he dared not look away.

"No boy of mine is running off, shirking his duty, leaving his mother." He put his nose close to John's. "Are we clear about that?"

"Yes, sir."

"Good." The air seemed to go out of him then. "Be off now. Uncle Elijah wants to see you at the farm."

John's muscles loosened. He left for the farm, the resentment he usually felt evaporating with each stride. Nearing the property, his steps quickened. At the tree line, he crossed the road, walking away from the farm, toward the knoll on the other side of the creek. John hopped across the stream, his foot slipping on a rock into the shallow water. He didn't care. He would have waded through higher water if he had to. He hopped onto dry land, and there she was. For a moment, his breath left his body. She sat slumped with her back against the tree.

Her head had fallen forward, her hands folded in her lap. He tiptoed closer, squatting down. The sun shone through the leaves, creating a speckled pattern of light and dark on her face. A wisp of air raised the curled tendrils of hair that had escaped from her braid. Her chest rose and fell with each long, slow breath.

He forgot about House, Matt, and Leah. The only person in the world was right in front of him.

AFTERNOON

COBB CLIMBS TO SECOND PLACE IN BATTING LIST

George Sisler Leading American Swatters, With Baker Third

The "Jawjaw" Jewel is back again. Once more Ty Cobb is perched amidst the American League performers who are holding the upper berths in the race for battling supremacy.

Though Cobb is not leading the league, he is only four points behind Sisler, who tops the list with an average of .346. Ty is second with .342, a considerable improvement over his total of a few weeks ago, while Baker follows him with .339.

—*The Tennessean*, July 7, 1918

~~~~

David watched the boy with the skinny arms. The kid held the stick in his hands, one on top of the other. He swiveled his hips and settled into his stance. David liked watching the kid play. Slight and gangly, he was an unlikely ball player, but he could hit anything. The faster the ball, the better. The pitcher threw the ball, and it bounced across the plate. Ball one. The second pitch sailed past the skinny boy. One and one. The kid wiggled his hips again. The pitcher drew his arm back and slung it. The ball flew hard and fast. In one fluid motion, the boy swung the stick and stepped forward with his left leg. The ball hit the stick with a smack. All eyes followed the ball as it flew through the air and over the outstretched hands of the player in the outfield. The boy rounded the bases to the hoots and hollers of his teammates.

"Mr. Kennedy?" David looked around. It was Theodore, one of the older boys in the neighborhood. "Mr. Kennedy? Do you want to play?"

"C'mon, Mr. Kennedy." A couple of the other boys chimed in. "Sammy has to go home, but the game's not over yet. Can you play?"

After a quick glance up at the sun, David shed his suitcoat and rolled up his sleeves. "Only for a few minutes, boys. Getting close to suppertime."

A red-haired boy rubbed his belly. "Don't I know it," he said with a laugh.

David picked up the spare glove and trotted to the outfield. Baseball hadn't fully caught on in the South, not the way it had in the big cities up north, but that didn't change his love for the game. When the Giants had won the World Series the year before, he'd cheered along with the New Yorkers. The war had shortened the 1918 season, however, and in the last month, dozens of players had been drafted into the armed services. Still, there was plenty of baseball to go around, and the young player Babe Ruth was making the most of his opportunity to shine.

The pitcher called out to the other boys on the field. "One out," he said. "Two to go."
~~~~

At the plate, the ball whizzed past the batter. Strike one. The second pitch sailed high and the third was outside. David bent forward at his waist and punched his fist into the well-worn glove. The batter at the plate connected on the fourth pitch. Bouncing hard, the ball sailed past the shortstop and skittered toward David. He rushed forward, scooped up the ball, and threw it to second base, holding the runner at first. His heart beat faster, and he trotted back to his position in left field. The inning closed out with a fly ball and a ground out. Game over, David returned the glove, wiping his hands on his pants.

"Gee, thanks for playing, Mr. Kennedy," Theodore said. "That was a nice play you made back there."

"Thank you, Theodore." He'd stopped several times before to watch the boys and occasionally joined them in play. Theodore and the skinny kid were the two best players he'd seen in the bunch. "Do you ever think about playing on a real team?"

"Do I? That would be the best." His face fell. "But my father says I have to finish primary school first." He shuffled his feet, banging his fist into his mitt. "He doesn't like baseball like you do."

"Ah," the older man said with a slow nod. A boy who didn't like school—like John George. Theodore didn't look anything like David's son though. This boy had a shock of blond hair and skin as pale as the moon to John George's brown locks and ruddy complexion.

"Do you think you could talk to my father?" Theodore asked now. "He doesn't like when I play, but he doesn't understand like you do. He thinks playing baseball is being lazy. He wants me to come to work with him after I finish school."

"He wants you to be a mechanic, eh?" Theodore's father worked on the railroad. He'd been a mechanic for close to two decades now.

"Yes, sir, but I don't want to. If I can't play baseball, I don't want to work on the trains like Father. I want to drive them—like you."

"An engineer, then?"

"Yes, sir."

David rolled down his sleeves. "How many years of school do you have left?"

"One."

David considered. It wasn't his place to usurp another father's wishes. "Well, why don't you finish that last year of school and then see?"

The boy's eager smile slipped. "Sure. Thanks anyway." Theodore slung his stick and bag over his shoulder. "See you, Mr. Kennedy."

David stood on the side of the road watching as the boy crossed to the other side. "Theodore."

The boy spun around, bag bobbing on his back. "Yes, Mr. Kennedy?"

"Finish school, then come down to the station and we'll talk."

"Yes, sir."

"And don't ever quit playing baseball."

"I won't, sir." Theodore grinned and waved, half running, half skipping down the street to his apartment.

Alone, David watched as the last of the boys left the makeshift field. He took off his glasses and rubbed his eyes. "Don't ever quit," he whispered, the words soft as a breeze, floating across an empty street. Sighing, he walked in the direction of home, his heart an ocean away.

~~~~

LETTERS FROM OUR BOYS

Since arriving on this side I haven't stayed, so far, in one place longer than two weeks; have been nearly all over France and part of England.

—*The Tennessean*, July 7, 1918

~~~~

Sabina woke with a start, her body jerking to one side. Seeing him, she calmed. "How long have I been asleep?"

"Not long."

Dark shadows hung under her thick lashes. "The baby was up."

John wasn't sure what that meant, and she didn't explain. Instead, she reached into the folds of her dress and pulled out a handful of pages. "Robert's letters. It's easier for you to understand if you read them." She paused, holding them out to John. "They're from France."

He didn't move. These were letters between a husband and wife. They weren't his business.

"Please," she said, pushing them into his hand.

Nodding, he looked down at the first page. Robert's handwriting, small and precise, filled the paper. He began to read.

Dearest Sabina,

We're in France now. The lines are close and I expect we will be attacking any day now. Last night, I had to sleep in the trenches. There was water at the bottom so I mostly slept standing up. I don't think any of us got much sleep, but at least I was better off than the guys that tried to sit down. All they got was wet shoes and pants! Most men don't have extras, so I doubt they'll be doing that again.

John laid the letter down. "It sounds awful over there."

"Keep reading."

He picked up the next letter, similar to the first. "Do his parents get letters like these?"

"Yes. Not as bad, but almost."

Uncle Elijah had been edgier than usual and Aunt Ruth withdrawn. He thought maybe he understood better now. John read on.

Gerry, the one I told you about from South Carolina. He got shot yesterday by a Kraut. The bullets were flying, and we made a run for the trenches. Gerry tripped or something. I didn't see, but he didn't make it back.

John paused. The neat writing had grown spidery.

We forced them back, but it took a long time. We tried to force our way through the front, but we couldn't. The enemy kept coming. Eventually, we held, pushing them back, but by then it was close to dark. While we were still fighting, some of the guys crept out and pulled Gerry in. I couldn't really see what was going on, just that he was alive. There was so much shooting that I couldn't get to him. We'd already been fighting for almost three days. After it finally ended, I went over to check on him, but he wouldn't speak to me. He moaned and cried, pushed me away. Said he wanted to die. Daniel, the guy who does the doctoring, shook his head. When I asked him what was wrong, he said it was Gerry's legs. Said they were ruined. No more walking or anything. Do you remember me telling you about Gerry? Fastest guy I've ever seen. All you had to do was ask and he'd show you. Now, he won't be showing anything. When I woke up today, Gerry was gone. They must have taken him away, but no one knows for sure. That's three guys in the last two weeks and the Krauts keep coming. They say we're winning though. I keep thinking about Gerry and his legs. No wonder he wanted to die. Sometimes I think I should go ahead and get it over with.

John dropped the letter in his lap, thoughts and memories of Robert filling his mind. John had admired his cousin from the time he was old enough to walk. Robert had taught him how to fish, how to throw a ball, how to do the things John's daddy would have if he'd lived. It wasn't that House hadn't made a show of trying once or twice, but his heart had never been in it. It was a duty, a way to make Essie happy, but a boy knows.

After John went to work at the farm, he'd been glad to see more of his older cousin, but Robert was different by then, moods careening from strangely frantic to sullen. Then he'd married Sabina.

She sat next to him now, near enough that he breathed in the musky scent of her skin. "He's not coming back," she said.

"How do you know?"

She pulled a folded page from the pocket of her dress. Dated the first of June, the final letter was short, the words written unevenly.

My Dearest Sabina,

I hope this letter finds you and our son well. I've had little sleep, the fighting going on for too many days. We take turns resting, but it's hard to sleep in the trenches. Most of us have lost weight, lost track of time. It feels sometimes like I've been in this same trench for months, other times like years. It's a good thing I'm strong, can still handle a gun when I need to. There are fewer of us now although more men come every day. They don't know what it's like yet, but they will.

I'm sorry I haven't been a good husband. I would like to tell you that I will be, but I don't want to say things that aren't true. I want you to take care of our son. I know you will be a good mother to him. When you tell him about me, remember the good things.

With love,
Robert

Sabina took the letters back. "There's something else." She bent forward, hugged her knees to her chest, and closed her eyes. His heart fluttered like a jackrabbit. "The marriage," she said in a whisper. "It was a mistake."

CHAPTER THIRTEEN

Summer 1988

GINNY SLID FORWARD to the edge of her seat, her hand resting on her belly. "Did she tell John she should have married him instead? What did he say?"

"Young love. It's quite complicated sometimes, isn't it?" Anna Mae reached for her tea, the tremor in her hand quieter than usual. She sipped, frowned, and set it aside. "I'm afraid I've let my tea grow cold."

"Would you like me to get you another cup?"

"Oh, no. You're very kind though." She patted Ginny's hand. "I'm a bit tired. I may have overdone it yesterday." She sighed. "But it was so lovely to be outdoors, wasn't it? This room is so tiresome."

Ginny looked around at the empty, drab walls made dingier under the florescent tube lights. Instead of curtains, blinds hung on the windows, the cheap plastic kind that rattled when raised or lowered. The plain chair and bed might best be described as institutional.

As for décor, that was limited to the digital clock and transistor radio that sat atop the scarred surface of the nightstand. If the room radiated any warmth, it came from Anna Mae herself. The only personal belongings seemed to be the quilt and the locket the old woman wore around her neck. It occurred to Ginny that there were more personal items in that trunk than in this entire room. She thought about her grandmother's house, filled with framed photos and mementos.

"It's not much," Anna Mae said. "I can imagine how this room looks to someone so young, so full of life." Anna Mae's hands caressed the folds of her quilt. Her gaze swept past Ginny to the walls. "I had things once, but when you've been alive this long, you start giving them away until there's not much left." When she looked back at Ginny, her faded eyes shimmered. "You might think that's hard, but sometimes we have to let go of the things we love most. In the end, no trinket or painting is as valuable as what's inside your heart." She angled her head as she spoke. "Someday, you'll understand."

Ginny almost brought up the trunk and the things she'd found, but Anna Mae switched on the radio then. Her fingers spun the dial past static and music until a man's voice filled the air.

"Mattingly has certainly earned his paycheck this year, folks. Another single. And now here comes Randolph to the plate."

Anna Mae held the radio in her lap. "My father would have liked Don Mattingly, I think," she said as though they'd been discussing that very thing. "Do you follow baseball?"

"Not really."

"I like to listen now and again." She leaned back against the chair, her eyelids fluttering closed.

Ginny remembered Anna Mae talking about her father and his love of baseball. "The Yankees?"

"Well, New York anyway. He followed the Giants," the old woman said sleepily, words fading. "I'm the Yankees fan."

Silently, Ginny picked up her purse and slipped out the door, the animated voice of the radio announcer ringing in her ear.

"And around the bases he goes. How about that, folks? How about that?"

Ginny's curiosity as a child had driven her to ask more questions than most. At one time, she'd considered journalism as a career until she'd realized current events weren't as interesting to her as those from the past. That same curiosity landed her on the floor in front of the trunk once again. She loved Anna Mae's story, but she wanted to know more. She wanted to know everything.

On this night, she rifled through the sheet music and the box of photographs. She pulled out a pair of silk purses, turning them inside out. Nothing more than a bit of lint. Opening a jewel box, she lifted out a tiny golden cross on a delicate chain. Ginny held it up, admiring the way it caught and held the light. The child-sized necklace didn't appear particularly valuable, but presumably, it had once meant something to Anna Mae. Had Katie Belle had a similar necklace? Had they worn their crosses until they'd grown too big?

Ginny's mind wandered to her own childhood. She didn't have any sisters or brothers, something she and her father had bonded over. They had overbearing mothers in common too. How many times had her father told her about Grandma Betty's hovering and fussing? Ginny had always assumed that was the reason he left Nashville, so she was surprised to learn it was Grandma Betty's idea.

"It's time to spread your wings, Michael. Go to a big city. Go far away," she'd said, according to her father. Of course, he'd been eager to make his mark on the world, but he'd hesitated, concerned his mother was putting on a brave front. He needn't have worried. "Your father and I will visit so often, you'll wonder if we've moved in. Take that job, Michael. It will be good for you."

He never went home again. Even when Ginny visited her grandparents in Nashville and then just Grandma Betty, she traveled alone. She didn't think it odd at the time, but she wondered now.

With a sigh, she let the lid of the trunk fall closed. She was no closer to unraveling the mystery of the letter or predicting how Anna Mae and Milton's story would end, but the next morning, as she settled in to hear another chapter in the story of the five men, Ginny shivered in anticipation. What would happen next?

CHAPTER FOURTEEN

Sunday, July 7, 1918
Afternoon

LETTERS FROM OUR BOYS

One of his last actions was to drag a wounded private, under heavy fire, back to a place of safety.

—*The Tennessean,* July 7, 1918

~~~~

Sabina tucked her feet under her legs and whispered the words, "The marriage was a mistake."

John's heart lurched. These were the words he'd longed to hear, and yet, it didn't feel the way he'd thought it would.

"When we first married, he made me laugh, and he listened to me as though I had something to say. My father liked him and invited him to supper. You know how he has that big smile and laugh. He was so easy to be around then." She paused, facing him. "But there was another side to Robert, one I didn't see until later. There's sadness and anger and something dark in his soul that's eating him up inside. It's funny though. Even after
~~~~

everything, even after I saw the worst, it was hard to be mad at him. He would be Robert again, and he was my husband. I sometimes thought if I could just make him happier, things would be better."

The lump in John's throat bulged. His voice croaked when he spoke again. "Your little boy looks like him."

"He does, doesn't he?" She blinked, tears threatening again. "I'm glad of that. Whatever happens, a piece of Robert will always be here."

Stunned, John said nothing. He wanted her to be wrong, but he didn't know Robert anymore. He'd heard his cousin was difficult: sweet one minute, explosive the next. But he'd never thought about what it must have been like for Sabina, not really.

"I'm sorry."

"Don't be. I chose to marry Robert. I did that on my own." She got to her feet, wiping away the dust and twigs. He stood, too. "I knew I didn't love him, but I cared about him—enough that I thought I might love him in time." His mouth fell open, and he started to speak, but she cut him off. "Let me talk." She paced the grassy knoll as she spoke, her voice flat. "When he started coming around, I was flattered. Everyone loved Robert. You remember?"

John knew that to be true. More than one girl in town had been brokenhearted when Robert chose Sabina.

John stood and took her by the shoulders. "Whatever Robert did or how he acted, that wasn't your fault. It isn't your fault."

She shook her head, her mouth set in a grim line. "I shouldn't have married him."

With all his being, he wished she hadn't, but it was done, and there was a son now. "You can't change the past, Sabina."

"No." She stepped closer, voice quieter. "Did you ever wonder why I married Robert? Why I would do that when it was you and I who had grown up together?"

The swollen lump in his throat hardened. "Yes," he said, the word no more than a squeak.

She laid a hand on his arm, her fingers resting on the folds of his shirt. “I was tired of waiting.”

A rush of blood pounded in his ears. “Waiting for what?”

Her lower lip trembled. “For you.” She slumped as soon as the words were out, as if simply the act of saying them was all she could do, her energy spent.

He wanted to wrap her in his arms, but an image of his cousin filled his mind. He didn’t move. “I didn’t know.”

Her hand fell away, and she lifted her chin. If he’d expected to see anger or disappointment, he realized in an instant how wrong he was. There was only sadness and resignation.

“My life is different now. I have a child. I’m married.” Her voice caught. “It’s hard in that house now.”

“What will you do?”

One shoulder lifted and dropped. “My mother isn’t well, you know.”

He inhaled sharply. “What’s wrong?”

“She’s coughing. Burning up all the time. I can’t take the baby around her.” Sabina sighed. “Daddy and Earl are doing their best to take care of her, but I don’t know. Things don’t seem better.”

“What about the doctor?”

“He came once, but you know how my mother is. Stubborn.” She half smiled, but there was no joy in it.

John wrapped his arms around her then. She fell into him, the top of her head finding the soft spot just below his shoulder the way it used to. He stood frozen, afraid to move. When she pulled away, his arms and chest felt cold and empty.

“I need to go.” Sabina reached out, her fingers trailing over his cheek. “But thank you for being here. For listening.”

He caught her wrist in his hand. “Wait. What if I had asked?” His blood pulsed under his skin. “Before Robert? What would you have said?”

Sabina blinked back tears.

“Don’t you know?”

~~~~

George knew Engineer John Nolan to run a tight crew, and this day had been no different. They'd left the station on time, hitting every stop exactly as the schedule promised. It helped that the Number One had arrived early for a change, and no one had been forced to watch for the overnight train or wait at Shops for the single track to clear. Those days were always better than the ones where the train sat idling and waiting. Not that it was always the engineer's fault. They all did their jobs in the best way they could under the tighter timetables.

George didn't ride with Engineer Nolan as often as he rode with Engineer Kennedy, and that was fine with him. Nolan wasn't a bad man. He had an even enough temperament. He wasn't unfriendly, but he wasn't friendly either. Although George had worked Nolan's trains more than two dozen times over the last year, he doubted Nolan knew him. The engineer wasn't one to notice anyone or anything that wasn't directly his concern. To him, the porters were the conductor's responsibility, and that was the end of it.

As the train drew closer to Union Station, George took inventory of the passengers. He made his final round, starting at the back of the train. The children had lost their initial sparkle of awe and wonder. Most struggled to stay put, bouncing their little legs against the seats. Their mothers warned them to sit still, shooting stern looks as they found their hats and smoothed their dresses. George took in the sticky handprints and the crumbs on the floor and seats. The coach would need a good cleaning.

As they approached Nashville, the ladies had their own demands. "George, can you get my hatbox?" "George, can you take this for me?" "George, can you mind little Harrison while I freshen?" Young Ben's words came back to him. *I see the way you're always jumping to get things or carry things . . . at some white lady's beck and call.* It wasn't that simple, and he forced his rising resentment down. No amount of feeling sorry for himself would get the job done.
~~~~

The train slowed, and George went to work. After the last passenger had gone, he patted his pocket, satisfied it had been a better day than some. Being on time helped with the tips.

Engineer Nolan took off toward the dispatcher's office, leaving the conductor, Albert Bruner, to wait for George to finish his work. Farther down the track, the mechanics and machinists gathered to begin their check of the train. George climbed back on board. Again, he started at the rear of the train, gathering blankets and cups. He collected the trash and wiped down the seats, swept the floor of dirt and debris. As he worked his way to the front, his mind wandered to Sunday dinner. With the war, meat was harder to come by, but he knew his wife would have something wonderful. Maybe meatless stew with fresh cornbread. Even with the rations, she could cook a grand meal in his book. His mouth watered and his stomach rumbled.

After cleaning the passenger coaches, he entered the Jim Crow car. Unlike the other cars, this one smelled of stale, burnt tobacco. He hated to close the windows, but the Number Four would not run again that night, and it was a porter's job to close up the cars. Lowering the glass, he saw a man standing in the shadows, his arms crossed. George peered through the smoky window. The man was alone, chin low to his chest. A low moan sounded, and as George watched, the man's shoulders shook. George drew back, his own chest heaving a little. The man was in pain, but he was a white man. It was not a porter's business. He went back to closing the windows. Job completed, he climbed down and found the conductor.

"Ah, there you are, George." Conductor Bruner pulled his pocket watch from his vest. "Are the cars clean?"

"Yes, sir."

"The water closets?"

"Yes, sir."

Bruner eyed the train another long minute. The porter waited. Shorty often followed George around the train, ordering him to wipe something again or straighten an already neat stack of blankets. Bruner rarely did, but occasionally, he gave it a second walk-through. George knew better than to take this personally. On this night, Bruner's mood was almost jovial. "Very well, then," he said. "I believe we can call it a day." He put on his hat and strolled toward the wide stairs, whistling as he walked. George hung back, knowing the conductor did not expect—or want—a porter's company.

After the conductor disappeared up the steps, George took off his hat, shrugged out of his porter's jacket, and folded it over his arm. A crash sounded nearby, followed by a sharp cry. He spun around. It was the weeping man. He stumbled from the shadows, staggering past George, his words unintelligible. George drew back, the sour odor of liquor trailing after the man. He watched as the man climbed the steps, nearly falling more than once. Only after he'd gone did George remember. He'd seen the man before, knew him from the train. He wasn't a railroader exactly, but he was there most days, in the postal car, sorting the mail. He frowned. There was no mail on Sundays and no reason for him to be at the station or hiding in a corner of the platform. George ran his hand over the length of his face.

"That is one troubled man," he said aloud. "Very troubled."

~~~~

"Father, does it ever bother you that some people don't accept people who are different?" Anna Mae asked.

David laid down his newspaper. His daughter had posed questions like this before, and each time, he did his best to give them attention. "How do you mean?"

She set aside her knitting, her hands clasped in her lap. "Like when people have different religions, for example. I mean, we're Catholic, but not everyone is."

"That's true, but we're not all that different. We are all Christians. I believe we're an accepting lot."

"Yes, but not everyone is Christian. What about them?" Anna Mae said. Katie Belle scooted closer to her sister and held her hand.
~~~~

"Well, I suppose non-Christians are referred to as heretics, though I can't say I know anyone who admits to being one."

Her mouth fell open for a brief second. "B-But what about Jews? Are they . . ." The word seemed to stick in her throat. "Heretics?"

David's head began to ache. These questions had taken a turn he hadn't anticipated. "Where is this coming from, Anna Mae?"

She glanced at her sister before saying, "Well, there are so many different people here in Nashville now. I'm trying to understand the world a little better."

David thought about that a moment. It was true that Nashville had grown. Even the papers reported on the growing population. But David had little knowledge of those lives.

He'd worshipped in the same parish for as long as he could remember, and his friends—like him—were all members of the Knights of Columbus. He rarely socialized outside of his circle. He picked up his pipe and wrapped his fingers around the stem, eyeing his daughter. "So, you're curious about Jews?"

Face pale, she nodded. "A little."

Mary looked up from her sewing, sensing a new tension in the air. David offered a smile and a wave of his hand. "Your daughter is very inquisitive tonight. Maybe it's because she's a teacher now," he said, hoping to erase the creases of concern he saw on his wife's face.

Looking back at Anna Mae, he tapped his pipe against his palm, considering his words. "Well, they are mostly a devout lot, I think," he said slowly. "They have their own houses of worship, their own Sabbath." He stopped then, not sure what else he could add.

"Are Catholics and Jews friends?"

"Friends? I suppose so. There are both Jews and Catholics in government and in business, same as there are Baptists and Methodists."

Anna Mae frowned. "Doesn't sound like close friends. More like it's convenient for everyone to get along." Before he could respond, she asked him another question. "Father, do you have any Jewish friends?"

The lines of his brow deepened, and again, he wondered about her questions. And then he remembered: the Women's Center. She would have met women from other neighborhoods, women she'd never known before. She might hear stories of hardship and difficulty. Of course, Anna Mae would worry if someone were to be mistreated or dismissed. He swelled with pride at the realization.

"Anna Mae, if you've made a new friend that is Jewish, I would expect you to be as kind to them as you would be to anyone."

"I would, Father, but you didn't really answer the question. Does this mean you do have Jewish friends?"

David cast a wary glance at his wife. "Anna Mae, what is this about?"

The tone of his voice was harsher than he'd meant it to be, and she lowered her head. It was Katie Belle who spoke up then.

"We do have a new friend, Father, and she's met a man, a Jewish man."

He tapped his pipe against his palm. "A friend from the Women's Center?"

"Yes, and she's very fond of this man."

"Ah," he said, relaxing a bit. "Am I to assume that the young lady is not Jewish?"

"Baptist," Katie Belle said.

"I see. Well, that is difficult, isn't it?"

"Why is it difficult?" Anna Mae again.

He added more tobacco to his pipe, tucking it in with his fingertips. "Well, I cannot presume to speak for the young lady's family or the young man's for that matter, but I'm sure it would be considered highly improper by most folks."

Anna Mae inhaled sharply. Katie Belle, though, lifted her chin. "And what about you, Father? Do you also find it improper?"

He crossed his legs and lit his pipe again. Drawing on it, he watched the smoke curl up, drift across the room. "It is not my place to judge," he said, finally. "Of course, I know you want the best for your friend, but I think it's best we leave such matters to others, don't you?" He looked to his wife and nodded, a sign the subject was closed. "How about some music now, Anna Mae?"

His daughter played, but the tunes were more mournful than usual. Listening and smoking, David chalked it up to the female disposition, but catching his wife's curious glance, he wasn't as sure as he'd been a few minutes earlier. He wished, not for the first time, that his girls had suitors, men who wished to take care of them, wished to start families and give them purpose. The ache in his head spiked, and he sat back, his eyes closed. He blamed the exhaustion of the days and nights before. Forcing slow and steady breaths, he let the melancholy music wash over him, calm the ache. One tune ended and another began, and he breathed easier. After a time, his muscles went slack and his head drooped, and blessed sleep carried him away.

~~~~

John shut the barn doors. Weary, he leaned against the rough wood. The horses had been tended and the chickens fed. He smelled of sweat and straw and dirt. It was the odor of hard work, the same as he'd been doing for as long as he could remember. Every day after school, he'd come to the farm to help with the chores. When he'd gotten older, he'd worked in the fields, helped with the harvest when school was out. Just shy of his fifteenth birthday, House had spoken to Essie about John quitting school.

"The boy can read and write. It's enough—more than most. Elijah needs him at the farm."

His mother hadn't given in easily. "He's got Robert. One more year of school will do John good."

It was true that Robert had been a big help to Elijah. But the farm's owner, Mr. Hadley, had informed Elijah that there were extra acres to work, more crops to grow. It was easier with Robert there, but Elijah wasn't a young man anymore. Robert couldn't handle the work alone. House sent John as often as he could, as often as Essie allowed.
~~~~

"Elijah asked for him, Essie. There'll be a share of the money from the crop. There'll be chickens and food too."

She chewed her lower lip. John could see her calculating what it would mean to the family, and he'd been expecting it. He was already one of the oldest boys in the school; most left before their twelfth birthday—if they stayed that long. But Essie wasn't only his mother, she was his teacher, and she liked having her children with her at the school.

"But I'm not done teaching him."

"You taught him what he needs. He can read the tickets at the shops and count bushels and barrels. He'll make a fine farmer. It's time for him to work now."

He lay in bed listening to them talk about him, decide for him. In the end, she relented, as he knew she would. Across the room, Leah rolled over and whispered, "I wish you didn't have to go to the farm. I wish you could stay."

"It's okay," John said, speaking the truth. "I like farming." He wasn't as big or as strong as Robert, but he liked planting and bringing things to life. Matt had never understood that.

In the distance, he heard the rumble of an automobile, and the memory faded. Spinning around, he saw a shiny black roadster coming from the direction of town, dirt flying up behind the wheels. He raised his hand to his brow, squinting as the automobile turned toward the farm. Mr. Hadley had a house on the other side, but the car didn't take that road, coming to a stop near the barn instead. The door opened, and a tall man in an army uniform climbed out. He left the automobile running and walked over to John.

"Do you know where I can find Elijah Johnson?"

John stood straighter and wiped the dirt from his shirt. He hadn't seen many soldiers in Hernando. The men who'd signed up from town left for training, like Robert, and then shipped out to the front. With the war ongoing, none had returned. This man wore a uniform made of a drab green material and a wide brown leather belt. There was a gun hanging from the belt and a multicolored bar pinned to his chest.

The young man pointed in the direction of a small house. "Uncle Elijah lives down there on that side road."

"Thank you," the soldier said and motored off, dust trailing behind him. John half walked, half ran after the soldier, then hung back out of sight. The soldier stopped at the house and after getting out of the car, seemed to waver, pacing the dirt path. The door to the small house opened and Elijah came out onto the porch, Ruth behind him, clutching his arm. The soldier stepped up to them, speaking and gesturing. John strained to hear, but it was no use. He was too far away.

"No, no, no," came a cry, and Aunt Ruth fell against her husband, beating him with her fists. Elijah grabbed her wrists and held on. Her scream, when it came, pierced the air. Over and over, she screamed, until she slid down to the ground, her cries fading to a long, low wail. A cold chill swept through John.

Sabina appeared on the porch, the baby in her arms. Elijah guided Ruth back inside the house where the thin walls couldn't entirely muffle the sound of her sobs. The baby burst into tears, too, and Sabina hugged him tighter, facing the soldier. John watched the exchange, his blood running cold. After a moment, she nodded. The man held out a paper and she took it.

She stayed there on the porch, holding her baby, long after the soldier's automobile was out of sight of the farm. Frozen, John watched as she swayed from side to side, mouth close to her son's ear. From inside the house, the sound of Ruth's wails rose and fell and rose and fell. Raising her head to the sky, Sabina drew in a breath, hugged her son, and opened the door.

John stumbled backward, the ugly truth slithering into his mind and his gut. Shaking, he leaned over, the remains of his lunch splattering over the ground. He wiped his mouth before he straightened again. Glancing once more at the house, he ran as fast as he could toward home.

Later, his mother rode next to House on the bench of the wagon, her chin high, her small body rigid. Leah scooted closer, her cheeks already stained with tears.

House had railed against the war and the Germans until John's mother made him stop.

"You screaming about President Wilson or the war isn't going to bring Robert back," she'd said as she sliced bread for the food basket. "When we get to Elijah's, there will be none of that talk."

"Humph." House had slapped a hand against the table. "Don't tell me what I can and can't talk about."

She'd whipped around, eyes blazing. "Elijah and Ruth have lost their son. Ruth is my sister." Her tears flowed through the words. "None of that helps. Do you understand?" Whatever anger she'd harbored slipped away, and she dropped the knife. "Not today." House's shoulders slumped, too, and he blinked hard.

Now, the small family remained silent as they approached the farm. John thought even the rows of corn sagged in the wake of the news, their leaves curled and wilted, as though standing tall was too difficult to manage. Next to him, Leah half coughed, half sobbed. He put his arm around her shoulder, pulling her close. There were other wagons near the house, and he knew that word had spread quickly through town. The Johnsons and the Burnettes. Reverend Hawkins. Even Mrs. Hadley had come down from the hill.

"What's that?" Leah whispered, leaning in close.

John listened to the low, plaintive moan, and the sound sent fresh chills up his spine. "Aunt Ruth," he said, his voice a croak.

House tightened the reins, bringing the buggy to a stop. Essie squared her shoulders and marched straight up the porch steps. Anyone in her path stepped aside. The door and windows were open. Friends and family spilled out of the small house. They crowded around the steps and in the living room and the tiny kitchen. John's mother bypassed the main rooms, moving straight to the back of the house, to her sister. The wailing died down after a few minutes, and John exhaled. He deposited the food in the kitchen. Finding an empty corner in the living room, he stood awkwardly, hands tucked in his pockets. Uncle Elijah sat on a threadbare sofa, surrounded by the rest of the men. House joined the group, clapping Elijah on the back.

"Poor Sabina." John didn't know the voice and moved closer to listen.

"Widowed with a young baby. Going to be tough going."

"Elijah and Ruth won't put her out."

"Of course not, but she's young. She'll be expected to work, find another husband."

"Hush now. There she is."

John's head jerked around. Sabina stood across the room, her small son in her arms. She rocked from side to side, whispering in the baby's ear. Her gaze settled on John for one brief moment before moving past him again. He drew himself up, took a step toward her.

A different voice made him stop and turn around. House. With a flick of his wrist, he steered the young man toward the door. "John. I could use your help right now."

~~~~

LIQUOR BY PARCEL POST

Atlanta, Ga. — Bone-dry law violators have conscripted Uncle Sam into their service to secure liquor. Whisky houses in Chicago and other places, it is said, now neatly wrap two quarts of booze in a strong cardboard carton, label it "Fragile: Handle with Care," and trust the parcel post to get it to parched customers in Georgia and other states in the Southern "Sahara." Several of the packages have been located here.

—*The Tennessean*, July 7, 1918

~~~~

DARK

~~~~

Milton leaned in close, keeping his voice low. "I don't trust him."

Frank lifted one brow. "Who? Carl?"
~~~~

From the corner of his eye, Milton watched Carl. The stranger stood with the Smythe brothers, a cigar between his teeth. Hank was telling a story, his hands punctuating the words, his features animated. Carl threw back his head and laughed. Milton cringed, the shrill sound reminding him of a sharp-toothed animal, snarling and deadly.

"He's up to something," Milton said.

"You're either a seer or bonkers, that's what I say."

Hank launched into another tale. Carl, wearing a bemused smile, chomped on his cigar and drained the rest of his drink. A thump sounded from somewhere down the hall and the men looked around. Another thump and the door flew open. Larry staggered in, tripping over his own feet.

A chorus of "Larry" rang out. He pushed past the brothers and grabbed the nearest bottle of whiskey.

"Good to see you, too, Larry," Hank said, jabbing his brother in the ribs.

"Wha's it to ya?" Larry slurred, liquor sloshing from his glass.

Frank shot Milton a sideways glance. "Haven't seen him like this since his momma died."

Milton remembered. Larry and his widowed mother had been close, sharing a house until her death. Not long after, his only sister had moved to Kentucky with her new husband, and Larry was suddenly alone. But as of late, things had been better.

His sister had come home when her new husband got called up to the army. Larry had been good since she'd arrived—even drinking less—although he enjoyed a couple of whiskeys now and then. They all did, but not like this.

Carl intercepted Larry. "Glad to see you could make it tonight. I was getting worried."

"S'not to worry." Larry waved an arm in the air. "Not a welcher. Pay my debts."

Carl considered the man a moment, then pointed at the table. "We're getting a game going. Want to play first?"

"Can't s-stay."

"Fine. Why don't we step outside? Settle up our business?"

"Wanna drink first," Larry said, stumbling.

"You think that's a good idea?"

Larry tipped his glass, drained it in two long swallows, and wiped his mouth with the back of his hand. His eyes rolled back, and he swayed on his feet, falling backward against the wall and sliding down to the floor.

Milton crossed the room and crouched down next to the slumping man. "You okay, Larry?"

"Fine," he slurred, his head wobbling atop his narrow shoulders. "Jus' need somethin' to drink."

"Maybe in a minute," Milton said. He hooked his arms under Larry's and dragged him to his feet. "I'm taking him outside to get some air," he told the room.

"I'll do it," Carl said.

"No." Milton's grip on Larry tightened. "He's my friend. I'm taking him."

"I'll go with you."

"No need," Milton said, not liking the predatory gleam in Carl's eye. "I've got him." Again, he found himself wondering what Larry had gotten himself into with the stranger. "Keep playing. We'll be back soon."

"You sure?" Frank asked.

"I'm sure."

He guided Larry to the door, down the hall, and through Rowena's, stopping every twenty feet to tighten his grip. Outside, he propped Larry against a tree and bent over to catch his breath. Larry wasn't a large man, but he was like dead weight in his drunken state. Swaying unsteadily against the tree, Larry's hair flopped over his forehead. His shirttail hung over his pants and his shoes were splattered with whiskey and something that smelled vaguely rotten.

"Did something happen today, Larry?" Milton asked. "Are you okay?"

"Wanna drink." Larry slid down the tree.

"Later." Milton glanced back at Rowena's. Dark curtains covered the windows. Two men came up the street and went to the door. They knocked three times, waiting. The door opened. Milton heard laughter and clinking glasses. The door closed, and it was quiet again. Milton took his friend's arm. "Let's get you home."

"Can't. S'Carl. Gotta pay my debts." His words ran together as though they were one. Milton ignored him and tried to pull the man to his feet.

"You can do that later," Milton said. His muscles burned and he strained to hold the man upright.

"Ya don't understan'."

"Tell me while we walk."

"Is 'Licia."

Milton stopped short. Larry's sister? "What about her?"

Before the man could answer, he fell backward and landed against the tree again. "Oomph."

"How's he doing?" came a voice from behind.

Milton straightened. Carl. "Not too good," he said, wondering how long the other man had been standing there. He moved in front of Larry. "Game over already?"

"We didn't play." Carl craned his neck to see around Milton. "I don't really have time tonight."

"That's a shame."

Carl stepped to the side. Milton mirrored him. Glaring, the man stepped to the other side. Milton followed.

Carl growled, his gaze flicking past Milton. "I got business with Larry. It doesn't have anything do with you."

"I don't think he's in any state to do business tonight." He lifted a palm, trying to keep his voice steady. "Maybe tomorrow night, friend."

Carl stepped closer, his nose inches from Milton's face. "That's not for you to decide," Carl said.

He pulled aside his coat, his hand dropping to his waist, flashing the gun he carried on his hip.

Milton's heart skipped a beat. There was no mistaking the threat in Carl's voice or the menace in the way his eyes narrowed to slits.

"Keep out of this," Carl sneered, stabbing Milton's chest with his finger. "Friend."

LETTERS FROM OUR BOYS

Death must have been instantaneous, and I am glad . . .

—*The Tennessean*, July 7, 1918

Darkness hovered over the road, and John and Leah walked faster.

Leah sniffled and blew her nose. "It doesn't feel real, does it?"

John wondered if death ever felt real. "No," he said.

She leaned into him, resting her head under his shoulder, and as they walked, he put his arm around her. They clung to each other like that—brother and sister—for a long while. They knew about death. Their father. Their siblings. But this was different. How could someone like Robert, someone larger than life, be gone—just like that?

"Are you afraid?" he'd asked Robert in the week before he left for training.

"Sure. A little. But not of war."

John studied his cousin, his brows drawn together. "Of what, then?"

Robert walked through the rows of corn, his fingers trailing over the new stalks. "I don't want to let anybody down."

John didn't say anything. He and Robert worked the fields, more apart than together. Since he'd married Sabina, they'd spoken little. But Robert was leaving now. "I'm sure that won't happen."

"I don't know," Robert said, mumbling. "It seems to be my specialty lately." He flicked his hand toward the house and grinned. "Enough talk about war. Bet you can't beat me back." He took off then, running slow enough for John to catch up. They ran stride for stride until they burst from the rows of corn, landing in the open field and Robert pulled away.

John didn't see Robert much after that. He left a week later.

He thought about the letters Sabina had made him read. He hadn't seen the brash and swaggering Robert everyone knew on those pages. No, "Army Robert" was a quieter version, more introspective, even fearful. Sabina knew both Roberts, knew him better than John did. And now he was gone.

When they arrived home, Leah went to bed, seemingly weary with the weight of the news and tired of crying. Unable to sleep, John stood by the window, staring out at the shadows. His mind raced with the things he wanted to say but couldn't.

John's momma and House had stayed behind to console Elijah and Ruth. He would have stayed, too, but Sabina hadn't wanted him there. It was a blow he hadn't seen coming.

"I need to be alone," she'd said, before he could speak. John had followed her outside, cornering her near a large tree. She was alone, the baby asleep in the house.

"I'm so sorry, Sabina. I really am. I saw the army man come today, and I didn't know what to do."

She half sobbed, and he reached for her without thinking.

She pushed him away. "Please, don't."

The skin under his shirt and on his face burned. "I didn't mean anything."

"I know you didn't," she said, voice softer. "I meant what I said. I need to be by myself."

"If that's what you want. I could come by tomorrow."

"You don't understand. I don't mean only tonight. I need to be alone for a while. I have a baby to take care of, and there's my mother, and now Elijah and Ruth."

"But I thought . . ."

"You thought what?" In one angry motion, she wiped away her tears. "You don't know me anymore, John. I've changed. I'm not the girl that used to fish with you and run with you and sit by our tree. Today, I thought maybe I could be her again, but I can't." Her voice cooled. "That girl is gone now."

What was she saying? "No. Today meant something."

"It did." She looked away. "But that was before."

She didn't finish, but she didn't have to. Before the man from the army had come. Before they knew the truth about Robert.

She stood up taller. "I'm not a girl anymore. I'm not who you think I am—who I was. That part of my life is over, and I can't go back. Not ever."

"You haven't changed, Sabina."

She wasn't having it. "Look at me," she said, putting more space between them. "Really look."

At first, he could only see the girl he'd always known. Her hair still hung in a long braid, her nose still turned up at the tip, and her pointed chin still jutted out as though leading the rest of her face. These were things he knew by heart.

She waited, silent, and so he looked harder. There were new lines around her mouth and her eyes, like delicate starbursts. Her face was thinner, longer, as if the soft angles had melted away. Where there'd once been lightness, there was something harder now. Her eyes, still the color of caramel, no longer danced with laughter but shimmered with grief, and something else—determination and strength.

He lowered his head, his heart heavy. Sabina was right. She wasn't the girl he'd known as a boy. She wasn't a girl at all. She was a woman.

"I need time to figure out my life, to figure out what's best for me and my son, and I need to do that alone."

He nodded slowly. "How long?"

She answered slowly. "I don't know. Months. Maybe as long as a year. People need me."

"A year," he repeated, numb.

"My son needs me," she said, making no apology. "Now more than ever."

John wanted to tell her he'd take care of her, take care of them both, but he didn't. He had nothing to offer. No farm of his own. No home.

She walked away from him, back to her new life as a widow and mother, a life that didn't include John Lang.

He laid his head against the window now. The moon shone clear and bright against the dark sky, and he touched a hand to the glass. Sabina had changed. Everything had changed. Everything and everyone but him.

~~~~

BITS OF BY-PLAY

By Luke McLuke

(copyright 1918)

NO JOKE

The hypocrite stings other men,
When piety conveying;
For he is always preying, When
He lets on he is praying.

—*The Tennessean,* July 7, 1918

~~~~

Milton brushed Carl's hand aside. "Look, I know Larry lost a bet," he said, hoping Carl couldn't hear the tremor in his voice. "But he's not in any shape to settle up now."

Carl hooked his thumbs into his waistband, his fingers caressing the ivory handle of the gun. "It's none of your business."

A hand clawed at Milton's pants, grabbing at his jacket. Larry. Struggling to stand, he hugged the tree. "Do business now," Larry grunted.

Milton did his best to distract him. "Hey, Larry, did I ever tell you the one about the German and the Austrian?"

Carl stepped between them. "Enough, funny boy. The man said he wanted to do business."

"Larry?" Milton ignored the other man, his attention focused on his friend.

"S'okay. Pay my debts."

"Did you hear the man?" Carl asked with a smirk. "You can leave now."

Milton hesitated, his gaze swinging between the two men.

"S'okay," Larry said again.

Reluctantly, Milton stepped back. "If that's what you want." He gestured toward Rowena's. "I'll wait over here, and when you're done, I'll walk you home."

Carl steered Larry to the far side of the tree, several yards away. Milton tilted his ear toward them but heard nothing more threatening than the buzz of crickets and the occasional hoot of an owl. Most of the short, squat buildings around Rowena's were dark, their doors closed. But if a man looked, he'd catch the occasional glimpse of soft light glowing around the edges of the windows, same as Rowena's. The minutes passed.

Carl clapped Larry on the arm and pulled a fresh cigar from his pocket. "Good doing business with you, Larry. Damn good." He laughed then, walking off, his cackle trailing after him.

Larry stumbled, mumbling something Milton couldn't make out. His chin sank to his chest and his shoulders shook. Milton waited. The sobs faded and Larry, face streaked with tears, pushed off the tree, half walking, half falling down the road.

Milton caught the man in a few strides. "Larry?"

He kept walking and mumbling, unaware or uncaring that Milton was there.

Steps sounded on the street, and Milton looked over his shoulder. Frank trotted up the road.

"Doesn't look like he's doing so good."

"No." The pair walked side by side, a few paces behind Larry.

"Thought you were gone when you didn't come back. Figured you took him home to sober up."

"That was the plan." Ahead, Larry rounded the corner, lurched, and caught himself on a streetlamp. "Carl showed up. Not sure he would've gone anyway. Said he had to pay his debt to Carl."

Frank seemed to accept that. "Well, I've never known Larry to let a debt go. Even after his momma died, he showed he was a man of his word."

"It could have waited," Milton said. He jerked his chin in Larry's direction. "Look at him. He's a wreck. There's something not right." He told Frank he suspected Carl of cheating. "How else could he have had that hand?"

"I didn't see anything," Frank said with a shrug. "Look, I don't like this either, but no one made Larry play. And you don't know that Carl cheated."

It was true that Milton couldn't prove Carl cheated, but he knew it, as sure as he knew his uncle would sooner take a knife to the heart than live a life without making hats. "He did."

"You just don't like Carl."

"Do you?"

"I don't really know him. The Smythe boys do though. He's staying at the Hermitage." Frank kicked at the ground as they walked. "Some kind of sales, and he likes to play cards. It's enough."

Milton didn't agree. What would a man like Carl sell? He started to tell Frank about the gun, but Larry pitched forward then, landing on his knees. Larry hoisted himself back to his feet and continued down the street. They followed him five more blocks to his apartment building, waiting until he disappeared inside.

"He'll feel better after he sleeps it off," Frank said.

"Maybe." At the corner, the pair went their separate ways. Milton climbed the steps to his uncle's house and let himself in. He slipped off his shoes and padded down the hall to the small bedroom at the back of the house. Lying in bed, he stared into the darkness, the last hour playing on repeat in his head. A faint breeze blew the curtains aside, and shadows danced across the ceiling. He couldn't be sure what had happened between Larry and Carl, but whatever it was had left a bad taste in his mouth. Milton didn't know Carl, but he knew one thing: Carl Lewis wasn't anyone's friend.

PART 5

BETS ARE IN

CHAPTER FIFTEEN

Summer 1988

THE MORNING LIGHT shot through the window, warming the already warm room. Anna Mae leaned toward Ginny, the lines deepening between her brows. "Is something wrong, dear?"

Ginny looked up from the Styrofoam cup in her hands, blinking.

"You look tired," Anna Mae said. "Have I bored you so much these last few days?"

"Oh, no. I'm not bored. I didn't sleep well last night, I guess." It was her own fault. Another fight with Shawn. Another night staring at the walls.

"Would you like to talk about it?" The old woman's voice was quiet, with none of the morbid curiosity and suspicion she would have heard from her mother. "I'm a very good listener. You might not know that with all the talking I've been doing, but I'm here for you if you want me to be."

Ginny lifted her head. "I don't know."

Anna Mae nodded. "I understand. I wouldn't want you to share something you're not ready to, but when you are, do you have someone to talk to? Your mother maybe?"

That made Ginny snort. "Definitely not my mother. She'd mean well, but she'd go on and on, and it wouldn't help. She used to say Grandma Betty was the one who wasn't a good listener, which was kind of true when it came to my parents, but she always listened to me. Maybe because I'm named after her. Elizabeth Virginia. Ginny is my nickname."

"Elizabeth?"

"Everyone called her Betty, but her real name was Elizabeth. Elizabeth Piler."

"Piler?" Anna Mae's hand rose to her throat. "Elizabeth Piler was your grandmother?"

"Yes, why? Did you know her?"

The old woman's hand found the locket at her neck, her fingers rubbing the golden surface. Her head turned slowly from side to side. "I don't believe I had the pleasure of meeting anyone by that name."

"Oh. It seemed like maybe you did."

"I did think I recognized the name for a minute, that's true, but I don't think so after all." She dropped the locket and clapped her hands. "Enough of me. We were talking about you, and the fact that something is bothering you. I don't want to intrude, but should you decide you want to talk, I'll be here. As your friend."

Ginny's lips parted.

Friend. It was a luxury she hadn't considered in a while. At least not in a good way.

She thought about the last words Lila had said to her.

"Why don't you do the right thing and let Shawn go? We both know he's only staying with you out of pity." Her former friend clucked her tongue. "He's too nice for his own good. The kind of guy willing to sacrifice his own happiness just so he doesn't hurt you. Is that what you want? To stay in a loveless marriage? To stay with a man you know would rather be with someone else?"

She stepped close enough that Ginny could smell the sweet florals of her perfume.

"Shawn doesn't need to know we talked, Gin. That would only make him feel worse than he already does." She tucked her hair behind her ear and said in a low voice, "The thing is, you and I both know that eventually he'll resent you if he stays. And the baby. If you don't tell him to go, all you'll be left with is a husband who hates you. Do the right thing."

Ginny shuddered, remembering Lila's words. "It's sort of personal."

"Hmmm. Yes, those are usually the most difficult, aren't they?"

"And embarrassing," Ginny said, her face flaming.

"Well," the old woman said in a knowing tone, "I've lost count of the embarrassing things in my life."

Ginny ran her finger over the edge of her cup. "I haven't told anyone about what's been happening."

"Only if you're sure."

Was she? She didn't know if it would make her feel better, but she did know she couldn't feel worse. "I think my husband is in love with someone else."

"I see. That is quite a difficult situation, isn't it?"

"The other woman is—I mean was—a good friend, another teacher at the school where I worked." Her voice shook as she spoke. "I still can't believe it, but he didn't deny it after I saw them together. Well, he did and he didn't. He admitted he cared about her, but that was all. He says he never slept with her, that he wanted to but didn't." Her lower lip quivered. "I mean, what am I supposed to do with that?" She lowered her eyes. "I think he loves her though, and if things were different, he would have already left. I probably should have told him to. But I didn't. I haven't. I think I've been afraid."

"Afraid of what?"

"Of being alone." Ginny stared at the cup in her hands. Powdered creamer dotted the coffee like snowflakes. "I sound like a child, don't I?"

"You sound like someone who's doing her best to figure it out."

Ginny bit her lip to keep from crying. Her husband didn't love her. "There really isn't that much to figure out. The only reason he's stayed with me is because of the baby."

Anna Mae's mouth dropped open. "You're pregnant?"

"Yes. I'm not all that far along, so I'm not really showing yet."

"That's wonderful," the old woman said, her eyes brightening. "Truly wonderful. A baby. Now, of all times."

Ginny frowned. She'd been thrilled to discover she was pregnant, but that was before the dance, and now the timing seemed less than ideal. "That's kind of the problem. Now isn't the best time. I found out I was pregnant the day before I saw them together, and then, well . . ." The words spilled out of her, then—that last conversation with Lila—all of it. "That's why I'm so confused. Lila seemed so sure about everything, about them."

"I see." Anna Mae tapped a nail against the arm of her chair. "And she asked that you not mention your conversation to your husband?"

"I guess she wanted me to end things, so he didn't have to."

"And what has he said?"

"That he ended it with Lila before it went too far." Tears threatened then. "Lila's right about Shawn though. He'll stay because, in spite of everything, he's a good guy. But that doesn't mean he loves me or won't resent me and the baby, that he won't wish he was with her."

Anna Mae pursed her lips. "Is she an old friend—this Lila?"

"Not really. I've known her a couple of years, I guess. She joined the faculty after me. She was dating someone back then. Jed. We had dinner together—the four of us—a few times before they broke up. I thought it was too bad. I liked him. Shawn and Jed played golf. They were friends too."

"And why did they break up?"

"I don't know exactly. She missed a couple of days of work, and when she came back, she said she'd ended things. She asked Shawn and I not to see him anymore. She said if we saw him socially, it would only remind him of her and she felt bad about hurting him."

"Hmmm."

"What?"

"Well, I don't mean to overstep, but unless I missed something, your friend didn't want to hurt the man she broke up with, but didn't mind hurting you—someone who is supposed to be her friend."

Ginny's jaw snapped closed. "Oh. Wow, I never thought of it like that." She half shrugged after a minute. "Does it really matter though? Lila's beautiful and fun. Men are always looking at her, doing things for her. That's how it started with Shawn, I think. She needed some help fixing things at her apartment, and I asked him if he could do it since Jed was out of the picture. He was pretty busy at work, but he went anyway. She's hard to resist. I can see why Shawn fell for her."

Anna Mae gave a slow shake of her head. "You're beautiful and fun, Ginny Campbell. I know I'm only an old woman, but I have eyes."

Tears threatened then, and Ginny blinked hard. "That's nice of you, but he's in love with her."

"Oh." Anna Mae's lips parted and her hand went to her throat. "He told you that?"

"Well, no. He says he's not, but he has to say that, doesn't he?" Ginny swallowed the lump in her throat. "Lila said—"

"Yes, Lila said. She has quite a lot to say, doesn't she?" Anna Mae's sharp tone made Ginny gasp. "I'm sorry, dear," the old woman said quickly. "That was unkind, and it's not my place. I just hate seeing you so upset."

"It's okay," Ginny said with a sniffle. She didn't know why, but Anna Mae's loyalty—no matter how biased—touched her heart.

The old woman's face softened. "Look, I don't know whether things with your husband can be fixed or not. That's something only time will tell, I suppose, but I do have to wonder. Obviously, I don't know Lila the way you do . . ." The woman's forehead scrunched as if considering what to say. Ginny leaned forward. "But it seems to me a woman who didn't mind hurting you once wouldn't hesitate to do it again—if it got her what she wanted."

"Meaning Shawn." Anna Mae arched a single brow, saying nothing. Ginny turned the suggestion over in her mind, but no matter how much she wanted Anna Mae to be right, Shawn had admitted there'd been something between them. "What difference does it make? If he was happy with me, it wouldn't have started at all."

“Maybe and maybe not.” Anna Mae ran her gnarled hands over the quilt. “But what your husband wants now seems to be the question on the table. This Lila thinks it’s her.” Ginny flinched. “But he says it’s not. One of them is lying and one of them is telling the truth. I believe when you find out which, you’ll have a clearer picture.”

Ginny wasn’t sure she needed a clearer picture, but she kept the thought to herself. “Thank you for listening. I do feel a little better,” she said with a yawn, surprised to find she meant it.

“I’m glad.” Anna Mae set her cup on the side table. “Would you mind if we continued tomorrow? I think we’re both a bit tired today.”

A wave of relief washed over Ginny. “Yes,” she said, rising. “Until tomorrow.”

~~~~

“How did you find me?” Jed’s voice softened before she could answer. “Not that I’m not glad to hear from you, Ginny, but I’ve kind of been keeping a low profile. I moved a few months ago and changed my number.”

“I’m sorry. I hope I’m not bothering you,” Ginny said in a rush. “I called your mother. I remembered you said she lived over in Ridgeville and when you weren’t listed, I thought of her. I hope you don’t mind.”

“I don’t mind. I guess you’re kind of in the same boat as me now, huh? It’s Lila, right? I heard she took up with Shawn.”

“How . . . ?” She couldn’t finish. Of course, Jed knew about the affair.

“Lila sent a letter to my mother’s house about Shawn and her. Said they were getting married soon.”

Ginny gasped. She wanted to be sick, her stomach churning.

Jed didn’t seem to notice.

“I wouldn’t have figured him for the type, but she’s pretty good at fooling a guy. I gotta give her that. That letter is classic Lila. Wanted to make sure I knew what I’d lost when I dumped her and got the heck out of there. At the time, I didn’t—”
~~~~

"Wait." Ginny shook her head, unsure she'd heard right. "Did you say *you* dumped *her*? Not the other way around?"

Jed's voice rose in indignation. "Is that what she's saying? Doesn't surprise me. Sorta goes with everything else about her."

"Everything else?"

Ginny heard a sigh followed by the click of a lighter and a hard inhale. "Look, when I first met Lila, I was blown away. I mean, who wouldn't be? She's a looker, and we were having fun. But after a while, I started to wonder."

"About what?"

"Well, she didn't have many friends, for one thing. There was you and Shawn, but no one else. It got to be that she wanted to be with me all the time. She'd get mad if I wanted to go out with the guys or stay home alone. She wanted to know who I was with every minute of the day. Then she started talking about setting a wedding date and what kind of ring she wanted. I hadn't even proposed. When I pointed that out, she went through the roof. I almost ended it then, but she started crying, so I let it go. Big mistake. She was like a spider after that, tightening the web. She started calling me at all hours of the day. The middle of the night. The only time I could get away from her was when she was at the school. I couldn't take it anymore, so I broke it off."

"That's not . . ." Ginny started, then faltered. What had Lila really said? She said she'd ended it, and Jed had taken it hard. There'd been no other details.

"Not what she told you, right? She probably didn't tell you that after I broke it off, she wouldn't leave me alone. She would show up at my apartment, banging on the door. That's why I moved, why I changed my number. I didn't even visit my mother for almost two months because I was worried she would show up."

Ginny pulled on the phone cord, wrapping it around her hand in tight circles. It didn't make sense. Lila was so beautiful, so fun.

"Sorry about you and Shawn though. I guess I should've warned him, but I never thought of it. You have no idea how much I wanted to get away from her. I figured when I got the letter about her and Shawn, it was more lies trying to get me to take her back. But here you are, tracking me down, so I guess it must be true."

"I—I don't know if it's true. That's why I called you."

"Well, I'm sorry I can't help you. I haven't spoken to her or Shawn in a long time."

"Thanks anyway, Jed."

"Sure. But do me a favor. Don't tell anyone you got this number, okay?"

"I won't."

"Thanks. And Ginny, for what it's worth, I hope it's not true. I don't know what's going on, but I can tell you one thing, if she set her sights on him, he's a dead man."

~~~~

"Are you feeling better today, dear?" Anna Mae smiled warmly, eyes searching.

"A little, I guess." She'd lain awake until two, the conversation with Jed playing on repeat in her mind.

"I'm glad. You have a baby to think of now," Anna Mae said. "Which reminds me, I have a gift for you." She lifted a tissue-wrapped parcel from the windowsill and handed it to Ginny.

The young woman's mouth opened. "A gift? For me?"

"Yes." Anna Mae beamed at her. "Open it."

Ginny peeled back the tissue paper. Inside was a faded blue cotton flannel blanket with tiny yellow ducks stitched along the border.

She touched a finger to one of the ducks, stroking the soft threads. Tears threatened, and she took a shuddering breath.

"Oh, Anna Mae."

"I hope you don't mind it isn't new. As I told you, I didn't keep much, but this particular blanket is a family heirloom, and . . ." Her words caught and her voice shook. "Well, let's just say I couldn't let it go."
~~~~

The young woman looked down at the soft blanket nestled in the fine tissue. *A family heirloom.* Considering David's estrangement from his family, she decided it must have come from Mary's side. She could imagine Mary passing this to her daughter in the hope she'd one day use it to swaddle her own son or daughter. How heartbreaking for them both that Anna Mae had never had the opportunity to use this treasure.

Ginny's fingers trailed from the delicate embroidery to the soft fabric. "It's so beautiful. But shouldn't this stay in the family? Go to one of your niece's children maybe?"

"No, no," Anna Mae said with a shake of her head, voice firm. "I spoiled them plenty when they were young. I want you to have it, and I won't take no for an answer."

Ginny's heart swelled. She did love the blanket, and not just because it was the first baby gift she'd received. The tears flowed now.

"I'm so sorry. I can't seem to stop crying these days."

"Perfectly natural. I'm just glad you like it."

Ginny thought she caught sight of tears in Anna Mae's eyes, too, but they were gone before she could be sure.

When she spoke again, her expression was as placid as ever. "Shall we get back to our story?"

"Oh, yes," Ginny said, wiping her cheeks.

"Good. Well, the morning of July the eighth started like most of the others that summer. It was hot and humid with not a speck of rain in sight."

CHAPTER SIXTEEN

Monday, July 8, 1918
Dawn

DRY WEATHER HURTING CROPS IN MONTGOMERY

The continued dry weather is becoming real serious, as most everything is being affected. Early corn seems to be suffering very much, and without an early rain will be almost worthless.

—*The Tennessean,* July 8, 1918

~~~

John put his feet on the floor, uncurled his rounded shoulders, and stretched his legs. Standing, he pulled a shirt over his bare chest and ran a calloused hand over the rough skin of his chin. The first rays of light streamed through the small window, but they couldn't dent the sadness in his heart. Body sagging, he pressed his ear to the glass, listening to the chirping of the birds, a reminder that even tragedy couldn't stop time, couldn't stop the dawn. From somewhere inside the house, he heard the low rumble of House's voice, followed by the sound of the front door slamming. He closed his eyes and breathed.
~~~

In the kitchen, his momma sat at the old table, a mug of black coffee in her hands. She didn't seem to notice him pad across the room to pour a cup or hear him come up behind her. When he sat down, his voice was soft. "Momma?"

Looking at him with red-rimmed eyes, she touched a hand to her matted hair and sniffled. "Yes, baby?"

He reached out and placed a hand over hers. "Are you okay?"

Her lips trembled. "I'm fine, baby, but Ruth is hurting something awful."

John stroked her hand. The sisters had always been close. They were the youngest children of Samuel and Nellie Jones. John couldn't remember a time when Ruth and his mother weren't carrying on about something or someone. It was Ruth who'd suggested Essie look to House when John's father had died. House had been married to their oldest sister, Patsey, before she succumbed to typhus. He was family already. John was small then, and Leah wasn't much more than a baby. He understood how it had made sense at the time. There'd already been too much loss in their lives. His momma needed steady, and House was nothing if not steady. Even John recognized that.

"She'll be okay," John said. "She's got you to take care of her."

Essie tried to give him a smile, but her mouth quivered with the effort not to cry. "You're a sweet boy."

He sank lower in the chair. Would she think so after she heard what he had to say next? He considered stalling. He could ask about Uncle Elijah, Sabina, and the baby, but it wouldn't change anything, and she deserved better. He rubbed his large hands against his thighs. "Momma, I need to tell you something."

She wiped her face with a handkerchief. "What is it, baby? Is something wrong?"

"No, not like that." His hands shook, but he pressed forward. "I can't keep sitting here day after day, doing nothing."

"You're a farmer, John. That's not nothing."

"I mean sit here in Hernando. Doing nothing."

Her mouth puckered. "Is this that Matt Toles putting ideas in your head?"

"No, Momma. I don't want to go to Chicago. But I need to do something on my own. Like Robert."

Her hand froze over her cup. "You will not sign up for this war, John Lang." She poked him with her finger, her ragged nail catching the fabric of his shirt. "The only way you're doing that is if they come and drag you away. Do you hear me? No war." Her voice, high-pitched one minute, dropped low the next. She grabbed him by the arms, shaking him. "How could you even think such a thing? After Robert? After everything? No son of mine is going off to die. Do you understand me? Do you?"

"I'm not joining the army, Momma. I'm going to Nashville."

It took only a moment for his words to sink in. "I don't think so," she told him, voice steely. "You're needed here."

"Elijah doesn't need me on the farm until harvest—if there is a harvest. You've seen the fields, Momma. You can't deny it." She pressed her lips together, and he leaned forward. "I've been thinking about going since those men came to the picnic to talk about the gunpowder plant."

"No." She got to her feet. "It's not a good time."

"There's never gonna be a good time."

She wagged a finger at him. "I won't have it. This war has already cost our family too much." She swept up the dishes, took them to the sink. "We can't lose anyone else."

"I'm going."

"You're not." With her back to him, she rinsed and washed. He watched her, knowing she wouldn't make it easy. Stacking the plates, she tossed the next words over her shoulder as though he hadn't spoken of leaving, as if he hadn't spoken at all. "Elijah will be expecting you at the farm soon. Be on your way."

It was just like his momma to end the conversation, taking the last word. Pain and loss made her seem smaller on that morning, her shoulders stooped and her head hanging low. John sighed. He hated to leave, hated to add to her heartbreak. He wished more than anything that he could have just one more day, but the DuPont man had been clear. The train left Monday. There would not be a second opportunity, and he would be on that train. He got to his feet.

"Robert went to fight for this country willingly, and now he's gone." She stiffened with each word he spoke. "I won't sign up for the war, but I'm not going to sit here and stare at a dying field of corn day after day. I'm going to do something for this family."

"Farming isn't nothing," she said again.

"I'll be gone three months. That's all. It's good pay, Momma, and if there's anything to harvest, I'll be back in time."

"House won't allow it."

"I'm not asking House. Or you, Momma."

She raised a hand to her mouth. He went to her, taking her hands in his. "I'm going whether you give me your blessing or not." His voice was soft. "But I'd rather have your blessing."

Her chin quivered as she spoke. "You're a man now? Is that what you're telling me?"

His stomach clenched. He hated hurting her, but he couldn't see any other way. If the crops were bad, they would all need the money. Sabina and her baby would need the money. Robert was gone. They all needed time to heal—even him. "I'm trying, Momma. I'm trying."

Her forehead touched his shoulder, and he wrapped his arms around her. She held tight for several minutes, then stepped back. "When are you leaving?"

Telling her he was going had been hard enough. "Today, Momma." He gulped. "Today."

LIVE COALS FROM ENGINE FIREBOX IGNITE FAT PINE.

The extreme drouth was responsible for a conflagration on the Tennessee Central Railroad, the first trestle beyond Riverside, catching fire about 2:30 o'clock Saturday afternoon and again that night. Five bents were burned and several more so badly injured that they will have to be replaced. It is supposed that in emptying the firebox live coals ignited the fat pine of which the trestle is built.

Another fire of similar origin occurred on the L.&N. in the region known as Hell's Half Acre, near the freight yards, a little later. The fire engines responded promptly and the flames were extinguished with little loss.

—*The Tennessean*, July 8, 1918

Staring up at the ceiling, David lay motionless, willing the pain to stop. Next to him, Mary rolled onto her side. David blinked in the gray light of the morning, black spots blurring his vision. He waited another minute before climbing out of bed, moving slower than usual. Slipping from the bedroom, he shuffled down the hall to the small kitchen. He found a clean cloth and dipped it in cool water. Holding it against his forehead, he lowered himself to the wooden bench.

The headaches baffled him. He'd had very few health issues during his lifetime and counted himself a man of few complaints. He wondered briefly if he should visit the railroad physician but dismissed the idea, reasoning the pain was most likely due to stress and worry. Each day, the papers were filled with lists of more casualties. Each day that passed without a letter added to his heartache.

When the cloth warmed and the pain had dulled, he got up and went to the window in the front room, laying his head against the glass. Looking out at the street, he whispered a prayer of thanks. He'd lived a long and comfortable life.

He loved Nashville and the trains and his family most of all. Yet, he couldn't shake the feeling that all wasn't right, that he carried the weight of the world changing around him. Stepping back, he smoothed his beard with his long fingers. What was wrong with him? He had a train to drive, and it wasn't like him to dwell on maudlin thoughts.

By the time he arrived at the train station, the fresh air and brisk walk had improved his spirits, and he felt more like himself. As he did every morning, he admired the sleek lines of the cars and the imposing size of the engine. Some men took pleasure in drink or women, but David's first love had always been trains. He drank in the sight of the hulking locomotives, the smell, the sheer power as they rolled over the tracks. Breathing in the oil-scented air, he tucked his hands in his pockets. It would be a good morning after all.

"Hey, Uncle Dave." Shorty hurried toward him, his short legs making him appear to waddle rather than walk. Instantly ashamed of the unkind thought, David did his best to wipe away the urge to laugh. "Did you hear about the fire?" Shorty asked. Deep lines bracketed his mouth.

David had heard the talk among the railroaders, but he also knew that both fires had been contained and no one had been hurt. He might have been a stickler for rules and procedures, but he didn't consider himself an alarmist. Shorty, however, quaked at the drop of a pin.

"Not to worry. That won't happen on our train." He wasn't surprised to see that Shorty wasn't immediately convinced. "Luther is the best fireman I've ever had, and you know me, I'm a careful man."

"That's true," the conductor said slowly, his scowl growing more pronounced. "But the coaches are old."

"Not all." David bristled. It was true that his passenger coaches were wooden, not the new steel cars that some of the larger, overnight trains pulled, but they were serviceable. To David, this worrying was pointless, and as if to put an end to the conversation, the platform vibrated and both men looked around. The Number One. David checked his pocket watch. Ten minutes early. It didn't happen often, and David was glad, his mood instantly lifted.

"Time to get going," David said with a smile. He laid a hand on Shorty's shoulder. "See you in Hickman."

A moment later, he climbed into the engine car and set aside his railroader's box. Luther lifted one hand in greeting. David opened the box and took out his clock. Five minutes more. His hand hovered over the box. Like many of the men he worked with, he kept a family photo inside. His—more than five years old now—bore a crease across one corner. He traced one long finger across the edge. Mary stood by his side, the children in the front. John George was sandwiched in the middle, one sister on each side. How old had the boy been? Eleven? Twelve? In the photo, his arms and legs were long, his chest still concave. The boy's sisters pressed in close, no space between the three. It had always been that way, both Anna Mae and Katie Belle doting on John George. In truth, the boy had been born with three mothers rather than one. It was David who was hardest on him. He sighed, placing the picture back in the box.

The fireman straightened and pulled his bandana down from his mouth and nose. "Was that the Number One?" Luther asked.

"Early today."

"Good," Luther said. He raised his bandana again and returned to his work at the firebox.

David touched a hand to the pocket of his overalls. The orders were brief on this Monday. The train would stop in Harding for the mail and continue on to the scheduled stops. There would be no need to wait at Shops on this day, no reason for his train to be late, and no worry about too many trains running and not enough tracks. He pulled the cord to sound the horn and pushed the lever high. The train chugged forward, and his breath quickened as the Number Four left the station.

~~~~

Near the front of the train, the combination mail and luggage car stood open. A long table was centered in the car, and two postal workers stood sorting through the piles in front of them. George slowed. One of the workers was the man he'd seen the night before, the one he'd heard crying.
~~~~

The postal worker lifted a shaky hand, wiping it across his mouth. Haggard, his face wore the shadowed look of a man who hadn't slept in days. His partner waved a hand in front of him and said something that made him blink hard. He stood up straighter, but his movements remained sluggish. George watched another minute, then moved on. It was none of his business, but as he worked, the man's sadness and pain haunted him. Men weren't supposed to cry. It wasn't right. Of course, he didn't know all the rules of white men, but as far as he could tell, the rule about crying was the same for any man.

"Must be something terrible," he said to himself with a shake of his head. "Something terrible."

~~~~

LETTERS

An Observation Worth While.

The American Negro, though encompassed by enumerable handicaps, is in like manner as the white man, sacrificing in support of the Government, to the extent of his life, that the long-wished-for and talked-of democracy may come and abide with us. And this is as it should be. July 6, 1918 A. C. PRICE

—*The Tennessean*, July 8, 1918

~~~~

"Nashville," Sabina said, repeating the word.

In spite of her declaration that she needed to be alone, he couldn't have her hear he'd gone to Nashville from anyone but him. She may not want him, but she'd suffered enough.

"Do you mind if I write to you?" he asked. "You don't have to write back."

"I don't know," she said. "What will Ruth and Elijah think?"

He hadn't thought about that but decided he didn't care. "Does it matter?"

"Is this what the new John Lang is like?"

His stomach fluttered, but it wasn't disdain or laughter that he saw in her eyes—only interest. "I guess it is."

"It suits you," she said, shifting the baby from her right hip to her left. "How long will you be gone?"

"Three months."

Her body sagged, but her voice was strong. "It'll go fast," she said, brushing a hand over the boy's curls. "Three months is gone in a blink now. Seems like only yesterday, Ivan was a newborn, crying every minute." She smiled at the boy, and John noticed she looked different with the baby, younger and happier, the shadows vanishing. "Now look at him. Growing like a weed." She half laughed when the baby tugged at her braid. "Look at him, John. Isn't it funny how he loves my hair?"

"You have beautiful hair."

Silent, she studied the house behind them. She took a step back. "They're watching us."

"I figured." He shoved his hands into his pockets.

"I've never been to Nashville, or any city, really. Are you worried?"

John shrugged. It wasn't really an answer. It was true he didn't know what city life was like. He'd never been on a train. He didn't know how to work in a factory. Surely, that was the reason for the pit in his stomach. Eagerness and excitement—and maybe a little nervousness. That had to be it. A plant wouldn't be like farming.

He expected the workdays would be long and pass slowly. He'd get used to it, and when it was over, he'd come back and work the harvest—if there was one. That's what he'd told himself during the night. That's what he told himself now.

"How's Essie taking you leaving?"

He wasn't surprised by the question. Sabina had known his mother since they were small. She'd seen the way Essie protected the children she had left, the way she took care of them. "She understands. Leah too. I think she wishes she could go."

"That sounds like Leah." Sabina rubbed the baby's back in a steady, circular motion. "And House?"

House, a man who could change with the wind, or more accurately, with the wind that suited him best, had been less than pleased:

"How long have we known Robert was gone? Not even a day, by my calculations. And what do you go and do? You start talking about leaving." House's golden eyes darkened. "What kind of son leaves his momma at a time like this? I'll tell you. A selfish one, that's what kind." Spit flew from his mouth. "If I had my way, I'd take you out back and tan your hide just for thinking of running out. But your momma says she wants you to go."

John bit his lip, his heart breaking at his momma's lie. He knew it for the act of love it was.

John didn't say any of this to Sabina.

"He's accepted it."

"Why, John Lang, I do believe you've changed."

Heat rose to his cheeks. He wasn't sure it was true, but her words gave him a sliver of hope. "The times call for change, don't they?"

"I suppose they do." Neither spoke for a minute. "They're expecting me," she told him. "Take care of yourself, John."

John squinted up at the sun. It was noon. Time to gather his things for the trip. The train from Memphis would be leaving that night, and he didn't want to be late. "You, too, Sabina."

He walked past the withering fields and up the dirt road back to town, a new lightness in his step.

Leah sat on her bed, watching him as he threw a few clothes and his journal into a knapsack.

"I'll miss you."

He crossed the room and wrapped her in a hug. "I'll miss you too. Very much."

Her warm tears dampened his shirt, and she laughed as she pulled away. "Couple of big babies. That's what we are." She gave him a playful slap on the arm and backed out of the room. "Finish now."

Alone, he stuffed in the last of his things. There wasn't much to take because there wasn't much in the first place, but that didn't make it easier to leave.

He would miss his momma, Leah, and Sabina. Home wasn't the things he packed or even the bed he slept in. It was the women in his life, the ones he loved.

He threw his bag over his shoulder and closed the door.

His momma waited in the front room. She smelled of freshly baked bread and sweet honeysuckle. He pulled her into his arms, surprised at how small she felt. After a moment, she pushed him away. "We'll be having none of that sappy stuff. Time doesn't stand still, you know, and the sooner you get going, the sooner you'll be back."

"Yes, Momma."

Leah joined their mother and slipped her thin arm around Essie's waist. He wavered, fresh doubt flooding his mind. He couldn't move, his feet suddenly as heavy as cinderblocks.

"Get going," his mother said, holding tight to Leah. "Don't drag it out, now."

He picked up his sack and walked out the door. The man from DuPont would be waiting in front of the post office.

His steps quickened.

In less than a day, he would be in Nashville.

~~~

SELECTMEN LEAVE IN SPLENDID SPIRITS

Selmer, Tenn., July 7 – (Special.) – Seventy-nine McNairy County boys entrained for Fort Thomas, Ky., this morning. All were in fine spirits, and were anxious to do service for their country.
~~~

NASHVILLE BOYS TO ENTRAIN FOR CAMP

Eighteen men from Davidson County exemption boards Nos. 1 and 2 and thirty men from Nashville division boards Nos. 2 and 4 will entrain at 9 o'clock tonight for Fort Thomas, Ky. They will go over the L. & N. Railroad.

—*The Tennessean*, July 8, 1918

An automobile rolled around the corner, veering toward them. Milton jumped back, pulling Anna Mae with him. She laughed, her fingers closing over his arm. "That was close." Blushing, she dropped her hand again.

Wishing he could take her hand in his but knowing he couldn't—not here—he changed the subject. "I love that we're taking a picnic during the week," he said. "The best part is, I feel like a schoolboy playing hooky."

"That's the best part?"

He flashed her a grin. "Well, maybe not the best part." How he wished they were alone, and he could take her in his arms—if she allowed it. So confident, so lacking in pretense, Anna Mae made him forget the rest of the world when he was with her, and he didn't think he ever wanted it to end. "What's in the basket?" he asked now, pointing at the wicker basket swinging from her arm.

"Oh, that's a secret, Mr. Lowenstein. I'm afraid you'll have to wait and find out."

A streetcar sounded from the end of the block, and they exchanged quick glances. "Let's hurry," he said. They rushed up the street and climbed onto the trolley just as the bells rang again, their breaths heavy under the hot sun.

Standing so close, he could smell the sweet scent of her hair and almost taste the tiny beads of perspiration that dotted her forehead. As the streets rolled by and they traveled farther from their home neighborhood, their bodies moved even closer. At Shelby Park, he jumped off, holding out his hand for her. Even after she'd climbed down, he held it longer than he needed to, reluctant to let go.

The pair walked under the sign marking the entrance to the park.

"Are you hungry?" she asked.

"Only a little." They moved deeper into the park. "Do you know where you'd like to sit?"

Her voice was soft when she spoke. "Someplace quiet."

He led her past a lake to a shaded corner of the park, surrounded by trees and bushes. "Is this quiet enough?"

"Oh, yes. It's perfect."

He laid a blanket on the ground. She sat, tucking her skirt under her legs. Her hair fell across the soft line of her jaw, and he reached out and tucked it behind her ear. He heard the sound of her gasp, and his hand faltered. She reached up and took his hand in hers.

"I don't want you to leave," she said.

"I wish I didn't have to."

"How many days will you be gone?"

"I should be back Thursday, Friday at the latest."

"And when do you leave for the army?"

"A week more."

A cloud passed overhead and for a brief time, they were cloaked in cool shadows. Neither spoke, the looming date of his departure there in front of them, unthinkable, unmovable.

"I should have waited to be called up," he said, surprising himself. He'd registered, like the other young men over twenty-one. Some had gone in right away, but most waited for their number. He'd waited, too, for a while, but the stories had made him want to do something more. He still wanted to serve his country, and he would, but he wished now he'd met Anna Mae earlier. They had so little time.

She lifted her chin. "I'd like you to kiss me."

He froze, his pulse racing under his skin. A beautiful woman had uttered the most amazing thing he'd ever heard, and he couldn't move. He was not a prude. He'd known women, some his aunt would not have approved of, and yet, the slightest touch from Anna Mae, even the tilt of her head flooded him with new feelings. "I may be mistaken, but it sounded like you asked me to kiss you."

"You're shocked."

She started to pull away, but he held on to her hand. "If I am, it's happily so." He inched closer. "Very happily."

"Do you think I'm terribly forward?" She raised her face to his, her pink lips parted.

"Never." He kissed her then. She tasted of honey and mint, and he pulled her closer. Anna Mae wrapped her arms around his neck and pressed her body to his, fitting herself against him. He heard the rush of blood through his veins, and he wanted to hold her forever.

"I wish you weren't leaving today," she said when they pulled apart.

The words were out before he could stop them. "I don't have to."

She lifted her head. "What? I thought you said your uncle expected you to get to Memphis?'

"He does." Milton planned even as he talked. "I have appointments the day after tomorrow. He wants me to make calls tomorrow, but I can do them after my appointments. I don't have to take the overnight. I can take the morning train out of Nashville, change lines, and be there in plenty of time."

"You would do that for me?"

"I would do anything for you." He caressed her cheek, his fingers brushing over her soft skin. He buried his face in her hair, inhaling the scent of her. "I want to be with you as much as I can."

She hugged him tight, whispering in his ear, "How will you do it?"

"I'll go by the shop and collect my samples. I'll take my bag like I'm planning to catch the overnight train, but I won't go. I can meet you instead."

"After dark? Where?"

It felt suddenly like a conspiracy, like a grand plan. "I know a place. I can bring some food." He gave her the address.

She lowered her lashes and sucked in her lower lip. Her silence made him wonder. Had he gone too far? Or was the idea so abhorrent? "Unless you don't want to. I would understand. I do understand. What I'm asking is, well, I don't know what I'm asking. I've never done this before. I want to be with you, Anna Mae. I've never felt like this, and . . ." He plucked at a blade of grass, unable to face her. "I'm the one being too forward. I'm sorry."

"No. Don't be sorry." She hesitated. "It's just that all my life, I've done what I was supposed to do. For my parents, my sister, my brother."

He waited.

"What you're suggesting is the opposite—of what I'm supposed to do, I mean."

Milton swallowed his disappointment. "Forget I said anything. It wasn't right to ask that of you." He lifted his head and smiled at her. "How about that lunch?"

"No, Milton. Listen." Her voice was soft. "I've had a good home, a good life, and before, that was enough." She brushed her fingers over her skirt, her face somber, the laughter from earlier gone. "The war has changed so many things, hasn't it? And it's gotten me thinking."

The air left his lungs. Could she mean what he thought? "About what?"

She reached up and touched her fingers to his lips. "That maybe there's more to life than always doing what you're supposed to."

~~~~

The train rolled on toward Hickman, hot air rushing through the windows. George pulled a handkerchief from his pocket, tipped up his hat, and wiped his face. His young cousin, Ben, was scheduled to take his first ride in a few days. He would take the short routes to start. It was easier to learn the ropes that way. Since accepting the position, Ben seemed a different man.

"I haven't been up north or out west before," he'd said, his fingers drumming on the old kitchen table.

"Well, you won't be going far at first," George reminded him.
~~~~

"I know, but I've put in for working overnights as soon as I'm ready. I'm going to go to as many places as I can."

George smiled at that. He knew many a porter who'd once been restless, eager to travel around the country. That was usually before the reality of the long hours and the weeks away from home set in. But Ben was young, and maybe it would be different for him. "You do that, Ben."

"George?"

The porter's mind snapped back to the present. "What can I do for you, sir?"

"I'm parched. I need something to drink now, George."

"Yes, sir." He delivered the water even as the man leaned toward the passenger in the seat next to him. "These porters aren't what they used to be, are they?"

George backed away. He knew that at the end of the trip, there would be no nickel from the small man, no tip at all. He thought he should be upset, but he wasn't. Instead, he found himself wondering if he might bring Ben to the next backroom meeting of the porters. All the men shared a longing for better conditions, better hours, better pay. But longing wasn't getting.

He caught sight of Shorty coming toward him from the opposite end of the car. Even as he put on his smile, he made up his mind. He would talk to Ben tomorrow, when the train got back from Hickman. He'd show him they were on the same side. The decision, now made, lightened his heart and his mood, and his smile, automatic a moment earlier, widened with satisfaction. Tomorrow would be a new day. A better day.

~~~~

LUKE MCLUKE SAYS.

There are 98,000,000 ways of getting into trouble. But talking too much seems to be the favorite way.

—*The Tennessean,* July 8, 1918
~~~~

~~~~

Grand Central Station loomed over the road, a hulking structure taking up an entire block. John stutter-stepped forward and pushed his hat back on his head. His mouth hung open. Wide concrete columns at the base of the building supported several stories that rose into the sky. The air behind the station was thick with smoke.

"Let's go, boy," the minder said, tapping him on the shoulder. "No time to be wasting if you want to make that train."

The minder from DuPont was called Mr. Winfield. He'd brought John and two more men to Memphis. The men, brothers, were from Olive Branch. Although they seemed pleasant enough, they kept to themselves, leaving John to his own thoughts.

Automobiles zipped past as they waited. Crowds of people swarmed the street, talking and laughing. Trolleys stopped on the corner. There was no open space to be seen, no quiet. John wondered if this was how Nashville would be.

Mr. Winfield raised a hand, and they followed him across the street. Outside the station, they waited for a group of white folks to enter first, then followed them to the interior of the station. Inside, he saw long wooden benches and a ceiling that stretched up high over his head. The late afternoon light bathed the main concourse in yellow and white. There was a large clock on one wall. Underneath, he saw a list of cities—destinations, he learned. Next to Nashville was the time of departure. His pulse quickened. It wouldn't be long now.

The small group continued on through the station. Mr. Winfield led them down to a platform where he saw tracks and men in overalls. They passed white ladies with large trunks and hatboxes. John kept moving.

"Our cars will be up here," Mr. Winfield said. He took them around a large group of white men, some in army uniforms. Soon, they came to the far end of the platform.

A man near John whistled. "Must be fifty, sixty men here."
~~~~

Mr. Winfield raised his hand in the air again. "Everyone here for Du-Pont, gather around." The minder was soon surrounded. "Got a few rules." The uncompromising tone of his voice made John stand up taller. "From here on out, everything you do is representing DuPont. Anyone sees you, they're gonna know you're a DuPont man, that you're working at DuPont to support your country and the war effort. There will be no slacking. No cussing. No drinking. No gambling." He scrutinized each and every man around him. "More than that, you are representing your people. You're doing the right thing for your country."

Next to John, an older man muttered under his breath.

Mr. Winfield put a hand to his ear. "What's that? Somebody say something?"

The man shuffled his feet but kept his mouth shut. The next minute passed in silence, and Mr. Winfield let it go. "Okay, men. This is how it's going to go. We'll be here in this second car. Mr. Leonard and his group will be in the first car. I will hand each of you a ticket that you will give to the conductor when he comes around. After he takes the tickets, I will give you the rest of the rules and . . ."

A loud noise drowned out the rest of his words. John whirled around to see an incoming train, thick gray smoke billowing from its chimney. The steel wheels squealed, and the locomotive slowed to a chug. The group shrank back from the edge of the platform as the train rolled to a stop.

Mr. Winfield herded the men away from the cars. The doors slid open. John watched all the activity with interest and awe. Around him, the circle of DuPont men grew, and he guessed the crowd had swelled to a hundred—maybe more—and he wondered if there would be room for all of them.

There was a flash of movement, and John caught sight of a familiar grin. "Matt?" He pushed his way through the crowd. "Matt?" he said, reaching out with his hand. His old friend whirled around and laughed out loud.

"You made it."

John had almost forgotten his promise to Matt. "I guess I did, but what are you doing here?"

Matt shrugged. “Taking a detour on my way to Chicago. I started thinking about how this is a sure job and sure pay, and I don’t know what will happen when I get up north. Seemed like the smart thing to do. But I’m still a Chicago man. I’ll be there soon enough.” He punched John in the shoulder. “You made it, John,” he said again. “You promised you would, and here you are.”

John’s smile dipped. “Did you hear about Robert?”

Matt’s forehead creased. “Yeah. My momma was heading over to see Ruth and Elijah when I was leaving. I wanted to go, but I was afraid if I stayed another day, they wouldn’t let me leave.” He shook his head. “I can’t believe you’re here. We’re doing it, John. We’re getting out.”

The DuPont man stepped forward again. “Back to your groups, men.”

Matt started to move.

“Wait.” John grabbed his arm, and without thinking, pulled his old friend into a tight embrace. The two men stood like that, arms around each other, for no more than a second or two, breaking apart as quickly as they’d come together. John flushed, unsure why he’d done it.

Matt, always more sure than John, didn’t seem to wonder at all. “Losing Robert is a terrible thing. For you and Sabina and everyone. I really am sorry.”

John only nodded, eyes stinging, the losses of the last few days stealing his speech.

Matt’s mouth turned up in a smile. “It’ll be you and me in Nashville, John. Like old times. You’ll see.” He spun around with a wave of his hand and was soon swallowed up in the crowd.

Staring after his friend, dozens of men swarming around him, John felt suddenly alone. He stared at the spot where Matt had been, cold inside.

Mr. Winfield’s voice behind him and a hard tap on his shoulder brought him back to the present. “Get back with your group.” After being sure the men were all in their place, the minder raised his voice. “As I was saying, you will give your ticket to the conductor when he asks for it. After he’s gone, we will gather again, and I will tell you what you can expect upon your arrival in Nashville.” He raised his finger, pointing it at each man in turn. “Until then, remember, you are representing DuPont, a great and patriotic company." He gestured up at the clock. "We'll be boarding soon, so pay attention." Finished with his speech, Mr. Winfield walked away to shake hands with the man leading the other group.

John watched the railroad men as they hustled to load luggage and mail into the two cars behind the tender car. He saw more men, women, and children come down the platform and fan out in front of the rear cars. He angled his head for a better view. The cars at the back of the train were shiny silver, not wooden like the cars in the front. More men in uniforms waited there, hovering near the women and children.

"Where you from?" asked a man standing nearby. Shorter than John by a foot, he was as wide as he was tall. His neck was the size of a small tree, and his muscles bulged under his shirt.

"Hernando," John said.

"Can't say I know it."

"Mississippi."

"I'm from Arkansas myself. There's five of us from around my place. You alone?"

John thought about Matt and the brothers from Olive Branch, but he didn't see them anywhere. "I have a friend in the other car."

The muscled man stuck out his hand, pumped hard. "Armstead is my name, but everyone calls me Ames." When he smiled, he flashed large white teeth.

"I'm John." He took his hand back, relieved he could still feel it.

From down the platform, the conductor called out, "All Aboard."

The low hum on the platform rose to a high-pitched buzz as everyone shuffled forward.

Ames clapped him on the shoulder, and John nearly stumbled. "See you on board," the man said and melted back into the crowd.

Mr. Winfield appeared before the group again, directing them into the second car, reminding them to do so in an orderly fashion.

"That's it," Mr. Winfield said. "Keep moving."

John stepped into the crowded car. There were a handful of seats, but only a few could be called usable. Following the men in front of him, John worked his way to the middle of the car, edging closer to the windows. Finding an empty spot, he pressed his back against the wooden wall. Around him, men huddled, clutching their paper tickets. John tapped his fingers against the wood. This was it. Matt was right. He'd made it.

~~~~

OUR HONOR ROLL

Army.

Washington, July 7—The army casualty list today contained 117 names, divided as follows:

Killed in action, 25; died of wounds, 17; died of disease, 9; died of airplane accident, 2; died of accidents and other causes, 3; severely wounded, 48; missing in action, 13.

—*The Tennessean*, July 8, 1918

~~~~

David left the train shed shortly before dusk, his workday finished. Walking home, he wondered if his own father had ever ridden trains and taken in the beauty of the countryside from a window, if he'd ever relished the speed and power of a locomotive. He hoped so, although he would never know. His father had been gone many years now, as had his mother. There'd been a letter from his sister when they'd passed, but it had come too late for David. The break from the family had been so long ago, he couldn't remember his life back then.

Surely, there were nieces and nephews he'd never met. A brother-in-law. Maybe they'd all stayed to live and work at his father's cotton farm. Maybe the farm was gone, like the family he once knew. Anna Mae had asked him about it once, but he'd only told her he had no family left. They were gone or dead. He'd spoken the truth as he knew it.

He slowed at the corner, the past weighing on his mind. He'd never liked farming or cotton much. Farmers were always waiting. Waiting for seeds to grow, waiting for rain, waiting for the harvest. He supposed now that he might have been an impetuous sort. Rebellious even. But never more so than when he'd left to join the Union Army. His mother had cried, unable to speak. His father, though, had plenty to say:

"I forbid it. We are Southerners, David. You are a Southerner, and you will fight as such." He pounded his fist against the table.

David's legs almost gave out on him, and it took all his strength not to sink to the floor.

"No son of mine will wear the uniform of those traitors. Make no mistake. The Union Army is a traitor to all that we stand for, to all that we have built and achieved." The veins of his neck bulged, doubling in size. "Do you understand me?"

David's mouth tasted of the cotton he despised, and his skin grew hot and prickly.

"I asked you a question."

He wanted to retch, but he held his ground. "Not all Southerners are joining the Confederate Army, Father."

"What did you say?" His father, voice gritty and coarse as sandpaper, stepped so near that David felt his breath on his cheek.

David struggled to keep his voice even. "Not everyone is joining the Confederate Army."

"Name one."

"Bobby Sadler."

"That yellow-bellied good-for-nothing? Is that what you want to be known as, David? As a worthless, useless man like Bobby Sadler?"

David flinched. He'd expected his father's anger, even his derision, but not the vitriol. David didn't really know Billy or what his reasons for running away were. David had his own reasons. "No, sir," he said, willing it to end.

His father relaxed. "It's settled, then. When you're of age, you'll fight for the Confederacy." He stomped off, satisfied.

David packed during the night and slipped out of the house. He was sixteen. He hadn't seen Tuscaloosa or the farm since. He tried writing his mother, but after his letters were returned unopened, he stopped.

Now there was another war, and his only son had gone to make his own way. As he walked home, he whispered a prayer that this time would be different.

Inside his Aberdeen Flats apartment, he set his railroader's box on the bench. Katie Belle sat in a chair near the window, her sewing in her lap.

"Hello, Father."

"Hello." Katie Belle was alone in the parlor, the apartment quiet. "Where's your mother?"

"Oh, she and Anna Mae are still over at the Red Cross. I expect them to be back before dark." She started to rise. "Mother made you a plate. I can get it for you if you're hungry."

He waved the idea away. He sat down across from her and stoked his pipe. "Maybe in a bit. I'd rather sit here with you awhile first." Her pale skin glowed under the light of the lamp. "Why aren't you at the Red Cross with your mother and sister?"

"I didn't want you to come home to an empty house, of course."

"How did I get so lucky?"

"We're the lucky ones, Father."

His throat swelled and he concentrated on his pipe. What was wrong with him? It wasn't in his nature to be so emotional, so easily stirred. The silence stretched out. Pipe lit, he watched Katie Belle's fingers move the needle over the fabric. "What are you working on?"

"Oh, I'm letting out the hem on these pants for John George. Mother is sure he'll be inches taller when he gets home."

"That's so like your mother," he said. Although Mary worried, he knew her to have a hopeful heart. She spent her days at the Red Cross and her evenings planning for John George's homecoming, thus keeping her mind from the same darkness that came to him in the night. He was grateful for that at least.

David sucked on his pipe. A trail of smoke floated upward, and he pinched the flesh between his brows. Between the headaches and the nightmares, he'd been on edge, as if there was something just out of his grasp, something tapping at his brain he couldn't see or understand. Perhaps he was overtired.

Katie Belle smoothed her hair, tucking it behind her ear as she worked. Although not as tall as Anna Mae, the sisters shared the same profile, the same Roman nose and pointed chin. But where Anna Mae was decisive and strong-willed, Katie Belle was softer, more pliable.

"Have you noticed anything unusual about Anna Mae of late?" asked David.

The needle faltered, and Katie Belle cried out when it stuck her finger.

"Are you hurt?"

"Not really." Finger in her mouth, she assured him she was fine. "So clumsy of me. It did smart a bit though." She held up the finger. "See? It's already stopped bleeding." Katie Belle pressed the finger into a rag. "Was it a good day today, Father?"

Thoughts of Anna Mae forgotten, he told her it was. They'd been able to keep the trains on time after the Number One arrived early. It didn't happen often.

"When is your friend retiring?" Katie Belle asked.

"Bill Lloyd?"

"Yes, that's the one."

David inhaled the smoke from his pipe. A fellow engineer, Bill often drove the overnight train from Memphis, the Number One. "Tomorrow will be his last train."

"And he's younger than you?"

"I suppose he is." Bill was only in his early sixties, but he'd been talking about quitting since early in the year. No one quite believed he would do it, but according to Bill, there was no changing his mind. "He's been doing it a long time."

"So have you."

"That I have." Tendrils of smoke wafted over them.

She leaned her head to one side. "Father, do you ever think about stopping?"

"What? Being an engineer?"

"Yes."

"No, I don't. I was born to drive a train."

"But . . ." She bit her lip.

"But I'm old? Older than Bill Lloyd?"

Katie Belle blushed. "I'm sorry, Father. It's just that you work so hard."

"No harder than the next man." He could see by the worry lines etched into the skin around her eyes that she wasn't satisfied.

"You could be home more. With us."

"That would be nice," he said, and he thought it might. What would happen if he decided not to drive the train to Hickman in the morning? If he up and retired, like Bill Lloyd? For a brief moment, he allowed himself to entertain the idea. More days with Mary and the girls. But just as quickly, he knew it was impossible. The railroad was short of engineers as it was, and the family relied on his railroad pay. He might not be a young man anymore, but he had a young man's responsibilities. A family. Children who depended on him. He said none of that.

"I love the railroad. I love being an engineer. I really can't imagine anything else I'd rather be doing." He reached out and took her hand in his. "I hope to be doing it until the day I die."

~~~~

The conductor came and went, taking their tickets as quickly as he could. Mr. Winfield kept a sharp eye on the process until the last man had finished, and the conductor left the coach. He pulled them into a tight circle.

"It's a long ride, men, and since it's a long ride, I aim to remind you that you're representing DuPont every minute you are on this train and every minute you aren't." He spoke loudly to be heard over the rumbling of the train. "Like I said before, there will be no drinking and no gambling.
~~~~

There will be no cursing and no troublemaking—of any kind. Have I made myself clear?"

John caught sight of Ames, the stocky man he'd met before they'd boarded. Ames stood in the front of the circle, on the other side of Mr. Winfield, his muscled arms folded across his chest.

"All shades will be pulled upon dark. I recommend getting some sleep. We will not be waiting for anyone lagging behind." He pointed a finger at the group. "I'll be watching the lot of you. Don't forget that." He pulled his jacket tighter around his waist before making his way to the back of the car.

Around John, the men talked quietly among themselves, each eventually making their way back to whatever small space they'd claimed. Spotting Ames coming toward him, John waited, glad to see his new friend.

The two shook hands. "How are you doing, young John?"

"Okay, I guess." In truth, his stomach had an unsettled, queasy feeling, but he couldn't be sure if that was only the motion of the train or something else.

"You look a little white. You the sensitive sort, John?"

John felt the blush creep up from his neck to his cheeks. More than once, he'd heard House say the same about him.

"How is that boy ever going to be a farmer if he can't stomach a little blood now and then?" The head of a fat chicken had fallen to the ground, the body in House's hand. His momma had defended him.

"Abel, you have the boy feed those chickens every day. Surely, it's not unusual for him to get attached. It's only him and Leah."

And when he'd grown older. "That boy needs to spend more time with Robert if you ask me," House had said one night. "Would toughen him up a bit. You spending all that time worrying about his book learnin' ain't going to make him grow more corn or cotton, Essie. You need to stop babying him."

John's stomach swirled. Was it the train or the memories?

Ames laughed. "Don't worry about it, young John. I been called worse."

John's mouth dropped open in surprise.

Ames spread his hands wide. "I know you wouldn't think it to look at me, but well, my wife says it's a good thing when a man has a soft spot, and if she says it, then it must be true." He leaned in closer, the lines around his eyes crinkling. "Don't pay no mind to that Mr. Winfield. Nobody's here to cause any trouble. Lord knows I didn't leave home so I could have a run-in with a man like that."

"Why did you come?" The question was out before John could stop it. He flushed again. "Sorry. It's none of my business."

Ames laughed again. "Don't be sorry, son. It's a good question. I'm here for the same reason as my friends over there. We need the pay. Like I said, I got a wife at home, and Lord willing, someday there'll be a little Ames running around." He grinned. "Don't hurt that we get to be patriotic to boot."

The queasy feeling in John's stomach quieted. "That's true, I guess."

"You got a wife at home?"

"No."

"But there's a lady. I can tell." The older man chuckled. "Ain't no better reason to be here, son." He jerked a thumb toward his friends. "Well, gotta be getting back. You can join us if you like." He gestured toward a group of men in the middle of the car. They'd staked out a spot near a block of broken seats.

"Thanks," John said, "but I'm gonna stay here."

The man lifted a beefy shoulder. "Suit yourself. I'm there if you need me."

John watched his new friend make his way back through the mass of people crammed into the car. He thought about the group that had assembled around Mr. Winfield. There had to be sixty or seventy men he'd given tickets. The other DuPont boss had a smaller group, Matt's group. They had boarded the first car behind the baggage. The sickly feeling returned. There were so many men. Would there be enough jobs for all of them?

He pressed his nose to the window, peering through the grimy glass. The world outside the train whizzed by, the fields and trees a blur of green and brown. They'd stopped once since they'd left Memphis, and while no one got off, several more folks had climbed into the already crowded car. Most of the windows were stuck closed. The few that did open barely moved the stifling air.

The train rumbled on.

"You ever been on a train before?" John looked to his left. A man was squeezed between the windows. He was older than John, wisps of gray already peppering the hair at his temples.

"Nope," he answered.

"Me neither," the man said. "I've never even been outside Memphis before. This is my first time."

Tired, John was tempted to nod politely and move away, but he thought better of it. It was going to be a long night, and it wouldn't hurt for him to get to know some of the others before they got to Nashville.

"John Lang. From Hernando, Mississippi."

The man shifted to look at him. "Lem Hudson."

"What made you decide to go to Nashville for DuPont?"

"I didn't. My wife did." Lem half smiled. "Carpentry work has been slow, so when they came around looking for men, she decided I could do that. 'It's only temporary,' she said."

John let his gaze wander over the other men crowded into the car. "Probably the same for most everyone."

"Yeah. Most likely."

They lapsed into silence. Outside, the light faded to gray, and the sun sank lower in the sky. A band of orange stretched over the horizon.

"Gonna be dark soon," Lem said.

John's stomach grumbled and he realized he'd forgotten to eat. He reached for his knapsack and withdrew the cold meat and bread his mother had packed. He offered a bit to Lem.

"Thanks. Marlee—that's my wife—she gave me food."

Watching the others in the car, he ate slowly, taking his time. Young men and old men filled the cabin, but there were others. A handful of women. Even a few children. His attention was drawn to the back of the car. A porter stood near the door that connected the cars. A half dozen white men had gathered there, smoking. He watched as another group knelt on the floor in a circle.

Lem leaned over. "They're playing craps." John frowned. "It's a game," Lem told him. "Gambling."

Curious, John thought he might watch, but the circle was quickly swallowed up by the men standing around them. A bellow went up from the group, and Mr. Winfield made his way over.

"There's another game over there," Lem said, and pointed to a front corner of the car. "Behind those men. So far, seems quiet though."

John stood up on his toes, craning his neck. There were several men crouched over the floor. He scanned the group for Ames but didn't see him. Relieved, he glanced back at the DuPont minder, but he seemed more interested in the white men's game.

"Marlee won't let me gamble," Lem said. "Nor drink. Not since I cracked my head open last year after a bit of a night." He reached up and parted his hair to show John the scar. "She's right though. Always is."

Both men quieted after that. John finished the cold meat and wrapped the rest of his bread in paper. He drank one long swallow of water from his jug and wiped his mouth with the back of his hand. Darkness settled over the coach. The few working lights in the cabin cast shadows across the floor.

The porter came around, instructing them to pull the shades. "It will be morning when we get to Nashville. Get some sleep," he said. He had a kind voice and a pleasant way about him, and John admired the buttons of his uniform, shining like gold coins against the dark fabric.

Around him, men got tired of standing and dropped to the floor. John sank to his knees and leaned back against the wood of the wall. The train sped over the tracks, the clacking noise loud in his ears. The water in his belly sloshed. When his shaky stomach settled, he wrapped his arms around his legs and laid his head against the wall. Night fell over the train.

~~~~

Clyde lingered over his food, pushing his plate away when Carl plopped down in the empty seat, knocking against the table.
~~~~

"How ya doin', Brother?" Carl asked, his voice thick with liquor.

"Take off your hat," Clyde hissed. "People are looking. And keep your voice down."

"Sure, sure." Carl did as he was told. He picked at the food on Clyde's plate, stuffing bites in his mouth, then licked his fingers, one by one. "I didn't know I was so hungry."

Clyde stood, pulling Carl up by the shirt. "Let's go." The last thing he needed was a reason for people to remember them.

"Hey," his brother said, stumbling. "I'm eating."

"We'll get something sent up to the room." He steered Carl toward the stairs.

Once in the room, Carl fell onto the bed and kicked off his boots. "Jus' gonna lie down for a bit."

It was all Clyde could do to hold his temper in check. In a few short hours, they would meet with the boys. How could he expect the men to be ready, to be alert, when even his own brother couldn't do the same? He lit a thick cigar and crossed the room to the window. The streetlamps glowed over the quiet street. The anger seeped from him with the smoke. Rest would do them both some good.

A few hours later, Clyde rose and washed his face in the darkness. Crossing the room, he studied the horizon. In the distance, he could just make out the silhouette of Union Station's clock tower. Soon, the sun would rise over the city, and the marble-and-stone turrets would shimmer in the morning light. Passengers would board the morning train, holding their tickets, not knowing what was to come. The money would be loaded into the mail car and locked in the safe. Clyde could see all of it, and the knot in his belly hardened. It was time.

A moment later, he slid both arms under his brother, lifting and rolling him off the bed. Carl's body hit the floor with a thud.

"Hey, what'd you do that for?"

Clyde handed him a washcloth and a fresh shirt. "Clean yourself up. We leave in a half hour." The men were expecting them. It was time.

PART 6

TWO AND ONE

CHAPTER SEVENTEEN

Summer 1988

GINNY PUSHED OPEN the front door of her house and flicked on the light. She was halfway down the hall before she noticed the suitcase. When Shawn stepped out of the kitchen, a dish towel over his arm, the mail she carried clattered to the floor.

His smile started on the left side of his face, the way it always did, then spread to the right, until his whole face erupted into a broad, goofy grin. She remembered that once upon a time, the sight of it had made her weak. Now it made her sad.

Shawn's smile faltered, and he raised his palms. "Surprise."

~~~~

"I like what you've done with the place. It looks good."

She tried to look at the living room through his eyes. He was right. Cleared of boxes, the sofa and chairs that flanked the fireplace were welcoming and the new rug cozy. With the old drapes gone, soft light from the big window warmed the space. "Thank you."
~~~~

They settled on opposite sides of the room, eyeing each other from their respective corners. She watched him rub his hands back and forth over his legs, the motion dizzying. How many times had she seen him do that before? She knew what it meant. He was nervous, or maybe uncomfortable, or afraid. Dread rose up from her toes, creeping up her body until she had to grip the arms of the chair to keep from shaking. He'd made his decision, then. She'd known this was coming, but it didn't lessen the hurt. In spite of everything.

"I know why you're here," she said finally, breaking the silence. "You don't have to say anything. I won't fight you."

For a moment, he only stared at her. "I'm not sure what you think, Ginny, but—"

Her anger flared, eclipsing her earlier grief. "What I think is that you've come here to tell me we can't do this anymore, that *you* can't do this anymore." Somehow, she kept her voice steady and her expression neutral—or as neutral as she could. "I appreciate you trying to do the right thing before by staying, but I'll be okay." She swallowed hard. "I am okay."

He stared at her, jaw flexing. "What the hell are you talking about?"

How dare he be angry at her? She was trying to make this easy for him. "Look. We both know if I weren't pregnant, you'd have left already. I'm not stupid. It's why you didn't fight me when I said I could do this move on my own. We've been going through the motions since I"—she paused—"since I saw you at the dance together. I wanted to believe it wasn't true. I wanted to believe the things you said. Maybe we both did. I was afraid before, about being alone. But I'm not anymore. I'm making friends. My parents are coming to stay with me. I'll be fine." She pushed herself up from the sofa. "I can't believe I'm saying this, Shawn, but I want you to go. There's a hotel about a mile away. You can stay there. It will be easier on both of us that way."

"No, Gin." He reached for her, but she backed away, her hands raised in the air.

"I mean it, Shawn. Don't make this harder."

"I'm not leaving." He came toward her. She tried to sidestep him, but he caught her arm. "Ginny. I love you."

She jerked her arm from his grasp. "I'm trying my best here, Shawn." Tears threatened again. "Why are you doing this?"

He laid his hand on her shoulder and spun her around. "Ginny, look at me. Please." She shrugged off his hand, but stayed, poised to spring away. "I'm not leaving you for Lila. I never was. I don't know why you think that."

Ginny blinked. "Then why are you here?"

"Because I can't stand being apart from you anymore. And it's not because of the baby. It's because I almost made the worst mistake of my life. That's what I've been trying to tell you for weeks. It's true that Lila and I, well, there was something. It started when I went over to fix that leak under her sink, remember? After that, she asked me to come over and fix something else, and then the next thing I knew, she was making me dinner. I'm ashamed to say, I liked the attention. But I ended it before it ever really started. I never slept with Lila, not one time. She didn't take it well. Told me I'd led her on, and maybe she was right." He took her hands in his. "I wish like hell I could take it all back. It's my fault. I shouldn't have let it go that far. But it's you I can't lose, Gin. It's you I love."

She didn't know what to say. Everything was a jumble in her mind. Lila's words and Jed's accusations and Shawn's confessions. She'd spent weeks building up the strength to let Shawn go, and now she didn't know what to think or believe.

"Can you ever forgive me?"

She pulled her hands from his, trying not to see the way his face fell. "I—I don't know." She walked past him to the window. The glow from the streetlight on the corner brightened and dimmed and brightened again. A man walked his dog along the sidewalk, and a car door slammed in the distance. She touched the glass with her fingers. Life wouldn't stop whether she forgave him or not. She faced him again. "How did we get here?"

"I wish I knew, Gin."

She heard sorrow in his voice, but it wasn't an answer. She lifted her face, her chin jutting forward. "You were never home."

"You're right. I wanted a promotion, bigger clients, all of it—even if it meant being gone for weeks at a time, but I shouldn't have put my career ahead of you, of us. I see that now," he said.

How long had she waited to hear those words? But were they only that? Words? "That doesn't explain Lila."

"No. I missed you. I should have told you instead of . . ." He stopped short of rehashing the details, but his next words didn't help. "Ginny, the thing is, on the days when I was home, we barely saw each other. That was hard for me."

"What?" Her nostrils flared. "You're blaming me?" It wasn't her fault that when he flew in, she was likely to be at a car wash for the chess club, sponsoring the yearbook kids, or at the library tutoring. She had responsibilities. She'd missed him, too, but she hadn't sought to soothe her ego in another man's arms.

"No, that's not what I'm saying." Again, his voice cracked, and he drew himself up. "What I meant is that I missed us and didn't know how to handle it. I shouldn't have acted the way I did. I shouldn't have expected you to drop everything for me. It wasn't fair." He looked at her, eyes pleading. "I wish we'd talked more. It's my fault. I should have said something, tried harder."

It was true they hadn't talked enough. They'd become ships passing in the night. She'd chalked it up to life, to a phase. She hadn't seen the cracks, the fissure growing wider in the months leading up to Lila. But Lila wasn't to blame for the choices her husband had made. Maybe if they had talked, really talked, things might have been different.

"When did you end things with Lila?"

"Right before you saw us at the dance." Ginny frowned. "I know you don't believe me, but it's true. That night, chaperoning, I was trying to be nice, nothing else. She said Jed had been harassing her, and she was scared."

Ginny shook her head. "Jed wasn't harassing her."

Twin lines popped up between his brows. "He was, Gin. I mean, we both liked Jed, but she told me he was saying horrible things about her when she wouldn't take him back. She had me put in a new lock and alarm system."

"I talked to Jed last night."

"What?"

"He went to the police because she was stalking him. He had to move, change his phone number. She never broke up with him, Shawn. It was the other way around."

Shawn fell back onto the sofa. "Wow. I had no idea. It makes sense though. She was doing the same thing to me. Calling me all the time. She even showed up at the airport once because I made the mistake of telling her when my flight got in."

Ginny didn't know when she would stop being surprised by the lengths Lila had been willing to go to in order to win Shawn, but she said nothing now.

"For once, I was glad I was gone so much. I wanted things to end. I needed them to."

"That's not what Lila said."

"What Lila said?" He raked his hand through his hair. "I have a feeling this is why you thought I was leaving you, so let's hear it."

Ginny didn't hold back. She told him about the confrontation in the teachers' lounge, about the letter to Jed's mother, about the phone calls that didn't stop until she'd moved to Nashville. The more she talked, the paler he got, his pink skin bleached of color.

"My God, Ginny. I had no idea."

The truth hit her then. "She played us both."

His lips parted but no sound came out.

"And it almost worked."

Anna Mae visibly shuddered with relief when Ginny dashed through her door.

"I'm sorry I'm late."

"No apologies," she said warmly. "I was worried though."

"Shawn's here."

"Ah. Well, that was a surprise, wasn't it?"

"He wanted to talk, to clear the air." Anna Mae's gaze strayed to the ring encircling Ginny's third finger, but Ginny shook her head. "I don't know what's going to happen. We're figuring it out."

"And Lila?" The lines around her eyes pinched when she said the other woman's name. "She's out of the picture, is she?"

"Yes."

Anna Mae's expression cleared. "Well, your husband may be stupid, but this means he isn't a complete dummy. There's hope for him yet."

Ginny's laughter rang out in the quiet room. Anna Mae chuckled along with her. When she caught her breath, Ginny said, "We're going to take it slow and see."

"Well, if taking it slow makes you smile and laugh like this, keep doing it, I say."

"Please, Anna Mae," she said in a warning voice. "You make me sound like a teenager who just got a note from a boy she likes. One night can't fix everything."

"True, but it can be the first step. Besides, we're all teenagers in our hearts, dear. Love is forever young, eternal for those fortunate enough to know it. In the end, it's only our bodies that betray us." A shadow fell over her face then, her expression no longer teasing. "Well, this seems as good a time as any to get back to my story. We're nearing the end now."

Ginny's smile slipped. She didn't want the story to end, and she didn't like the way Anna Mae sounded when she said it.

"I hope you won't be too disappointed when you hear the rest." Anna Mae's gaze shifted to the window, to the land rolling away toward the city. "Not all stories turn out the way we want them to, do they?"

Ginny's pulse quickened, and fear snaked through her belly. There was the letter she'd found, the one Anna Mae had written but never sent. *So much loss here and in the world. I fear it got to be too much for me. If I ever needed another reason for the decision I made, that is surely a good one.* She wanted desperately to ask Anna Mae if something had happened with Milton, but the old woman made sure she didn't get the chance, diving back into her story.

"As you may recall, John was on his way to Nashville. He fell asleep along with the others in the car. I imagine it was quiet enough save for some snoring and the wheels rolling over the tracks." Anna Mae's voice trembled with emotion as she traveled back in time. "Not everyone was asleep though. Not in Nashville."

CHAPTER EIGHTEEN

Tuesday, July 9, 1918
Before Dawn

DRAFTEES LEAVE FOR FORT THOMAS, KY.

Quite a large crowd was down at the Union Station, and it gave the boys quite a send off. Many sweethearts, wives and mothers were there, all waiting to see the train leave, taking their loved ones from them. But they stood it bravely, no crying, but an earnest effort to smile and make it appear that the boys were going on a picnic instead of a fight for freedom. When the whistle blew announcing the train's eagerness to be off, one and all grabbed his or her own in one last fond embrace. Then the boys were off, off on their errand of mercy and right.

Many of the draftees were from Murfreesboro and other towns on the line.

—*The Tennessean*, July 9, 1918

~~~~

David woke with a start, his breathing ragged and his chest covered with sweat.
~~~~

"Did you have the nightmare again?" Heavy with sleep, Mary's voice was more garbled than usual.

David rolled toward her, and she cradled his head in her hands. Knowing she wouldn't be able to read his lips in the darkness, he nodded slowly. She pulled him closer, stroking his back with gentle hands. He didn't move, grateful for the warmth of her embrace. Her lips touched his forehead, and he exhaled, stomach unclenching. He didn't know how long they stayed like that, their bodies entwined, their chests rising and falling. When he woke again, Mary had moved away, her back to him. He touched the space where she'd been, the bedsheet still warm. Later, when they were alone—perhaps after dinner—she would ask him about the nightmare. He would tell her the same as he had the other times, leaving out the worst of it. And he would never tell her about this one. He winced at the memory.

The heavens had opened, rumbling, louder and louder. He ran, searching every inch of ground. Cornstalks shot up from the earth, surrounding him. He whacked at the stalks with his arms until he could lift them no more, and on he searched, crawling through mud and death. He wouldn't give up. He couldn't. And then it happened. He found John George, his only son.

He shuddered again and clutched the sheet to his chin. He squeezed his eyes shut tight, banishing the horrible images from his mind. He would speak of this nightmare to no one. Not to Mary. Not to the girls. Not to anyone.

~~~

Anna Mae moved her head, burying it in the crook of Milton's shoulder. He didn't dare move. Just the flutter of her lashes over his skin or the slightest touch of her hand was magical. Even the sky seemed in on it. Through the window, the moon glowed silver, and the stars, shining bright, cast a soft light over the tiny room. He wished he could make it last forever.
~~~

Her lips moved against his skin, and he shivered. "What are you thinking?" she asked.

"I'm thinking how I don't want this night to end."

"Me neither." She lay on her side, propped up on one elbow. "There can be other nights, if you want there to be."

He sat up and reached for her. "You know I do." The air stirred, caressing his bare skin. How could he ask her for anything when he was leaving? "But I have to be on that train in the morning."

"You'll be back Thursday?"

"Friday at the latest."

"Three days."

"I'll hurry. I promise."

He saw her nod, look away. They lay down again, shoulder to shoulder, not touching. When she spoke again, her voice was tinged with resignation. "How much time do we have after you get back?"

She'd asked before, but he told her the date again. She didn't comment, curling up against him instead. He listened to the sound of her breathing until it slowed, grew steady with sleep. He rested his head against the pillow, marveling at her presence and thinking of the time they'd already missed. How many dances had he been forced to attend? How many daughters had he been introduced to when she'd been there all the time? Only a few blocks from his house. His Anna Mae.

"Is there someone you've been waiting for? Someone already in the war?" he'd asked her.

"No one."

He found it hard to believe and said so.

"Before the war, there were a few," she admitted, "but not so very many. I told you about my last suitor. He said I was too much for any man to be forced to handle. I said I didn't care to be handled at all, thank you very much. He didn't come back after that." She sighed. "My father worries that I won't ever marry, but I told him I'd rather be alone than betrothed to a man I don't love."

"So, it's not marriage you're opposed to, then?"

"Of course not. Only a loveless one. A lifetime is a long time to spend with someone you don't like all that much."

He looked back at her. "You're absolutely right, Miss Kennedy."

"You don't find me outspoken or full of new-fangled ideas?"

"I like new-fangled ideas."

She smiled. "Tell me more about your life, Milton, about your parents." And he did. They talked and talked and talked, opening up their hearts a little more with each passing hour.

Now, his own smile widened at the memory. He sighed. He would have to wake her soon. His bag and his samples were packed. He would go to Memphis to show hats and dresses and take orders, but his heart wouldn't be in it. His heart would be here, in Nashville.

He brushed her soft hair with the tips of his fingers, leaned over, and touched his lips to hers. Her body arched and one arm came up over his shoulder. The warmth of her skin and her mouth set his pulse racing. She stirred, opening herself to him again. After, he traced the sharp line of her hips, the curve of her breasts. Fear made him pull away.

"What's wrong?" Anna Mae asked.

"Do you hate me?"

He didn't know what he expected, but it wasn't the relief he saw reflected back at him. "Of course not. How could you ask me that?"

"I've done everything backwards. This isn't the way it's supposed to go."

She watched him, her forehead creasing again.

"I should have insisted on meeting your father. I should have brought your mother flowers. I shouldn't have cared what my aunt and uncle think. I should have—"

She put a finger to his lips. "Shhh. It wasn't only you." The quietness of her words stopped him short. "We've known each other only a short time, Milton, but it feels like I've always known you. Surely, you know there is not one thing I would change about these last hours."

"Me neither," he said, surprised to realize how much he meant it. "I should have come to the apartment."

She shook her head. "My father is a good man, but I don't know that he wants to meet you or even know about you. It shames me to say this, but I don't know if he can get past the fact that you're . . ." Her voice trailed away. She couldn't look at him.

He was quick to fill the silence. "A hat salesman? We're an unsavory lot, you know." He waited. Was that a smile? After a minute, he admitted, "My aunt and uncle are no better."

Her voice trembled. "Thank you for that."

Milton took her hands in his. "Did you mean what you said before? That you wouldn't change a thing?"

"Yes."

"I wouldn't either." He took her by the shoulders. "But when I get back from Memphis, we'll tell them. Your father. My aunt and uncle."

Her face clouded. "I don't know."

"I'm leaving for the army, Anna Mae. I want this settled before I go."

"Settled?"

"I want to marry you. I want you to be my wife."

"Oh, Milton." She raised a hand to her mouth. "I would very much like to be your wife."

He showered her with kisses and wiped away her tears. He touched his lips to her ear. "If I could stay, I would. If only this war would end."

"I know that," she said. "No one wants war, Milton, but it is here anyway." She laid a hand on his cheek. "I've seen the way my mother cries. I've seen the ladies at the Red Cross, how hard they work and how they wait for their husbands and their sons. There are rations now. But we are strong—all of us—and we will get through this. America will win. John George will come home. And you will come back to me."

He covered her with more kisses. She was truly an amazing woman. "I meant what I said before. This isn't the way it's supposed to go."

Anna Mae tipped her head back. "You mean this? Being here tonight?"

"Yes."

Anna Mae tucked a lock of hair behind her ear and lifted her chin. "I'm not ashamed, Milton. I've never been happier in all my life." There was no apology in her voice, nor accusation. "I would do it all again."

~~~~

The men rode in silence, the only sound the horses' hooves clomping across the dirt. Clyde led them toward the cornfields and slowed. The orphanage stood on the hill, a shadow against the dark sky. He squinted, searching each window for a sliver of light, but saw none. Satisfied, he moved on again.

He stopped near a stream and led his horse to the water. The rest of the men did the same. When the horses were done, they climbed on again. Clyde followed the line of the stars, picking his way to the edge of the field. When the sun came up, he would measure their distance from the train track, move the men if necessary. Harper was behind him, with Cooper bringing up the rear. The newest men followed in the middle.

"Need to go slow through here, boys," he said, his voice a whisper in the wind. He pulled on the reins, halted. Harper repeated the words to the man behind him and that man did the same. After a minute, Clyde could no longer hear the words.

Nonetheless, he waited. When he was sure the last man had gotten the message, he urged his horse forward, holding tight to the reins. They plunged through the field. A horse behind him snorted, the brittle leaves tickling its nose. He counted the steps as they trotted ahead, gauging the distance they traveled. When he thought they'd gone far enough, he pulled back on the reins, bringing his horse to a stop.

"We'll wait here," he said. Same as before, the men repeated the message until they'd all arrived, forming a dark circle in the field. He couldn't make out the features, but he could see the whites of their eyes, the gleam of their teeth. He slid off his horse. "Hold tight to your horses."

"How long do you think before the sun comes up?"
~~~~

Clyde strained to see who had spoken. It was one of the new boys. "An hour maybe."

"That long?"

"What's the matter? You scared o' the dark?" Harper asked.

There was silence. Another voice chimed in. "What do you know? Spark is scared of the dark. He's chicken."

"Nobody calls me chicken," the boy said, his voice rising. There was a rustling of leaves and the sound of steps. A body hit the ground.

"Enough," Clyde said, hissing. "We don't have time for this." He pointed in the direction of the men fighting. "Cooper you take the rear flank. Spark, you go with Cooper. Now." The corn rattled as the men passed. It wasn't much space between them—twenty-five yards, maybe thirty—but it would do. Patting his horse, he fixed each man with a long stare. "We'll need to wait here a little longer. I'll be coming around to each of you. We don't have much time now. We have to be ready."

The men spread out in a semicircle, their horses by their sides. Cooper came up behind Clyde. "It's been a long couple of weeks," he said. He held the reins with one hand. The other was tucked into the waist of his pants. "The men are anxious."

"We can't afford for them to be anxious. One mistake and this doesn't work." Somewhere in the distance, an owl hooted. A breeze blew up the hair on his arms. "Is the kid really afraid of the dark?"

Cooper spit on the ground. "How should I know? The job's in the daylight, not the dark."

Clyde didn't say anything. Cooper was right, and yet, the last thing they needed was some guy losing it in the middle of the cornfield because he got nightmares in the dark. There was nothing to be gained by reminding Cooper of that, but he couldn't help saying, "We should have known about Spark."

"It won't happen again. Next time, I'll make sure."

Clyde rubbed a hand over the shoulders and backside of his horse, his thoughts unspoken. There wasn't going to be a next time.

~~~~

WEATHER FORECAST

Washington, July 8—Tennessee—Fair Tuesday, slightly warmer northeast portion; Wednesday fair.

Normal precipitation for this date . . . 16 ins

Deficiency since first of year . . . 7.31 ins

Sunrise . . . 5:37 a.m.

—*The Tennessean*, July 9, 1918

~~~~

John peeked out from under the window shade. The clouds parted to reveal slivers of white-blue sky, and a purple-pink light stretched over the land like a promise. Beyond, he saw distant barns and dry, empty fields. It wouldn't be long now before they arrived in Nashville. Around him, bodies stirred and shifted.

In the rear of the coach, a man laughed. Others joined in. The white men had played all night, rolling the dice hour after hour. A porter sat nearby on a stool, watching and waiting. John yawned. The night had passed slowly, sleep snatched in short stretches. Even in sleep, his mind had raced, skipping from home to Nashville to Sabina and back again.

He thought about the letters he'd written and tucked into his bag. One for his momma and one for Leah. Another for Sabina. He might not send that one. At least not yet.

John spotted the minder standing with another white man at the back of the car. There was nothing offensive about the man exactly, but the way he eyed them made John's back stiffen and his stomach lurch. He hoped it wouldn't be that way at DuPont.

He let go of the window shade, slid down the wall of the wooden coach, and pulled his knees to his chest. The rumble of the train rattled his teeth. His eyes burned and his muscles ached. He tried to ignore the clawing hunger in his belly, but his thoughts drifted to his momma's cornbread, dripping with butter, hot and sweet. He licked his lips thinking about it.

"Hey." Lem touched him on the shoulder. He'd been quiet since midnight. "Got any idea how much longer?"

John lifted his head and blinked. Sunlight peeked through the slats where the wooden car had splintered and peeled. According to the minder from the DuPont company, the overnight train was due to arrive in Nashville shortly after 7:00 a.m.

"Shouldn't be too much longer," he said.

"I surely hope so." Lem ran a hand over his face. His skin, soft and beardless, had taken on an ashy pallor. "I'm not feeling so good."

John nodded but didn't comment. The coach was hot and crowded. They were all exhausted and hungry. There were no sleeper cars like the white folks had and no dining cars either. The hours of wall-to-wall standing and crouching had taken their toll. The nervous smiles worn at departure had long since faded, replaced by bloodshot eyes and surly expressions.

One man after the other stirred, stretching stiff limbs, waking to the new day. The car rocked under them, the wheels clacking, and the train rolled on.

~~~~

"Can I get a shine, George?"

The porter looked around. "Mr. Lowenstein. Good to see you this morning."

"Thank you, George. Got here a little early today. Hoping you aren't too busy for me."

George smiled—the first he hadn't had to think about that day—and pulled out his brushes. "Never too busy for you, Mr. Lowenstein," he said and meant it.

"You're a good man, George."

"Thank you, sir."
~~~~

Mr. Lowenstein sat down, propping his feet up on the small ledge. With deft hands, George buffed one shoe and then the other. Mr. Lowenstein wasn't one of his regulars for a shine, but he traveled often enough that George knew him. He'd seen him in the smoker, most times playing cards or dice.

None of that mattered to George. A good porter had to be able to read a man, serve without getting in the way. Mr. Lowenstein was quick to lend a hand to a friend, tell a joke, offer a kind word. He also liked to talk.

"You a married man, George?"

"Yes, sir."

"I guess you've got children."

"Five, Mr. Lowenstein. My oldest daughter is set to graduate high school this year."

"Well, that's quite an accomplishment, George." Mr. Lowenstein tapped one foot on the box. "Family and a good woman. There's nothing like a good woman, I always say. You're a lucky man, George."

The porter glanced up at the man. Dark circles hung under the young man's eyes, but he didn't seem tired. In fact, George thought he was in fine spirits. Aloud, he said, "That I am." His hands moved over Mr. Lowenstein's shoes, whisking and brushing.

"It's a fine day, isn't it, George?"

The porter grinned. It was clear to him now. Mr. Lowenstein had found a woman. "Yes, sir. A very fine day."

A shadow fell across Mr. Lowenstein's shoes. "Hey, you there." George's hands slowed their motion. "George? Can I get a shine, boy?"

The porter inhaled, waited a beat before looking up at the man. With a massive chest and a block-sized head, the man loomed over the pair. His eyes, flinty in their gaze, matched his cool tone.

"Are you done with him yet? I'm in a hurry."

"Sir?"

"Are you slow, boy? I asked if you're almost done giving this man his shine?"

George's shoulders tightened. He gritted his teeth, kept his voice even. "I just started, sir."

The man huffed. "Oh, for Chrissakes." He checked his pocket watch. "How much longer? I don't have all day."

George had bags to load soon. He didn't want to give the big man a shine, but he could use the tip. "One quarter of an hour, sir."

"Fine," the man said with a grunt. He pulled a cigar from his pocket "I'm going for a smoke. Don't let anyone get in before me. You understand?"

"Excuse me." Mr. Lowenstein cleared his throat. "I'm Milton Lowenstein. And you are?"

The large man scowled and lit the fat cigar, smoke streaming from his mouth. "What's it to you?"

"Oh, nothing really. I was trying to be polite, but I'm sorry to inform you that George can't give you a shine today."

The porter kept his head down, his mind racing. What was Mr. Lowenstein talking about?

The big man sputtered, "What's that you say?"

"I've already booked George for my partners." He pointed toward a group of men standing nearby. "They're waiting over there. You'll have to find another porter."

George couldn't breathe, glad he was on the ground, his legs suddenly weak.

"Is that so?"

"It is definitely so." Mr. Lowenstein waved at the men. After a moment, one lifted his hand in return.

The man looked from George to Mr. Lowenstein to George again, his ruddy skin turning purple. He waved his cigar under the porter's nose. "Why didn't you say so?" He shook his head. "Goddam porters." Grumbling, he stalked off, the sound of his steps heavy on the concrete.

George held the brush in his hands, unable to speak for a moment. He didn't mind not having to give the rude man a shine, but he did mind losing the tip.

"Sorry about that, George. I'll double your tip today. No, I'll triple it," Mr. Lowenstein said as though he'd read the porter's mind. He winked at George, who gave a shake of his head. "It's too fine a day to put up with people like that, don't you think?" The man leaned forward. "Can I show you something, George?"

Mr. Lowenstein was surely in good spirits. "If you like, sir."

Milton pulled a golden locket from his suitcoat and dangled it from his fingers. The locket swung back and forth. He opened it. Inside was a picture of a woman with light red hair.

George said nothing. He didn't know what he was looking at or why.

"I'm getting married."

"Ah." George grinned then. He'd been right. There was a woman. "Congratulations, sir."

"Thank you, George. It's a very fine day indeed."

~~~~

OUR HONOR ROLL

Washington, July 8.—The army casualty list today contained 50 names, divided as follows:

Killed in action, 6; died of wounds, 13; died of accident, and other causes, 2; wounded severely, 29.

—*The Tennessean*, July 9, 1918

~~~~

David rose, body and mind weary. He crossed the room, his footsteps silent on the floor. With practiced hands, he pulled up his overalls, grimacing as he hooked them over his shoulders. The ache in his joints and the hammering in his head served as a reminder he wasn't as young as he used to be. He picked up his boots and glanced at his wife. She looked younger as she slept, softer than she did during the day. He tucked the sheet around her shoulder, leaned over, and touched his lips to her soft cheek. He pulled away quickly. He was not a demonstrative man. What had made him do that?

Outside the girls' room, he stopped. He would need to speak to Anna Mae soon, perhaps that night. There was something changed about her, something he wasn't sure he understood. One moment, she was practically giddy, giggling like a schoolgirl with Katie Belle, and the next, she grew pensive, quiet. The previous evening, he'd caught her staring out the window, her knitting abandoned in her lap.

"What is it, Anna Mae?" he'd asked. "Is there something on your mind?"

He had to ask twice.

"I don't think so, Father," she said, not meeting his eye.

"You seem very far away." Mary watched the exchange with interest, her head turning from side to side, watching them.

Anna Mae laughed, but there was no lightness, no joy in it. "No, Father, I'm right here where I'm supposed to be." Anna Mae smiled at her mother and picked up her knitting again.

He considered pressing her but changed his mind, content to listen to the sound of knitting needles clicking in the quiet.

Now, as he stood outside her door, he decided that had been a mistake. He would speak to her that night. Perhaps one less thing to worry about would ease the pain battering his skull.

After lacing his shoes, he collected his railroader's box and left the apartment. From between the buildings, golden stripes of light shone on the road. Catching sight of the clock tower, he hurried to the station, his steps quickening. He made his way to the dispatcher's office, finding Shorty along the way.

"Is it me or are we waiting more and more for the Number One?" Shorty asked after they'd received the day's orders.

"It's not you." As they walked, Shorty's litany of complaints compounded. David's head ached again, and he stopped listening. He slowed to watch the cluster of railroaders who huddled near the tracks, each finishing his tasks before leaving for home. He felt a flash of envy. A fresh weariness settled over him. He knew without seeing that his eyes were shot through with red. He rubbed at them, trying to ease the sting and clear his vision.

"Uncle Dave? You okay?" Shorty asked, his square head angled downward.

David forced a smile. "Never better."

"As it should be." The conductor gave a small salute.

Nodding, David said nothing. They'd both recited their lines, the same as they did every day. So much of David's life was routine. He got up, walked to the train station, got his orders, boarded the train. He drove the same route day after day, with rarely a change. He walked home at the end of each day to his wife and daughters. On the occasional weekend, he joined his friends for a game of cards or played street ball with the boys. He went to church. He was a man who liked structure, liked predictability. Maybe it was being a railroad engineer. A train was expected to leave on time and arrive on time. He didn't like surprises or unpredictability. Not like his first wife.

"Why, David, you might be the most disciplined man I've ever met," she'd remarked once.

He stood in front of his small chest, arranging the few clothing items he had. "Is that a good thing?"

She peered into the drawer as he sorted. The shirts were folded into flat quarters, sorted by color. "Well, I don't know, really."

His heart pounded faster. He remembered the first time he saw her. He was young then, but she was younger—a vision in a dress the color of sunshine. She glided across the floor with her dance partner, lips parted, loose blond tendrils dusting her pale cheeks. When the dance ended, he managed to land at her side, unaware how he'd gotten there. His hand found the small of her back and she tilted her head to look up at him.

They were married a short time later.

David soon learned his new wife was anything but disciplined. Her dressing table stayed crowded with combs, bows, and lotions. More than once, she neglected to tidy up their rooms. He didn't mind at first, assuming she'd get better, but as the months rolled into years, he realized she didn't care to be better. Even so, her laughter filled their small apartment, and she'd been born to be young Birdie's mother. It occurred to him more than once that maybe his beautiful wife didn't see his fastidiousness as a positive quality.

"We have different ways," he said. "I hope you don't mind too much."

"Well . . . not too much." She stood on tiptoe, putting her lips to his ear. "Let's not be disciplined today, my love."

He inhaled the scent of her lotions and knew he didn't stand a chance.

David shook away the memories now. What was wrong with him? Why was he dwelling on the past? He was remarried now, had grown children. Perhaps he would always be a disciplined man, a creature of habit. Would his first wife be disappointed? He wondered. Birdie had never quite gotten over the loss of her mother. When she was alive, their apartment had been bright with colored pictures and filled with conversation and booming laughter. But she had died, and the color had faded, the laughter gone.

He sighed. Mary was a good woman. Dependable. Strong, too, in her own way. Like David, she craved routine. They were a good match. Perhaps their marriage lacked the fire of his first, but it wasn't littered with spats and hurt feelings either.

David stopped to check the time. Less than fifteen minutes until the train was set to depart. The Number Four train—his train—waited on the tracks. From where he stood, the black metal engine loomed large in front of the tender car. He didn't have to look to know Luther was already hard at work, loading the coal to fire the train. Behind the tender car, two baggage cars stood open. Outside the first, a crew loaded mail and baggage.

"Why, as I live and breathe, if it isn't the famous engineer, David Kennedy."

David spun around and wagged his finger with a laugh. "That's Uncle Dave to you."

"I'm riding your train today," John Nolan said. The ends of his waxed mustache twitched as he spoke.

David had long admired the young engineer. Although not a tall man, Nolan had a compact build and powerful arms, reminding David of a strong bull. "I heard. You're driving tomorrow?"

"That I am." They walked farther down the platform, away from the growing hubbub near the passenger cars. "Looks like it's going to be a full train today."

"I believe you're right."

"On time today?"

David would have flinched if the question had been asked by anyone else. His reputation for being on time was legendary, but the new orders in recent months had affected all the engineers and schedules, particularly David and his routes. Nolan, having driven the route himself, understood better than most. "Need to watch for the Number One," David said.

Nolan frowned. "Getting to be more of a problem, I hear."

The growing knot in David's gut hardened. An engineer had to rely on his conductor, who relied on the porter, who in turn relied on the flagman. Each relied on the other, and if things went the way they were supposed to, that should be enough. That's what David had been telling himself anyway.

"I hear the powers that be might increase the number of trains again," Nolan was saying. David's attention snapped back to the other man. "I've heard the same now that there's that gunpowder plant. Don't like it one bit, if I'm being honest," Nolan continued. The Irishman made the sign of the cross. "I'll be praying for you, Uncle Dave."

Head aching, David could only muster a single nod. "Thank you. Can't have too many prayers these days."

"No," the younger engineer agreed. "That we can't."

~~~~

BITS OF BY-PLAY

By Luke McLuke

The Wise Fool

"It is sad to think that every man has his price," observed the sage.

"And it is sadder to think that he can't get it," commented the fool.

—*The Tennessean*, July 9, 1918
~~~~

~~~

The sky shifted, sending pink-gray clouds floating overhead. Clyde lifted his face toward the rising sun and pushed his hat back with the flick of a finger. The men, speaking in hushed voices, quieted, all watching the sun creep over the horizon, warming the air.

Cooper stood at his side. "How much longer?"

"Soon."

"Should we move?"

Clyde looked back at the orphanage to measure their distance, then back to where the track cut through the cornfield. He made a decision. "Gather the men. Keep it quiet." One by one, the men and their horses surrounded him. He licked his lips and addressed the group. "The train will be coming through in a little over an hour." He waved his hand in the air. "We're going to move closer to the track now, but not here."

"Where, then?" Harper asked.

"Just past the curve. We'll be waiting a few hundred yards down. As soon as the train rounds Dutchman's Curve, Cooper will raise his rifle and fire a shot. That will get the engineer's attention."

"What if it doesn't?" one of the men asked.

"He'll fire again."

"It will work," Cooper said.

Spark, the young man afraid of the dark, spoke up. "I don't want to be a sitting duck on that track."

There was a low grumble among the men. Clyde pressed his lips together. He didn't need any doubts at this stage of the game. "No one is going to be a sitting duck. Carl is on the train." The men exchanged glances. "If the train doesn't slow, he'll hold a gun to the conductor's head."

"That's more like it."

"Leave it to Carl."

Cooper stepped forward. "We're ready to move. Follow Clyde. Single file. I'll bring up the rear."
~~~

Clyde took the reins of his horse and began walking through the corn. They lined up behind him, single file. He walked until he got a visual on the track, keeping it in his sights. Five minutes' more walking, and he could see where the track veered sharply. When he'd walked far enough, he led his horse away from the track, farther into the corn but only seconds from the track on horseback. When all the men had joined him, he spoke again. "Cooper will stay here with you. I'm going back to the bridge. When I see the train, I'll whistle and ride. You'll cover the track and stop the train. Remember, Carl is on that train." There was no response. He expected none.

Clyde took his horse and walked back, keeping his mind clear and focused. They had a half hour now. Maybe less. Moving farther down the track had cost them time, but it had been the right decision. He knew it.

~~~~

Shorty read the orders. "Meet Number Seven at Harding Station to pick up mail. Number One being hauled by Engine Number 281—hold at double tracks until Number One passes."

"Yes, sir," George said to his boss.

"I'm going to need you to watch out for that train." The conductor nodded toward the passengers. "This train is as full as a cow getting ready to spill her milk." His voice rose an octave. "And let that new flagman know the orders too. He needs to keep a lookout."

The horn sounded, and the train rolled forward. George and Shorty leaned into it, practiced at absorbing the changing motion. The wheels made a sharp *clack clack* as they rotated, briefly drowning out any conversation. The train picked up speed and shot out of the shed.

"Don't forget," Shorty called over his shoulder. "The Number One is coming. I'm counting on you, George." Before the porter could respond, Shorty scurried to the front row of seats, his hand out, ready to take tickets.

George glided through the cars. He spoke to the new flagman, sharing the orders before working his way back through the train.
~~~~

"Would you like me to open your window for you, sir?"

"Splendid idea, George. It's going to be a hot one today."

Each time he unlatched a window, he scrutinized the land ahead, searching for the Number One. Each time, he saw nothing but an empty track. In the second car, he spotted Mr. Lowenstein.

"Very nice shine, today, George," the man said, pointing at his shoes. "Thank you again."

The porter felt the weight of the tip in his pocket and thought about the man's wedding announcement. It had been an unusual morning. "You're welcome, Mr. Lowenstein."

George opened window after window, listening and watching for the Number One. As he made his way toward the smoker car, his heart sank. If the Number One was as late as he guessed it was, the Number Four would be waiting at Shops. Again.

~~~~

Milton stuck his shoes out in front of him and admired his reflection in the glossy leather—blurry, but him. He nudged the man next to him.

"George gives the best shine," he said. The stranger grunted and pulled his hat lower over his face.

"Hey, fancy seeing you here."

Milton looked up to find Frank grinning down at him. "Hello, Frank. I didn't know you were on this train."

"Yeah. In the last row today. I'm not going all the way though." He stuck his hands in his pockets. "I thought you left yesterday on the overnight."

"I changed my mind."

"Then why didn't you come by the game? We could've used you."

He evaded the question. "Did you win?"

"I didn't do too bad, but we didn't play long. Larry didn't show again, so it was just me and the Smythe brothers."

Milton's gut twisted, a sick dread washing over him.
~~~~

He'd been by Larry's home. The postal worker hadn't been home in two days, according to his sister, and he hadn't been on the mail car that morning either. "What about Carl?"

"Wasn't there," Frank said. He leaned closer, lowered his voice. "I thought I saw him earlier though."

Milton rose from his seat, scanning the faces and heads around him. "Where? On the train?"

"No. In the waiting room. I thought I heard him laughing. You know that laugh he has."

Milton shivered. He did know. It reminded him of crows fighting—nothing funny about it. "But he wasn't there?"

"Not that I saw. It was so crowded that by the time I worked my way across the room, he was gone—if he was ever there." Milton thought about the other men he'd seen board the second passenger car. Carl hadn't been among that group. If he'd been in the station that morning, maybe he'd taken a different train.

The man in the seat next to Milton grumbled, "Are you going to stand there gabbing all day? Why don't you move on already?"

"Care to get a smoke?" Milton asked.

Frank grinned. "Is it a smoke or a game you're looking for?"

"Both," he answered, his hand rising to his jacket pocket. "I'm feeling lucky today."

The men moved through the car, slowing as they passed a row of soldiers.

Frank nudged Milton. "That'll be you soon. Getting nervous?"

"I suppose I am." All the reasons he'd wanted to sign up had faded in importance these last few days. Even so, his impending departure for the army couldn't dent the happiness he felt or his resolve to return as fast as he could.

"You're a better man than me," Frank said. His nose wrinkled as they entered the smoker. "It's crowded today."

The African Americans occupied the front of the car, their bodies squeezed together. At the back of the car, there were two loose circles of white men. A half dozen stood smoking their pipes and cigars and talking. The second group, the gamblers, had taken the far corner, some on their knees rolling dice, the others standing over them, watching.

Frank faced his friend. "So, you didn't say where you were last night?"

Milton couldn't stop the smile that spread across his face. He'd already told the porter, and Frank was one of his oldest friends. "I have some news." He lowered his voice as he spoke.

Frank listened and smiled back. "The girl from the park? I knew it. I guess congratulations are in order, then."

"Thank you, Frank." Milton pulled out his pipe and shifted his gaze to the group of men standing at the rear. Among the talkers, a dark-haired man with a curling mustache caught his attention. He looked familiar, though Milton couldn't place him. He moved closer, drawn in by the faintest trace of an Irish accent.

"And so, I drew my gun," the man was saying. He stoked his pipe, taking his time about it.

"And then what happened?" another man asked, unable to wait any longer.

The Irishman's mustache twitched. "What do you think happened? I shot that beast." He sucked in the smoke and blew it out again in a stream. "That was the end of him."

There was back pounding punctuated by broad smiles and Milton found himself smiling, too, in spite of not knowing a word of the story the man had told. The door opened again, and two white men came in followed by George. After leaving their hats with the porter, they joined the gamblers.

Voices rose among the men huddled over the dice. One man stood, looking down at a sea of angry faces. Milton caught snatches of angry words and accusations, but the man only laughed, the cackle sharp as claws in dirt. The hair rose on the back of Milton's neck.

"Carl," Frank said.

A few of the men got to their feet, their mouths set in hard lines. "I want my money back," said one.

Carl stepped close to one of the men, his voice a snarl. "Oh, yeah? What are you gonna do about it?"

The man stammered something Milton couldn't hear. Carl laughed again. "Tell you what. I'm feeling generous today." He threw some coins on the ground. "I don't need your money, boys," he said with another laugh. Milton's stomach roiled. The other white men had gone silent, watching.

Frank looked at Milton. "It's too crowded in here for me, old friend. I'm going back to my seat."

"Sure." Milton and Frank shook hands. "I'll catch up with you later." Milton caught sight of George as Frank went through the door. The porter watched the gamblers, his expression wary, but he stayed near a window.

Carl ignored all of them, pushing his way toward the back of the smoker. Milton stepped in front of him.

"Well," Carl drawled. "If it isn't the hat salesman."

"Hello, Carl."

The gambler's face hardened. "What do you want?"

"I want to talk about Larry."

"He lost. Paid his debt. End of story."

"That's not the end."

Carl's nostrils flared. "What did he tell you?"

"What did you say to him? He hasn't been home in two days. His sister's worried sick."

Carl snorted. "Is that all? He probably went off somewhere on a bender." He brushed by Milton, slamming him hard on the shoulder. "I don't have time for this."

Regaining his balance, Milton lunged for Carl, grabbing him by the arm. "Then make time."

~~~

John stole another glance at the minder. The DuPont man had joined the smokers.
~~~

"Maybe I shouldn't have come," Lem said. His voice cracked as he spoke.

"It'll be okay. It's only for three months." John did his best to sound confident, older than his years, but the sentiment rang false in his ears. Three months hadn't sounded long when he'd taken the job—it had sounded like freedom. But now, hours from home, all he felt was alone. Even as John said it again, he wondered which one of them he was trying to convince. "Three months will be over soon, and we'll all go home with pay."

"Home with pay," the man repeated. "Yeah, okay." His shoulders drooped. "I just want to get there."

"Soon."

Mr. Winfield emerged from the circle of smokers, making his way to the center of the car. He held a single sheet of paper in his hand. "Men from DuPont, gather around." He waved his arm, shouted the orders again.

John and Lem shuffled forward.

"You all heard the speeches on the Fourth, did you not?"

John remembered the man in the brown suit and nodded along with the others.

"I have a very important message for your kind, written by your kind. As such, it should be read by one of you." His gaze wandered over the men, landing finally on John. "You, can you read?"

"Yes, sir."

"Step forward, then." John entered the circle. The minder handed him the paper with a nod. "Read it out loud."

Heart drumming under his shirt, he began to speak. "'Why he failed! He did not report on time.'"

"Speak up," Mr. Winfield interrupted.

John cleared his throat and raised his voice to a near shout. "'Why he failed. He did not report on time. He watched the clock. He loafed when the boss was not looking. He stayed out with the boys all night. He said, "I forgot." He did not show up on Monday and he wanted a holiday every Saturday. He lied when asked for the truth.'" John lowered the paper, his face hot. He understood now why the man in the brown suit had not read this part of his speech.

"I want you to remember those words," Mr. Winfield said, taking the paper from John. He pulled a pocket watch from his vest. "We'll be arriving in Nashville soon. When we're called, we will leave this train in an orderly manner." His voice took on a more threatening quality. "You're DuPont men now. Don't forget it." If the minder noticed the anger simmering on the tired faces, he didn't show it.

Back on the floor, John hung his head. Lem laid a hand on his shoulder. "I've heard it before. Most have. It's been at all the factories in shops this year."

The young man nodded, but that didn't make it sit any better in his gut.

"No one's going to fail," Lem said. "Not me and not you. None of us."

Matt's voice rang in John's ears. *You can be your own man. You can be your own man.* He said the words out loud now, his fists clenched: "I am my own man. I will not fail."

~~~

David leaned out the window of the train and winced, the bright light of the sun hurting his eyes. It was going to be another hot one. Behind him, Luther worked in silence. David hadn't missed the troubled look on his face that morning.

"Wait for the Number One again?" he'd asked after hearing the orders.

"Can't be helped," David had said.

He touched a hand to his forehead now, reminded he'd slept little the night before. The nightmares and the headache. Neither had faded as the morning wore on.

David leaned out the window again, searching the tracks ahead. Still no Number One, but Shorty would pass the orders on to George and the flagman. Surely, one of them would spot the other train before they got to Shops. His fingers tightened over the throttle. They'd left the station five
~~~

minutes late that morning. He could make that up, but it would be harder if he had to wait at Shops.

David slowed the train. Shops sat on more than twenty acres, a sprawling site with offices, repair shops, maintenance buildings, and most impressive, a giant turntable. The turntable was used to aid a locomotive in changing direction. It was also used to move engines to one of the more than forty stalls for repair or maintenance. On this morning, as David drove the Number Four through Shops, his head throbbed, the pain intensifying. He struggled to breathe and bent over at the waist. A train lumbered past. He unfolded and looked over at Luther. "The Number One?" he asked, his voice half drowned out by the roar of the train.

Luther grunted.

"What?" David couldn't see the other train, black dots blurring his vision. He stumbled, catching himself before he landed on the floor of his own engine. The dots faded and his shoulders loosened. He pulled back on the throttle, wheels grinding as the train slowed. Ahead, he saw the signal tower. The arm on the tower was pointed up, indicating he could proceed. He felt some of the tension drain from him then. Must have been the Number One they'd passed. Just in time.

~~~~

George stood at the window, scanning the parallel tracks for the Number One. The sounds of a fight made him look around. Mr. Lowenstein had his hands on a larger man, one who didn't look friendly at all. George gasped. He knew that man. It was the same man who'd bumped into him a few days earlier, the man with the greasy hair and dead eyes.

Before George knew what was happening, Mr. Lowenstein landed on the ground with a great thump. Wearing a nasty grin, the greasy-haired man rubbed his knuckles. George rushed over. Blood trickled from Mr. Lowenstein's nose. He tried to push himself up but faltered, using his hands to steady himself.
~~~~

"Mr. Lowenstein? Are you all right?"

Carl laughed. "Got your boy George to help you, friend?" He spit on the floor. "Not telling any jokes now, are you?"

George helped Mr. Lowenstein to his feet. The train slowed at that moment, and a second train rumbled past. In the hopes of spotting the Number One, George rushed to the window in time to catch sight of the back of a switch engine hauling ten cars. Putting his face up close to the window, he searched the tracks but saw only train stalls and repair stations.

Another bang, and another crash. George swung back around to find Mr. Lowenstein and the greasy-haired man rolling across the floor now. The passengers jumped back, spreading out in a circle to give the two men a wider berth. Others clamored to the front of the car, eager to get far away from the fight.

George's frantic gaze darted back and forth between the window and Mr. Lowenstein. They had not yet passed the Number One, and in another minute, they would reach the signal tower. Engineer Kennedy would be forced to slow the train, stop, and wait. As expected, the wheels of the train squealed. George exhaled. They would wait now. The two men tumbled toward him, and the porter leaped out of the way, his blood pumping. "Lordy," he cried.

The tall man picked Mr. Lowenstein up by his lapels, tossing him aside like a sack of potatoes. "It's time you learned to keep your snotty nose out of my business." Mr. Lowenstein scrambled to his feet at the same time the other man curled his fingers into a tight fist. Mr. Lowenstein's head snapped back with the blow. He fell backward, legs splayed out in front of him, his skull bouncing off the floor. The train sped up again, and George spun around, Mr. Lowenstein forgotten. At the window, he glimpsed an empty signal tower, its arm up. That didn't seem right. Had they passed the Number One? He thought maybe there'd only been the switch engine. Doubt rose in his mind.

Seconds later, the train left Shops and the parallel tracks, rolling smoothly onto the single track headed west. George looked through the window, trying to see in all directions, his breath fogging the glass. Should he find Shorty? Again, he was plagued by doubt. It was the conductor's job to pull the emergency valve if they missed the Number One. But Shorty would be collecting tickets, not watching for the Number One. He relied on George for that.

His breath came in great gasps now. He told himself that Engineer Kennedy was an excellent engineer. He'd have stopped if the track wasn't clear. Maybe in the heat of the fight, George had missed the other train. That had to be it. He craned his neck to see ahead and saw nothing, but instead of relief, he felt only a prickly dread as the train picked up speed again, heading straight toward Dutchman's Curve.

~~~~

Clyde's horse stamped and bristled under the reins. He leaned forward and brushed his hand over her mane. He spoke to the animal, his words soft. "There, there, girl. Only a few minutes more." The horse calmed enough that Clyde steered her back toward the north. The men had done as they were told. They waited farther up the track, on the other side of Dutchman's Curve. Raising a hand to his brow, he scanned the horizon. Time seemed to slow while he waited. He sat up in his saddle. In the distance, he spotted a plume of dark smoke. He gave the signal, his whistle cutting through the silence of the morning. He stole a quick glance at the orphanage. Seeing nothing, he dug his heels into the horse's flanks and rode.

He raced through the cornfield, the stalks whipping across his arms and legs. He slowed once and whistled a second time. He waited. There it was. Cooper's return whistle. He rode on. The men would mount their horses now and take their places across the track. The engineer would have to stop the train. If he didn't, Carl would force the conductor to pull the cord. He snapped the reins, urging his horse to gallop faster. In another minute, maybe two, the train would be there. His shirt flapped, and the clomping of hooves sounded in his ears.
~~~~

Clyde burst from the corn and raced parallel to the single track. He rode toward Dutchman's Curve, his horse pounding ahead. Seeing the men, he slowed his horse to a trot and loosened his grip on the reins. Cooper had taken the lead and waited at the front on the tracks.

Two more men lined up behind him. The others were on either side of the track. Clyde rode up next to Cooper and pulled up his bandana like the others. Almost time.

~~~~

Milton moaned, struggling to sit up. He caught sight of the back of Carl's head as he pushed his way through the crowd. He rubbed a hand across his jaw, his head already pounding. The gamblers had gone back to their game. The others had returned to their cigars and stories. George, the porter, had taken off his hat and was holding it against his chest. The whites of his eyes shone and sweat poured down his face. His lips moved, but there was no one near him to hear. Rising, Milton staggered toward the porter.

"George, what's wrong?" he asked. The porter only stared out the window at the world whizzing by. Milton grabbed him by the arms, shaking him. "What's wrong?"

"I don't know. Maybe nothing."

"You don't look like it's nothing."

In answer, George returned to the window, pressing himself against the glass. Milton leaned in, looking over the porter's shoulder, but saw nothing other than empty track and rows and rows of drying corn. He took a step back, not understanding. It was a beautiful day outside, and despite George's strange behavior and the run-in with Carl, he wouldn't let anything dampen his good mood.

The train began to slow and Milton glanced toward the window again. A bend in the track. He didn't know why George seemed out of sorts, but he decided he'd had enough of the smoker car. A little rest before he switched trains would do him some good. He started to tell the porter he'd be on his
~~~~

way when George let out a small cry. Milton stared at the man, who was now visibly shaking where he stood.

"George?"

The porter didn't look around at him, only touched a finger to the glass. Milton followed the direction he pointed, searching for whatever was frightening the other man. There was the corn and track—same as before. Then he saw it. Smoke rising up in the air ahead. Another train.

"Only one track," George said, his voice no more than a whisper.

Milton's mouth went dry. The wheels screamed, and George fell to his knees. He didn't look at Milton, nor did he make a move to get up. He bowed his head, clasping his hands together. Barely hanging onto the wall of the car, Milton looked wildly around the crowded smoker. The gamblers got to their feet. Voices rose higher. He understood then.

Taking the golden locket from his coat pocket, he pressed it to his lips, a calm settling over him. "I love you, Anna Mae. Always."

~~~~

Facing the city, Clyde cocked his head, listening. In the distance, he heard the familiar rumble of locomotive wheels. He stiffened and twisted around in his saddle. Farther up the track, he could see a train, but it wasn't coming from Nashville. The realization hit him with a jolt. This train was headed straight toward them. His head whipped back around. The smoke from the Nashville train could be seen just beyond Dutchman's Curve. They were coming too fast. Two trains. One track. A shout rose from his throat. "Ride." He dug his boots into the flesh of his horse. "Get off the track. Off the track."

~~~~

The train moved smoothly over the single track, picking up speed since leaving Shops. David shook his head to clear his vision and caught a glimpse of the orphanage on the hill. He saw the cornfields, a sea of green-and-brown stalks rising from the ground. A light breeze blew and the corn swayed. He slowed just enough to guide the engine around Dutchman's Curve. A blur of motion caught his attention. There were horses plowing through the cornfield, the stalks bending and snapping beneath them. A horn sounded, and David jerked his head back toward the track.

"Holy Mother of God."

~~~~

John's body rocked with the rhythmic clatter of the train, his eyelids growing heavy again. His mind drifted to sunny skies and wide-open cornfields. The shiny green leaves caught the breeze, flapping against his face. Around him, the stalks rose higher, grew closer. He walked faster and faster until he was running, legs pumping, the sun beating down on his back. He ran toward the last row, where the land opened to the north road. He stopped short. It wasn't there. Had he gone the wrong way? He spun around, plunging through row after row of corn. Screeching birds circled overhead. He looked to the left, looked to the right. Everywhere, there was nothing but corn. Sweat dripped from his temple and his chest heaved. He raised a hand to the glare of the sun, squinting up at the dark-winged birds. All at once, they dove straight down, their pointed beaks like arrows, their shrieks filling the air.

His eyes snapped open. The forward motion of the train seemed to jerk, still careening ahead but the sudden shift made him tumble backward. The horn blasted, and John's heart beat faster. He reached out, scrambling to his feet. Screams punctured the air. He heard the thunderous boom before the grinding crunch of steel. His body flew forward, his arms and legs flailing. The crown of his head slammed against the floor of the coach. Lem landed across his back, his elbow smacking into John's nose. Blood gushed, warm and sticky. Pinned, he couldn't move, couldn't see. The sound of his breathing, ragged and shallow, roared in his head. He saw the faces of his momma, his sister, Sabina. He saw the light. Then there was darkness.
~~~~

PART 7

END OF THE LINE

CHAPTER NINETEEN

Summer 1988

GINNY CLASPED HER hand to her heart. "They crashed," she said, half question, half whisper.

"Yes, they crashed."

Ginny followed Anna Mae's gaze to the single track that ran out of Nashville and under the white bridge. It followed the line of the creek before veering sharply out of sight. The hollow pit of her stomach churned. "Is that where . . ." The words died on her tongue.

"Dutchman's Curve." Anna Mae's voice broke, and she stared down at her hands. A long minute passed. "Oh, dear, this is harder than I thought."

Ginny reached out and took the old woman's hands in hers.

"Milton?"

Anna Mae shook her head.

"I'm so sorry, Anna Mae."

"Silly, isn't it? After all this time." Anna Mae lifted her hand to the locket around her neck. "It belonged to his mother, the only thing he had left from her. I'd given him my picture to put inside. He was holding it in his hand when . . ." Her hands trembled and her voice faded.

Ginny glanced back at the closed door. "Can I get you something? Some more tea?"

"Yes, dear, that would be nice." When Ginny came back with the cup, Anna Mae patted her hand and thanked her. "That should do the trick nicely. Now, where were we?"

"There's more?"

"Oh, yes." The old woman wore a sad smile. "I wasn't far from where it happened, and I went down there as fast as I could. You could see the smoke for miles. And the smell. I can't forget it. Even now." Her stooped shoulders shuddered. "There were nuns and children on the hill and railroaders and doctors and so many people. It felt like all of Nashville showed up at Dutchman's Curve that day."

"It must have been horrible."

"Oh, it was." She shuddered again. "But we'll get to that." She took the tea and drank. Setting it back on the table, she lifted her chin. "Not everyone died that day, although there were some who wished they had. The Lord, though, had other plans. Clyde didn't put too much stock in religion—he never had—but sometimes what you think you believe is different from what's in your soul." She eyed Ginny as she spoke. "Clyde saw it all. He had to live with that, didn't he?"

"Knowing his brother was on the train, you mean?"

"He'd put him there, insisted on it, even. Waiting in that cornfield didn't turn out exactly how he'd planned. As I said, he saw it coming. He sounded the alarm among his men, and they rode as fast and as hard as they could. But riding couldn't stop those trains."

CHAPTER TWENTY

Tuesday, July 9, 1918

CLYDE PULLED BACK on the reins, whirling around. The two trains sped over the track—two bullets aimed at one another. He couldn't tell which of the trains recognized the danger first. He only heard the sharp squeal of brakes, the sound splintering the air, but it was too little, too late.

In the seconds before the iron and steel collided, Clyde covered his ears. One engine plowed into the other, their forward motion suspended. The mail car. The Jim Crow car. Both rolled on, folding in on each other, one by one, like a telescope. Clyde recoiled in his saddle, his body trembling. The wooden cars closest to the engine broke apart. Others slipped off the track, sliding sideways. Steam hissed. There was the sound of an explosion. He couldn't move, frozen in the saddle.

Clyde didn't know how long he sat there, how many minutes had passed before Cooper came up beside him: "What do you want the men to do?"

Clyde looked over his shoulder and saw the men waiting out of sight of the wreck. Seeing the fear and shock on their faces, he wanted to say something to reassure them, but he had no words. "Get them out of here," he said.

"What about the safe?"

Both men looked back toward the train. Most of the rear cars were intact. Already, those passengers who could were crawling from the wreckage. "It's no good," he told Cooper. "Clear out the cabin. Get out of Nashville."

Nodding, Cooper waved a hand at the men. They didn't need to be told twice. They rode hard, the horses' hooves pounding through the corn. Cooper leaned over toward Clyde. "What about Carl?"

Clyde hung his head. His brother would have been in one of the front cars, not the rear with the women. "I don't know." Swinging down to the ground, he handed his reins to his friend. "Take my horse. I'm going down there."

Cooper started to say something, thought better of it. "See you, Boss."

Clyde walked slowly through the corn. He heard the voices of other men as they rushed toward the wreckage. He wasn't surprised. Smoke choked the air, and the noise of the crash had been deafening. He looked back to see automobiles stopped on the bridge just past the corn. Word would spread quickly. Anguished cries came from one of the broken cars, but he kept walking, holding his bandana to his nose.

As he got closer, he slowed. Bodies thrown from the train lay near the wreckage, contorted in ways that weren't natural. Clyde had never considered himself a sensitive man. He was not easily cowed. He'd seen dead men, been the cause of their deaths even, but this was different. The destruction of the cars, the scent of charred flesh, and the sounds of death assaulted his senses all at once. Only the knowledge that Carl was there—somewhere—kept him moving.

He stepped over the body of one man, then another. Blood glistened in the sun, flowing over the ground. He tightened the bandana over his nose. Some of the injured seemed to be lost, wandering around. Others stood in clusters. More were doing what they could.

"This one's alive."

"Pull him out, if you can."

A huddle of men hurried down the line, and he spotted the conductor, gesturing and pointing. Clyde scanned the faces of the men surrounding him, anyone near him, but recognized none. His hands curled to fists. Carl should have been there, in the white coaches with the conductor, but Clyde knew in his heart, he wasn't.

Clyde moved toward the center of the wreckage until he came to the engines. Smoke and steam poured from the hulking mass of metal. There were four bodies among the wreckage there. He caught a flash of overalls. An engineer. There would have been two men in each engine.

More people arrived on the scene. "Is anyone a doctor? We need help down here."

At the baggage and mail cars, he slowed, unable to stop himself. The safe, tantalizingly close, lay on its side, half-buried under broken baggage and scraps of letters that would never arrive. There were more bodies here. Legs twisted, bones protruding through skin. Tearing his eyes from the safe, he kept walking.

He came to the Jim Crow car. Masses of bodies filled what remained of the wooden coach. Farmers and laborers. There was the porter, his hat gone, his coat buttons catching the light of the sun. There was a white man with a curling mustache, but he didn't see Carl, couldn't see him in the rubble.

A few good Samaritans had already begun hauling bodies from the car, lining them up one by one in the cornfield. He followed as if pulled by an invisible string. It was there that Clyde found his brother. He spotted his hat first, then his boots.

"This is a big one," a man said, laying Carl on the ground. His brother was stretched out, his boot tips pointed upward. Blood soaked his left arm, shoulder, and temple. A large gash in his head matched the scar on his face. Clyde wanted to look away, but stood, transfixed, unable to move.

A voice next to him made him look around. "Is this someone you know?"

The man wore a black shroud with a white collar and a cross around his neck. There was a knot on his forehead, and he held a red-speckled cloth in his hand.

"Were you on the train?" Clyde asked.

"Not this one. The other one, the overnight from Memphis." He gestured toward Carl's lifeless body. "I'm giving last rites to the dead, offering blessings. If you know him, I could give a special prayer."

Clyde lowered the bandana he held in his hand. Carl wouldn't have liked the holy man, no matter how good his intentions. "No, Father. I don't know him."

The priest studied Clyde a moment and then lowered his head. "God bless you, young man," he said before moving off.

Clyde's gaze drifted down the track. Men lifted metal shards and cleared broken wood. They called out as they worked. "Is anyone there? Does anyone need help?" They scrambled forward. "There are people trapped in here," one man shouted. More men rushed forward.

At the rear of the trains, women and children huddled together, shaken but safe from the devastation. The dead were confined to those coaches closest to the engines.

Clyde took one last look at his brother. "So long, Carl."

He retreated to the hill to watch. Nuns and children from the orphanage stood holding hands. Hundreds more trampled over the corn. The gunpowder money was supposed to be his last job. He couldn't understand it. He thought he'd been so careful. How could he have forgotten there was another train?

What was it his brother had said? *We're going to be famous.* But he'd been wrong, and now he was dead. Clyde took off his hat. There was nothing but cloudless sky above—a bright, vast blue space that stretched all the way back to Memphis. His brother, his only family, was gone. Clyde heard more shouting then, the voices of the men at the crash site drifting up from the cornfields below.

Railroaders lifted broken steel from the track, and civilians carried makeshift stretchers. He blinked hard and ran a hand over his chin. He watched another minute before his feet carried him back down the hill, to the wreck.

~~~~

William Jones made his way to the engines. He gawked at the smoking metal, torn away from the engine wherever it wasn't crushed. Hot coals had ignited, catching fire. The boilers had toppled, sending scalding liquid splashing across the coach. But it was the mangled bodies that drew his eye, and he had to swallow hard more than once.

A man caught up to him. "Are you the embalmer?"

"Yes." He pointed toward the engines. "David Kennedy—the engineer for this train—is my father-in-law. Have you found him?"

"I'm sorry to hear that, sir. I didn't know him myself, but I'd heard of him. I work at the switching station. I'm told he'd been with the railroad a long time."

"Yes. A long time."

"Well, I guess you can do the identifying, then." He led William to the front. "Up here."

David lay under the battered engine, only his upper body visible. His glasses were bent and hung from one swollen ear. His skin shone a shiny pinkish red, and by the look of it, William guessed David had been caught by the boiler.

Crouching low to the ground, he blanched. David's lower body sat a few feet away, severed above the hips. He took several deep breaths before rising again. "That's him."

"Lucky he wasn't burned worse." The man pointed at a line of charred bodies only a few feet farther down the track.

"It's best if the family doesn't see him like this," William said. "Is there someone who can help me get him out from under there?"

"Should be coming now," the man said. He rolled up his shirtsleeves and mopped his face with a dirty cloth. "All my years with the railroad, I've never seen anything like this."

William turned his back on the train and took in the growing crowds. "Any idea how this happened?" he asked.
~~~~

The man waved a hand at the piled-up and broken coaches. "Nope. Somebody blundered, I guess." William followed the line of his outstretched finger from the wreckage to the bodies lying among the corn, many with their faces covered. Others lay exposed, their mangled limbs darkened with blood and soot. "Hell of a blunder though, wouldn't you say?"

William's throat grew tight, his mind and heart numb. "Yes. Hell of a blunder."

CHAPTER TWENTY-ONE

Summer 1988

GINNY SNIFFLED AND wiped her nose with a wad of tissue. "I—I don't know what to say. It's so terrible."

Silent tears ran down Anna Mae's face, sliding into the crevices and creases of her pale skin. "Yes, quite." She looked out at the empty track. "The Jim Crow cars were the worst, of course. They were closest to the engines and bore the brunt of the collision."

Ginny thought about what she'd heard. Those cars were overcrowded with passengers on both trains. The timber would have collapsed on impact, exposing all of them. She couldn't imagine the chaos, terror, and heartache. And Anna Mae. Her father had been driving that train. And Milton had been in the smoker car along with George and Carl. Her head came up.

"John and Matt were on the other train?"

"Yes. By the time the trains were aware of each other . . ." She raised her hands and dropped them again. Her cloudy eyes slid back to the window and the field. Ginny waited.

She had so many questions, but this wasn't the time. This was Anna Mae's story, and she would let her finish.

When the old woman spoke again, her voice shook with grief. "I knew where my father would have been—in the engine—but I wasn't brave enough to go there at first. I thought Milton would be able to help me handle that, and so I hurried to the coaches."

CHAPTER TWENTY-TWO

Tuesday, July 9, 1918

ANNA MAE RAN through the crowds, calling for Milton until her voice grew hoarse, but he was nowhere to be found. Fear mixed with dread, coiling deep in her belly, and she thought she might be sick.

When a man with a gash across his forehead grabbed her wrist, she let out a scream.

He lessened his grip but didn't let go. "Are you Anna Mae?"

Her mouth dropped open but no words came out.

"I'm Frank Danielson. A friend of Milton's." Relieved to find someone connected to Milton, she could have wept with joy. Even better, he'd been on the train and he was alive. "He told me about you, that you were to be married."

She was clutching his hand now. "Where is he? Is he okay?"

He shook his head. "I left him in the smoker."

Her hand flew to her throat. The smokers were at the front of the train. "All the more reason to find him. He could be hurt or bleeding."

"I've been up there. There's nothing left of the smoker," he said, his voice unsteady.

"We have to try." Anna Mae's hands tightened over his arm. "I won't leave him alone. I can't. We can't. He deserves that at least. Please."

He stared past her for a long minute before nodding. Frank led the way. Everywhere she looked, there were dazed passengers and men with rolled-up sleeves offering strong shoulders or tending to wounds. As they got closer to the front of the train, men were carrying bodies and laying them on the ground in rows. Most of the dead were passengers in the Jim Crow cars, but it was hard to tell who was who through the smoke and grime.

Frank slowed. "Do you see him anywhere?"

She shook her head, unable to speak.

"I'm going to check the men over there," he said, pointing at another line of dead and injured on the ground. "Wait here."

"I'm going with you," she said, her voice stronger than she felt.

"Are you sure?"

She told him she was. They walked on, picking their way through the men sprawled across the grass lining the cornfields. More than once, she had to look away, the blood and broken bones making her stomach swirl. At the end of the row, they still hadn't found him.

"He's not here," Frank said.

Relief flooded her body, but it was short-lived. More bodies were being pulled from the car, one after another. She'd lost count dozens ago. Now, she found herself drawn to the remains of the smoker car, to the piles of splintered wood and shattered glass. Frank pointed at men who stood two by two near what was once the car, each pair waiting to carry another poor soul from the wreckage.

Silent, Frank and Anna Mae waited, searching each face that went by. Anna Mae spotted him first, carried out feet first, his head flopping awkwardly. She ran forward, Frank at her heels. The men carrying Milton slowed as she approached, the tragedy of the day etched into the lines of their faces.

"You know him?" one asked. He was tall, his face hardened by weather.

"His name is Milton," she said. "We were to be married."

"Sorry," the other man mumbled.

Anna Mae and Frank followed them, watching as they laid him out on the ground, straightening his broken legs. His waistcoat, soaked red with blood, flapped open. His eyelids were shut and swollen, his face bruised as though he'd been beaten. She fell to her knees.

The tall man lingered, bent toward her. "He's got something in his hand, Miss."

She tore her gaze from Milton's face. His hand was closed tight in a ball, but a gold chain dangled from between his fingers.

"Oh, Milton," she breathed. Heart thumping under her skin, she took his hand in hers and pried each finger open until the locket dropped to the ground. The golden chain glinted in the hot sun. Sweat dripped from her brow and mingled with the tears on her cheeks. She put the locket around her neck, the metal cool on her skin. Bowing her head, she whispered a prayer for the man she loved.

When she opened her eyes again, she found Frank and the tall man waiting. Frank helped her to her feet and the tall man nodded once, saying "ma'am" before returning to the broken car.

"Anna Mae? What are you doing here?" She looked around to find William, her brother-in-law. He shot Frank a curious look and then held out his hand.

After introductions, William wiped his face with his handkerchief and gestured toward Milton. "Anna Mae? Did you know this man?"

She met his worried gaze. Birdie's husband was a good man. Her father had often commented on that very thing.

"Yes," she said, "but I'll tell you about it later." She turned back toward Frank. "Thank you for helping me." She pointed at the gash on his forehead. "Are you going to be all right?"

"I'll be fine." He leaned in close and lowered his voice. "He was the happiest I've ever known him."

She inhaled, the pain slicing through her heart like a knife. "Thank you," she whispered. He touched a hand to his head and left her, hobbling back in the direction of the coaches until he disappeared into the crowd. Anna Mae straightened her shoulders and faced William. It was time to learn the rest. "My father?"

"It's not good news," he said, lips set into a hard line. She blinked hard and waited. "It's best you don't see him. The boiler . . ." His words trailed away.

"Oh," Anna Mae managed to say before clamping both hands over her mouth. She staggered, gulping the acrid air. The boiler. William was right. That wasn't the way she wanted to remember her father.

"I had him put in my wagon," her brother-in-law said. "Please tell your mother I'll do my best to take care of him."

Her heart sank again. Mother. And Katie Belle. Did they know about the wreck? What would they say when they heard the news?

"Thank you, William."

He waved a hand toward the train. "I have to get back."

"How many are there?"

"A hundred. Maybe more." He paused, his face pained. "And lots more injured."

"Can I help?"

He frowned. "I don't know. There are some ladies bringing water and washing wounds."

"I can do that."

William raised a hand to his brow and searched the field. He pointed at a spot farther up the track, where the train from Memphis lay buckled. "There were a lot of wounded in those cars."

She saw a second mass of bodies and more passengers being pulled free, many broken bones and bleeding heads. She saw water being carried down the hill in pails to tend to the injured. A large woman in a heavy, plain skirt directed those that could help. She made up her mind. There was no time to waste.

~~~~
~~~~

Anna Mae dipped the fabric she'd torn from her dress in the water. The man had come from one of the Jim Crow cars, a worker headed to the gunpowder plant. His already dark skin was made darker with blood and soot and bruises. Hesitating, she touched the rag to the man's forehead and cheeks, wiping away the blood. The shallow sound of his breath didn't surprise her given his injuries—those she could see anyway. She thought his nose was broken along with his arm, and then there was his leg. He stirred then—mumbling something she couldn't understand, his head rolling sideways, his eyelids fluttering. She drew back.

"Wh-where am I?"

"Nashville."

"Nashville." He tried to sit up, then howled in pain and fell back to the ground.

"Be still now," she ordered. "You've been in an accident."

He touched a hand to his chest. "It hurts to breathe."

"Take small breaths," she said, hoping that would help. She dipped the cloth in the cool water again. "What's your name?"

"John Lang," he managed to choke out.

"I'm Anna Mae."

"My leg," he said, struggling to lift his head to see.

"Don't move," she told him again. Anna Mae didn't need to look to know the awkward bend of it.

She didn't know if it was the pain or shock, but his eyes closed again. She leaned closer to hear his breath. This man needed a doctor. Anna Mae got to her feet and, raising a hand to her brow, scanned the men and women hurrying about, moving bodies, carrying water, and removing wreckage but saw no one that could help. Tears pricked her eyes, and she brushed at them angrily. Now was not the time. Then, reminded of a war story her father had once told her, she gathered up her skirt and ran toward the train. It didn't take long to find what she was looking for. Picking up a wooden slat from one of the train's cars, she carried it back to the man and laid it next to his leg. Working quickly, she tore several strips from her dress. She stole a glance at the man's face, but his eyes remained closed. Straightening his leg as best she could on the wooden slat, she tied it to the board.

The sound of his voice made her jerk back in surprise. "What happened?" His eyes searched hers. "There was a terrible noise and I fell, I think. I don't remember anything after that."

"Yes. Hush now," she told him. "You need to save your strength."

His hand fell on hers. "Please," he said. "I need you to find someone."

Her heart clenched. He, too, had someone on the train.

His hand tightened over hers. "My friend was in the other car, the first car. We were going to the plant."

DuPont. She knew of the gunpowder plant, had heard her father speak of it and the workers riding the trains.

"His name is Matt Toles," the man said.

She gave a shake of her head. "The first car was . . . bad."

He tried to sit up again. "Please, I need to know. To tell his mama."

Anna Mae didn't know how she would find this man's friend among the bodies. There were so many, and she wouldn't know where to start. She started to tell him so, but the anguish on his face—the same she bore—made her change her mind.

"How will I know it's him?"

John didn't think long. "His initials are carved into the soles of his boots. MT. He always says that way no man can ever steal 'em. He's my best friend." His voice broke on the last words.

She nodded. "I'll be back as soon as I can."

Anna Mae walked toward the line of dead. At each pair of boots, she knelt closer, inspecting the sole. After the tenth man, she found him. She forced herself to look at his twisted and broken body. She didn't know why. She didn't know the dead man, but John did, and for reasons she didn't understand, that was reason enough.

She knelt down beside John. "I found him."

"Alive?"

"I'm sorry."

The young man's face contorted in pain.

"Was it bad?" he asked.

She did the only thing she could, the thing she hoped was true for Milton, for her father, for all of them. She lied. "I don't think he suffered too much."

~~~

The day wore on, the sun blistering those that came to look at the carnage. The severely injured were rushed to the hospitals—the whites to Vanderbilt, the rest to City Hospital. Red Cross workers, doctors, and railroad men rushed around. The volunteers carried buckets of water. Doctors bandaged what they could. The railroad men worked to remove the cars, hitching them to working engines to be hauled away. Thousands of spectators gathered in the cornfields and on the hill.

By the afternoon, Anna Mae's back hurt, and her hands were raw. Her dress clung to her body, and she wiped beads of sweat from her upper lip. The railroad company had almost finished removing the mangled steel and coaches. Bodies had been loaded into wagons and taken to their respective morgues. And people kept coming. Looking for loved ones. Looking to help. Looking.

She'd been at the site for hours, but it felt more like days or weeks. It was time to go home, to hug her mother and her sister. She trudged up the hill, back toward New White Bridge. A man stood nearby, his hat in his hand.

She stopped. It was the tall man who'd carried Milton off the train.

"Sorry for your loss, ma'am."

"Thank you."

"Hard day for a lotta folks."

His voice was deep, with a twang she didn't recognize. "You're not from around here, are you?"

"No, ma'am. But I'm headed home now."
~~~

Something about the way he spoke made her study him again. "Were you on the train? Do you know what happened?"

His head dropped along with his voice. "My younger brother was on that train. I was supposed to look out for him." It was her turn to say she was sorry. "It was bound to happen sooner or later. Carl couldn't get out of his own way. This time, though, was my fault." He shook his head and shuddered. "This was a mighty hard thing today."

When she spoke, her words were no longer a question. "You saw it happen."

His hooded eyes glistened in the afternoon sun. "Yes, ma'am, I did."

CHAPTER TWENTY-THREE

Summer 1988

"CLYDE TOLD ME everything that day, about what he was planning, what he witnessed when the trains hit." Anna Mae sighed. "I think he was a changed man after that." She shifted toward the nightstand, opened the drawer, and pulled out the letters tied with string. Rifling through, she pulled one and held it up in the air. "Clyde wrote me once. Told me he'd taken a job in a town in West Virginia, was living a quiet life. I don't know if that was true or if that's what he wanted me to believe, but I do hope so. I wrote back, more than once, but I never heard from him again."

Ginny's eyes were drawn to the rest of the letters Anna Mae held in her lap. She knew the one on top, the one from Milton. It occurred to her now that he must have mailed it that very morning, his last, after he and Anna Mae had agreed to marry. She blushed at the intimate words she'd read. Now she knew what those words had meant to the woman in front of her.

"You're wondering about these?" Anna Mae asked, holding up the stack again.

"Yes." Heat rose on Ginny's cheeks. "I hope you don't mind."

The old woman's smile was gentle. "Not at all. I would wonder, too, if I were you." She touched the letters with gentle fingers. "John was the first to write me."

"He survived?"

"That he did. He was taken to City Hospital. After he healed, he went to work for DuPont. And then his three months were up."

"Did he go home after that?"

"Not exactly." Her pale lips turned up in a sad smile. "He went to Chicago. That's where his friend Matt had wanted to go, and so he said he was going to try it out for him. His mother wasn't too happy, but like Clyde, John was a changed man after the accident. The John Lang I came to know was a very determined man, and if he set his mind to something, a person would do well to get out of his way." She chuckled. "I always did admire that about him. They wrote me when they left Chicago to buy their own farm in Upstate New York, and that's where they stayed. I think Mississippi and Tennessee just held too many bad memories for those two."

Ginny sat up straighter. "They?"

"Oh, dear, didn't I tell you? Sabina waited for John until he finished at DuPont. They got married the very next day. Then they packed their bags, took the baby, and headed up north. They had three boys of their own along the way." She plucked out another letter, extracting a photograph. She held it out to Ginny.

Holding it by the corners, Ginny looked down at a handsome family of six: a man with a wide smile, a woman with a long braid, and four boys of varying heights.

"That was right after they bought their dairy farm. They grew crops, too, but it was mostly dairy." She took the picture back, returning it to the envelope. "I would have liked to have seen John again, but in those days, even writing a letter to a man who was . . . well, you understand. It might have been misunderstood. I don't know what happened to the family after the kids grew up, but I'd like to think they were happy. They'd already been through some terrible things. They deserved some happiness at least."

"So did you, Anna Mae." Ginny reached out and placed her hand on the old woman's. "So did you."

Anna Mae was quiet a moment. Her voice, when she spoke, was tinged with sadness but no regret. "I had happiness, dear. A lot of good years. But those days with Milton were something."

Ginny sniffled. "I'm sorry," she said. "You don't have to talk about it."

Anna Mae shook her head. "I don't mind. It's quite an amazing thing, really. A beautiful thing." Ginny lifted her brows. "We spend so much time trying to forget what hurts that we miss out on remembering what's good. Perhaps I didn't know love long, but I knew it, and not everyone can say that, can they?" Anna Mae swatted the air with her hand, sweeping away any unhappy thoughts. "Enough about me. What else do you want to know?"

Ginny didn't hesitate.

"Yes, George Hall," Anna Mae said with a slow nod. "I was told his funeral was one of the best attended in Nashville, but of course, I wouldn't know. Another thing that would have been frowned upon. Not surprisingly, he was quite popular among the other porters. He left behind his wife and his children, but I'm sure he would have been proud. His daughter finished at the high school and went to Fisk University, as her father had hoped. She was a professor there for many years." Anna Mae rubbed the knots on the back of her hands. "Her younger brothers all grew up, got married, and moved away. It wasn't my place, but I went to see George's wife after the accident. My father had spoken of him, and there'd been so much loss."

Ginny thought about how difficult that must have been for the young Anna Mae.

"Celeste was polite, but I wasn't her favorite person, as you can imagine. I didn't blame her really. Especially later, after the trial."

Ginny leaned forward, pulse skipping. Was this what Anna Mae had referred to in her letter? *The days in court and the trial itself took their toll. The testimony, so very cruel, was especially difficult.*

"What trial?" she asked now.

"That came later," Anna Mae said, the words slow. "The papers called the wreck a blunder. There were stories. My father . . . he was blamed. Even his friends at the Knights of Columbus shunned his memory. My mother took to her bed. It fell to my sister and I, but before long, I couldn't help either." She drew in a shaky breath. "We didn't know when John George would come home from Europe, and my father's army pension wasn't enough for us to live on. He'd spent his whole life with the railroad and got nothing for it. My mother had no choice. She took the railroad to court, but it nearly broke her. She needed me. Katie Belle needed me." Anna Mae's voice dropped to a whisper. "It took all I had to be a part of it, to speak of that terrible day. The train crash, that was an accident. That was bad. But for my mother, the trial was worse."

CHAPTER TWENTY-FOUR

Thursday, October 21, 1920

121 PERSONS ARE KILLED AND 57 INJURED IN TRAIN COLLISION. DEATH AND DESTRUCTION WROUGHT WHEN CRASH ON N.C. & ST.L. RY. OCCURS.

Engines Demolished and Express Car Driven Through Coaches Laden with Human Freight, Other Cars Being Telescoped and Piled High in the Air. THOUSANDS FLOCK TO SCENE OF CATASTROPHE

Washington, July 9.— The Railroad Administration announced tonight that George L. Loyall, assistant to the regional director for the South, has been ordered to Nashville to investigate the wreck on the N.C. & St.L. Railway. Mr. Loyall is especially charged, the administration said, with fixing individual responsibility for the wreck, if that be possible.

Because somebody blundered, at least 121 persons were killed and fifty-seven injured shortly after 7 o'clock on Tuesday morning, when Nashville, Chattanooga & St. Louis Railway passenger trains No. 1 from Memphis and No. 4 from Nashville crashed head-on together just around the sharp, steep-graded curve at Dutchman's Bend, about five miles from the city near the Harding Road.

Both engines reared and fell on either side of the track, unrecognizable masses of twisted iron and steel, while the fearful impact of the blow drove the express car of the north-bound train through the flimsy wooden coaches loaded with human freight, telescoped the smoking car in front and piling high in air the two cars behind it, both packed to the aisles with Negroes en route to the powder plant and some 150 other passengers.

Just where lies the blame is impossible now to say. Officials of the road are silent.

—*The Tennessean*, July 10, 1918

Anna Mae walked beside her mother and Katie Belle, her insides knotted and her palms sweating. As though one, all three women slowed outside the Davidson County Courthouse. This would be the site of the trial, the one Mary had initiated. Anna Mae wanted to believe it would be worth it, but she didn't hold much faith in the outcome. Not when so many had already decided where blame belonged.

Inside the courtroom, they sat shoulder to shoulder, linked in a show of solidarity. Mary's health had been precarious for months. Only recently on the mend, she'd rallied to pursue this case, a suit arguing for monies owed to her late husband's beneficiaries under the Federal Employee Liability Act. She'd engaged two lawyers, both young and ambitious, who assured her they could prove David's death met the criteria: that he'd been performing his railroad duties at the time of his death and that his demise could, in part, be blamed on the negligence of the railroad itself or another in its employ. The suit asked for damages in the amount of $25,000. However, while the family did need the money, that was not Mary's primary motivation. Above all else, she wanted to clear David's name.

After the railroad's investigation, the papers and the general public had begun referring to David as The Blunderer. In the Kennedy apartment, the nickname rankled. It wasn't only his Knights of Columbus friends who'd disassociated themselves from his memory.

Their railroad family had all but disappeared too. Less than half a dozen friends were still willing to speak to the girls and their mother, and even then sometimes only grudgingly. For Mary, who'd always been a proud woman, this was unacceptable.

And thus, Mary had initiated the lawsuit. On this morning, she sat with her head held high, her spine straight, and her hands folded in her lap. If she could not testify with words, she would do so with her manner. Anna Mae tried to follow her mother's lead, but she had other worries, not limited to a gnawing concern that her mother hadn't fully recovered, that the ordeal of the trial might be too much for her already precarious health. Yet, she knew what was expected of her. She would sit quietly and be her mother's ears, listening to every word.

Often tedious and littered with railroad rules and time schedules, the early bit of testimony took the better part of the first day. It wasn't until James Preston "Shorty" Eubank took the stand that the air in the courtroom grew charged. William Norvell, her mother's attorney, didn't waste any time getting to the heart of his questioning.

"Mr. Eubank, we've heard the orders you received on the morning of the accident. The Number Four train was to wait for the Number One train before moving onto the single track. Is that correct?"

"Yes, those were our orders."

"You and Engineer Kennedy got those orders together?"

"Yes."

"And did you share those orders with anyone else?"

"I read them to the porter, George Hall, who shared them with the flagman, Sinclair."

"Did anyone else on the train receive the orders?"

"Meadows, the fireman. Uncle Dave would have told him."

Norvell looked back at Mary before letting his gaze wander over the jury. "So, five crewmen on the train knew the Number Four had to wait at Shops for the Number One. There is no mistake about that."

"That's true."

"But you didn't wait for the Number One, did you?"

"No, sir."

Angling his head to his shoulder, Norvell asked, "What were you doing when the trains hit, Mr. Eubank?"

Shorty swallowed, his face pink. "I was collecting tickets."

"And had you seen the Number One pass?"

"No."

"Had you seen any train pass?"

"I heard a steam engine go by, but I was busy, so I wasn't looking."

"Correct me if I'm wrong, but you had the orders, didn't you? Had you forgotten to look out for the Number One?"

"No, sir. But I counted on Uncle Dave and George and the flagman for that. I couldn't take tickets and watch at the same time."

Beside Anna Mae, Mary blanched. Shorty was putting the blame back on the others, on David.

"Besides the engineer, who has the ability to stop the train?"

"The conductor—me—I suppose. He can pull the emergency valve if he needs to."

"And before that, he can pull the bell cord asking the engineer to stop, can't he?"

"Yes, that's true."

"But you didn't do either of those things, did you?"

"I was taking tickets. That was my job."

"As was watching for the Number One. Five people had that job, didn't they? Not one, but five?"

Sitting forward, Anna Mae's fingers found Mary's. She could feel the racing of her mother's pulse, hear her quick breaths.

Shorty didn't answer right away.

When he did, he spoke so softly, Norvell had to ask him to repeat his answer.

"Yes. Five had the job."

~~~~

The trial lasted three days. Norvell made his point, but in the end, he wasn't able to get everything. The jury awarded Mary $8,000, the same that had been given to the beneficiaries of the white victims of the crash, but well below what she'd asked for. In contrast, the families of those in the Jim Crow cars received only a fraction or just over one thousand dollars. In spite of the settlement in Mary's favor, the jury did not clear David's name. Instead, negligence was assigned to all the railroaders aboard the Number Four. It was exactly as Anna Mae had feared. David Kennedy would always be The Blunderer, and nothing short of a full exoneration could have soothed the ache in her mother's heart.

A few years later, the State Supreme Court reversed the decision, stating that David's beneficiaries were not entitled to an award for the accident he helped to bring about. For the small family, it was another loss, adding to their shame.

On a cool morning not long after the decision, Anna Mae rose early, her feet light on the bare floor. In the darkness of the room, Katie Belle's breath whistled softly. Careful not to wake her sister, Anna Mae slipped out. Padding down the hall, she skirted the boxes and bags piled throughout. Today would be their last day in the apartment. At her father's desk, she pulled out the chair, sitting slowly. Blinking back tears, she ran her hand across the smooth surface, remembering how he'd dip his pen in the ink, always careful not to blot the pages.

Anna Mae slid open the top drawer and searched inside until her fingers closed over the wooden pipe. She held it in both hands, inhaling the lingering scents of David's tobacco. Rising, she carried it to the trunk, this last item. With a shaking hand, she wrapped the pipe in paper and slid it into
~~~~

the corner of the case, where it fit like the last piece of a puzzle. *Maybe it is,* she thought.

Hands trembling, Anna Mae tightened the buckles and stared once more at the trunk that bore her initials in gold lettering. Inside were the memories of her life, her years in the apartment with her parents, her sister, and her brother, the brief time she spent with Milton, the wreck, George, John, and Clyde—all of them. Fighting tears, she latched the lock. It was time to put this part of her life behind her.

She wiped away the tears and lifted her chin. The words she spoke were a whisper and a prayer. "Goodbye and Godspeed."

CHAPTER TWENTY-FIVE

Summer 1988

ANNA MAE'S VOICE faded away, and she looked over at Ginny. "Not quite the outcome you expected, was it?"

"So, you moved on? Is that it?"

"No. Even if I'd wanted to, it wouldn't have been that easy." She clasped her hands together. "There seemed to be no end to it all. *The Defender* had a story calling the crash murder. Of course, it was an accusation borne out of injustice and steeped in emotion—understandable, really—but that didn't make it hurt less. And as I said, the trial did nothing to stop the rumors from swirling."

Ginny thought she understood. The railroads and the government had accepted no blame. David, as engineer, should have looked out for the Number One, but that same responsibility also rested on the shoulders of Shorty, Luther, the flagman, and George.

But there were other causes, not the least of which was an untenable timetable set by a government and a railroad ill equipped to handle the demands. Wooden cars. Crowded trains. Single tracks. An elderly engineer. Signals that weren't checked. It was a perfect storm no matter how one looked at it. Worse, the government and the railroad, absolved of any guilt, didn't do the right thing after the fact. The settlements fell short and were pitiable when it came to the majority of the victims. The discrepancy in the payments between the races, the unfairness of it, overwhelmed her. She couldn't help thinking of George's wife and children, young Ben, Matt Toles, and Lem Hudson, and dozens and dozens more.

"It's awful," she said at last.

"It was that." Anna Mae's head bobbed up and down. "It took some time for all the attention to die down. Mother never really recovered. After John George came home, she was better for a while, but the stigma of it all wouldn't end." Twisting her hands in her lap, the old woman gave a small smile. "I did my best to be a comfort, though I'm sure I only added to her pain in the end. After Katie Belle married and then John George a year later, they both moved away. Even Birdie and William left Nashville. I couldn't blame them. I taught music when I could, but mostly, mother and I worked as housekeepers. After Mother died, I missed her terribly. This may sound odd since she didn't speak much, but the house grew too quiet. That's when I started taking in boarders."

"I'm so sorry, Anna Mae."

"That's kind of you, dear, but don't be. As I said, I've had a good life, even if it wasn't what I'd once dreamed it would be. Besides, that isn't why I told you this story. It was never about me. It's about sharing what happened that day, about what things were really like and how so many lives were lost and changed. It was a tragedy—a horrible tragedy—that should never be forgotten."

Objectively and as a history teacher, Ginny agreed, but she couldn't help feeling for Anna Mae, a woman she'd come to know and care about. She'd lost Milton because he'd made his way to the smoker, but if he'd been in his seat, things might have been different. John Lang was luckier than most. George Hall and Matt Toles weren't. Even with the massive number of deaths, the accident itself remained overshadowed by the very war that had brought about the circumstances of the crash.

Life had gone on. That's how it worked, she guessed. The accident became a footnote in history, one she as a teacher had never heard of. John and Sabina had built a family, but they'd left their home to do it. Like Anna Mae, Celeste had been forced to take on additional work to keep her family fed, but in the end, Anita had fulfilled her parents' dream and then some. After the war, railroad safety did improve. Wooden cars were replaced with steel ones. Automatic signals were installed. The porters formed a union. Maybe those things would have happened anyway, but there was no way of knowing. Tragedy was like that sometimes. Death and loss aren't always the end. Sometimes they're the beginning.

Sliding closer to the old woman, Ginny reached out and took Anna Mae's hands in hers. "Thank you."

"For what, dear?"

"For choosing me to tell your story." Tears dripped down her face as she squeezed the old woman's hands. "It's a gift I'll treasure all my life."

Anna Mae's face glowed with pleasure now. "Well, that is all I ever wanted."

~~~~

Ginny sat in front of the trunk, her legs crisscrossed in front of her. She pushed the lid back and pulled the items out one by one. She took out the straw hat that Milton had given Anna Mae, admiring the red flower and ribbon.

Her fingers brushed across the purses, handkerchiefs, and music sheets. She held up a soft wrap, inhaling its musty scent. They may have only been things, and most held little monetary value, but they were the physical memories of a woman's life.

Shawn sat down on the sofa nearest her, a cup of coffee in his hand. "What are you doing?"

He'd been home almost a week now, and while there had been more than a few awkward moments, they were less frequent, and she was glad of
~~~~

that. They'd agreed to take their time, to talk and, most important, to listen. If they were going to make it, they'd have to learn from the past.

"I don't know. I still can't figure out how this trunk got in my attic."

"Grandma Betty's attic, you mean."

"Right. It guess it could have been here when she moved in," Ginny mused out loud.

"True. Or she came across it somewhere else and kept if for some reason."

"That doesn't really sound like her," Ginny said. Grandma Betty may have been a hurricane talker and an overenthusiastic mother, but she was also organized and the opposite of a hoarder. She'd been known to throw out an item before you were even finished using it. Besides, Grandma Betty rarely did things without purpose, so why had she kept a strange trunk? She had to know it was there.

Slowly, she let her gaze wander over the items lined up on the floor. Stopping at the jewel box, she picked it up, admiring the tiny cross.

"What's that?" her husband asked.

Ginny showed him the jewel box. "I forgot to ask Anna Mae if Katie Belle had a matching one. Isn't it beautiful?" She held it out for him to take, but it slipped through his fingers, landing on the floor. Scooping it up, he held the box in one hand and the necklace in the other. Ginny, though, wasn't looking at either. Instead, her eyes remained on the cushion that had fallen out and landed upside down. Tucked into the folds was a tiny slip of paper.

Fingers shaking, she unfolded the note. She read the words slowly, her voice soft.

"My Dearest Son, may you know I loved you more than life itself. God Bless you always."

"I don't understand," Shawn said. "I thought you said the cross belonged to Anna Mae."

"I thought it did." She looked down at the note again, the writing as familiar to her now as her own. *My Dearest Son.*

Her mind raced and she jumped to her feet, running to her room and grabbing *Anne of Green Gables* from her nightstand.

And there was the letter.

My Darling, I saw you in Centennial Park today.

She read it all the way through, her breath quickening.

"Are you okay, Gin?"

She jumped. She hadn't heard him come in the room. Unable to speak, she shook her head slowly, lifting the letter in her hand. He took it, reading.

"You told me about this, right? It's a letter to Milton?"

"That's what I thought," she said, a tear leaking from her eye. The trunk in the attic. The letters. It all made sense now. When she spoke at last, there was wonder in her voice. "I should have guessed before, but I didn't see it. I didn't know."

It was Shawn's turn to shake his head. "Should have guessed what?"

"The most wonderful thing of all," she said, smiling broadly now. "Truly wonderful."

~~~~

Ginny pushed open the door to Anna Mae's room. The old woman, resting in her chair in much the same way she had on the first day they'd met, gazed out the window at the old railroad tracks.

"Anna Mae."

The old woman's head came around. "Why, Ginny. What a wonderful surprise. I wasn't expecting you until tomorrow."

She stared at the old woman. Anna Mae had no fewer wrinkles. Her hands were still knotted with arthritis. Her hair was still white, and yet, she looked more beautiful than ever to the girl.

"I know," she said, finding her voice, "but something came up and our plans changed."
~~~~

"Oh? Is everything okay with you and Shawn?" She waved a hand before Ginny could answer. "Never mind me. That's none of my business. Look what I got this morning," she said, pointing at a chair that hadn't been there before. This one had deep cushions and arms. It was as inviting as the hard, wooden chair had been uncomfortable. Anna Mae couldn't contain her joy. "A new chair. I couldn't have you sitting on that old chair another day now that I know you've got a baby on the way. Isn't it lovely?"

It was, and Ginny said so.

"Sit down, dear, and tell me how you're feeling."

When Ginny remained standing, Anna Mae's smile wavered. "Is something wrong?"

"No. At least I hope not," the younger woman said. "But there's someone I want you to meet."

"Oh, my. Is Shawn here?" Anna Mae raised a hand to her hair. "Of course, I'd love to meet him, so long as he doesn't mind if an old woman has a few words of wisdom to share."

Ginny's laugh sounded nervous even to herself, but she pulled the door open. There was Shawn, waiting, a bouquet of pink flowers in his hands. She pulled him in.

"This is Shawn."

"It's nice to meet you," he said.

"And nice to meet you." She looked up at him, white brows rising. "Ginny didn't mention you were so tall."

Ginny held the door as the two introduced themselves, her gaze shifting to the second man waiting in the corridor. With a crook of her finger, he came forward, his steps hesitant.

"Are you sure?" he whispered.

In answer, she reached out and took his arm, dragging him into the room. Anna Mae looked from Shawn to the man to Ginny, brows arching higher. The younger woman wondered what Anna Mae saw in that moment. Did she see her own snow-white hair, all trace of golden-red gone now? Did she see the long fingers of a musician and a surgeon? Did she see Milton?

"This is my father, Michael Piler," Ginny said. "Your son."

~~~~

Anna Mae stared at the man, the color draining from her face. Her mouth fell open, but no words came. Ginny's father seemed to falter behind her, equally unable to speak. Shawn shot Ginny a questioning glance. Seconds ticked by, no one speaking. Only when the old woman's chin quivered and shook, followed by her whole head and then her shoulders did Ginny move. She knelt down in front of Anna Mae, holding her hands until her sobs faded.

"This is all a bit overwhelming," Anna Mae said finally, her voice small in the quiet room.

Michael, standing awkwardly behind his daughter, cleared his throat. "That it is."

Whirling around, Ginny pushed him into the new chair. "Sit down, Dad."

Anna Mae, unable to stop looking at the man in front of her, trembled as she asked, "How? I don't understand." She swung toward Ginny. "How did you know?"

"I didn't until last night," the young woman admitted. "It started with the cross and the note in the jewel box." She explained about finding the note.

"The cross. I'd forgotten about that." Anna Mae's voice softened with memory. "And the note. It was tucked into the box, I think."

"It was, but there was another letter, too, one you wrote but didn't send. I found that one hidden in *Anne of Green Gables*." She looked back at Shawn, and he pulled the letter from his pocket, handing it to Anna Mae.

Reading the letter, the old woman gave a shake of her head. "I'd put it in the book, planning to finish it later, but I guess I never did, did I?"

"No, I guess not. When I first found it, I thought you were writing to Milton. But now that I know what happened, that didn't make sense. The letter was written years after the crash, after the trial. So, then I thought maybe
~~~~

there was someone else you hadn't told me about, another man," she paused, "until I found the note in the jewel box. *My Dearest Son.* You'd written the letter not to another man, but to your son." She hesitated. "Milton's son."

"Yes," Anna Mae whispered. "A miracle. I didn't know . . ." She stopped, looking at each of them in turn. "With everything, I didn't know. I'm so sorry," she said, bowing her head.

It was Ginny who spoke then. "You have nothing to be sorry for."

Anna Mae gave a half-hearted nod, her chin still low.

"But I'd love to hear the rest. We all would, I think—if you want to tell it."

Lifting her head, Anna Mae's eyes glistened once more. "I do want to." She reached for a tissue and sat up a little straighter then, her gaze landing on Michael. "I'll do my best," she said. Her son leaned forward, and she began.

"Not long after the accident, my mother took to her bed. Katie Belle and I tried to take care of things, but before long, I fell ill, too—or thought I did. It was Katie Belle who figured it out first. I was terrified, of course. Already, we had lost so much, but in a way, the scandal, which had been like a black cloud hanging over our apartment, did have one silver lining. No one called on us. No one thought about us at all." She paused to catch her breath. "It wasn't hard to hide my condition. We rarely left the apartment, and when we did, I'd taken to letting out my gowns a few stitches at a time. No one knew. Not even Mother for a while." Fresh tears shimmered. "The cross was mine once. You wore it in the days after you were born, and I wanted you to have it."

Ginny inched closer. She'd known her father was adopted. He was much older than her mother, born in 1919. It was the right time, and yet, it had never occurred to her.

"Anna Mae, why didn't you tell me?" She looked over her shoulder at her father. "Tell both of us?"

For a long minute, Anna Mae didn't answer. "In the beginning, I didn't know myself. I couldn't understand why my trunk would be in a house on

Sunset with someone named Betty. Until you reminded me Betty was a nickname for Elizabeth. And then you said the name. Elizabeth Piler."

Most of this Ginny had figured out, though not all. "But you said you'd never met her."

"That was true. The adoption was arranged through the church. I was told about the Pilers before your father was born, about how they'd been unable to have children."

"That doesn't explain why you didn't say anything after you knew who she was, who I was," Ginny said carefully.

"I couldn't by then." Anna Mae squeezed her granddaughter's hands. "How could I upset your lives? It would serve no purpose. And I'd already received the most wonderful gift. Your friendship."

Michael, who'd been listening, spoke then. "It makes sense now, why my mother didn't want me to stay in Nashville, why she wanted me far away."

Anna Mae's lips curved upward in a sad smile. "I suppose she was frightened I'd show up one day and try to take you back. I don't blame her. I didn't want to give you up. You have to know that. An unwed mother after the scandal of the wreck was bad enough, but Mother was bedridden. We had no money. John George wouldn't be home for years. I thought it was the best thing I could do for you. Give you a good life." She regarded him now. "It was a good life, wasn't it?"

"It was," he assured her.

Her hunched shoulders sagged, but her eyes were glad. "After I signed the papers, I was no use to anyone. Katie Belle carried the load until the trial. Mother needed both of us then. It may have been the only good thing to come out of that infernal time. I came back to the land of the living, made peace with the choices I'd made. But I never stopped wanting you to know where you came from and who you were—when you were ready. Selfish of me, really, when I think about it now. You had a life."

"It wasn't selfish," Ginny protested.

"But it was. It is," Anna Mae said, her expression somber now. She shifted toward Michael. "I had the trunk delivered to your parents—they lived near Centennial Park in those days—with a letter asking them to share the trunk with you when you were older."

"They never told me about it," he said.

"No, I don't imagine they did. But they didn't throw it out, did they? They kept it, even moved it to Sunset, which is quite extraordinary, really."

"I didn't know I was adopted growing up. I don't think people spoke of it much in those days." He nodded toward his daughter. "It was an accident that I found out, a blood test after my father fell ill, but by then I wasn't a young man anymore. I told my wife and Ginny, of course. I tried to broach the subject with my mother once, but in the end, I couldn't."

"You didn't want to hurt her."

"I figured she would have told me if she'd wanted me to know. Being my mother was everything to her, and I couldn't take that from her."

"You did the right thing. She was your mother after all."

Ginny sat frozen between them, listening and watching. Anna Mae and her father. So alike. The quiet manner in which they spoke. The long, graceful fingers. The red hair turned to white. How had she not seen it before?

"But I had another mother, one I never dreamed I'd meet."

"Are you very angry with me?"

He slipped from the chair and fell to his knees next to Ginny, placing his hands on theirs. "Never. You gave me life in more ways than one. For that, I will always be grateful."

For once, Anna Mae had no words.

Michael moved closer. "But there is something I want. I'd like to know you the way Ginny does. I want to hear about your life, about the train crash, about my father, about my grandparents, about everything."

Tears leaked from Anna Mae's bright eyes.

"I don't want to forget the past," Ginny's father said. "Not a bit of it."

Anna Mae fell forward, and they wrapped their arms around one another, pulling Ginny to them. Grandmother, son, and granddaughter. The three huddled for a long time before the old woman pulled away, pushing Michael up and back to his chair.

After tucking her quilt around her legs, she rested her hands in her lap, fingers poised to play an imaginary tune. Winking at Ginny, she once more brought her gaze to rest on her son, a tiny smile on her pale lips.

"Michael, do you like stories?"

THE END

ACKNOWLEDGMENTS

IF THIS IS the first book you've read by me, you may not know that I have previously written (and still write) mystery and suspense. If it's not your first book by me and you know my mysteries (thank you!), you might be wondering why I've ventured into historical fiction. The reason is simple. A friend in Nashville, BR, showed me a sign—a historical marker really—at Dutchman's Curve. The sign read:

DUTCHMAN'S CURVE TRAIN WRECK

The deadliest train wreck in US history occurred on July 9, 1918, when two crowded trains collided head-on at Dutchman's Curve. The impact caused passenger cars to derail into surrounding cornfields and fires broke out throughout the wreckage. Over 100 died, including many African-American workers journeying to work at the munitions plant near Old Hickory.

BR went on to tell me that the accident was largely unheard of outside of Nashville and even there, the site of the crash wasn't awarded the marker until 2008, on the ninetieth anniversary of that horrific event.

He had me at "deadliest train wreck."

I went home, brain buzzing and determined to learn more. As a writer, I immediately looked for books on the wreck and found only one, Betsy Thorpe's *The Day the Whistles Cried: The Great Cornfield Meet at Dutchman's*

Curve. Her excellent book, a work of creative nonfiction, focuses partly on the day of the wreck and primarily on the aftermath and trial that followed. Through Betsy's writing, I was introduced to David Kennedy, George Hall, Milton Lowenstein, and Matt Toles. I understood the events as they were described and yet, the "whys and hows" remained a mystery to me (see what I did there!). And thus, I embarked on my own research journey.

Actually, Betsy herself was an amazing source. I was lucky enough to meet with her several years ago when she walked me down to the site of the wreck. Thank you, Betsy! Later, over lunch, we tossed around several theories as to why the Number Four train didn't wait at Shops, why no one sounded the alarm, and why the accident happened at all. But that's all they were—theories. All these years later, there is still no definitive explanation. As a mystery writer, however, my head was filled with what-ifs. As you might have guessed, I had some ideas of my own, and so I began to build my story.

This is the part where readers ask: What is true and what isn't? While this book is inspired by a true event—one that more people *should* know about—it is ultimately a work of fiction. For example, nowhere did I find any evidence that Anna Mae and Milton ever met. Still, they did live very near each other and Anna Mae never married. These were facts that bled into possibility. There is also no evidence that David Kennedy suffered from blinding headaches, but because he was the oldest engineer with the railroad by several years, it's reasonable to assume he may have had some underlying health issues. Perhaps he had a heart attack or a stroke. Perhaps he was distracted. Short of being there with him, it's hard to know why he didn't stop his train. What I do know is that the timetables created by the government after they took over the railroad caused difficulties for the railroaders and created potentially dangerous situations on a daily basis. One might argue the accident could have been avoided, but one could also argue those timetables were necessary to support the war effort. If the coaches had been steel rather than wooden, the loss of life might have been significantly less. If the signal at Shops had been automated, the Number Four train might not have ventured on toward Dutchman's Curve. If segregation hadn't forced so many to ride in the smoky front coach, the loss of life might have been different. If, if, if . . . either way, hindsight can't bring back those who were lost.

What is true is that Matt Toles died that day along with the popular porter, George Hall. While there is some information to be learned about George, there is very little to be found on Matt, only nineteen at the time of his death. Like Matt, a large number of the young men who died that day were destined for the gunpowder plant, however, unlike him, many were never identified. John Lang is my fictional representation of those men. While he lost his friends, he got the happy ending they all deserved.

Like John, Clyde and Carl are also fictional. As would-be outlaws, they represent the end of an era on trains. Most people have heard of Butch Cassidy's Hole in the Wall Gang, Jesse James, or the Newton Gang, all of whom robbed a train at least once between the late 1800s and the early 1900s. The last significant train robbery attempt took place in 1937 on a Southern Pacific Railroad train.

Each of these characters had already started living in my head when I plunged into the research. The greatest challenge in this book was to honor all who died when there was so little recorded information for so many. In some cases, the documents I found were limited to census records or birth or death certificates, and those seemed to take me in circles. So, I ordered books on trains, World War I, the clothing of the time, etc. I scoured the internet. I spent countless hours on ancestry sites and combing old newspapers. Of course, the clips included in this book wouldn't have been possible if it weren't for access to these publications, particularly the *Tennessean* and the *Crisis*. However, there were many more clips I didn't include. I read the ads, the social columns, and the editorials. I toured the former train station, now a beautiful hotel, Union Station Nashville Yards. I studied the events leading up to the crash to build the world where two trains could collide on a beautiful July morning in 1918.

While this book is a work of fiction, I've included some other true moments in the story. For example, both the speech given by the stranger at the Fourth of July picnic in Hernando, Mississippi, as well as the "Why He Failed" speech read on the train to Nashville can be found in the U. S. Department of Labor's report, The Negro at Work During the World War and During Reconstruction. In addition, when William refers to the accident as a blunder, that is taken from a story that appeared in the *Tennessean* on July 10th, 1918, the day after the wreck. It read "Because somebody blundered, at least 121 person were killed and fifty-seven injured shortly after 7 o'clock on Tuesday morning, when Nashville Chattanooga & St. Louis Railway passenger trains No. 1 from Memphis and 4 from Nashville crashed head-on together just around the sharp, steep-graded curve at Dutchman's Bend, about five miles from the city near Harding Road." The next day, the headline read, "Crew of Train No. 4 is blamed."

As for the trial itself—another real event—the scene as I've imagined it is only a representation of a part of the proceedings. The real trial included testimony from many of those working on the train that day as well as at Shops, L&N officials, the railroad physician, detailed explanations of routes and rules, and more. However, the outcome as I wrote it is true. While Mary "won" an $8,000 award as a beneficiary, she was unable to clear her husband's name, and ultimately, even that small win was overturned.

It goes without saying that the Great Train Wreck at Dutchman's Curve should hold a place of importance in our nation's history. The loss of all those lives is too great for us to forget. Since the historical marker of 2008 and more recently, the 100-year anniversary in 2018, there has been more interest in the history of the crash, and I sincerely hope that continues. We can't turn back time, but we can honor and remember.

Bringing each of the characters to life was a labor of love. I chose to begin not with the day of the crash but on the Fourth of July, a day when the city and the country celebrated even while others fought in Europe. It was especially important to me to have Anna Mae share her story, someone who might have connected—even in the most tangential way—with some of the other characters. That she finally got a kind of happy ending (in my version) felt satisfying to me, and I hope to you.

As for the writing process itself, that was done in stages. There were drafts and more drafts. More research. Stops and starts and more drafts. Some of my early readers were Marcia Palmer, Doug Ehlers, and my daughter, Cameron Murphy. Their comments and feedback were spot on and I'm grateful to each for their input. Also instrumental in helping me craft a better version was Rebecca Scherer. Her insights always help me to see the bigger picture.

I owe a huge debt to Helga Schier, my late editor, who chose to take on this saga. Thank you, also, to Elana Gibson for carrying the torch and helping me to make this book the best it can be as well as Ellen Leach for all your hard work. I'm so lucky to have had you both to edit this story. Along with Helga and Elana, I also want to thank the late Sue Arroyo for believing enough in this story to ask to see more. Thank you to Maryann Appel for an incredible cover. I'm not sure I could have imagined a better one. And thank you to Bill Lehto for all your support, to Abigail Miles for your marketing know-how, and to the whole team at CamCat Books. You are the best!

Thank you to all my friends who have asked about this book (for years) and who never fail to support my writing. This book has been particularly special to me. Although I'm not a trained historian and *The Great Forgotten* is a work of fiction, the tragedy at the heart of this story and the state of the world in 1918 are very real. So many lives were lost that day: young, old, black, white, men, women, and children. That so many were never identified is heartbreaking. It is because of that marker at Dutchman's Curve, Betsy Thorpe, and so many others in Nashville that more people finally know about this tragedy. Thank you to all of them for making that happen.

Thank you to my amazing children, Cameron, Thomas, Luke, and Meredith, for your endless support (and teasing) and for reading my words. Thank you to my late husband David who had a special love for Nashville, our wonderful friends there, and this story. I hope I got it right.

ABOUT THE AUTHOR

THE FIRST THING K. L. Murphy wrote was a modified screenplay of a 1970s TV show. She and her siblings performed that show for their own built-in audience (mom and dad) to rave reviews (mom and dad again!). Later, she moved on to high school journalism before graduating from the College of William and Mary and taking a detour into banking and finance. Once she began writing again and focusing on fiction, the process felt like coming home.

K. L. is the award-nominated author of *Her Sister's Death,* a 2023 Silver Falchion Finalist for Best Mystery and the January 2023 Once Upon a Book Club Pick. She is also the author of the Detective Callie Forde Mystery Series, including *Last Girl Missing* and *The Murderer's Girl* as well as the Detective Cancini Mystery Series: *A Guilty Mind, Stay of Execution,* and *The Last Sin.*

Her short stories are featured in *Deadly Southern Charm, Murder by the Glass, First Comes Love, Then Comes Murder, Friend of the Devil: Crime Fiction Inspired by the Songs of the Grateful Dead,* and *Crime in the Old Dominion,* which she also co-edited. In addition, K. L. (an avid fan of recording personal histories) is the author of *The Center: From Generation to Generation,* a coffee-table book that chronicles the seventy-year history of the Richmond Jewish Community Center.

A member of Mystery Writers of America, International Thriller Writers, Historical Writers of America, Sisters in Crime, and James River Writer, K. L. makes her home in Richmond, VA, where she loves spending time with her family, friends, and amazing dogs.

If you enjoyed
K. L. Murphy's *The Great Forgotten,*
consider leaving a review to help our authors.

And check out another book by K. L. Murphy,
Her Sister's Death.

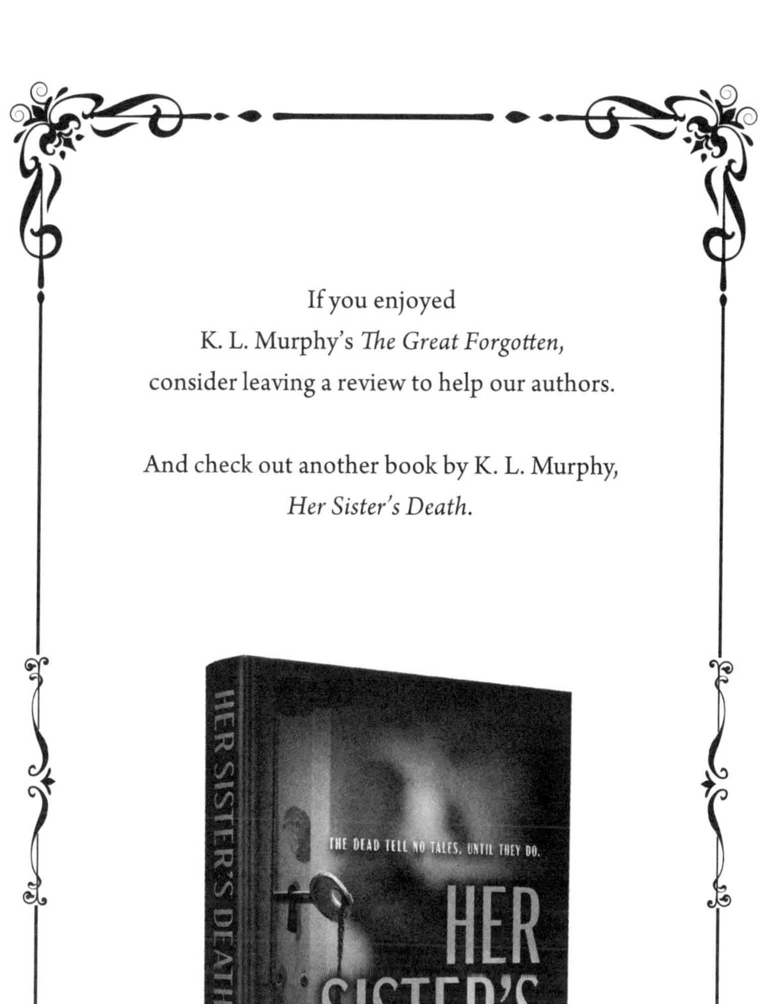

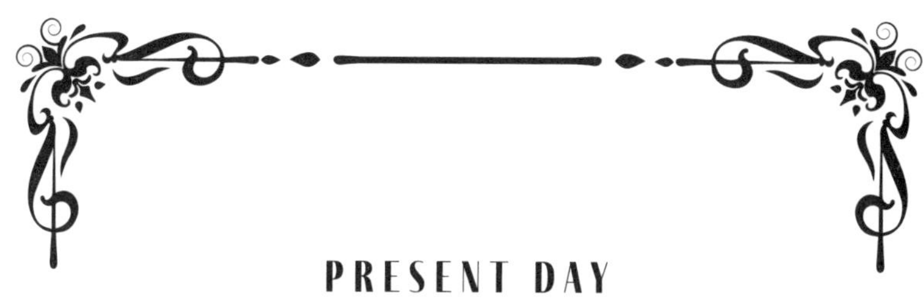

PRESENT DAY

CHAPTER ONE
VAL

Monday, 9:17 a.m.

ONCE, WHEN I was nine or maybe ten, I spent weeks researching a three-paragraph paper on polar bears. I don't remember much about the report or polar bears, but that assignment marked the beginning of my lifelong love affair with research. As I got older, I came to believe that if I did the research, I could solve any problem. It didn't matter what it was. School. Work. Relationships. In college, when I suspected a boyfriend was about to give me the brush-off, I researched what to say before he could break up with me. Surprisingly, there are dozens of pages about this stuff. Even more surprising, some of it actually works. We stayed together another couple of months, until I realized I was better off without him. He never saw it coming.

When I got married, I researched everything from whether or not we were compatible (we were) to our average life expectancy based on our medical histories (only two years different). Some couples swear they're soul mates or some other crap, but I considered myself a little more practical than that. I wanted the facts before I walked down the aisle. The thing is, research doesn't tell you that your perfect-on-paper husband is going to prefer the ditzy receptionist on the third floor before you've hit your five-year anniversary. It also doesn't tell you that your initial anger will turn into something close to relief, or that all that perfection was too much work and maybe the whole soul-mate thing isn't as crazy as it sounds. If you doubt me, look it up.

My love of research isn't as odd as one might think. My father is a retired history professor, and my mother is a bibliophile. It doesn't matter the genre. She usually has three or more books going at once. She also gets two major newspapers every day and a half dozen magazines each month. Some people collect cute little china creatures or rare coins or something. My mother collects words. When I decided to become a journalist, both my parents were overjoyed.

"It's perfect," my father said. "We need more people to record what's going on in the world. How can we expect to learn if we don't recognize that everything that happens impacts our future?" I fought the urge to roll my eyes. I knew what was coming, but how many times can a person hear about the rise and fall of Caesar? The man was stabbed to death, and it isn't as though anyone learned their lesson. Ask Napoleon. Or Hitler. My dad was right about one thing though. History can't help but repeat itself.

"Honey," my mother interrupted. "Val will only write about important topics. You know very well she is a young lady of principle." Again, I wanted to roll my eyes.

Of course, for all their worldliness, neither of my parents understands how the world of journalism works. You don't walk into a newsroom as an inexperienced reporter and declare you will be writing about the environment, or the European financial market, or the latest domestic policy. The newspaper business is not so different from any other—even right down to the way technology is forcing it to go digital. Either way, the newbies are given the jobs no one else wants. Naturally, I was assigned to obituaries.

After a year, I got moved to covering the local city council meetings, but the truth was, I missed the death notices. I couldn't stop myself from wondering how each of the people died. Some were obvious. When the obituary asks you to donate to the cancer society or the heart association, you don't have to think too hard to figure it out. Also, people like to add that the deceased "fought a brave battle with (fill in the blank)." I've no doubt those people were brave, but they weren't the ones that interested me. It was the ones that seemed to die unexpectedly and under unusual circumstances. I started looking them up for more information. The murder victims held particular fascination for me. From there, it was only a short hop to my true interest: crime reporting.

The job isn't for everyone. Crime scenes are not pretty. Have you ever rushed out at three in the morning to a nightclub shooting? Or sat through a murder trial, forced to view photo after photo of a brutally beaten young mother plastered across a giant screen? My sister once told me I must have a twisted soul to do what I do. Maybe. I find myself wondering about the killer, curious about what makes them do it. That sniper—the one that picked off the poor folks as they came out of the state fair—that was my story. Even now, I still can't get my head around that guy's motives. So, I research and research, trying to get things right as well as find some measure of understanding. It doesn't always work, but knowing as much as I can is its own kind of answer.

Asking questions has always worked for me. It's the way I do my job. It's the way I've solved every problem in my life. Until now. Not that I'm not trying. I'm at the library. I'm in my favorite corner in the cushy chair with the view of the pond. I don't know how long I've been here. How many hours. My laptop is on, the screen filled with text and pictures. Flicking through the tabs, I swallow the bile that reminds me I have no answer. I've asked the question in every way I can think of, but for the first time in my life, Google is no help. Why did my sister—my gorgeous sister with her two beautiful children and everything to live for—kill herself? Why?

~~~

Sylvia has been dead for four days now. Actually, I don't know how long she's been dead. I've been told there's a backlog at the ME's office.
~~~

Apparently, suicides are not high priority when you live in a city with one of the country's highest murder rates. I don't care what the cause of death is. I want the truth.

While we wait for the official autopsy, I find myself reevaluating what I do know.

Her body was discovered on Thursday at the Franklin, a Do not Disturb sign hanging from the door of her room. The hotel claims my sister called the front desk after only one day and asked not to be disturbed unless the sign was removed. This little detail could not have been more surprising. My sister doesn't have trouble sleeping. Sylvia went to bed at ten every night and was up like clockwork by six sharp. I have hundreds of texts to prove it. Even when her children were babies with sleep schedules that would kill most people, she somehow managed to stick to her routine. Vacations with her were pure torture.

"Val, get up. The sun is shining. Let's go for a walk on the beach."

I'd open one eye to find her standing in the doorway. She'd be dressed in black nylon shorts and neon sneakers, bouncing up and down on her toes.

"We can walk. I promise I won't run."

Tossing my pillow at her, I'd groan and pull the covers over my head.

"You can't sleep the day away, Val."

She'd cross the room in two strides and rip back the sheets.

"Get up."

In spite of my night-owl tendencies, I'd crawl out of bed. Sylvia had a way of making me feel like if I didn't join her, I'd be missing out on something extraordinary. The thing is, she was usually right. Sure, a sunrise is a sunrise, but a sunrise with Sylvia was color and laughter and tenderness and love. She had that way about her. She loved mornings.

I tried to explain Sylvia to the police officer, to tell him that hanging a sleeping sign past six in the morning, much less all day, was not only odd behavior but also downright suspicious. He did his best not to dismiss me outright, but I knew he didn't get it.